MW00936682

THE TESTAMENT OF THIRTEEN

THE TESTAMENT OF THIRTEEN

SARA M SCHALLER

DESIGNS BY SERAPHIM

The Testament of Thirteen

Published by Designs by Seraphim

ISBN 978-1-7325162-6-7 (hardcover)
ISBN 978-1-7325162-7-4 (paperback)
ISBN 978-1-7325162-8-1 (ebook)

Cover design by Sara M Schaller
Interior design by Sara M Schaller
Symbol Artwork by Anthony Liguori Sr.
Edited by Double Vision Editorial
Maps by Lizard Ink Maps

First Edition: September 2022

www.saramschaller.com

To the angels

Who gave me courage and inspiration.

AUTHOR'S NOTE

In this book, I've added some guides for you to use as references, specifically a cast of characters and glossary. They are not needed in order to read and enjoy the story (there's enough within these pages to keep you informed), but I wanted to include them anyway as an added bonus. If you decide to use them, they will be featured at the back.

HEAVEN
HIGH HEAVEN
MIDDLE HEAVEN
LOW HEAVEN

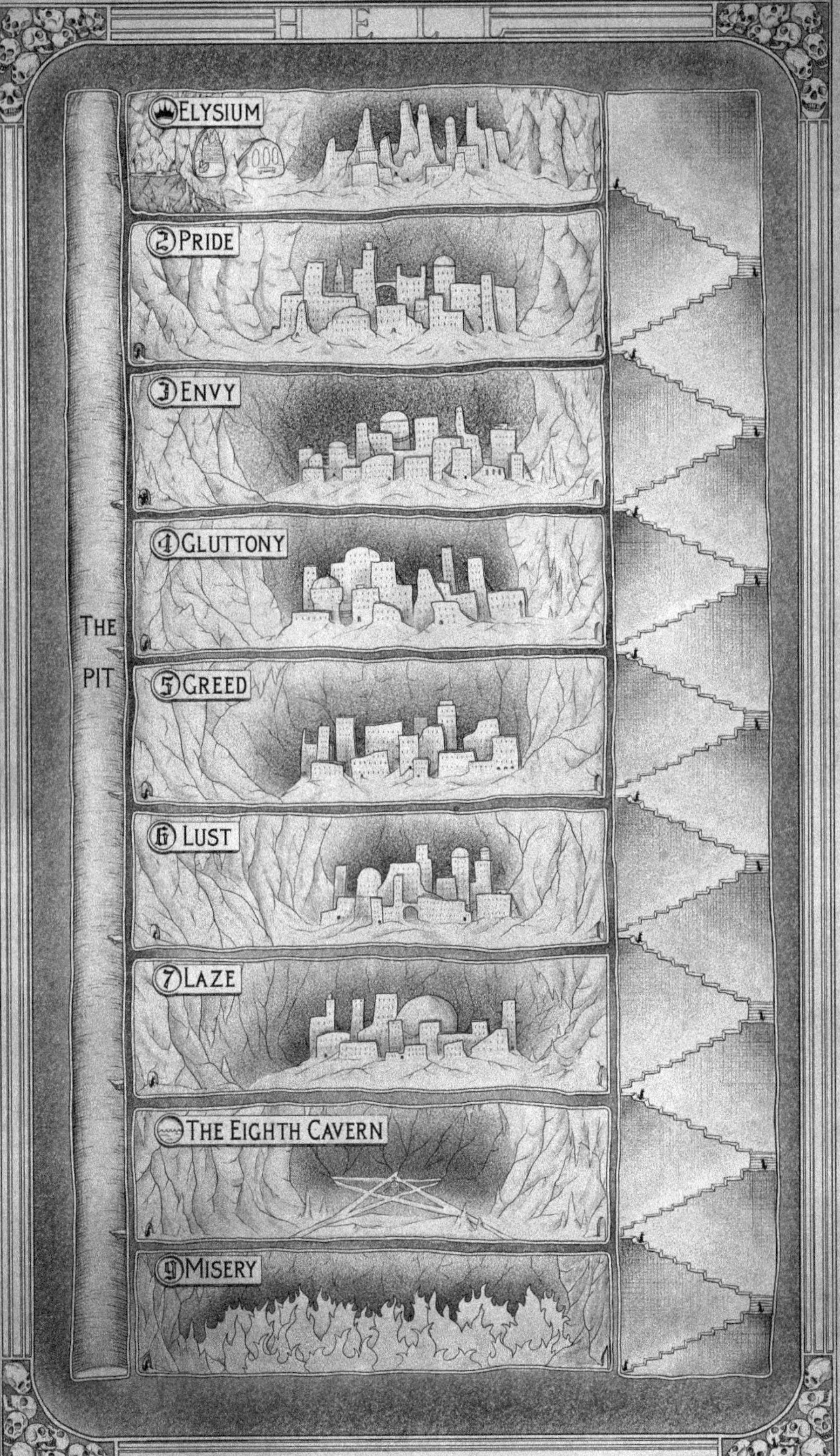
HELL
ELYSIUM
2 PRIDE
3 ENVY
4 GLUTTONY
5 GREED
6 LUST
7 LAZE
THE EIGHTH CAVERN
9 MISERY
THE PIT

TO FIGHT AS ONE
IS TO UNITE AS ONE.

1

GABRIEL

Heaven, Present Day

For the first time in my centuries-long existence, I cursed the sight of Heaven. This was not where I wanted to be, upon the clouds of High Heaven, staring at the grand castle.

No, I wanted to be with Jordan. Actually, I *had* to be with Jordan. He was in danger, and I had been stolen away right at the moment he needed me most.

Jordan, Sophia, and Dane had fixed the Tree of Life tapestry and had been given instructions on how to unbind themselves, something Sister Delphine had kept secret to prevent any of them from knowing who they truly were. Each of them had traveled to a particular location in the United States to perform the unbinding, and the seven of us had split up among them to protect the children. But just as Jordan had completed the process, the Fallen had attacked, and in the thick of battle, a bright shock of light appeared, one that had swept me away and brought me here.

I eased up from my hands and knees and glanced over my shoulder only to see that the rest of my brothers were similarly sprawled around me.

"What's going on?" I demanded, a touch of hysteria in my voice. It was one thing for me to be called back, but for all seven of us to be called at once meant two things: something had gone terribly wrong, and the children had been left with no defense.

Jophiel rubbed his head. "I'm not sure."

"This can't be happening!" I shouted as I rose to my feet. "We can't be here! They need us!"

A hand touched my shoulder. "Gabriel, calm down. We'll figure this out."

I lashed back. "This is no time to be calm, Chamuel! So cut the antics."

"Fine, but losing your composure won't get us out of here any faster."

"I suggest the both of you cut it out," Michael said. "We have Seraphim incoming."

My eyes trailed away from Chamuel's face to rest on the castle. Sure enough, there were dozens of indistinct figures running along the parapets taking defensive positions.

"Do they really think we're here to fight?" Raphael asked.

"No." There was a grim tone to Michael's remark. "They're preparing for something worse."

Before he could elaborate, Seraphim angels descended from the sky, forming a circle around us and barricading us in with their shields.

"Surrender your weapons!" one of them shouted.

Uriel drew an arrow from his quiver. "That won't be happening."

In one swift movement, the Seraphim drew their staffs, inching closer and reducing the already confined space within the circle.

"Stand down!" Michael commanded. "We're not a threat."

"That is up to the Council of Seraphim to decide," one of the Seraphim said. "Now drop your weapons!"

None of us made any attempt to do so because most of us weren't even holding weapons. Certainly, they were attached to our bodies, but we had no inclination to use them. Except for Uriel, perhaps, but Michael had him backing down with one sharp glance.

"This is ridiculous!" My frustration got the best of me. "Take us to Seraphiel." I knew she must have been the one who had called us back. She had been the one responsible for sending us down in the first place.

After a moment, the staffs dropped and one Seraphim stepped forward. "Fine. I'll heed your command. But it seems you've been gone so long that you've forgotten the hierarchical choirs and who takes orders from whom. So this is my warning to remember your place."

My fist clenched. I was ready to take a swing.

"Gabriel, there's no time for that," Michael whispered. "Think of Jordan."

He was right. I relaxed my hand and composed myself. "I'm sorry for overstepping. Would you please take us to Seraphiel?"

"Of course," the Seraphim angel said. "That's where you were going all along anyway."

They jabbed their staffs toward us, forcing us into motion.

My frustration rose again. *We're being treated like prisoners!*

We followed the Seraphim along the marble walkway and shuffled up the stairs to the grand doors. Now that we were closer, it was easy to see that they were preparing for battle. Spears and arrows lined the parapets, and cisterns of holy water and oil sat next to them, ready to be dipped or set aflame.

Zadkiel must have seen the supplies, too, because he asked, "Is there going to be an attack?"

"Quiet! I'm done with your commands and questions. You will not speak unless spoken to," one of the Seraphim ground out.

We all fell into silence, internally simmering over their foul behavior. Answers would be given soon. We just had to wait. At least, that's what I kept telling myself.

There was no one in sight as we entered the castle. The Seraphim led us up the grand stairs and stopped directly in front of the gathering room, where our Seventh Day Gatherings were typically held. Granted, we had convened outside among the clouds at the last one. But this room was meant for a large number of angels, not just the Council of Seraphim. Why were they bringing us here?

One of our escorts pounded on the ornate doors three times before they opened. We filed inside at a quick pace, and I instantly realized *every* angel council—all nine of them—was in attendance. This was no gathering. It wasn't an audience with Seraphiel, either. It was a tribunal. And we were about to be judged.

Benches filled with angels lined each side of the aisle. All of them stared at us with disapproving expressions. It wasn't until I was faced with a room full of my brothers and sisters that I realized how much the seven of us had changed—most noticeably in our attire. We were wearing human apparel, not heavenly robes, and we were fresh from a fight, looking a little rugged instead of pristine and untouched. And those were just external differences. There were plenty of internal ones, too. Those were far greater grievances in their eyes since our entire way of thinking had changed during our time on Earth.

The Seraphim escorts abruptly stopped and stepped aside to line the aisle, leaving us face-to-face with the Council of Seraphim at the front of the room.

Seraphiel rose from her seat, golden robes ebbing and flowing as she moved to loom over us on the altar. All that stood between us were seven short steps, yet it felt like each represented a millennium, a more accurate estimate of our absence than the generalized terms I usually used to describe it.

The entire room was eerily silent, but Seraphiel didn't wait long to fill it with her voice. "It's sad to see who you all have become." She paused to emphasize her words and purse her lips. "Such rogue ruffians who freely do as they please."

"Excuse me, we might be ruffians," Michael said, "but everything we have done is what you and Father bade us to do."

"Really? Because we never authorized you to unlock the gemstone keys, cause unrest among the human world, or steal human artifacts."

"It's not stealing," Uriel growled, "when the object in question was rightfully ours." He challenged Seraphiel's hard gaze, knowing full well we had discovered one of the secrets she had tried to hide for so long—the fourteenth sphere.

"Well, whatever you call it, your meddling has unleashed a dark force, one much stronger than Satan and his army, one that is already knocking on our gates for revenge."

"If you called us back because of Lilith," I said, "then no one is to blame but me. I broke the sphere and unleashed her. I am responsible for her reemergence."

The whole room gasped, but I continued. "I did it because the boy who is the bloodline was in danger. I did it because I thought it would destroy her. My negligence should be punished, but my brothers should not suffer. If anything, they should be sent back. The boy is in Hell's clutches. He and his friends require help. He is the sign you sent us to wait for, and now that we know who he is, he must be protected at all costs."

My words did little to sway Seraphiel. If anything, they seemed to enrage her. "What you are speaking of is not for everyone's ears!"

"Then you shouldn't have made this so public!" Uriel gestured to the benches. "This wasn't our choice. You brought us here."

"Besides, aren't we beyond that?" Zadkiel asked. "Before we left, everyone was making changes to be more transparent, not to continue the secrecy."

Seraphiel broke and lost her composure. "Well, nothing is the way it was anymore!"

It seemed something other than an impending battle was afoot, but it was hard to guess what it could be.

"We are sorry for our foolishness," Raphael said. "But we were told to wait and watch for a sign. The sign came, yet no further instructions did. We were trying our best to honor Father's wishes and to act as we thought Heaven would want us to. You told us yourself we were chosen to be sent down because we could make decisions even in difficult circumstances. So that is what we continue to do. And while those decisions are sometimes unwise, they are executed not only with Heaven's best interests in mind but also humanity's."

Seraphiel's entire face relaxed, and her eyes were filled with sadness. "I understand. It's hard to make decisions when no one is there to guide you. None of you will be punished for your actions, but all of you will remain here."

My heart dropped. "What? Seraphiel, please. They need our help."

"As do we," she shot back. "Lilith has breached our northernmost gates and is making her way through the celestial realms. She is attacking quickly and ruthlessly, her main aim to arrive here and claim the other five sets of keys needed for the Union of the Spheres. Dispatchers from the other realms have sent word to inform me of her intent, and since you all are responsible for her freedom, you should be present for the battle."

"Fine," Michael said.

"But can we return after?" I asked. It was alarming that he didn't have the urge to show some haste. Who knew how long it would take for Lilith to arrive? There were six other realms within Heaven that she had to fight through before she arrived at ours.

"Perhaps after our victory," Seraphiel said, "I'll grant your wish. For now, join your brothers and sisters as we discuss strategy."

Those words must have been some hidden command for the Seraphim along the aisle to wrangle us over to an empty bench among the masses of angels.

I sat down next to my brothers and couldn't fight off the sense of dread that filled me. We weren't going back. Not unless we returned on our own, without permission, which meant disobeying Father. And we all knew how far the last angel who betrayed Him had fallen. But if it would get me to Hell, it would get me to Jordan. Which is exactly where I wanted to be.

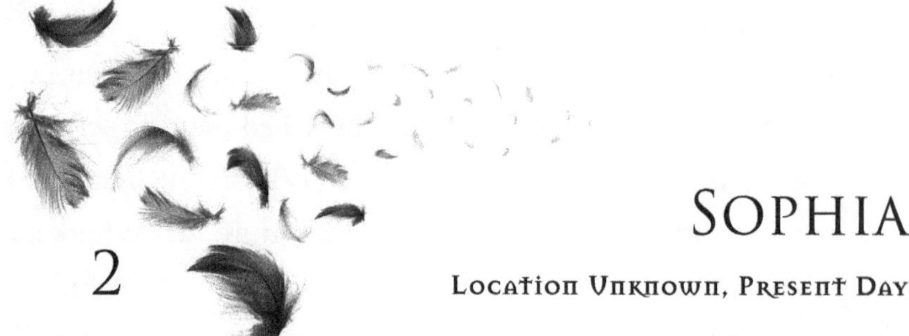

2 SOPHIA

Location Unknown, Present Day

My back ached. The wings wouldn't go away. I didn't know how I'd hidden them for so long. Maybe it had been the trauma that had closed off that part of my mind. Maybe it had been Sister Delphine's binding. Either way, they were here to stay. I was a Nephilim, and there was no hiding from it now.

After my wings appeared, Penelope bound my hands with a zip-tie and threw a hood over my head. I didn't struggle as someone led me to a vehicle. As soon as I was in her clutches, I was a five-year-old again, too scared of her to fight, too scared of myself to try. There was simply no fight left in me.

My only hope was that Jordan and Dane were safe, that the other angels were still around. Chamuel and Uriel had vanished. To where, I had no idea, but I prayed they were unharmed after whatever burst of light had taken them.

I sobbed under the hood. The thought that any of them might be hurt—or worse—was too much to bear. I couldn't handle losing any of them. I'd already lost Sister Helen.

The van stopped. I still had enough wits about me to guess we were in a van since I didn't hit any seats when I had been thrown into the back of it. Penelope must have thought this was the best way to transport me given my wings were fully outstretched and I had no idea how to control them. I'm sure she would teach me. I'm sure I had no choice in the matter. That's how it had been before. Why would it be any different now?

The doors opened, and hands grabbed my arms. I slid out of the van and stumbled onto the ground, which was surprisingly smooth. Definitely not rough dirt, yet too smooth to be pavement. Maybe concrete?

I shook my head, stunned at how critical and technical my mind was being. I had never thought like this before, so affixed to tiny details. Considering I had essentially been kidnapped, though, I guessed my instincts were taking over.

My captors led me forward for a while until I heard a beep and a door open.

"Thank you, gentlemen. I'll take it from here."

Penelope.

Instantly, the hood was pulled from my head. I squinted against the artificial lights and shook the hair out of my face.

"There, there," Penelope said, reaching out and pushing away the stray tendrils. "I don't intend to harm you."

I pulled back from her touch. "Leave me alone."

She only persisted, placing her hand on my cheek. "You've been crying. Why, sweetheart? You're home now."

Stepping back, I said, "This *isn't* my home. And you're *not* my mother."

She smirked. "I'm afraid I am. Where else do you think those wings came from? But you believe what you want. You're only making this harder by denying the truth."

I didn't have anything to say so I stayed quiet.

"Why don't I show you to your room?" Penelope looped her arm through mine and guided me down the hall.

The whole place was white and sterile—obviously one of her labs. We were the only two people in the hallway, and from what I could see, there was only one lone door at the end.

As we drew closer, a muffled sound filled my ears. It was hard to tell what it was, as the vibrations were inconsistent, sometimes weaker sometimes stronger.

Penelope stopped abruptly. She pulled her phone from her pocket and dialed a number, all the while keeping her arm looped through mine.

What was on the other side of the door?

I heard the call connect, but before anyone could actually speak on the other end, Penelope barked, "Why don't you have control of the situation yet? I've given you plenty of time."

"I'm trying!"

The words were so clear it was as if they had been spoken in my ear.

How could I hear their conversation? What was going on?

Then I realized something. Nephilim had the aptitudes of angels. And that meant I had celestial hearing just like them.

I focused, trying to listen more carefully.

"There's no way to sedate him. Every needle breaks. Nothing can penetrate his skin. He's far stronger than I estimated!"

Fear raced through me.

Who was *he*? Was it Dane? Was it Jordan?

It had to be one of them, and I wasn't about to let them get hurt.

My fear shifted to adrenaline and instincts kicked in. I tugged my hands apart, snapping the zip-tie bond. Before Penelope could react, I kicked out and hit her in the abdomen, sending her sprawling. I swiped her key card, raced down the hall, and smacked the badge to the scanner.

The door opened, and piercing screams hit my ears. Those must have been the vibrations I heard. They had just been muted because of the soundproof door.

What were they doing to him?

I kept running down the hall, passing by several doors. A quick glance into one on my right showed an empty room with a bed and toilet. Almost like a jail cell but nicer and cleaner. More like holding rooms for Penelope's experiments, yet it didn't seem like there was anyone there since all the rooms were deserted.

I followed the screams until they led me to a nurses' station similar to the ones in a hospital. No one was there, but when I looked around, people were frantically rushing to a large room.

A room with clear glass sliding doors. A room where a boy lay on the ground convulsing in agony, his dark hair and tattooed arms the only recognizable things about him with his face contorted in such pain.

Dane.

An ache shot through my chest seeing him like that, but it didn't stop me from moving closer. It didn't stop me from pushing through the nurses who were too focused on finding a way to sedate him to notice me. It didn't stop me from kneeling down next to him and reaching out to touch his hand.

"Sophia, don't!"

Penelope's warning came too late.

My fingers closed around his, but rather than calming him down the way I thought it would, the touch only sent me into a fit of screams, too.

Fire. My whole hand was on fire, the skin literally burning before my eyes. Yet no flames could be seen. I tried pulling back, I tried letting go, but his grip was like iron, strong and unbreakable.

Out of the corner of my eye, I saw Penelope bickering with an Asian woman, the other one from the gala. Her name was Jazema. They were fighting over some object. A loud bang revealed it was a gun.

She was going to shoot him! I had to do something.

"Dane!" I shouted.

He opened his eyes at the sound of my voice. They were full of pain and sadness, but those emotions were quickly replaced by fear when he realized he was hurting me. He pulled his hand free and released me.

I fell back to the ground, cradling my arm.

He crawled into a fetal position and was eerily still.

Penelope and Jazema stopped struggling, the former lowering the gun.

"He's our greatest asset and you almost killed him!" Jazema screamed, prying a bullet out of her arm.

"She's worth more to me than him," Penelope growled back. She dropped the gun and met my gaze.

I stared at her, eyes full of hate. In that moment, I didn't regret shooting her at the gala. I just wished it had killed her because then Dane wouldn't be suffering like this. "What did you do to him?"

"Nothing. And that's the truth. His parents are the ones who did this to him."

Parents? Who were his parents?

Jazema came closer and knelt in front of him. "Clearly, his Hellfire is stronger than Daddy's." She glanced over her shoulder at Penelope. "Let's just hope he didn't get anything from Mommy Dearest."

Penelope joined Jazema, looming over Dane's immobile body. "Mark my words, if he did, he's getting a bullet right between the eyes."

Jazema rocketed into a standing position. "Penelope, you can't!"

"Oh, but I can, Jazema! Trust me, we won't have any control over him if he has Lilith's magic."

Lilith's magic? Hellfire? Were Dane's parents Satan and Lilith?

A sting to the neck brought me back to my senses. The nurses were surrounding me, and one had injected me with something. My eyes began to droop closed, and the last thing I saw was Dane screaming as he stretched his arm toward me.

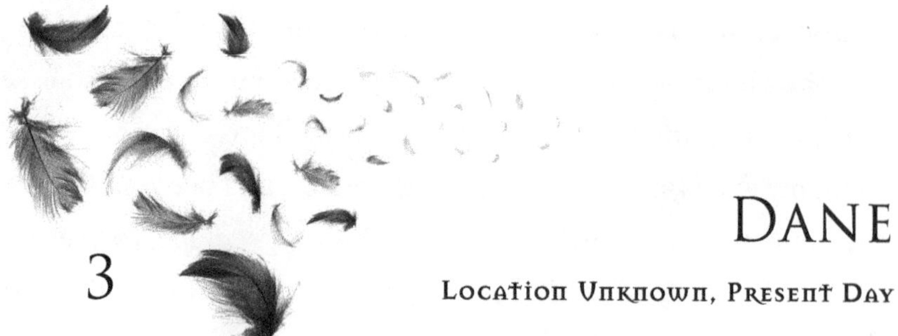

3 DANE

Location Unknown, Present Day

I watched as they carried Sophia away, unable to help her. Every motion erupted seething spasms in my body, even curling my fingers into a fist, the only way I could manage to express my rage. I squeezed my eyes shut, finding solace in stillness. But the reprieve was brief.

First comes the fire, blazing through bones.

My eyes flashed open. No matter how hard I tried, I couldn't get Lilith's voice out of my head. She kept repeating the same thing over and over again.

I brought my outstretched hand to my face, the small movement eliciting another cry of screams.

Why did this have to happen to me? Why did I have to carry this burden?

You can handle it, Ace.

Satan's words of encouragement raced through my mind, the same ones he had said when he was pretending to be Samuel, the man I had met at the gym who had promised to train me in exchange for nothing but a little ink to grace his arms.

I pulled my hand away from my face and pounded it against the ground. I didn't care about the ache I knew it would create because

I didn't want to hear his voice, either. Satan had acted as if he didn't know me when we'd met, but he had been the one to save me from the brutal mugging I had experienced on the street. Why he had rescued me made perfect sense now. Because I was his son. He must have known all this time, yet he never once tried to intervene until I was faced with near death.

Then again, maybe he had.

I wondered if he had sent Lucifer to come get me when I was a kid.

First comes the fire, blazing through bones.

Lilith was back.

How she was in my head, I didn't comprehend. It wasn't the way it had been with Jordan. She had actually made a connection with his mind in the present moment, whereas this was something different. She wasn't here tormenting me as she had done to him. It was simply her voice hardwired to meddle with my mind by repeating the same words. Almost like a spell. I wouldn't have thought that on my own if Jazema and Penelope hadn't mentioned her magic.

Then I remembered something.

Jordan. Shit!

Where was Jordan? Was he here, too?

"Ah!" I shouted, trying to let out the rage. But all it did was send a shock of searing heat down my throat. I grimaced and went still.

I hoped Jordan wasn't here. Maybe he was safe somewhere else and would come rescue us. That was more his style. Although, I had a strange feeling he wasn't out of danger, either.

Nothing from the past few hours made any sense. Raphael and Jophiel had disappeared. The unbinding was a horrible nightmare that I was still living. Jordan was missing, and Sophia was here with wings sprouting from her back.

I hadn't missed that detail, nor how her white, speckled wings made her look even more beautiful than she already was.

When she had yelled my name, I opened my eyes thinking I'd had a terrible dream. Yet my reality only grew more horrendous when I'd realized I was hurting her.

I had always felt like there was no place for me in this world. Like my body didn't match my soul. The unbinding had given me hope that there might be a way to fix that feeling, but it had only made things worse.

My body was now a cage, and I was its prisoner.

There had to be a way to survive this, though. Satan had the Hellfire, and he lived with it every day without it immobilizing him. If anything, it had become a superpower.

I had to learn how to control it. It was our only chance of getting out of here. And more than anything, I had to get Sophia out of here. It killed me that I couldn't help her, couldn't protect her...couldn't touch her. Our relationship had only just begun and our chances of it sustaining all this seemed bleak, especially considering every inch of my skin was a burning inferno.

But I was getting ahead of myself. Right now, I needed to focus on commanding the Hellfire. Except the nurses were back again, inching closer to pinch my skin with a needle. I was surprised they hadn't learned their lesson with the twenty needles they had already tried.

"Don't you think they should try a different tactic?"

It was the annoying Nephilim girl, the one who had nearly stolen the fourteenth sphere.

"Rajani, there is no other way." Jazema sighed. "If there were, I would have done it already."

"Well, maybe you need to think more sinisterly and less ethically."

Jazema met her gaze. "I'm listening."

"You're trying to do this with science. Maybe all you need is a light or dark weapon to penetrate the skin. I mean, all you want is his blood anyway, and there are plenty of ways to shed that."

Blood.

The whole room shifted. My whole body trembled.

Blood. Blood. Blood.

I lashed out my arm and grabbed one of the nurse's wrists. Luckily for her, the cuff of her sleeve protected her skin from the Hellfire, but she was so frightened by the controlled movement that she jumped back and poked another nurse with the needle in her hand.

A small drop of blood fell to the ground.

The nurses went rigid, and Jazema stepped in front of Rajani to shield her. I just stared at the small speck of red.

Why did it fascinate me? Why did it whisper to me?

FIRST COMES THE FIRE, BLAZING THROUGH BONES.

I convulsed at the sound of Lilith's words, dropping the nurse's wrist and losing myself in the crushing blaze.

Obviously, there was an order to Lilith's chaos and she didn't like that I was trying to skip a few steps. I just wished she would move on to the next part. Maybe that meant the agony would end.

The others in the room relaxed.

"No one tell Penelope of this," Jazema demanded.

The nurses nodded and exited the room.

Rajani stared at me. "What exactly is he capable of?"

"I'm not entirely sure." Jazema bent down and wiped the speck of blood off the floor with a paper towel. "I just hope he's more like his father than his mother. If he has any of her powers in him…" Jazema went quiet.

"Then what?" Rajani asked.

"Then we're doomed."

4 JORDAN

HELL, PRESENT DAY

It was cold. Teeth-chattering cold. That was my first thought when my eyes slid open. I raised a hand to my aching head and heard the jangle of chains. Peering down, I noticed a shackle attached to my wrist.

"Are you all right?"

I flinched at the voice, then winced, the quick movement spurring a radiating headache.

"I'm sorry. I didn't mean to frighten you."

The cave we were in was dark, the only source of light coming from a small flame in the sconce on the far wall.

I let my eyes adjust and tried to make out the figure of my fellow inmate. I didn't recognize her voice, so I didn't think it was anyone I knew.

Slowly, her features became discernable. Long, straight black hair, amber eyes, and a tired face. The garments she wore were in complete tatters, and the skin at her wrists was irritated and red from the shackles. She must have been wearing them for a long time. The most astonishing thing about her was the pure white wings behind her back. The left one looked normal, but the right one was tilted at an odd angle.

"It's broken," she said. "It happened the night I was captured. No one here thought to reset it. Probably because it prevents me from flying, which is an advantage for them. It's healed that way ever since."

"Does it hurt?" I asked.

She bobbed her head. "Occasionally. It hurt more when the injury was fresh. I've grown used to it now."

"How long have you been down here?"

"About nineteen years." Her amber eyes met mine.

I couldn't help but think she reminded me of someone, but I couldn't figure out who.

Nineteen years. That was my entire life.

Then I thought of something. I remembered the conversation we'd had with Sophia about her trial of trust, how she'd explained that she worked with members of the Triune—a group of angels tasked to protect the holy bloodline—and that one such member had gone missing several years ago.

"You're Kat, aren't you?"

She smiled. "How do you know that?"

"My friend Sophia told me about you. That you disappeared…" I trailed off.

Sophia. Dane. The angels.

Where had they all gone? Were they safe? Were they hurt?

I had to get out of here.

"Calm down, Jordan," Kat said, seeing the sudden terror on my face. "Everything's going to be fine."

"How do you know my name?"

She gave me a sideways glance. "*You* are the holy bloodline, the reason for my existence. Why wouldn't I know your name?"

I grinned. "Fair point."

The holy bloodline. Which was what I was. I had to keep reminding myself of that.

"Do you know how we get out of here?" I asked her.

She pursed her lips. "I have a few ideas, but I was used to Satan's routine and I don't think he's in charge anymore. So we'll have to see how the new regime operates."

"What do you mean Satan's not in charge? What happened?"

Kat shrugged. "I'm not sure. Lucifer and Satan were fighting in the portal room." She pointed to the cave wall, but it didn't seem like there was a doorway there. "Then they must have taken it out into the throne room. From there, I'm not sure what happened. All I know is I heard Lucifer return, and he ordered the Fallen to do something for him on Earth. I didn't hear the command, so I didn't know he was sending them to capture you. But from what I can see, Satan's gone."

I wasn't familiar with the layout of Hell like she was, but there was apparently more to the Underworld than this small cave we were trapped in.

"Gone?" I asked. "Like dead?"

"The only way you can move up in rank here," Kat said, "is if you kill whoever is in the position you want to take."

I sucked in a breath. Satan was dead. Was that even possible?

This was a whole new playing field, vastly different from the angels who tried everything in their power to prevent violence, not enact it.

I shook my head. "What does Lucifer want with me?"

"Isn't that a great question…" The fallen angel appeared from out of nowhere and smirked at me. "Good morning, sunshine. Every time we meet, you're waking up from some unconscious daze. I suggest you try to avoid that down here. You never know who might sneak up on you when you're not looking."

"Leave him alone, Lucifer," Kat demanded.

He set his eyes on her. "I see you've already introduced yourself. Doesn't surprise me since you never shut up."

"If you didn't want her to talk to me," I intervened, "then why stick me in here?"

Kat's eyes widened at my boldness, then quickly sank into an expression of concern once Lucifer set his attention back on me.

He sauntered closer and hung his hands through the prison bars. "I'm afraid I'm running out of room. Too many of Satan's puppets still linger." A manic look entered his eye, and he grinned like a predator ready to eat its prey. "I guess I'll have to take care of that." He focused on me. "Would you prefer I move you? Perhaps to Misery where you can be tortured with those heartless spirits?"

I gulped. "I'll admit, that doesn't sound inviting. But I think the spirits might have better personalities than you do."

Lucifer pulled back his hands and pounded them on the bars.

Kat ran as far as the chains would allow, anticipating the fallen angel's rage. "No!"

Lucifer reached to his side for the cell key and opened it so fast I barely had time to hide my fear.

He grabbed my hair and lifted my head back, spitting in my face when he said, "You're just like her. That crotchety old nun who pretended to be brave by speaking fierce words to hide her weakness."

I froze.

"But I have every intention of tormenting you just as I tormented her before I slit her throat and watched her bleed."

My face contorted in horror while my fist came up and met his jaw. The chains at my wrist rattled, but he was so close to me that I could still reach him.

The move caught him off guard. I braced myself for his retaliation, which came in a series of three punches. One to the eye, one to the ribs, and the third I managed to block, his fist meeting the stone behind my head.

"Enough!" Kat screamed.

But I wasn't done. I went as far as the chains would allow and yelled, "You sick, twisted asshole! You did all that to her and still made her burn!"

He flashed a wicked smile. "It was the only way to cover my tracks and make it look like Satan did it. His means of murder are far more ethical than mine."

I took another swing at him.

"Jordan!" Kat pleaded.

It didn't matter. I wasn't in range to make contact with him anymore. He was backed up against the bars that joined the two of our cells.

I wondered how far Kat could go, though she seemed at her limit, too.

Lucifer rolled up his sleeves, ready to do some damage, until a figure appeared outside the cell.

"Your Highness."

Seriously? Did Lucifer really make them call him that?

"What?" he screamed. "Can't you see you're interrupting, Asmodeus."

"Yes, but there's activity by the rivers."

Lucifer blanched. "What kind of activity?"

"Swirling. Like something, or someone, might surface."

"Shit!" He raced out of the cell, barely remembering to lock it before he vanished along with Asmodeus.

"Are you insane?" Kat admonished me. "Why were you antagonizing him?"

I wasn't listening. I was following Kat's chains. They looked longer than mine, yet she couldn't reach the bars, either. Then I saw it. Hers were knotted together.

"Jordan, listen to me!"

"I am!" I snapped back. "I was egging him on because I wanted to see where he kept the key and I wanted to see how long it would take for him to back up to the bars."

She stopped.

"You said yourself that we needed to know more about the new regime. Now we do."

She nodded. "He's quick to react when you attack his ego."

"Mm-hmm. And he backs up *real* fast."

"Why does that matter? I can't reach him."

"You could if we can unknot those." I pointed to the twisted chains behind her. Granted, the large knot was close to the cave ceiling, which was several feet in the air.

Her gaze followed the metal serpentine bonds. "They've been that way for ages."

"No human could reach that high, but an angel surely could…" I trailed off when she gave me a stern look. "Oh, right…your wing."

She nodded. "Believe me. I've tried."

I thought it over. "Maybe we could trap him somehow."

Her eyes narrowed. "I've tried that, too. I managed to escape this cell only once and that was because they were trying to kill Satan and threw me a weapon hoping I'd do it for them."

"How did you get back in here?"

Sighing, she said, "I was too weak to go through the portal. I've been down here so long my celestial energy is waning."

"Then all the more reason to get you out of here."

"No. We have to worry about getting *you* out of here."

"Kat, please, it's either both of us or neither of us."

"You're far more important than you think, Jordan. But I'm not arguing with you. It's pointless." She slumped to the ground. "Who did he kill?"

I was quiet, the memory hard enough to face, let alone the possibility that Lucifer had tormented her.

"Sister Helen," I whispered, a few tears running down my face.

Kat sucked in a breath. "No—" She squeezed her eyes shut.

I rubbed the tears from my cheeks. "We have to do something to get out of here. Whatever it takes."

"Like taunting him again? That's not happening. Not at your expense."

"Kat, we have no choice. One of us has to do it. Have any of them ever taken you out of here for some reason?"

"No, but the demons are more gullible. They sometimes even carry weapons. If we create a ruckus, it might lure them to us. Then we could try to overtake them or even persuade them to move us."

Demons? What exactly was beyond this cave?

"Okay... Demons walk around with weapons?"

She shook her head. "Not all the time."

"All right. So we have the beginning of an escape plan." I peered over at the cave wall. "I just don't know what lies beyond there and how we get out of Hell."

"It's not that difficult. The portal room is on the opposite side of this barrier. We can use Satan's portal to take us to Earth. I didn't have enough energy, but you have plenty, even if both of us manage to get out."

Her use of the term *barrier* reminded me of something Jophiel had taught me about divine light—how it could be manipulated to do things like shield, barricade, or transport people. Which made sense given the fallen angels kept appearing out of thin air when, in reality, they were just walking through a divine light barrier.

"Wait…what do you mean I have plenty? Didn't you say it was celestial energy? Only angels have that."

"Correct, but you have divine energy, which is even stronger."

"Oh right. The bloodline. Keep forgetting about that."

"Are you okay?" Kat asked.

"Yeah, why?"

"You're bleeding."

I reached up to touch my cheek, and my fingers came back smeared with blood.

Blood.

My eyes rolled back in my head, and I sucked in a breath.

"Jordan!" Kat shouted, her voice full of alarm.

I wish I could have reassured her that I was only having a vision, something I had grown used to even though they were debilitating, but I couldn't control the words pouring from my mouth:

"First comes the fire blazing through bones,
But wait until your veins cool to take your throne.

"By the new moon, you'll be ready for flight.
Let the air rush through your wings, black as night.

"Like the Earth, rest your soul,
For when the full moon rises, you'll be whole.

"With the waters, you'll be reborn,
Nothing left to be mourned.

"Return to me, my son. Claim your birthright.
Stand as Darcel, blood mage full of strength and might."

When the vision ended, it took me a few minutes to fully come back to the present, but even then, I couldn't stop thinking about who the vision's words were meant for.

Dane.

He was in trouble.

Just as I thought about him, I could see him writhing in pain, and I knew it would only get worse. My gut told me I couldn't let this new prophecy come true, because if it did, he wouldn't be the same anymore. He would be someone else. A foe, an enemy, rather than my friend, my brother, which is what he had come to mean to me.

"She was right," Kat said suddenly.

I had completely forgotten about her, so lost was I in my thoughts. Rather than being distraught as I had expected, she was self-assured.

"Who was right?"

"Your grandmother. She didn't want your parents together. She warned them there would be great consequences if they were to have a child."

"Why?"

"Because you have the Conway sight and the Sinclair blood, which descends from a long line of prophets."

"Meaning…?"

"Meaning you can have waking visions, powerful ones that overtake your consciousness, sometimes even mentally transporting you to a moment in time as if you are witnessing it yourself."

"Well, I guess Granny was right because that's definitely what they do."

"This isn't the first?"

I shook my head. "No, and it wasn't the worst. I've already had to deal with Lilith attacking my mind."

Kat froze. "She shouldn't have the ability to use her powers from inside the sphere."

"Well, she did," I assured her.

"Did?"

I nodded. "She's out now. Gabriel smashed the sphere thinking it would annihilate her, but it unleashed her instead."

She clutched her right wrist. "Gabriel did what?"

Sensing it was a rhetorical question, I didn't answer. And just as I thought, I didn't need to, as Kat jumped up from the ground and began climbing her chains. I could tell she had tried it before, knowing exactly which places to grab hold, but unlike when she had first arrived here, she had grown weak, barely able to make it even a foot up.

She dropped to the ground and paced back and forth as far as she could. "No, no, no." She kept repeating it and rubbing her brow. Then she climbed onto the chains again.

"Kat, stop!" I yelled. "You're wasting your energy."

"No, I'm not! We have to get out of here because she's coming, and if she knows you're down here, she'll only take advantage of you, especially without having control of your visions. We have to escape before she arrives. She'll slaughter me the moment she sets eyes on me, and I can't leave you without any defense!"

"Whoa, whoa, whoa," I said. "Take a breath. We're going to get out of here. Besides, I do have a defense against her." I reached into my pocket and pulled out my fleur-de-lis necklace.

Kat moved as close to the bars as she could get. "You need to put that on. Now."

"All right." But I hesitated. If I put it on, I couldn't help Dane. I wouldn't be able to see him. My mind wouldn't be open to the visions. I wouldn't be able to find a way to stop the prophecy. "I can't do it."

"Why not?"

"Because the vision I had was about my friend, and he needs my help."

"Jordan, keeping the channel to the visions open won't help him. Getting out of here is what will help him. And once you do, you can find him."

She had a point. I could always take it off once we were out of here and stop the prophecy then. I just hoped we had enough time. Dane's transformation seemed to be linked to the moon phases, and it was hard to say what phase it was in now since I had no way of seeing it.

I slipped the chain over my head. As soon as the pendant hit my chest, it felt as if a ward rose around me.

"Thank you," Kat said. "I promise we'll help your friend once we're safe. Now get some rest while you can."

I sat down on the ground and slumped against the cave wall. I had some insight into what had happened to Dane but not much. I just wished I knew what had happened to Sophia and the others, too. None of it seemed good. None of them seemed like they were safe.

Glancing over at Kat, I couldn't help but think I was fortunate to have her with me. Even now, though, it surprised me how much she reminded me of someone. I just couldn't place who.

"Don't worry," she said, catching my gaze. "I'll watch over you."

I closed my eyes, hoping to get some rest, but no sleep came.

5 Sophia

Location Unknown, Present Day

Every part of my body felt sluggish when I opened my eyes. I went to move my arms, but they were stuck at my sides.

Glancing down, I saw that my wrists were in bonds attached to the railings of the bed I was lying in. I pulled and struggled against them with no luck.

At the beeping sound of the door, I whipped my head up and glared at the woman strolling through.

Penelope.

"Hello, darling. I see you've come to."

I pulled against my restraints and shouted, "Let me go!"

"Unfortunately, I can't do that. Not after the stunt you pulled."

Frowning, I said, "What did you expect me to do? You're hurting Dane!"

She shook her finger. "No, I'm not. Neither is Jazema. What is happening to him is entirely in his DNA."

I attempted to launch myself at her. "You really think I believe that?"

"Believe what you want, dear. Just know that I won't ever lie to you."

I wanted to scream. Her sickly-sweet demeanor repulsed me. I knew who she was, what she was capable of. Maybe she wouldn't lie to me, but she certainly had plans for me. She probably wanted me to be like that Nephilim girl who had chased us in Brazil and Australia. A perfect, albeit brainwashed, assassin ready to perform every command.

"How is your hand?" she asked me.

I looked down, having forgotten how Dane's touch had burned my skin.

Was there really some hidden power lurking inside him? Were his parents truly Satan and Lilith?

"Fine," I said.

Penelope came closer to inspect it. "Thank goodness you have my angelic blood running through your veins. Otherwise, you would have lost your hand. No human could have healed like this, and certainly not as quickly."

She was right. The severity of the burn should have disabled my hand. But already it had healed as if nothing had happened to it.

I swallowed, preparing myself to ask her the question racing through my mind. I didn't want her to think I trusted her, but I had to know. "Are Dane's parents Satan and Lilith?"

She gently set down my hand and looked me in the eye. "Yes."

"And he has Hellfire running through his veins?"

"Indeed."

My jaw tightened. I had learned about Hellfire in my Sacrarium training—at least enough to know Dane would suffer. His life would be full of pain. And that's if he made it through the transition.

He didn't deserve this. Dane wasn't a monster. Dane was kind and clever and artistic.

He was someone I loved.

The thought made me smile briefly. Maybe it was too early to start using such serious words to describe how I felt, but after almost four months of being in a relationship with him, I definitely had deep feelings for Dane. I didn't want to see him hurt.

My heart seized in pain, thinking about what he was going through. Then I reminded myself that Dane was strong. He would get through this. As would I. Because we would help each other get out of here.

I didn't care who Dane's parents were, or that I may never be able to touch him again. Nothing mattered but protecting him and keeping him safe, especially since he had no way of doing that for himself right now. Dane was counting on me, and the only way I could help him is if I tricked Penelope and won enough of her trust to get me out of these bonds.

"Do Nephilim inherit all angelic abilities or just some?" I asked Penelope.

My question caught her off guard, the corners of her eyes relaxing just enough to eliminate her stern gaze. "It depends. If a Nephilim is descended straight from a Watcher, then yes, they do have all angelic abilities."

Fast regeneration. Heightened hearing. Superstrength.

Those were some of the angelic abilities I knew about, which means I should be able to break through these bonds.

Penelope smirked. "I know what you're thinking, but this is reinforced titanium. You're not getting through these." She brushed a stray hair from my face. "There are plenty of unruly patients around here who have tested them with no success, so I suggest you get comfortable with your fate. The quicker you do, the easier this will be." She strode away from the bed.

Seething, I demanded, "And just what *is* my fate? To be imprisoned like this forever?"

She turned to face me. "No. Just until I can trust you."

Which might as well be forever because I would never become her ally.

"An intern will be in shortly to draw your blood. Please be nice and get some rest."

And just like that, she was gone.

I had to form a plan, some way to get out of here, because the trust scenario wasn't going to cut it. It was impossible for me to get close to her, even if I was pretending. I hated her too much. There had to be another way.

The beeping sound at the door drew my attention. A bulky man dressed in all black entered the room. He wasn't what I was expecting an intern to look like.

"It's all right, Ivan. You can wait outside."

Someone else had followed him in the room, but it was hard to say what they looked like since the large man hid the other person's features from view. That was, until the man turned and shuffled back the way he had come.

That's when I came face-to-face with Naomi, the girl who lived next door to Jordan. Her parents had tried to set them up, but they both had felt they were better friends than potential love interests. However, when she admitted to Jordan that she worked for Geneloom, he was unsure if their friendship would last. And this would certainly be all the evidence he needed to make up his mind.

My eyes turned to slits. "You backstabbing traitor."

She ignored my comment and stepped closer to the bed. "I'm here to draw your blood." She looked over her shoulder at the door. "If you don't cooperate, Ivan will come in to assist." She set her gaze back on me. "Please don't make him come in."

"Are you really going to act like you don't know me?"

"I *don't* know you. We were never properly introduced. I just know *of* you and that you're Jordan's friend."

I wanted to correct her and say *cousin* instead of *friend*, but I was too floored at how stone-cold she was being. It was a far cry from the sweet girl who I had seen at Sister Helen's funeral.

Naomi placed a small pouch at the foot of the bed, opened it, and took out the supplies she needed—needle, vial, tourniquet, alcohol wipe. Then she came close to my side.

"Why are you so heartless?" I asked.

She tore open the wipe and brushed it over my vein. "I'm not heartless. You just don't know me." She wrapped the tourniquet around my arm.

"Should that matter? You see me, a helpless person trapped in this lab, and you don't have the urge to do anything?"

She picked up the needle. "Of course I do, but there are many helpless people in this lab, and it's not my right to choose who gets saved and who doesn't. Because if I picked you and only you, none of the others would have a chance."

Naomi stunned me into silence with her words. There must be more patients than just Dane and me. I hadn't seen them, but first Penelope and now Naomi had mentioned them.

She poked my skin, and I watched as my blood started to fill up the vial. Then something occurred to me. "Naomi, if you're here, that means we're close to your house, right?"

"I can't disclose our location."

"Ugh! Why do you have to be so frustrating? Just tell me."

She pulled out the needle, capped it, and placed it aside to focus on bandaging me. When she was done, she packed up her supplies. Before she left, though, she met my gaze. "What's frustrating is your assumptions of me. If you would only cast them away, you would see my true intentions."

Naomi walked out, rejoining Ivan, and the two of them disappeared down the hall.

What did she mean? Was she trying to tell me something?

I sighed and glanced down at my arm. Instead of focusing on the taped bandage, my eyes narrowed on a small device beside my hand.

I grabbed it and clicked the button. My bonds sprang open. I rubbed my wrists and smiled. I guessed I'd misjudged Naomi after all.

6 DANE

Location Unknown, Present Day

"Is he even alive?"

Darkness.

I refused to open my eyes, my whole world encased in shadow with only the occasional voice making it through to mock me.

"He is, but barely. His body temperature is skyrocketing."

"You mean he has a fever?"

"Yes, but it's much worse than that. He's nearing two hundred degrees. No human can handle that heat."

Heat. Too much heat.

A drop of sweat dripped down my nose.

"This isn't normal. From what I know, Satan's Hellfire paralyzed him to the point of immobility because of the pain. That isn't the case here. At first it seemed to be following that pattern, but now the fever is overtaking him."

"Perhaps Lilith was wrong. He isn't her greatest creation. He's not strong enough to handle the fire."

Strength.

The muscles in my back contracted, spasming in pure agony. I did not shout, for I had grown numb to the pain. Besides, my voice had all but disappeared to a hoarse whisper, so what good would it do to send out a cry for help when no one would hear?

"His demise might be the best course of action. No one should have to suffer like this."

"True. But his demise will come naturally, not prematurely."

Suffering.

It would continue.

Death.

My only salvation.

Let it come quickly.

7

GABRIEL

HEAVEN, PRESENT DAY

I stood outside the castle, my feet firmly placed on the marble of the landing circle, and gazed up at the Heavenly Gates I knew would be breached by Lilith. It was only a matter of time.

The whole moment was strange. I was on Heaven's parapets again, yet this place no longer felt like home. The most impenetrable structure in our realm was about to be attacked by an enemy that had no right to exist. And I was back in angelic robes, missing the comforts of a fine suit and tie.

Surely Earth had changed me. But I never thought it would change me so much that this place, this Paradise, would feel so foreign.

"You forgot this," Michael said from behind me.

I turned and saw the scythe in his outstretched hand, the rest of my brothers at his side armed and ready for battle.

"What are we doing?" I asked.

"Gabriel, we've been over this." Michael sighed. "We must stay and fight. Then we can return and rescue the kids."

"Do none of you feel like I do? Are none of you discontented?"

Raphael stepped forward. "Of course, we are."

Uriel pulled at the collar of his robe. "Especially since we have to wear these. They're a lot itchier than I remember."

Chamuel sighed. "Uriel, please!"

"What? I'm trying to enliven the moment. Isn't that what you want? Me looking on the bright side of things."

"Enough! Both of you!" Zadkiel chided.

We all grew silent.

"We've lost our synergy," Jophiel stated.

"What do you mean?" I asked.

"The last time we all saw one another, we had split up to go with the kids for the unbindings," Jophiel explained.

The rest of us nodded.

"Well, it seems the kids weren't the only ones unbound," he went on. "Our camaraderie seems damaged, too."

"Jophiel, please. We're fine," Uriel assured him.

"Are we?" Michael asked, glancing at me.

"We are… I just feel complacent," I explained. "We had so much free will to do as we pleased, and now we're here again, having to obey and take orders. It's hard not to feel like—"

"Samael," Zadkiel finished.

I nodded, unable to admit what I was thinking.

"I'm feeling it, too," Zadkiel confessed.

"You are?" I asked.

"We all are," Michael said. "We're all thinking that he was right. The better question is what would have happened if we followed him. Would we have been able to lead him down a path of nonviolence, a path where he could have voiced his concerns without betraying all that we were taught?" He paused. "None of this is right, Gabriel. None of us are fine. You're not alone. We all are questioning our existence. We all are questioning what is right and what is wrong. We all are suffering on the inside at the thought of Jordan, Sophia, and Dane being in danger."

Michael looked around at us. "But what is getting me through is knowing that putting a stop to Lilith will be putting a stop to one more enemy that has their sights set on harming those kids. That is the reason I'm here. That is the reason I'm staying. She is the bigger threat, and we must eliminate her."

I clenched my jaw and grabbed the scythe from Michael's hand. "The truth resides inside."

Michael nodded. "Deceit lies without."

"The journey to both is obscure," the rest of them finished.

Taking inspiration from the words of Sister Helen rather than Father or Seraphiel or even one of our heavenly comrades was another strange occurrence to add to this moment. But if anything, it reassured us we were acting in the proper manner.

"Speaking of which, we need to inform one another about the kids' identities," Chamuel said. "I was a little taken aback, Gabriel, when you proclaimed Jordan was the bloodline. Is that true?"

"Yes," I said. "What about Sophia?"

"Nephilim," Uriel stated. "Descended straight from a Watcher."

"Penelope, to be precise," Chamuel added.

"Really? And Dane?" I wondered aloud.

Raphael and Jophiel looked at each other. "Satan is his father," said the former.

"And Lilith is his mother," said the latter.

There were shocked expressions all around, but there wasn't time to say anything. The castle bells rang, announcing the arrival of our enemy.

"Speak of the she-devil," Uriel said.

We raced up the steps and entered the castle, heading to the staircase that would take us down to the dungeon. It was never used to imprison anyone, but instead it acted as a place to store extra supplies, be it as large as weapons or as small as writing quills. Michael had thought it was a good place to hide the remaining keys since it was a heavily fortified area of the castle with only one entrance and exit. Seraphiel had trusted Michael's judgment and agreed to the plan.

When we arrived, Seraphiel awaited us inside the dungeon with a message. "Greetings, comrades. Are you prepared? You all have the most important responsibility."

We nodded.

"Good. You're our best fighters so I wanted you down here with the keys because these objects only stand a chance if you are the ones protecting them. My hope is we will finish Lilith before she gets to you, but my mind will be more at ease knowing you're here if she gets through our defenses."

"I assure you," Michael said, "Lilith will not be getting these keys."

Seraphiel patted Michael's shoulder. "Good luck." Then she turned and exited the dungeon.

"How would you like us positioned?" Zadkiel asked.

Michael was quick to respond. "Three at the front, three at the back. Uriel, choose your best vantage point."

"Well if three of you are guarding the door and the other three are in the cell with the chest of keys, then I will position myself in the middle."

Since we were all gathered by the door currently, Uriel turned and walked down the narrow corridor lined with cells and stopped in front of the one where we had placed the chest of keys. It was also where the corridor branched off to the left and right. It was the perfect placement since it had a line of sight to the entrance and ample protection from a direct, face-on assault, as Uriel could take cover down the smaller corridors.

"All right," Michael said to the rest of us, "take your positions."

Chamuel, Jophiel, and Zadkiel walked down the corridor and entered the cell at the end, surrounding the chest and ready to defend it.

Raphael, Michael, and I remained by the entrance, bracing ourselves for the arrival of the enemy.

Except everything was eerily quiet.

The bells had rung, announcing an imminent attack, yet none had come. Either the alarm had been premature or the battle had ended before it had even begun.

I glanced at Michael. "This doesn't seem right."

He pursed his lips. "Because it's not."

His eyes shifted, and a faraway look crossed his face. It was easy to tell he was analyzing and calculating different scenarios and strategies.

"Perhaps it's a small attack team instead of an army," he said. "One scout might have been seen, which was cause to sound the bells, but it might have been a distraction."

"Why's that?" I asked.

"Because if she has a small team, her aims are infiltration and stealth, causing the need to draw attention elsewhere."

Uriel waved his hand to get our attention and motioned for silence.

He had his head cocked to the side, listening intently to a sound coming from down the left corridor. Raphael, Michael, and I did the same, trying to pick up what he might have heard. There was a rhythmic tapping noise, its tone growing louder. Meaning only one thing. Whatever it was, it was coming closer to us. Except it was such a dainty sound that it didn't seem like a threat.

Apparently, Uriel thought it was, though. He drew an arrow from his quiver and nocked it in his bow, stepping slowly backward until he was in front of the cell with the chest of keys.

"Damn it!" Michael drew his sword and ran to meet Uriel.

"What is it?" Raphael asked.

"They're footsteps!" Michael cried. "She's here! Seal the cell!"

Zadkiel grabbed hold of the door handle and pulled it closed, shutting the three of them inside with the chest.

Uriel held steady as the footsteps increased in frequency, indicating the person had sped up into a run. Michael rushed to the cell door, sheathing his sword and then reaching for the bar to lock it.

Raphael and I raced down to meet them, preparing to assist and defend our brother.

But we were too late.

Uriel fell to his knees, arrow still nocked in his bow.

Michael froze mid-action as he attempted to swing down the bar.

And as I rounded the corner and came face-to-face with Lilith, all it took was one twist of her hand and I stopped in my tracks.

She cackled. "Oh, boys. You underestimated me." She wove among our unmoving bodies. "It's so easy for me to control you. All I have to do is move my fingers. See?" She snapped them, and my scythe dropped from my hands, clattering to the floor. "I'm a blood mage—mother of blood magic to be precise." She crept behind me and stroked her hands along my shoulders. "The source of my power runs through your veins. All it takes is a simple gesture to command you." She twisted her hands through the air, which had Michael releasing the bar and stepping away from the door.

All of us were trying to resist her. You could tell by the exerted expressions on our faces. But it was to no avail.

"There's no point in fighting it." Lilith crossed her arms and faced the door to the cell. "There's no barrier that can protect you."

She was about to perform another motion with her hands, presumably to ensnare the others. But they were more clever. One of them swung open the door. Another swept the floor with their wings, sending up a cloud of dust.

Jophiel ran from the cell, carrying the chest and shouting, "There's nothing that can stop a blood mage but a break in concentration."

Sure enough, he was right.

Lilith choked on the dust and released her hold on us.

Chamuel and Zadkiel sprang from the cell, the latter swinging his club and the former sweeping the floor with his wing again and kicking up dirt and dust. The rest of us regained our composure. Within seconds, however, we were all frozen again, our weapons drawn and immobile in their path to slaying her.

"Ugh!" she screamed, snapping her fingers again.

Jophiel tripped and went careening to the floor, dropping the chest in the process. The wooden box rattled open, but no contents came sprawling out. It was empty.

"You're all so ridiculous and naive. I've been here for quite some time now. Enough to manipulate Seraphiel to my will. I had her call you all back. I had her act as if a grand battle was brewing to scare you all into complacency. She's already given me the keys. This here—" she motioned around the room "—is merely a ruse to trap you all."

She sneered at us. "I had her tell the whole heavenly host that I was attacking all the realms to get here, but all I did was use a portal. Everyone prepared for battle, the bells even sounded, but it was all a trick. All the other angels have been locked away in Middle and Low Heaven, so there's no chance of help or rescue. I even severed the connection to Father, for He would have tried to ruin my plans.

"There is no hope for you now. I have every intention of killing each of you because the seven of you are what stands in my way of getting what I want. Don't worry about the children. I'll take good care of them. The boys, at least. I couldn't care less about that Nephilim girl scum." She paused and smiled viciously. "Which one of you would like to die first?"

"Mistress!"

Lilith's face contorted. "Why are you interrupting me?" she shrieked at her accomplice.

It was the hooded man who had attacked us at the gala and in Norway. The man who should have died from his wounds but had miraculously survived, no doubt from Lilith's magic.

"There are angels in Low Heaven who have escaped," he reported. "The remainder of the team is engaging them to buy us time. We're all that's left. We've caused enough damage to devastate them. We must take the keys and go."

Lilith sighed. "I wanted so bad to kill you." She turned away from us and sauntered down the corridor. "I guess I'll just have to settle for one." She squeezed her hand into a fist.

Jophiel grabbed at his chest and cried out.

"I'll see you on the other side," she said to him as she passed, forcefully releasing her fingers.

A burst of brilliant light radiated through the dungeon, and we all dropped to the floor.

Slowly, the light receded. Slowly, we moved our limbs. Slowly, our voices returned.

"*No!*" I screamed, staring at an empty corridor.

A single charred spot along the stones was the only sign left of our brother.

We had lost Jophiel.

8 SOPHIA

Location Unknown, Present Day

Shortly after I unlocked the restraints, I realized a few things. One, I couldn't just get up and leave. I had no idea where I was, and I had no way to navigate out of the lab safely. I had to do more recon before I attempted to flee. Two, I had to figure out how to get Dane out of here. He was in a vulnerable state, and walking out on his own accord was not an option at the moment. Three, if there were other patients here, I had to find them. If I was going to hatch an escape plan, I wasn't going to leave them behind. Whoever they were, they deserved a chance at freedom, too. And finally, the whole scenario was a test. I was confident Penelope had given Naomi the device to unlock my bonds as a way to explore my trust. By using it, I would have ultimately failed.

Penelope was playing mind games, just as she had when I was younger. Except this time I had every intention of winning. I had to go along with it for now until I was fully prepared.

The next time she came to visit me, she didn't hide her enthusiasm. "Good morning, dear. I'm glad to see you're still here."

I handed her the device. "There's no need to involve the intern in whatever it is you're doing."

Penelope smiled. "Of course, there is. I'm testing her just as much as I'm testing you. There are only two interns left. Naomi is a promising candidate, but I have to be sure she is committed to Geneloom."

I laughed. "Don't you mean to you?"

She shrugged. "Perhaps. Now let's go. Your training begins today."

"Training?" I asked.

"Did you think I was going to let you rot away in here? No, you must learn how to use your Nephilim abilities so you can apply them."

I followed her through the door and out into the hallway. We walked down the corridor and entered the space where they were holding Dane. My heart seized at the sight of him. He was drenched in sweat, and his eyes were like glass, no life left in them.

I stopped in my tracks.

"Sophia." There was an edge to Penelope's tone, warning me to keep walking.

Moving my feet, I continued on but not without asking, "Is he all right? Will he survive?"

Penelope rolled her eyes. "I'm not sure. Jazema thinks he will—or hopes rather."

"And you? You don't care for his well-being at all, do you?"

"Why should I? In my eyes, he's a threat if he survives."

"Clearly, since you tried killing him."

Penelope stopped and faced me. "Because he was hurting *you*. When are you going to understand that you're my sole priority, that your safety is the most important thing in the world to me? I took you from that woman for a reason."

She resumed walking. I didn't.

"What has you stopping now?" she huffed.

"You took me from my mother? I thought she abandoned me."

Penelope's gaze turned cold. "*I'm* your mother. Besides, does it really matter? You don't belong with her. You belong with me."

"Yes, it does matter! I've spent my whole life thinking she left because she didn't want me. If that's not the case, what did you do with her?"

"Framed her for murder. Sent her to jail."

My eyes widened in shock.

"I told you I would never lie to you. If you don't want to hear the truth, stop asking hard questions."

Then everything clicked into place. The nightmares of the courtroom. The person screaming at me that I was a liar. Penelope had framed my mother for Preston's murder. That's the gunshot I had heard that day, and Gigi, his mother, had been the one calling me a liar. I wonder if Preston and Gigi were even their true identities. Knowing Penelope, they had been hired help or enemies indebted to her that she had promised salvation but had only betrayed in the end.

"Do you realize how many people you've hurt? How many lives you ruined?"

"All for you. I would do anything for you."

My face contorted in horror. "Except you've hurt me and ruined my life! You tore me away from my mother, from a happy home. You've put me through traumatic tests and mind games and ridicule. You made me suffer through a court case as a child that all but destroyed my self-esteem. Let alone that I've questioned my identity my entire life because of you!"

"I think you're being too harsh. You can't blame all that on me. Now let's get moving."

"Or what?"

"Or I'll get Ivan to move you along."

Fuming, I said, "Have I told you how much I *hate* you?"

Penelope slapped me across the cheek. "Have I told you how much I hate when you act like an unruly child? Let's go!"

I wanted to scream. But what good would that do, other than reinforce her words?

I shuffled my feet as we entered yet another hallway. The lab was like a maze, and there were no windows anywhere, which made it even harder to figure out where we were or remember how to move about from one area to another. The only thing I was able to gather as I followed Penelope was that we were underground. No windows were certainly a good indication, but when we entered an elevator, I knew for sure.

There were buttons for each level within the lab, and it surprised me how many of them were subterranean. "G" for the ground level was listed at the top, and numbers one through ten followed beneath it. Other elevators typically were the opposite. What this meant for me, though, was that there was only one aboveground level, only one way to get to freedom.

Penelope scanned her badge and pressed button "ten." It lit up, and the elevator descended. I watched the machine count the floors as we passed them, realizing that Dane and I were being held on level five.

I seethed on the inside, thinking about how Penelope was an evil bitch. She was taunting me by showing me everything, giving me glimmers of hope that I knew where cloaked in deception. In a way, she wanted me to attempt escape to see how far I would go, to see how far my Nephilim instincts would get me. Well, I certainly wasn't going to waste my shot right now. I had to perform more recon first. But who says I couldn't call her bluff?

"If you want me to know the inner workings of the lab, then you might as well explain each level."

She glanced over at me. "What makes you think I want you to know?"

I shrugged. "You haven't blindfolded me. When I arrived you did because you didn't want me to know where I was. Clearly, you're comfortable with me knowing about the lab because you haven't kept it a secret," I said. "Besides, I would have to steal a badge and remember the way we came to even use or find the elevator again. So what hurt would it do to just tell me?"

Penelope smiled. "This is the type of thinking I like to see."

The elevator binged, and the doors opened. We stepped out into a low-lit corridor.

Before we moved any farther, Penelope looked at me and said, "Levels one through three are research laboratories. Level four is a depository. Level five is typically abandoned. It used to be a treatment and triage center. Levels six through nine are patient wards, and level ten holds our training facilities." She held out her arms to indicate that's where we were.

"What kind of patients are in the wards?" I asked.

She placed her hand on my cheek and pinched it forcefully. "None that should concern you."

I grimaced. "You told me you wouldn't lie to me."

"I'm not lying. What I said is true. I'm simply refraining from answering your question in full." She let go of my cheek and walked down the corridor.

It was a single, long hallway lined with doors on each side.

"These are our small training rooms used by beginners," Penelope said as we passed the doors. She stopped at the last one on the right. "This is where you'll be today."

I glanced behind her at a double set of glass doors. "And what's in there?"

"That's the large arena for patients more advanced in their training." Penelope placed her badge on the keypad for the door in front of us. She walked inside and held the door open for me. "You'll start here."

I entered the room, or what felt more like a cell, and cringed at who stood before me. It was the raven-haired Nephilim girl.

"This is Rajani," Penelope said. "I believe the two of you have informally met. She will be your training instructor."

Oh, for heaven's sake...

I crossed my arms and stared at her.

Penelope patted my shoulder. "Have fun." She was halfway through the doorway when she stopped and said, "And, Rajani, be nice." Then she closed the door on us.

Rajani smiled viciously and crossed her arms, too. "What would you like to start with? Strengthening exercises or hand-to-hand combat?"

I thought it over. Penelope's cruelty and harshness had left me with enough pent-up anger that there was really no choice.

So I made my decision quickly.

Closing the distance between us, I tackled her onto the training mats, knowing that would be my only impressive move.

And sure enough, it was.

9

DANE

Location Unknown, Present Day

"The fever is subsiding. His temperature is returning to normal."

Why did I still feel like shit, then?

Maybe there was no more heat. Maybe there was no more pain. But my back ached. It felt like it might break in two right down the middle.

These bastards had me inside what looked like a treatment room in an ER, but they had left me lying on the floor. No barriers. No restraints.

Instead, people milled about, watching me like a fish in a tank.

Was I supposed to be some impressive specimen?

I didn't feel impressive.

You will rule the world. You will control them with the snap of your fingers. Just you wait.

Grabbing my head, I tried to shake out Lilith's voice.

Kill them. Snap their necks, break their bones, stop their hearts. Just kill them all.

I cringed because it wasn't Lilith's voice anymore. It was entirely my own. And the dark idea was so appealing.

They deserved to suffer. Everyone deserved to suffer just like me, for I had endured too much and they should know what it feels like.

Whatever was happening to me, I was being reborn. There would be no more inner struggle, no more dual voices trying to lead me down two paths. It was time for one of them to prevail. This was the perfect time to choose my own destiny and align myself with the darkness.

The thought made me smile. No more pretending. No more trying to be someone I wasn't. It was time to be who I wanted to be. My most authentic self.

It was time to be a little wicked.

A snapping sensation along the vertebrae of my back had me rethinking that plan.

I was lying to myself every time I thought the pain had receded or that it couldn't get any worse, because what I was feeling now was by far the greatest torture.

I grunted and groaned as the bones popped, cracked, and broke.

The nurses were alarmed, one of them shouting, "Get Jazema!"

I understood why. My skin completely tore down the middle of my back, as if someone had taken a knife and sliced it clean. My skin shredded apart as bones shifted and new ones grew, ascending out of my spine and taking shape.

Writhing in pain, I had a brief moment where I wished Penelope would return instead of Jazema so she could shoot me with that gun.

No one deserved this misery.

So make them all pay.

But not all of them were the enemy.

Revenge favors no one. That's what makes it easy.

I roared. At the pain. At the voices in my head. Rolling my head back and forth along the cold linoleum, I tried to shut out everyone and everything.

I tried ignoring the searing ache as the bones continued to rise out of my back. Then everything was silent, and a new sensation overcame me.

Small pinpricks, like the repeated poke of a needle. Not along my back exactly, but slightly higher up. Except what could be above my back that I could feel?

Opening my eyes, I glanced over my shoulder. Black, gargoyle-like wings filled my sight, the membranes and sinew still forming.

Someone let out a shocked gasp, and I turned my attention to them. It was Jazema, frozen in her tracks, with her eyes wide as saucers. There was a brief pause, the two of us staring at each other, and it was in that moment that I realized something: I wasn't in pain. The fever was gone, yet I could still feel the fire thrumming in my veins.

My wings settled along my back. I had survived. I was in control. I was free.

I smirked. It was time to let chaos reign.

Bracing myself on my forearms, I lifted my body slowly from the ground.

Jazema sprang into action at my movement. "Nurses, sedate him!"

I rolled my eyes. They were going to try this again, repeatedly poking me with a needle. When were they going to understand that nothing could penetrate my skin?

Suddenly, an oxygen mask was pressed to my face before I could get my bearings. Some kind of anesthetic filled my senses. I swayed on my feet, and my eyes fluttered. I tried fighting it. I wanted to stay in control. I *needed* to stay in control. For...her.

Slumping to the floor, I heard Jazema say, "Take him to level nine. He'll fit in nicely down there."

Her leopard-print heels where the last thing I saw before my eyes closed.

10 JORDAN

Hell, Present Day

Something was wrong. Lucifer hadn't returned for what felt like a few days now. Granted, I was happy not to be graced with his presence, but none of the Fallen had taken his place, either, which had to mean they were dealing with something else.

Like I said, in a way it was a good thing. I didn't want their attention on me. All that would have brought was pain and suffering. I was curious, though, to know what preoccupied them. I was hoping it might be the angels, but I knew it probably wasn't. They tended to make their arrival known whenever they were about to clash with the Fallen or rescue someone.

My stomach growled for about the millionth time, since I hadn't eaten anything in days, but I ignored it and pushed away the empty feeling of starvation. Glancing around the cell, I tried to find a way to break my bonds. Just pulling on them was no use, especially since I had little energy and had grown weaker from the lack of food. This seemed like the opportune time to attempt an escape, though, as the Fallen had to be dealing with another threat. But there was nothing that could help me.

I peered over at Kat, who was pacing in her cell. She chewed her lip and had a very thoughtful expression on her face. I guessed she was trying to figure a way out of here, too.

I smiled a little, thinking about how Gabriel would pace like that whenever he had to make a decision.

Wait a minute…

That's who Kat reminded me of! Gabriel!

She paced like him, she had the same dark hair and amber eyes as he did. Even their facial expressions were similar.

Did it mean something? It was like they were twins.

"Oh my gosh!" I exclaimed, as something occurred to me.

"What's wrong?" Kat asked.

I didn't have time to tell her, though. A fallen angel entered the cave, carrying a bowl and a bucket in one hand and jingling the key around in the other. He unlocked my cell and stepped inside.

"Who are you?" I asked.

Rather than answering, he threw down the bowl and bucket, and jabbed me in the side with something that sent an electric shock through my body.

"Murmur!" Kat was at the bars, ready to defend me.

"Oh, shut it, you bitch! Otherwise, you'll get a jab, too!"

I recovered from the shock and peered at the bowl. It was filled was some kind of mushy food. It looked like oatmeal. Glancing over at the bucket, it was full of water.

"Bring it on! I can take it!" Kat challenged.

Murmur sneered at her. "I'm not engaging you. Lucifer told me as much. He sent me here to check on the boy and feed him. He said to ignore your sassy ass."

"I'm surprised Lucifer showed some kindness," I said, reaching for the bowl.

Another unanticipated jab sent a shock to my ribs, which left me wincing on the ground.

"I'm done with the lot of you! I have better things to do, what with Lilith's army rising from the rivers! Her whole horde will overtake this place soon, and then I'll be answering to her." He squatted down and got close to my face. "My hope is that she'll just kill you so I won't have to keep nourishing you, and then, once you're gone, I'll feed your lifeless body to the hounds when they return."

That's it! I had enough of this.

I elbowed Murmur in the ribs, grabbed his Taser-like baton and pried it from his fingers. He punched me in the stomach, and I threw the weapon across the cell as I fell to a knee. Murmur lunged after it, turning his back to me and approaching the bars to Kat's cell, where she was ready to attack. She swiped a knife from his boot and was about to sink it in his abdomen, but he dodged backward, where I was waiting for him, holding the chain attached to my bonds, which I looped around his neck. I pulled snugly until he was so close that I could whisper in his ear.

But instead of taunting him, I silently choked him into complacency. Except it wouldn't knock him unconscious like a human because angels didn't fall unconscious. Instead, it would kill him. And I wasn't sure if I was ready to kill somebody.

I loosened my grip at the horrific thought.

Murmur pulled free, gasping for air and stepping forward, away from me and into Kat's reach, where she plunged the knife right into his chest.

He wheezed and fumbled, dropping to his knees.

I was expecting blood, and lots of it, but none came. Instead, he just kept gasping and clutching at his chest.

It was a terrible sight to see. He was suffering, and we had caused that suffering. It left me with an unsettling feeling, but rather than watch him struggle to live, I did the thing I knew was best.

I inched closer and reached into his pocket for the ring of keys. Then I went to grab the knife and drive it in farther to end the inevitable and put him out of his misery, but he beat me to it. Yet, he didn't push it in. He pulled it out and took a swipe at me. The blade grazed my shirt, and I leaped backward against the wall.

Murmur had me cornered, and he knew it, too, smiling as he raised the blade. I grabbed his arm, holding back the knife. His other hand came to my throat, squeezing tight. Rather than resist, I wheezed and brought my other hand to Murmur's face, pushing my thumb into his eye.

Uriel had taught me the move, and while I didn't enjoy executing it, it certainly worked in this scenario.

Murmur let go of my throat and stepped back. I choked in a breath but didn't stop. I kicked his hand and sent the knife sprawling. Quickly, I picked it up and spun it around, plunging it into his abdomen.

His face was frozen in shock.

"I'm sorry," I whispered, twisting the blade even deeper.

He winced, and slowly turned to ash, crumbling from sight.

I sank back, too numb to react.

A black feather lay on the floor. It must have fallen from his wing during the skirmish.

I dropped the blade from my hand. I had slain an angel. A fallen one, but an angel nonetheless. What had I done?

"Jordan! Jordan!"

Kat kept repeating my name over and over. I had forgotten she was there.

I looked at her with a blank gaze. She kept pointing to something.

Turning my head, I saw the ring of keys on the floor. They must have fallen from my grasp in the middle of the fight. I crawled over and picked them up, finding the one that would work on my bonds. When my wrists were free, I used a different key to open my cell.

"Go! Go!" Kat shouted.

I shook my head. "No, you're coming with me." After opening her cell, I stepped inside and knelt down to unlock her bonds.

"I'm sorry I couldn't help," she said.

I met her gaze. "You tried. I was the one who hesitated."

"It's a natural reaction," she assured me.

"It doesn't matter," I was quick to say. "What matters is getting out of here."

I reached for her right wrist and unfastened the shackle. I did the same for the left, but when the shackle opened, I stared at a tattoo that I had seen before on someone else.

The astrological symbol for Gemini.

"I knew it."

Kat pulled her arm back. "It's not what you think."

"Really? Because Gabriel has the same mark on his arm. And you two have many similarities. You're his twin, aren't you?"

She sighed in defeat and nodded. "Yes, but no one knows. They don't even know who I am."

"Why not?"

Kat didn't answer.

"This means you're part of the Council of Archangels," I said. "Which explains the fourteenth sphere. Every angel on the council has a sphere."

"I'm not a member of the Council of Archangels. I did have a sphere, but it was not needed for the Union, so I used it to trap Lilith. According to you, that sphere has since been destroyed by my…brother."

"Then what are you?"

She looked me dead in the eye. "I'm an archangel. An angel of power to be precise. Although I do not hold a seat on the council, I do share one with my brother. Together, we represent the constellation Gemini, but he is the twin who fulfills those responsibilities. I was given a different purpose, and as such, my identity is unknown to many who reside in Heaven. Father wanted it that way, so that is the way it will be. Now can we please get out of here and continue this discussion later?"

"You're right. Let's go."

We rose from the ground together and exited the cell. Kat continued on, walking right through the stone wall of the cave. I hesitated at first because I didn't realize it was possible to do that until she had disappeared. I followed after and was transported into a room with a broken stone table and two archways.

"This is Satan's portal room," Kat said. She turned around. "That is the barrier to the prison." I followed her gaze and saw another archway, presumably leading to the cells we had just escaped from. "That one is a shield that leads into Hell." She pointed to her right. "And that one—" she shifted her hand to point to an archway directly in front of us "—is the portal."

"Where does that go?" I looked to the left at a hallway.

"Out to the throne room." She stepped closer to the portal. "Are you ready?"

I nodded. "Yeah, but I've never done this before."

"Take my hand," she said, offering hers.

I grasped it.

"Place your other on the portal."

I did as I was told, and as soon as my fingers touched the invisible substance, I felt a rush of energy. "Now what?"

"You will say *terra* and the location you want to go to. I advise you to pick a generic place that can be compromised because they will be able to follow us."

"Aye! You're not supposed to be here!" someone yelled.

"Jordan, now," Kat urged.

I didn't have time to glance over my shoulder and see who had spotted us. Instead, I shouted, "*Terra* New York City."

A gleam of light flashed before my eyes, and a feeling of weightlessness overcame my entire body. There was a rushing sound in my ears that was soon replaced with the honking of a horn and the shout of a man. "Get out of the street!"

I opened my eyes, and sure enough, I was in Times Square, standing in front of an angry taxi driver who kept beeping his horn.

"Any day now!"

I glanced over at Kat, who was squinting against the bright, artificial lights, her hand still in mine.

This was my city. This was my home. I knew exactly where to go.

"Come on." I tugged Kat over to the sidewalk. "I'll take us somewhere safe."

11 SOPHIA

Location Unknown, Present Day

They had moved Dane.

It was easy to detect his absence as soon as I was brought back to my room after sparring with Rajani. They had completely cleaned up and shut down the treatment area where they had been holding him. Nothing remained. It was as if he'd never existed.

A part of me feared they might have killed him. Jazema seemed too invested in his power, though, to come this far only to destroy him. So I tried to remain optimistic. I kept telling myself he was alive, just moved to a different level within the lab. And now I had to add finding him to the list of things I needed to do in order to escape.

Ultimately, everything came back to figuring out the structure of the building—the ins and outs, the security, the identities of who or what was trapped within these walls. It was an overwhelming and daunting task. One that seemed impossible to do alone. But I had to make an effort.

I didn't know how long I had been here already, but in a short amount of time, I had gained enough trust with Penelope for her to unshackle me and let me train with Rajani. That was progress. Not completely the kind I wanted to make since all Rajani did was beat me rather than teach me. A black eye, split lip, and broken ribs were all I'd gained from her. No injury was permanent, though. In fact, mine only lasted an hour. Penelope seemed interested in my healing ability. Apparently, it was much faster than any Nephilim or angel she had known.

For me, it only solidified how much I hated what I had become.

A beeping noise came from the door. I sighed, despising that sound. I was sitting on the cold linoleum floor, knees to my chest and back turned away from the door, but I knew it was Penelope.

"Good evening, darling. I've brought you dinner."

I heard her place a tray down on the metal desk.

"I see you're in a mood today. No bother. The doctor just needs to take a look at your wings and then we'll be gone."

I flinched and turned to face her. Sure enough, another woman stood with Penelope. She was dressed in a lab coat.

"Don't touch me," I warned.

"Sweetheart, it's all right. She simply just needs to take a look. Your wings have been bound for too long. Whether that was your doing or that silly spell, I'm unsure, but in either case, the damage has been done. They are stunted and need to be fixed."

"Do they? Because I don't want them fixed. You do."

Penelope tsked. "It's a shame that you detest them. They're your greatest asset. Viewing them with negativity won't help. You'd be surprised how much your wings are connected with your willpower and psyche."

I rolled my eyes. "I don't care. Leave me alone."

Ever since my wings had unfurled on the night of the unbinding, I had pretty much ignored them. They were what I hated most. The thing that made me a freak. The feature I couldn't hide.

I had discovered them when I had been here as a little girl. That memory of feathers and blood had been haunting me in my sleep for years, but I didn't know what it meant until recently. I didn't remember how I had gotten them or what had made them go away. But deep down, I knew it was more than the spell Sister Delphine had woven into the tapestry.

Something had happened here.

"What will it take," Penelope said, striding to stand in front of me and kneeling down to look me in the eye, "to let the doctor examine your wings?"

I met her gaze and glared back at her. I knew what I wanted in exchange, but I couldn't seem too eager to bargain. After a moment, I asked, "Where is Dane?"

Penelope's eyes flashed. "Why are you so concerned about him?"

I sat up fast and got in her face. "Just answer the question!"

A smirk played at her lips. "Oh dear, you've fallen in love with him, haven't you?" She grabbed my chin with her hand and squeezed. "Mark my words, you will not think about him anymore."

Out of the corner of my eye, I saw her keycard hanging from her waist. This was my chance, but I had to keep her talking, so I didn't back down. Wresting my chin from her grasp, I said, "Mark my words, if you hurt him, it'll be the last thing you do." I genuinely believed what I had said, but it also distracted her long enough for me to gently pry the keycard from her waist.

Now, we both were silent, menacingly staring at each other. I slipped the badge up my sleeve. "Where is he?" I bit out.

Without breaking eye contact, she said, "Level nine. Satisfied?"

I nodded.

"Good." She stood up. "Doctor, please inspect her wings now."

The woman gently placed her hands on my back, and I cringed. The pain was brutal, but I had overlooked it until now. Survival was more important.

The doctor kept gently prodding, poking, and pushing on bones. Every time she would ask, "Does that hurt?" and every time I would answer, "Yes."

She moved from my back to the wings themselves. They didn't hurt at all. She brushed her hands over the feathers, felt the ligaments and bones.

Suddenly, she sighed and stood up.

"Well?" Penelope demanded.

"Her wings are fine. Full-grown, strong, real beauties actually. It's her back I'm concerned about. The vertebrae didn't shift so they're resting on top of one another. Normally, as young Nephilim children grow, so too does their spinal column, which allows the wing bones to develop and move into place. In her case, the wings sprouted when she was young but were then bound, causing a discrepancy in how the body naturally adapts to them."

Penelope shook her head. "How do we fix it? Surgery?"

"I'm not undergoing surgery for this!" I protested.

"You don't have a say in the matter," Penelope said.

"Yes, I do. I'm twenty years old. Definitely a legal adult who gets to make decisions about what happens to my body."

"Well, those rules don't apply here. I'm in charge."

Horrified, I said, "Is that the way it is for everyone?"

She shrugged me off.

"Clearly, it is," I continued. "If you can do it to me, your own daughter, then I guess you can do it to anyone."

"Enough!" Penelope shouted. "You're having this surgery!"

"Can I just say that there is an alternative treatment," the doctor inserted.

Penelope leveled her with a venomous look. "And what might that be?"

The doctor met my eyes. "Using your wings and letting them adjust on their own."

"I don't want to do that," I said. "Besides, it's not like I can fly around here."

"I beg to differ," the doctor replied. "Your mother has many training facilities. But it's not my decision to make." She turned to Penelope. "How would you like to proceed?"

"Surgery," Penelope commanded. "Tomorrow."

I was outraged. "Tomorrow?!"

"I'm doing this for your own good." Penelope motioned the doctor toward the door.

Taking the hint, she strode over and opened it, Penelope following after her and leaving me alone once again.

I shook my head. There was no way I was having that surgery.

Slipping my fingers down the sleeve of my shirt, I pulled out Penelope's ID card.

It wouldn't be long before she knew it was missing. So I had to act. Now.

I stood up and went over to the door. It beeped as I scanned the badge, and then I grabbed the handle and opened it. I stepped into the empty hallway, slinking past the deserted treatment area and down to the elevator that I knew would take me to the other levels.

I used the badge again and pressed the button to summon the elevator. Stepping back, I braced myself for anyone who might be inside.

Thankfully, it was empty when it arrived. I stepped inside, swiped the badge, and hit the button for level ten.

As the doors closed and the elevator descended, I whispered, "I'm coming, Dane. Just hold on."

12 DANE

Location Unknown, Present Day

My eyes slowly opened. I stared at the ceiling through an oxygen mask. I was in a different room, this one dimly lit. Everything was quiet, except for the clicks and beeps of machines. I tried moving my arms, but they felt heavy.

Suddenly, the room began to inch downward. Or maybe I was, because the next thing I knew, ice water rushed over my body.

My mind panicked, yet my body remained motionless.

"Don't worry," Jazema said. Her voice was dull and muted and came from my left side. Eventually, her figure loomed over me. "Your fever is returning. The ice water is the only way to fight it."

Glancing down, I saw that I was reclined on a metal platform that was attached to a tank of water. With the click of a button, Jazema lowered me farther until my body was submerged, leaving my head out for air.

I gasped as the freezing water touched my wings. My skin reveled in the cold, but my wings were sensitive to it. Or maybe I was sensitive to them since they were such a new addition.

I tried raising my arm to my face to pry off the oxygen mask, but it was hard to control my limbs. "Wh-wh-what a-a-are you d-d-doing to me?" I stammered.

"Sedating you with nitrous oxide, otherwise known as laughing gas. It's the only way to keep you calm."

I wanted to chuckle and retort, *More like keep me complacent*, but I couldn't form the words.

"You'll remain here until your condition subsides. I'm afraid your transition isn't over yet, if the fever is any indication." She paused. "The nurses and I will check on you regularly to make sure you're comfortable. We cannot proceed until we know your full capabilities and potential."

She stepped back and disappeared. The room was quiet so I figured she'd left it entirely.

I closed my eyes and couldn't help but sink into despair. Is this what my life was to become? Was I to be a prisoner, an experiment, forced to lie here numbly? Would I ever draw again? Would I ever see Sophia again?

A single tear escaped my eye and ran down my cheek.

My body was a cage, and I was its captive.

Hush, my son.

It was her again.

Dry your tears.

Lilith.

I'm coming for you.

I rejoiced at her words and settled back in the pool of cleansing waters, sensing I would soon be reborn.

13

GABRIEL

HEAVEN, PRESENT DAY

Numbness overcame me as I stared at the place where Jophiel had just been. It wasn't possible. He couldn't be gone.

Zadkiel was the first to move. He shuffled over to the charred spot and dropped to the ground, letting out a wail of anguish. Chamuel was the next, springing forward to comfort our brother. Raphael grabbed me by the shoulder and kept saying something to me. It wasn't until I flicked my eyes away and looked down at my hand that I realized I was gripping the blade of my knife. Blood trickled down my hand. As soon as I let go, the wound started to heal.

If only grief after death could mend so quickly.

I stood there, unmoving. My mind couldn't comprehend what had just happened, let alone figure out what to do next. Thankfully, Michael and Uriel seemed able to at least do the latter. Michael strode out of the dungeon with Uriel close upon his heels. I glanced at Raphael.

"You should go with them," he said. "I will remain here until they are ready."

I swallowed and tried to focus on the moment, on what came now.

"What if there are wounded?" I asked.

"Then another angel of healing can take care of it." He slipped by me to join the others.

Steeling my emotions the best I could, I exited the dungeon and let my feet guide me through halls to the place I knew I would find Michael and Uriel.

I stopped briefly before the doors to the council room, preparing myself for what might lay beyond them. The Council of Seraphim convened in a domed room at the top of the castle, which was much smaller than the gathering room where we had originally met. When I pushed them open, I was met with an unwelcome sight.

The Great Tree had been destroyed. It was our direct connection with Father, housed within the council room, as they were the ones who communed with Him the most. It stood at the far end of the circular room, its branches severed and its trunk slashed in two. The seats that surrounded the tree had been tossed out of their semicircle formation and instead lay toppled over. This place was typically full of serenity, its walls and ceiling made of beautiful stained glass. Now it was a crystalline casket of ruin.

I was devastated by the blatant desecration aimed at Father.

Michael and Uriel weren't alone in the room. A handful of our brothers and sisters milled about to assess the damage. In fact, they were in deep conversation with Tzaphkiel, a fellow member of the Council of Archangels. I joined them as they discussed the damage to the other realms.

"And the Tree?" I asked. "How do we repair it?"

"The angels of nature are already attending to it. They are working with the angels of healing to mend it," Uriel assured me. He turned to Tzaphkiel. "Is Sandalphon around? He is the most knowledgeable angel of nature. I'm sure he'll know what to do."

Tzaphkiel frowned. "You don't know?"

"Know what?" I asked.

"He resigned his post shortly after you all were sent down to Earth. Father had another task for him. Sandalphon no longer resides in Heaven."

"Where is he, then?" Uriel demanded.

Tzaphkiel shrugged. "I'm unsure. A lot has changed since you've been away."

"What else?" Michael asked.

"Well, Metatron and Raziel were elevated to Seraphim. Father gave them the vacant seats on the council after the war to recognize all they have accomplished in interpreting and documenting the divine wisdoms."

"I see," Michael said.

"And Ariel?" I wondered aloud.

Tzaphkiel grew serious. "She's gone. Many claim she's missing, but it's been so long that I imagine...she has met a darker fate."

"What do you mean?" I asked. "Where did she go?"

"She went after Lilith," Tzaphkiel explained. "Many years ago. Ariel believed she found a way to stop her. She presented her plans to Father, who sanctioned her departure. She told no one else of what she knew or where she was going. And she never returned."

"If hardly anyone is left," Michael said, "then who sits on the Council of Archangels?"

Tzaphkiel pursed her lips. "Me and four others. I was appointed interim Head of Council due to my seniority. The full council must be organized for us to vote in a new one. Your seats still remain, but Father did fill the four vacant ones."

"With whom?" Uriel demanded.

"Some great comrades," Tzaphkiel assured us. She glanced at Michael. "One in particular I think you would approve of—Cassiel. He's actually the one who freed us from Lilith's capture."

Michael let a quick grin flash across his face at the mention of his best lieutenant. "Where is he?"

"Not far off I'm sure," Tzaphkiel said. "Cassiel!"

An angel sauntered over to us. He had dark hair and golden-brown skin. "You called?" he asked.

"I was just telling our brothers here that you're one of the newest additions to the council," Tzaphkiel explained.

"And that you were the one who helped everyone escape," Michael added.

"Of course, Commander. You taught me well," Cassiel said.

"Indeed." They clasped arms in greeting. "Is there anything you can tell us about the attack?"

Cassiel crossed his arms. "It was calculated. She knew her way around this place. Knew every one of our weak points. She attacked quickly and quietly with a small group, but their attack involved little bloodshed initially. It was more manipulation." He paused, thinking it over. Then he seemed to suddenly remember something. He reached into his cloak and pulled out some device, which he handed to Michael. "Each of them was wearing one of these on their wrist. I think it's a teleportation tool. It would be the only way to explain how they entered and exited with such stealth and without detection."

Michael passed the device to me. It looked like a watch, except instead of a timepiece, it had a blank silver disc with several dials. I handed it to Uriel.

"Any guesses as to how it was made?" I asked.

Cassiel shook his head. "No."

"We'll figure it out. Just give it to Jo—" Uriel stopped, his usual stony expression cracking to reveal the grief underneath. He shoved the device at Cassiel, anger replacing sadness. "Just give it to the angels of art."

"Has something happened to Jophiel?" Tzaphkiel asked.

I nodded. "He's..." I shook my head, unable to say the words.

Everyone grew somber and silent. The others joined us, giving us an opportunity to change the subject. Zadkiel, Chamuel, and Raphael were soon filled in on the changes that had occurred in Heaven, as well as the mysterious device.

"Where are the keys?" Zadkiel demanded. "The box we were protecting was empty."

"What?" Tzaphkiel shouted in surprise.

"Lilith must have them," Michael said solemnly.

"Then we have to recover them," Cassiel said.

"No," I insisted. "First we must rescue our friends."

"And what of the keys?" Cassiel asked.

I met his gaze. "They will come after."

"And Lilith?" Tzaphkiel asked.

"She will pay," the six of us said in unison. It was an oath.

"You two will remain here and bring peace back to our home," Michael commanded.

Tzaphkiel and Cassiel nodded. "Of course."

Michael stayed Cassiel by grabbing his arm. "Wait for my call. A battle is brewing, and our armies must meet the fight."

Cassiel nodded. "Yes, sir."

"Now we must go," I said. "Lives hang in the balance, and our other family is depending on us."

"Of course," Tzaphkiel said. "These are desperate times. Do what you must."

With that, the six of us exited the council room and took the stairs to the tower. None of us hesitated when we entered the open-air gallery. We simply jumped off into the portal that would take us back.

It was time to finish what we had started. It was time to save the three most important beings that walked the Earth.

14 SOPHIA

Location Unknown, Present Day

When I arrived at level nine, I let out a breath of relief. The entire way down I was worried someone on another floor was waiting for the elevator. I imagined the doors opening and me trying to fight off whomever was on the other side, only to lead to my chances of escape being blown. But none of that had happened. I hadn't been intercepted.

Now my mind filled with new fears. What lay ahead? Memories certainly. Was I ready to face them? I took a deep breath and stepped off the elevator. There was no going back. Besides, the memories didn't matter. What mattered was Dane.

The hallway was deserted and eerily quiet. I wondered what time of day it was because it seemed like early evening or night had fallen, given the lack of people milling about.

This entire floor was dimly lit, which only made the experience creepier. I came to the end of the hall and wondered which way to go. Flashbacks of the underground tunnels Sister Helen had sent me into came to mind. I forced myself not to think about them. I wasn't that person anymore. I paused. Actually, I *truly* wasn't that girl anymore. I was a Nephilim now, and whether I liked it or not, I had to get used to it.

So maybe I should put my new skills to the test. I closed my eyes and listened, hoping my celestial hearing might pick something up. I heard the faint sounds of breathing and let my feet trail in their direction. Opening my eyes, I continued down the new hallway, passing doors as I went. I stopped at one and gazed at the small screen affixed to the wall next to the door. It showed a live camera recording of the person inside. It was a girl. She was sitting on her bed reading a book. She looked about my age and had the most beautiful golden-brown wings. They looked similar to those of a barn owl. Who was she? Why was she here?

At least she seemed unharmed and cared for. A clean set of scrubs sat at the edge of her bed, and an empty food tray lay on her desk. The girl raised her head away from the book and stared at the camera as if she knew someone was watching her. She stood and walked over to the door, her face filling the entire screen.

Suddenly, I remembered her. Her pale skin and platinum-blond hair. Her face was nearly unrecognizable since we both had aged and grown, but her piercing blue eyes were still the same.

Siena. Her name was Siena.

I raised a hand to my mouth and stepped back as the memories started to flood my mind. She had attacked me when we were younger. Tore at my wings. That's where the feathers and blood in my memories had come from. But there was still more that wouldn't come to the surface.

"Well, well, well... Look who has returned."

I flinched at the sound of her voice. It was warbly through the monitor, which I thought was purely video, with no audio. "I never thought I would see you again, but here you are, Sophia."

How did she know it was me?

She cackled. "It's easy to sense you, especially your surprise. After all these years, I guess that's my spectacular gift."

What did she mean?

Then I remembered Penelope's words. How I healed quicker than any Nephilim or angel she knew. That must be my anomaly. Siena's must be her senses—all of them, not just hearing.

I pulled myself away from the screen and shuffled down the hall.

"Leaving so soon? Can't say I'll miss you." She cackled again.

I rubbed my arms, trying to chase away the sudden chill that had creeped up them. I needed to stay focused. I had to find Dane so we could get out of here.

Stopping in my tracks again, I turned around to glance down the hall. Who was to say Siena was the only one locked down here? There were other doors, other cameras. I just hadn't stopped to look. Who was to say that they didn't deserve a chance at freedom, too?

I would help them. Except I had to help myself first.

Continuing on, I headed in a new direction. I stopped at a door and scanned Penelope's badge. It led me into a large room full of monitors, each one dedicated to a patient. There were so many—at least twenty.

I drew closer to the screens, passing by a sealed chamber. Glancing through the glass window in the door, I realized it was a temperature-controlled specimen room. I imagined there were blood samples in there. I pulled my attention away from the chamber and noticed my dagger from the unbinding sat in a holder on the wall. They must have confiscated it.

I took it down and slid it in my pocket, then settled my eyes back on the screens. I approached them and took a seat.

Before focusing on the footage, I glanced over my shoulder to make note of the exits. There was the way I had come in, as well as a doorway on the far side of the room.

Feeling like I was safe enough, I took a moment to analyze the screens. There were girls and boys, some my age but most of them younger. They all seemed fine physically; however, it was hard to tell what damage had been done mentally. As the screens panned from footage to footage, I realized there were classifications among patients. Most were designated Nephilim. Two were labeled Pure Form Nephilim. There were some that were classified as Watchers, which was surprising but also impossible to identify since the rooms were vacant.

Then the screen flipped again. At the top, it read *Supernals.* There were four video streams beneath it.

One of which showed Dane.

Supernal? What was a Supernal?

"You never learned when to mind your own business."

I whipped around in my seat.

It was Jazema. Next to her stood Naomi.

"Always a pesky girl," Jazema said. "I guess you're a pesky woman now. Just like your mother."

My eyes narrowed. "I thought you were business partners."

"We are. Doesn't mean I like her, though. When I started Geneloom, I had a different business partner. We were much closer. Practically sisters. When she died, I had no choice but to ask your mother for help."

Jazema reached into a cabinet and pulled out a gun. She leveled it at me. "I've tolerated enough of her antics. I'm not about to endure yours, as well. You ruined enough the last time you were here."

I clenched my teeth and swallowed hard.

Jazema raised an eyebrow. "Nothing to say?"

I shook my head. "I don't remember my time here."

Jazema lowered the gun. "Then I should fill you in. When you were here, you managed to make all the girls loathe you, to the point that Siena nearly tore you to shreds. You had the best Nephilim aptitudes we have ever seen, yet you never wanted to use them. I couldn't kill you because I needed Penelope on my side, so I fiddled with your growth, gave you stunting supplements, hoping that Penelope would see you had no potential. No matter what I did, though, it didn't matter. She was determined to make you extraordinary.

"Your only friend was my Moriko. Except your acquaintance ultimately caused her death. When your father rescued you, he destroyed the lab, blowing it up with every other patient inside it."

I shook my head. "No…" It was too horrific.

"Yes. You cost me my daughter." She raised the gun again. "So I've had enough of you."

"Wait!" I shouted. "Why did you capture us?"

Jazema rolled her eyes. "You're here because when Penelope saw you at the gala, her interest in you renewed. Dane is here because he has the potential for power, and I want to use it desperately."

"And Jordan?" I asked, hoping for news.

Jazema tsked. "Neither Penelope nor I wanted him. Lucifer did, though."

What?! Lucifer had him. That meant he must be in Hell. Which was probably a million times worse than this lab. "Why did he want him?" I asked to keep her talking.

"Enough!" she screamed. "The chitchat is over!"

I tensed and closed my eyes, waiting for the shot. None came. I opened them again and looked at Jazema. She had an evil smile on her face. "You do it," she said, not breaking eye contact with me and handing the gun to Naomi.

I forgot she had been standing there all this time.

"What?" she asked.

"Kill her," Jazema said, "and you won't be an intern anymore. I'll give you the open position and fire the other girl."

Naomi took the gun.

I met her eyes and pleaded with her through my gaze.

She raised the weapon. I tensed again but kept my eyes open.

Naomi put her finger on the trigger and then suddenly shifted her arm, setting four rounds into Jazema. She shrieked and fell to the ground.

"Do you really think I'm a stone-cold backstabber?" Naomi tucked the gun in the waist of her pants. "Help me tie her up before she starts to heal."

Shocked, I rose from the chair and looked around the room for something to use.

Naomi had Jazema's hands locked behind her back. "There are zip-ties in the third drawer," she told me, pointing to a cabinet.

I retrieved them and brought them to her. Naomi put them around Jazema's wrists and ankles.

"You bitch," Jazema wheezed out. "You'll pay for this."

"I'm sure I will, but I'll be long gone before you get a hold of me," Naomi replied. She rose and turned to face me. "I'm sorry for making you think I was a bad guy, but I had to finish my trial of trust."

Recognition dawned on my face. "You're Sacrarium."

"Just about," Naomi said. "My mom thought I'd be a good member."

"Your mom?"

"Yeah, she's the new Alpha." Naomi glanced at her watch. "The rescue team should be showing up any minute. I have two things I still need to do."

"How can I help?"

"You can go over there and press that red button, which will release all the patients. I'm going to place explosives in the specimen room to destroy their research."

She nonchalantly told me her plans, and I couldn't help but smile. Naomi was pretty amazing.

I hit the red button, and alarms started to sound.

"That's okay!" Naomi shouted. "It's part of the plan."

I watched the screens. Some patients were eager to flee, while others were hesitant. Eventually, though, everyone escaped.

The screens flashed, and I saw Dane's room once again. The door was open, but he was still lying immobile.

Naomi came close to my side.

"We have to help him!" I pleaded.

"Let's go!" Naomi grabbed my arm as a sudden explosion rocked the whole building. It sent us sprawling to the floor.

Dazed, I turned my head to look at her. "How many explosives did you use?"

"That wasn't me!" she yelled. "Mine aren't set to go off yet!"

We eased up off the floor, and Naomi fiddled with the monitor controls, bringing up the security cameras. She panned through them until she found a skirmish taking place on one of them. Hitting a button, she initiated the audio.

There were a lot of gunshots and smoke. It was hard to see what was happening. Then Lilith came into view. In one instant, she managed to shoot someone with the gun in her left hand and slit the throat of another with the blade in her right. She dropped her weapons and waved her hands, leveling another five bodies.

"Whoever she is," Naomi said, "she is *not* part of the plan."

"No, she's worse. She's chaos and destruction." My voice hitched. "And she's here for Dane." I met Naomi's eye. "Take me to him. Now!"

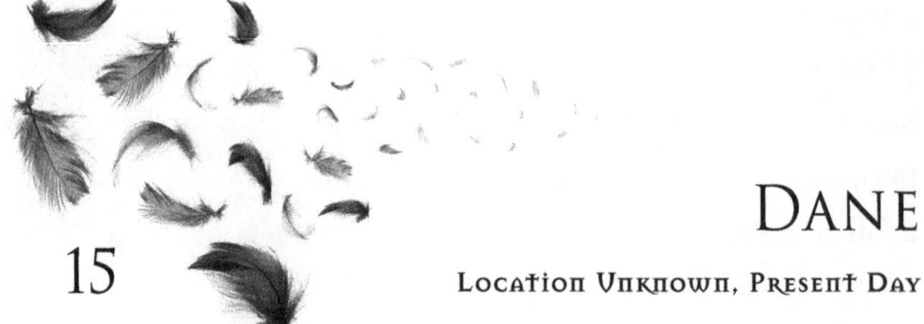

15

DANE

Location Unknown, Present Day

There was rumbling and then an explosion. My eyes eased open. The door to the room I was in had miraculously unlocked and rolled back.

I slowly lifted my arms, fighting the nitrous oxide. It was time to claim my birthright.

I ripped the mask off my face and threw it across the room. Then I dunked my head back in the ice water, clearing my dazed mind.

Never hold back, Ace.

Satan's words whispered in my ear, the ones he had said to me when he had trained me at the gym. I had savored those encouraging remarks at the time, but I didn't need them anymore. Instead, my mother's invocation rang through me.

Stand as Darcel, blood mage full of strength and might.

Opening my eyes underwater, I launched out of the tank, ready to kill whoever stood in my way.

16 SOPHIA

Location Unknown, Present Day

Naomi led me through the halls as best she could, but it was utter chaos everywhere we went. Some patients were fleeing; others were trying to enact their revenge. Security guards and lab technicians were trying to restrain everyone, while subsequently fighting off Lilith's henchmen and running for their lives.

A couple of times we had been confronted either by guards, attackers, or patients, but we had done well evading them or settling the matter quickly.

Naomi still had the gun in the waistband of her pants, and we both had picked up a few other weapons along the way—knives, scalpels, gun magazines. She seemed very well-trained in firearms whereas I had grown decently acceptable at hand-to-hand combat and had learned where to place a strategic strike.

Another explosion sounded.

"Okay, *that* was me!" Naomi yelled over the commotion.

"Now what happens?" I asked.

"Reinforcements arrive."

"We could have used them twenty minutes ago."

"I know, but this psycho chick was not part of the plan."

When we finally arrived at Dane's room, it was empty.

"Where did he go?" I shouted.

"He must have escaped," Naomi said.

"How? He was heavily sedated."

"You heard Jazema. He's supposed to be superpowerful."

A gunshot rang out. I flinched as Naomi dropped to the ground.

"Naomi!" I shouted. I went to help her but someone said, "Don't move."

Her voice was like ice sliding down my back.

"Turn around," Lilith demanded.

I did as she'd instructed and faced her.

She stepped over to me and stroked my cheek. "Pretty thing, aren't you? I can tell why he's besotted with you." Lilith jammed the gun under my chin. "Darcel cannot have any distractions, and you, my beauty, are certainly a distraction." She lowered the gun. "It's not my job to kill you, though. Just capture you. He must do the deed. You must be his first kill." She backed off. "Let's go."

I didn't move. My eyes were rooted to the blood spilling out from Naomi's abdomen.

"Did you not hear me?" she snapped. "Let's go!" She waved her hand in the air, and my body became hers. I lost complete control, my feet moving without my permission, following her every command. She was leading me straight to my death, and I had no say in the matter.

17 JORDAN

New York City, Present Day

Ever since Sister Helen had sent me to Gabriel's apartment, it had turned into a safe haven for me, and that trait was never more accurate than now.

When Kat and I entered the lobby, I was happy to see Benny manning the door.

"Jordan!" he shouted in greeting. Then his face sank into a frown. "Are you all right?"

"Hi, Benny. We're fine. This is Kat, Gabriel's sister. We came here to spend the night. Do you happen to have an extra key to the apartment?"

"Of course," he said. "Let me get it for you."

Benny went behind the security desk and found the spare key. He came back over to us and handed it to me. I reached for it, but Benny pulled back.

"You sure you're okay, kid?"

"Yes, I promise. We just had a rough night."

He nodded and handed over the key. "Okay. You take care of yourself."

"I will," I assured him.

Taking Kat's arm, I directed her toward the elevator. We entered, and I glanced at her. "Are you okay?"

She sighed. "It's been many years since I was last on Earth. I grew weaker in Hell, and now my celestial energy is trying to rejuvenate. The sudden transition is jarring, but nothing I can't handle."

The elevator dinged.

"Well, we should be able to rest for a little bit here," I said, steering her to Gabriel's apartment.

Kat shook her head. "There is no time for rest, Jordan."

"Then a regroup," I suggested, unlocking the door.

We went inside. Kat stopped in the foyer, eyes scanning the place. "This is where Gabriel lives?"

"Yes, he's acquired a somewhat lavish taste." I moved beyond the foyer and into the living room.

She followed. "We need a plan on how to get out of the city."

"Right. We can just go to my house."

"Sure, but how do we get there? Does my brother have a vehicle?"

He did, but it was currently sitting in my garage. "Good point." I sank to the couch.

"We could call someone," Kat suggested.

"I don't have my phone." I'd lost it somewhere along the way. Maybe Lucifer had taken it. Either way, it didn't matter.

"There isn't one around here?"

I glanced around the apartment. "No. Gabriel doesn't really like phones."

"What about the man downstairs? Can we use his phone?"

"And endanger an innocent person? No, I'm not involving Benny, or anyone else for that matter. We'll figure out another way."

Kat crossed her arms. "Really? I don't see you coming up with any ideas."

Offended, I said, "If you could just fly, all our problems would be solved."

We both fell to silence.

"I'm sorry. I shouldn't have lashed out," I said.

"It's fine. I was the one who started it." She sat down next to me. "We could take a bus or a train. We'd need money, though, for tickets."

I sprang off the couch and down the hall.

"Jordan!" Kat called. "Where are you going?"

I raced into Gabriel's office and sat down at his desk. There had to be cash or a credit card somewhere. I pulled open the center drawer of his desk, and sure enough, he had a card tucked in there.

Kat appeared in the doorway. "What—" I raised the card, and she stopped. "Okay, so we have money."

Turning to the computer, I said, "I can buy the tickets right now." I powered it on. It lit up and immediately went to the lock screen.

Hmm… I wondered what password an angel would use to secure their computer. Thinking about Gabriel's lack of technological savvy, I smiled and typed in, *Password*.

There was a brief pause, and then the laptop transitioned to the home screen.

When I saw Gabriel again, I had to remember to get him to change that. I was grateful for it in this moment, though.

"All right." I navigated to the internet and went to the Greyhound website. There was a bus leaving tonight that was headed for Ithaca. I showed Kat.

"Perfect. We have to keep moving so the Fallen won't find us. The faster we leave, the better."

I booked two bus tickets and printed them out. When I was done, I sat back in the desk chair, closing my eyes.

Alarmed, Kat asked, "What's wrong?"

I wasn't sure myself. I just felt like I needed a minute. My stomach growled.

"Of course, you must be hungry. Let me go get something for you to eat."

My eyes flashed open. "No, you don't feel good. I'll go."

Kat shook her head. "I need to reacquaint myself with this world."

"I'll come with you. We shouldn't split up," I said.

Kat placed a hand on my arm. "I'll be fine. Besides, you need to rest. I can sense this place is sanctified against the Fallen so I know you'll be fine in my absence, which won't be long. What would you like to eat?"

I thought it over. "I'm starving, but I shouldn't gorge myself. Maybe a turkey sandwich?"

"I saw a deli on our way here that wasn't too far." She reached for the card. "I'll be back soon. Just relax while I'm gone." She stopped at the office door and backtracked, grabbing a decorative knife that hung on the wall.

"You know that's probably some priceless antique, right?" I pointed out.

She nodded. "Most likely. It's certainly not celestial, but it'll do."

I grinned and watched her leave.

As soon as she was gone, I sighed and ran a hand through my hair. I didn't feel like myself. Maybe it was the hunger just throwing me off. Maybe a nice, hot shower is all I needed to feel better.

I walked down the hall and went into the bathroom. I looked like hell. My hair was a mess, and I had stubble on my chin, not to mention a black eye, split lip, and cut cheek.

I turned on the shower, then peeled off my coat and lifted my shirt over my head. My eyes grew wide when I spotted the small wound on my abdomen. It was just a graze from Murmur's knife swipe, but I was still alarmed. I had been injured with a dark weapon. Small black lines were already spreading from the injury. It wasn't deep, but the damage had been done.

Crap!

I needed holy water. Now.

Slipping out of the bathroom, I crossed the apartment and entered Gabriel's bedroom. I raided his dresser and closet to see if he had any holy water around. No luck. I tried his office next. Luckily, there was an old holy water grenade in his desk. I went back to the bathroom, turned off the shower, and wiped steam from the mirror. Unscrewing the glass ball, I braced myself and poured the water over the cut.

I cringed and gripped the side of the sink.

Damn, that hurts.

Clenching my teeth, I poured more and let out a scream. Even though it seared, I tipped the glass ball again. Nothing came out. Glancing down, I saw it was empty.

Great! I was screwed if I didn't find more soon. What I had poured had barely done anything.

I threw the glass ball in the trash and bent over to get my shirt. Just as I picked it up, something on my coat caught my eye. It looked like a small black fly.

"Shit!" I violently grabbed my coat and pried the tracker off it. I had to get rid of it. Thoughts of smashing it raced through my mind, but I would need something to crush it. Like a hammer or something heavy. My eyes landed on the bathroom sink, which made me remember that the kitchen sink had a garbage disposal.

I ran out of the bathroom and into the kitchen, ready to throw the tracker down the drain and flick the disposal switch, but I froze at the sink. Staring out the window, a full moon consumed my gaze.

When the full moon rises, you'll be whole.

Dane. He needed me.

I closed my hand over the tracker and sank to the floor.

My mind was racing, and I wasn't sure what to do. I felt backed into a corner with everything that had been thrown at me in the past minute.

I could leave the tracker here at the apartment and go find Kat. We could take the bus home, treat my wound, and find Sophia, Dane, and the angels.

But what price might Dane pay? The full moon was tonight. If I waited to help him, what would happen?

While the plan was logical, it wasn't what my gut was telling me to do.

Damn it, damn it, damn it! I had to save him. I had to try. Even if it landed me back in Hell.

I jumped up from the floor and returned to the bathroom. Maybe I could help both Kat and Dane. I put the tracker back on my coat and dressed myself again with the hope that I might be able to lead the Fallen away from the apartment. I slipped one of the printed tickets in my pocket and left the other on the counter for Kat. I scribbled a short note for her:

> *Don't come looking for me. Just take the bus and go to my house.*
>
> *The address is 520 Oak Harbor Road.*
>
> *The gate code is 0325.*
>
> *I'll meet you there. If I don't show up, assume I've been captured by the Fallen.*

I left the note with her ticket and figured I was ready to leave. Then my stomach growled again. I went into the kitchen, gulped down two glasses of water, and found a roll of crackers in the cabinet, which I shoved in my pocket.

That should be everything.

A sudden pain erupted in my side, and I doubled over.

I needed holy water, but I also needed to go.

Mustering through the pain, I ransacked the kitchen for something I could put holy water in. Luckily, I found a flask in one of the drawers.

Now I was ready. I just hoped my plan worked.

18 JORDAN

New York City, Present Day

There was a church several blocks away from Gabriel's apartment. The farther I traveled, the more I led the Fallen away from Kat, which seemed like a good idea to me.

I paused on the church steps, hand on the door. Could I even enter if dark matter was running through my veins?

Shrugging, I guessed there was no time to find out like the present.

I was grateful I didn't burst into flames the moment I stepped inside. My gaze darted around the dim interior of the church. I needed to find the well of holy water to fill my flask. I spotted it off to the left. I headed in that direction. The church was quiet, it was night, and there were only two other people inside sitting in the pews.

When I made it to the well, I reached in my pocket for the flask, unscrewed it, and dipped it in the holy water. It started to fill instantly.

"Young man."

I jumped and glanced over my shoulder. "Yes?"

"You know you shouldn't be drinking that, right?"

"I do, Father," I said to the priest. "It's just I need to take some with me, and I didn't know what else to put it in."

"So long as you know," he said, striding down the aisle.

Sighing, I removed the flask from the well, screwed the lid back on, and returned it to my pocket. One task completed. Now I needed to figure out how to help Dane. But I had no way of knowing where he was, and even if I did, I couldn't get there in time to save him.

I spied candles sitting in front of a statue of the Virgin and Child. Lighting one seemed like the right thing to do. I went over, grabbed a match, lit a candle, and knelt in front of the statue. Closing my eyes and clasping my hands, I thought about the most recent vision I had, reciting the words over again in my mind:

First comes the fire blazing through bones,
But wait until your veins cool to take your throne.

By the new moon, you'll be ready for flight.
Let the air rush through your wings, black as night.

Like the Earth, rest your soul,
For when the full moon rises, you'll be whole.

With the waters, you'll be reborn,
Nothing left to be mourned.

Return to me, my son. Claim your birthright.
Stand as Darcel, blood mage full of strength and might.

It seemed like Lilith had put some spell on him that would gradually reveal his powers and change him into someone else entirely. But didn't he deserve a choice? Didn't he deserve to choose if he wanted to be Dane or Darcel?

"Not everyone has a choice."

I opened my eyes. I wasn't in the church anymore. I was outside in a glen full of shimmering light.

"M-Mom?"

My mother was sitting on a log before me. She patted a place next to her. I rose and went to sit at her side. She immediately put her arm around me and pulled me close. "I didn't have a choice when I left you."

I hugged her close and said, "I know."

She rested her head on mine. "You think Dane deserves a choice, though?"

"Yes."

"Regardless of his lineage?"

"Of course. He didn't pick his parents. He didn't know the power lurking inside him, and I'm sure if he had a choice, he would choose right."

"You believe that wholeheartedly? Who's to say the dark isn't right in his case?"

I pulled back. "I'm not here to debate if light is right and dark is wrong. I'm here to try to find the gray area, the balance. Dane can be the balance."

My mom smiled. "Indeed. He can be. But not without you. He wasn't created to be the balance. He was created to be an apocalyptic force. You are what keeps him in check."

Shaking my head, I said, "No, I'm not."

She gave me a scolding look.

I thought it over. All the times I had interceded. He had hated me for most of them. Now I think he was grateful. "I guess you might be right."

She nodded. "And has he returned the favor?"

He had saved me from the hellhounds at Dafne's condo last spring. I didn't tell her that since I didn't think she'd want to hear it, though. "I can't say if he's returned the favor or not."

"Hmm..." My mom pondered what I had said. "You and he have a special bond. You always have."

"I know," I agreed, "which is why I need to help him."

"And help him you shall," my mom said. "But there is a burden that must be carried."

"I'll carry it. Put the burden on my shoulders. Dane has suffered enough."

My mom patted my cheek. "My boy, you are too good. Your request is granted. Be prepared for the consequences, though."

Consequences? What consequences?

Someone latched on to my shoulder, and I opened my eyes. I was back in the church, kneeling in front of the candles and statue. Except this time, it wasn't the priest who had intervened. It was the hooded man from the gala—the Sentinel.

"You're taking me back to Hell, aren't you?"

"Yep. There's a new queen in residence, and she wants to meet you face-to-face when she returns."

19 SOPHIA

Location Unknown, Present Day

Dane wouldn't kill me.

That's what I kept telling myself as Lilith sauntered down the halls and I aimlessly followed her. She defeated any opposition that stood in our way, which was hardly any at this point, as most everyone had fled the building.

It didn't take long to locate Dane. I was sure it would have taken me a while to find him on my own since he was isolated in some sort of solarium that I had never seen before. For Lilith, it had been easy. They were connected beyond the bounds of blood. They were linked through power.

Relief washed through me at the sight of him, despite what Lilith had claimed. He was standing alone in front of the window, looking out at the night and the full moon. He looked healthy and rejuvenated—unlike the last time I had seen him when he'd seemed to be in a miserable state of pain. He had black gargoyle wings now that suited his appearance perfectly.

Externally, he hadn't changed much. Internally, I hoped he hadn't changed at all. I wanted him to be broody and kind and artistic. I wanted to see his smile and hear his laugh. But as soon as he turned his attention to us, I knew I had lost him. His whole demeanor was foreign, his eyes full of menacing rage, his lips puckered in a scowl.

Lilith released her control on me. I felt it instantly, as if all the blood had rushed back into my limbs. I didn't run, though. I had to stay. I had to try to reason with him.

A proud smile graced Lilith's face as she strode over to Dane. "At last, I'm reunited with my son." She placed her hands on his bare shoulders, her gloves protecting her from the Hellfire running through his veins. "Since the day you were born, I knew you were bound for greatness. I made sure of it."

Dane wasn't paying attention to her. His gaze was fixed on me. He kept clenching and unclenching his jaw as if the sight of me was having some sort of effect on him.

Lilith turned around with a frown on her face. She venomously stared at me, her arm still around Dane. "Darcel, what are you feeling?"

He didn't answer. He stepped forward, closing the distance between us until he stood mere inches from me. He reached out his hand as if to touch my neck. My breath hitched, and he stopped. Our eyes met.

"Kill her, Darcel!" Lilith demanded.

For a moment, he considered it. His eyes narrowed, and a small smirk played at his lips. But then the Dane I knew resurfaced, fighting off the demon inside.

"I love—" He never got to finish. His eyes rolled back in his head, and he dropped to the floor.

"Darcel!" Lilith screamed.

Obviously, she hadn't been the one to stop him, given her shock.

Lilith knelt next to Dane's limp body and brushed the hair from his face.

Suddenly, a force like no other came over me, and I said, "You don't get to decide his fate, Lilith. He has been given a choice."

I don't know where the words came from, but I felt as if someone had taken over my body.

Lilith looked up at me. "Evangeline, you meddling bitch!" Lilith started to bring her hand in the air, and I knew what that meant. Not a loss of control this time, but death.

I didn't hide, or run, or back down from it. I was ready to face it. Except someone else didn't want me to die.

A body collided with mine, the force sending us both through the solarium's window and out into the open air. The drop wasn't steep but certainly would result in injuries, and for the second time in a matter of minutes, a force overcame me. This time it wasn't some higher power. This time it was pure instinct.

The wings in my back eased out, catching the wind. I gripped the person who had saved me more tightly in my arms and crested the air, slowly descending to the ground. My back was screaming in protest, but I ignored it and concentrated on landing. I was aiming for an open spot next to the building on the outskirts of a forest, and while I aimed correctly, I had no idea what I was doing.

We crashed into the ground. I let go of the person, and my wings wrapped around me to break the fall. I rolled a few times and came to a stop. That definitely had been an ungraceful way to end my first flight, but at least we would have bruises instead of broken bones.

Easing up onto my arm, I looked over to see if the other person was unharmed. It was a man, which explained the strong force he had used to tackle me through the window. He had wavy blond hair that was long enough to curl behind his ears. His eyes were green, and he had a short beard and mustache on his face. I had seen this man before. He was the one who had rescued me when I was five and had given me the St. Michael medallion necklace.

"Dad?"

His eyes widened, and he smiled. "You know who I am?"

I shook my head. "Not really. It was a gut feeling since I look so much like you."

He got up quickly and rushed over to me, squeezing me in a hug. I returned it. Not because I was happy to be reunited with him but because I needed comfort. I needed to feel safe. There had been so many unveiled secrets, deaths, and fears in the last hour, let alone the last few days, and I knew no matter what, my dad would protect me.

So I let my guard down, held on tighter, and cried. For everything and everyone I had lost. And when I thought of Dane, my cries turned to sobs because I had lost him, too.

Dane wouldn't kill me. But Darcel would.

Even though Dane had said he loved me, I knew it was one last declaration before Darcel took over. I knew it was his way of saying goodbye. Maybe he did have a choice, but to me, it was plain to see that he had already chosen.

20 LILITH

Location Unknown, Present Day

Kneeling over Darcel's limp body, I was afraid he might be dead. I had sacrificed so much to ensure his survival. He couldn't be taken away from me just as our journey to dominance commenced.

Luckily, his chest still rose and fell. I heaved a sigh of relief.

I wasn't entirely sure what had happened to make Darcel pass out. Had it been the girl? Had it been that Evangeline had used the girl's body to send a message to me? Her energy was easy to detect, and it had filled the entire room. Even in death, she was still strong.

My rage was rising. I hated her. I hated the girl. I hated this entire place. All this should have been mine. Those despicable Watchers had stolen it from me. Really, Katriel had robbed me of it by entrapping me in that sphere. Then the Watchers had picked at the leftovers like vultures picking at a carcass. They would all pay.

But for now, it was time to go. I didn't want to be here anymore, and the purpose of my mission was resting at my feet.

"Mistress, the building is now being overtaken by the Sacrarium," one of my team informed me.

"It's no bother. We're leaving. Has the Sentinel reported back?"

"Yes, he has secured his charge." He reached for his wrist. "Shall I take us to Hell?"

"No!"

He stopped. "Where would you like us to go?"

"We're going to Purgatory. I can't have both my son and the other boy together in Hell. They must remain separated. Besides, Darcel didn't make his first kill before midnight."

Sure enough, the watch on my assassin's wrist beeped, signifying the hour in question.

"Why must it be before midnight, Mistress?"

"Because the full moon has ended, and he needed to claim his power before it did."

"And a kill is the only way for him to claim his power?"

"No." I shook my head. "But regardless, he has never used blood magic before."

"I see. I'm sorry, Mistress."

I brushed him off. "There's no reason to express your sympathy. I will return to Purgatory and plead with the dark forces to grant Darcel his power. Mark my words, he will be a blood mage."

21 EVANGELINE

AFTERLIFE, PRESENT DAY

If he wasn't already.

Among the dark and watery depths of oblivion rested a body—that of Satan, former ruler of the Underworld.

He lay limp and immobile in death, content with his fate, until the stroke of midnight on a cold evening in November, when the power of a blood mage was born.

22 SATAN

The River of Hate, Present Day

I sucked in a breath and choked on a mouthful of water. My eyes flashed open, unprepared to see the River of Hate's waters surrounding me.

Bubbles came out my nose as I exhaled, but the inhale of water burned my lungs even now. I needed air.

Raising my arms, I had every intention of sweeping them through the water to swim my way to the surface, but my legs were trapped. I glanced down, and a black cocoon enveloped my lower body.

What the...

"Your body is mine," the river rasped.

Like hell it was.

I placed my hands on the cocoon and ignited the Hellfire. It burned through the black shell quicker than I had ever seen. Kicking free, I swam as fast as I could to the surface.

My lungs ached. I needed another breath.

Whatever lurked in these waters was angry, and they made sure I knew it. Ear-splitting shrieks consumed my senses, but I didn't stop. The waters grew choppy, making it hard to gain ground, but I pushed through them, steady and strong.

When I surfaced, I wheezed in a gulp of air and gagged. Something latched on to my ankle and tried to drag me under, but I wouldn't let it. I rocketed into the gray sky, severing whatever hold the river had on me.

I continued to choke and knew I had to expel the water from my lungs, so I landed a short distance from the river and heaved up whatever liquid toxin I had swallowed.

Gasping, I took a brief moment to regain myself. "Shit!" I shouted.

Where was I? And how was I even here?

I had been dead. Food for the fishes or whatever the hell lurked in that godforsaken river. I shouldn't have been alive, yet I was. I felt different. Not in a bad way. In a good way, actually. I felt strong, stronger than I had felt in a while. Almost like when I had been Sam…

I checked my wings and sighed in relief to see that they were still black. I wasn't about to go back to restriction and conformity when I had been free for so many centuries.

I glanced down my body to make sure everything was normal. No injuries or parasitic creatures. Just soaking wet.

I pulled off my shirt and bunched it into a ball to ring out the water. Out of the corner of my eye, something caught my attention, and I immediately dropped my shirt. Raising my left arm over my head, I inspected the tattoo Dane had given me. It was red, as if it had been freshly inked. What alarmed me, though, were the intricate symbols and marks that had suddenly appeared. I lifted my right arm, and it was in a similar state.

Dropping my arms, I stared off into the wasteland that sprawled before me.

Dane, what did you do?

Some of the marks seemed to be some sort of language, but none I knew or had seen.

For now, I couldn't worry about it, though. What I needed to do was figure out where I was and how to get back to Hell. The river was an obvious choice, but I really didn't want to tread those waters again if I didn't have to.

Wherever I was, it looked deserted, not a soul in sight. I guessed it was time to get up and explore. That was the only way I was going to find another way out of here.

I rose from the ground and slipped my shirt back on. I turned around a few times, trying to decide what direction to go. Everything looked the same, so I just stepped forward and started my journey into the unknown.

I walked for what felt like ages without seeing anything or anyone. I meandered along the river, thinking it might lead somewhere. Eventually, it did, but it was nowhere I wanted to be.

A mile-wide expanse was cut into the ground. It was like the Pit in Hell except larger and who knew how deep. Encircling the chasm were four bridges, which at one point had been connected but now were raised and impassable.

The closer I got to the edge, the stronger the river waters grew, becoming wild and raging. I wanted to see what was inside the deep expanse. Drawing nearer, an unexplainable force tried pushing me back. I dropped to the ground and crawled on my hands and knees until I came to the ledge and had a chance to glance over. What an incredible sight it was. The river gorged out into an intense waterfall.

One that no soul wanted to be caught in, as it meant dropping to an unimaginable death.

Looking out, I saw other methods of untimely doom. Directly to the north, a fierce windstorm. To the west, a forceful mudslide. To the east, a deluge of lava. All plummeting into a dark void. Above, the bridges scaled toward the cloudy sky, their structures impressive works of architecture.

Abruptly, I spied movement to my right. Sinking lower to the ground, I watched as a figure scaled down the edge of the void and disappeared into a cave cut into the side.

Whoever they were, they seemed experienced because they had moved fast and efficiently, using some kind of climbing axe to aid their journey. They also had been an angel, their wings easy to detect even though they were shrouded beneath a cloak.

Obviously, flying down there wasn't an option; otherwise they would have used their wings. But who needed a climbing axe when you could just use your hands and feet?

I rose from the ground and climbed over the edge.

The cave wasn't too far down. It was several feet to the right of where I was, though. This probably was a bad idea, but that angel had been the only soul I had seen in my entire time here. If they were a friend, I could gain information about where I was and how to get out. If they were a foe, I could still acquire the same knowledge after showing a little force. Either way, it ended in me getting something from the task, which would make me better off than I was currently.

I located some decent footholds and slowly maneuvered my way down. When I tried to find decent handholds, however, the situation grew tricky. It was as if all the various elemental climates sensed I was hoping to commit the impossible—forge the void—because they all picked up in intensity. Mist and lava globs spewed into my face while the wind whipped ferociously at my back and mixed with earthy debris from the mud.

Clearly, that's why the other angel didn't attempt to fly and, instead, used the climbing axes to stabilize themselves.

Oh well. I had started, and there was no point in stopping.

I found handholds and continued down, fighting against the elements. I had made enough progress that I was level with the cave, but now it was a matter of climbing sideways instead of down to reach it.

Inching to the right, I maintained my slow but steady pace until both my handholds and footholds gave out. I fell back, wings gliding out to catch me, except that ferocious wind must have sensed my vulnerability because a large gust caught them and sent me sprawling into the center of the void. I was caught up in a vortex of elements, all of them working together to tear me apart. I shouted and grunted in pain and frustration, stunned to see the mysterious angel watching my torment from their cave.

Bastard! They would pay when I got my hands on them.

A flash of silver sped through the air. I figured it was a knife or a sort of weapon, but shockingly, it was a grappling hook. It rose out high in the sky, eventually making a downward arc. I had to grab it before it fell too low; otherwise, I would be at the mercy of the angel to try again, which was no guarantee. For all I knew, I only had this one chance.

The tornado-like vortex kept spinning me round in its clutches, but I slid my hand free and raised it to grab the hook. Luckily, I was able to latch on, except gravity now pulled me free, sending me careening right into the outer wall of the void.

When I hit the solid rock, I hung there dazed for a few brief moments, trying to regain my composure. I felt a few tugs on the rope. Glancing up, I saw the other angel was trying to get my attention. "Climb up!"

The voice was indistinct, and I couldn't tell if it was male or female. It was also hard to detect any facial features from this distance. Either way, I would know soon enough who had come to my rescue. Obviously, they were a friend.

With my newfound strength, the rope climb was easy. I would have been able to do it in my prior state, but it would have taken much longer. As I finally worked my way up and over the edge, I took another moment on the cave floor to catch my breath.

A boot met my ribs the instant I had found safety.

"Ah!" I yelled.

The angel was evidently *not* a friend.

"You scum!" the angel yelled. Their boot descended again.

"Quit it!" I roared, getting to my feet.

"Still the same Samael," the angel said. "Quick to anger, eager to fight."

I froze. I knew that voice, those words. "Ariel! Shit!"

She laughed. "Didn't think you'd miss me much. I guess I was right." She attacked, knife at the ready.

I dodged and splayed out my hands in surrender. "Can we talk about this?"

"No!" She swiped and cut my arm.

Pulling back, I said, "Why'd you save me, then?"

"So I could kill you myself!"

I engaged her and swiftly disarmed her, dragging her into a headlock. "Are you really still holding a grudge?"

"Of course!" she huffed, trying to pry free. "You wrecked everything! You betrayed us!" She stopped. "You set her free!" she screamed, elbowing me in the ribs, twisting out of my hold, and throwing me to the ground. She turned and grabbed a sword, placing the blade at my throat and a foot on my chest. "You expect me to forgive you for that?"

Finally getting a good look at her, I realized she was missing her right arm and left leg. She wore prosthetics for both, but the pain of losing limbs never went away.

"Lilith? She did this?"

Her foot and sword sunk deeper. "Yes. If you hadn't unleashed her, I would still be whole."

"I never intended to free her. It was a mistake."

Blood pooled by her blade.

"If you want to be angry at someone, be angry at Him!" I protested. "He is the one who sent me. He is the one who knew how lethal Lilith was and did nothing to annihilate her."

The pressure on the blade eased.

Was I actually swaying her?

"Why are you here?" she demanded.

I sneered. "I assure you, I'm not here because I want to be. I was chucked into a river, and—" I stopped. No one should know about the tattoos that had resurrected me. Certainly not someone I didn't trust. "And left for dead but I was lucky to swim my way out. What the hell is this place anyway?"

Ariel took the blade away from my neck and grinned. "You don't know?"

"Would I be asking if I did?"

She returned her sword to her sheath and crossed her arms. "Welcome to Purgatory."

"Purgatory?" I was shocked. "It actually exists?"

"You're standing in it, so yes."

"How do we get out of it?" I asked.

Ariel stepped deeper into the cave and returned with a cloth. She handed it to me. "You don't, really."

I pressed the cloth to my throat. "There has to be a way."

"Be my guest. Go swim the river again and see where you get. It's a miracle you made it through once."

"I have to get back to Hell!"

"And I have to enter Qliphoth!" Ariel whined. "Sometimes we don't always get what we want."

Confused, I asked, "What? What's Qliphoth?"

"It's a place within Purgatory. Almost like Hell."

I shook my head. "Hell isn't in Purgatory."

"No," Ariel agreed, "but there's a passageway to Hell in Purgatory."

"The rivers?"

Ariel didn't answer and instead retrieved a map from her supplies. She rolled it out on the ground and knelt, pointing as she spoke. "Qliphoth is a dark realm. Lilith draws on the power of the dark forces that linger there. She's camped her army close by, although she's slowly expanding her reach." Ariel pointed to four bodies of water. "She has a small team stationed by the Ponds of Purgatory now, and she uses them to travel to Hell. The River of Hate is the only river in Hell that runs straight through to Purgatory, but it's not typically used as a means of transportation. And you've learned why."

The blaze inside me started to boil. How dare Lilith use my kingdom as a causeway! I ignored the intense emotion and asked, "How can she get through the ponds to the rivers?"

"Magic."

Figures.

"And what exactly lurks in the River of Hate?" I asked.

"A being that was imprisoned there. It seeks a corporeal form, so whatever goes in will most likely not come out since the being wants a body."

Oh… Well, I guessed I escaped that fate.

"How do you know so much?" I asked.

Ariel sighed. "I've been here a long time. I discovered a way to inhibit Lilith after the war in Heaven. I asked Father to send me here so I could find the blood mages to test my theory and ask for their help in stopping her. But they had all been slaughtered. I was nearly slain, as well. If it weren't for Sandalphon, I'd be gone."

"He's here?" I asked.

Ariel nodded. "Father gave him a new purpose. Sandalphon is the Warden of Purgatory. He's all that keeps this place from the edge of collapse."

Huh… A lot has changed.

Then a thought struck me. "Isn't Lilith a blood mage?" I remembered Abbadona had said as much. My chest squeezed. The last memory I had of her was when she'd been captured by Mammon. It hurt to think about.

"Yes, a self-made one. There used to be ones born with the power."

I glanced at the map. "How do we get to Qliphoth?"

Ariel chuckled. "Not sure. I haven't attempted it. There are five regions total in Purgatory: the Northern Region, the Southern Region, the Western Region, the Eastern Region, and the Core. There are passageways in each region to another realm. These passageways, though, are also prisons."

"Who are the prisoners?"

She shrugged. "I don't know. Father's enemies, I guess."

I lost myself in a fit of laughter.

"What's so funny?"

"If these prisons hold His enemies, then why aren't I in one?"

Ariel met my gaze with a deadpan stare. "Maybe you're not His enemy. Or maybe you're not His largest threat. Who knows why He lets you roam free and forces others to suffer."

She had a faraway look in her eye.

Hmm... That was the second time now she had showed animosity toward Him.

"Is there anything or anyone that guards the passageways?" I tried to bring her attention back.

"Yes. There are keeps at each passageway. The blood mages used to protect them."

"Who does now?"

"No one. But the blood mages sealed the keeps before being slayed, subsequently sealing the passageways, which is why I have never made it into Qliphoth. Not to mention traversing the Wastelands between regions is a treacherous journey."

I sighed and put a hand to my forehead. "And what godforsaken chaos resides in the Wastelands?"

"Lost souls, demons, wild creatures, temptations, slain angels."

My head bobbed up from the map. "Excuse me? When angels perish, their energies recede into the universe. Goes for both the Fallen and the Blessed."

Ariel nodded. "That's what we were told. But it's not the truth. Our energies don't recede into the universe. We come here. If we are slain here, *then* we recede into the universe. Otherwise, we roam and wander forever. Unless you become a Guardian of the Lost Souls. They help guide lost souls to Heaven or Hell, depending on where they belong. Both blessed and fallen angels are among their ranks."

Lies. So many lies we had been told. My hands clenched into fists. "Who's here?"

Ariel smirked. "No one who likes you. Most casualties of the war still linger."

Shit...

"I have to leave," I said.

"Probably, but we're back to where we started."

"No, we're not. You said Lilith made camp at the ponds. Let's attack and ransack the place. Find whatever magical thing is allowing her to traverse them."

"How do you know it's a thing?"

"I don't, but if she has her army traveling through the rivers, then it has to be a thing because not all of them possess the ability to wield magic like she does."

Ariel pondered my words. "You may have a point."

"So then lead the way to the ponds."

"I'm not taking orders from you. I'll never take orders from you."

"Oh, just wait," I assured her. "I'll grow on you."

23 Sophia

Location Unknown, Present Day

I pulled away from my dad and said, “My friend got shot in there. I have to find her.”

He placed his hands on my shoulders. “Don’t worry. She’ll be rescued. We have a lot of forces on the premises.”

“We?”

“The Sacrarium. They’ve overtaken the facility.” He stood and helped me to my feet. “Let’s get you to the hospital.”

He gripped my elbow, but I shrugged out of his hold. I didn’t want to be coddled or controlled anymore. “I’m not going to the hospital. I’m waiting until my friend is found.”

“Sophia, if she was shot, then they’ll just bring her to the hospital.”

I sighed. He had a point. “Fine.” Before I followed him, I reached behind my neck and took off my necklace. “Here,” I said, handing it to him.

He took it, unsure at first as to what I was giving him. Then he saw the St. Michael medallion. He handed it back. “Keep it. It’s yours.”

“No, it’s not,” I said. “It’s yours.”

“Sophia, I insist,” he urged.

Suddenly, I felt unsteady and faltered in my steps.

My dad grabbed my arm. "Let's get you out of here."

This time I didn't protest as a strong wave of exhaustion overcame me.

He loaded me in a car, and before I knew it, I was en route to a nearby hospital. Glancing out the window, I saw that the Sacrarium really had taken over, rounding up as many patients as they could. The group of patients they had gathered was small in comparison to the number I had seen on the monitors, which meant many truly had escaped and were now out in the world, free and loose to do as they pleased.

As far as I was concerned, though, Penelope or Jazema hadn't been caught, and nothing was over until they both were dead. They would never give up. They would never tolerate their plans coming to ruin. It was only a matter of time before they regrouped and retaliated.

When I arrived at the hospital, it was nearly one in the morning. I was rushed into a triage room and inspected for injuries.

"I'm fine. I really don't need treatment. I'm just tired."

Someone prodded my back, and I let out a scream. Alarmed, the nurses and doctors hurried about, prepping me for an X-ray.

When the image appeared, the doctor said, "I'll have to consult with surgery. Hang tight until I come back."

The nurses hurried about again, gathering supplies to start an IV.

"Please leave me alone!" I shouted.

They all froze. One was brave enough to say, "Just remain calm. Everything's going to be all right."

"No! I don't want treatment right now. I need a minute."

"Of course," the nurse said. "We'll check back in a bit."

Finally, they all left.

I took a few deep breaths and tried to settle myself. I had been at the lab for nineteen days. Almost another three weeks of my life wasted thanks to Penelope and her wish for me to be something "extraordinary."

I didn't feel extraordinary. I felt exhausted and weak, like I wanted to sleep for months. Shaking my head, I knew there was no time to relax, though. Not when Jordan was still missing. Dane might be a lost cause, but Jordan wasn't. He needed help.

There was a knock on the door. My dad walked in with two women. One of them was Sister Delphine. The other I thought was a doctor until I caught sight of her face.

It was my mom, Emily. She had aged a little since I saw her last at the library, but it was easy to tell who she was. I inhaled a sharp breath. What was she doing here? I didn't want her here. I squeezed my eyes shut as the night she abandoned me flashed before them. I tensed and brought my knees up to my chest. Penelope's declaration rang through my mind, how my mom hadn't abandoned me but had been purposefully taken out of the picture.

I didn't know what or whom to believe. The three people standing in front of me had turned out to be as deceiving as Penelope herself. Perhaps they were less dangerous, but their deceptions still stung. And I wasn't in the right state of mind to decipher the truth.

"Get out!" I shrieked.

"Sophia, please," my dad soothed.

"Get out! I don't want to see her! I don't want to see any of you!"

My mom opened her mouth to speak.

"Don't you dare say anything to me! I don't want to hear it!"

"All right, all right," Sister Delphine said. "Let's give her some more time."

“She doesn’t have time,” my dad replied. “She’s refusing treatment, and her back is a mess.”

“Aeron, I think it’s best to leave her be,” my mom suggested.

“But—”

Both women gave him a stern look, urging him to leave.

When they did, I relaxed a bit and thought about what to do.

I had to get out of here.

Getting off the bed, I faltered again but caught myself, approached the door, and stopped. My mom, Sister Delphine, and my dad were standing a few rooms over talking to someone. I thought it was Naomi’s mom. I had seen her once at Sister Helen’s funeral, but we had never met face-to-face.

I concentrated my hearing on what they were saying.

“Naomi is about to be taken up for surgery,” her mom said.

My mom put a hand on her arm. “She’ll pull through.”

Naomi’s mom wiped her cheek. “I hope so. I wouldn’t be able to forgive myself if she didn’t.”

All my attention was focused to the right that I hadn’t noticed the person who had come up on my left. “Excuse me,” she said, “you need to get back in bed.”

Wait… I knew that voice. Turning around, I shouted, “Dafne!”

I leaped at her and hugged her tight. She latched on and didn’t let go. I couldn’t help but shed a few tears again. Honestly, I didn’t trust anyone here. All these adults had kept too many secrets for too long. But Dafne was different. She was my best friend. My confidante. I could tell her anything.

Easing back, I met her eyes. “What are you doing here?”

She pulled me farther into the room. "My parents were called in to assist with processing the lab and the patients. Most of them are Nephilim, and that's kind of their area, not the Sacrarium's. Anyway, I've pretty much been on house arrest for months, ever since I told my dad I was quitting Harvard to attend fashion design school next fall. He freaked, took my phone, and forced me to work at the vineyard for the time being so I didn't 'waste my potential.' I think he secretly wants me to take a liking to it, but I like drinking wine, not making it. So I went into the city to live with my grandparents, who support my decision. Except my grandfather felt the same way, that I should be doing something during this break from school. His proposition was a million times better, though. He suggested I go into the family business."

"Isn't that the vineyard?" I asked.

Dafne shook her head. "No, the *real* family business. The Nephilim and Watcher and Ishim stuff. I've been training with him ever since. I overheard that my parents got called in, and I was too curious not to tag along. They don't know I'm here, but when I saw you at the lab, I freaked because I wasn't expecting you to be involved, but I followed you to the hospital and here we are."

I hugged her again.

"Are you okay?" she murmured in my ear.

"No," I whispered. Then I pulled back and told her everything that had happened.

When I was done, she sank into a chair. "Jordan's missing?"

I grabbed her hand and squeezed it. "We'll find him."

"Of course, we will," she said with conviction. "We have to get out of here, though."

"Agreed. But I need to see Naomi first."

I had to check on her. She had turned out to be a good friend, and the image of her getting shot kept playing over in my mind.

"Sure. I think she's a few rooms over, but they're about to transport her so we should go."

Dafne walked out of the room. She made sure the coast was clear and waved to me. I followed her as she led the way to Naomi's room.

Surprisingly, no one was inside. Then I thought about her mom. Naomi had said she was the new Alpha, which meant she was in charge and responsible for overseeing everything that was going on. She must be busy, and I was sure Naomi's dad was on the way, ready to stay by Naomi's side.

I entered the room and took her hand in mine. "I'm so sorry this happened, but thank you for being brave and doing what you did. You rescued everyone, and I'm so grateful."

Her hand squeezed mine. I looked at her face and was shocked to see she was awake. She let go and grabbed the breathing tube in her mouth.

"No!" Dafne cried, rushing forward to stop her.

I drew closer and tried to soothe her. "Naomi, it's all right."

She kept adamantly shaking her head.

"I think she's trying to tell us something," Dafne said.

Naomi nodded.

"Um…" I looked around, trying to find a way she could tell us without pulling out her breathing tube. I went over to the cabinets and searched for something to write with and write on.

There was a large gasp from behind me. I spun around to find Dafne had helped Naomi take the tube out.

"Dafne!"

"She wanted it out!"

"What about the machines?"

"She turned them off," Naomi rasped.

"I turn my back for a second," I chastised.

"What do you need to tell us?" Dafne asked.

"I can't have surgery. I need to get out of here."

"Naomi, you were shot," I reasoned.

"Yeah, but they pulled out the bullet." She struggled to sit up. "I'll be fine."

I put my hand on her shoulder and tried easing her back. "You won't. You're still bleeding."

"I know, but surgery won't work," she said, trying to get up again.

"Of course, it will. You're just having doubts," I tried.

"No, I'm not." She met my gaze. "I'm more like you than you think."

My eyes narrowed. "What do you mean?"

Then the lights shut off. Everyone outside the room started to panic.

"We need to go," Dafne said.

I reached for Naomi's IV and pulled out the needle. "Not without her." There was something she wasn't telling us, and she deserved a chance to come clean.

Dafne helped disconnect the rest of Naomi's machines, and together, we assisted her out of the bed.

Emergency lighting had kicked on, but it wasn't nearly as bright, which was a good thing for us as we sneaked out of the room and headed for the stairs. We slowly ascended them to the floor above us since Naomi couldn't go much farther. This entire wing of the hospital had been emptied for us so this level had yet to be occupied. I was sure they had intended to fill it with post-surgical patients, but now that the power was out, that wouldn't be happening anytime soon.

The three of us stopped in the hallway. I stayed with Naomi in front of a wall of windows while Dafne tried to break into a supply closet nearby. Naomi was bleeding through her bandage, and we needed to change it.

After breaking in the door, Dafne ransacked the closet for anything she could get. I made Naomi sit on the floor as Dafne rejoined us. I lifted Naomi's hospital gown and pulled back the dressing. Dafne had a new one ready and placed it over the gunshot wound. I stood and disposed of the trash in a wastebasket nearby.

A crack of lighting flashed, and a boom of thunder sounded.

Naomi perked up. "A storm is brewing." She peeked out the window just as it started to rain. "I need to get outside."

Dafne met my eyes. "Uh…I don't think that's a good idea."

"It's not," I said. "Not until we know the threat."

"You think we're being attacked?" Naomi asked, pulling her attention from the window.

I nodded. "Penelope and Jazema don't take defeat easily. I should know. Both have chased me far and wide for various reasons."

"What do we do? Wait for them—"

I silenced Dafne by placing a hand on her shoulder and putting a finger to my lips. My celestial hearing had picked something up.

We all listened.

I heard the thump of boots.

"They're on the roof," I whispered.

"We need to go back downstairs," Naomi said. "It's the only exit left."

Dafne and I nodded.

We helped Naomi up from the floor and approached the stairs. I opened the door, and an assailant jumped on me.

"Sophia!" Dafne yelled.

I wrestled my attacker down the stairs and bashed her head against the railing. Glancing down, I saw it was Rajani. She was dazed and paused her assault.

I tried going back upstairs, but she grabbed my leg. I kicked out, forcing her to let go. Rajani was regaining her footing, though, ready to start the fight again.

"Dafne, take Naomi and go! I'm sure there's another staircase!"

They disappeared back through the door.

Rajani cracked her neck and egged me on. "Let's see if you learned anything from me."

"Bring it on," I said, ignoring the twinges of pain in my back.

We launched at each other. I surprised her, and myself, with how I held my own against her.

I had her in a headlock when a loud ruckus came pouring down the steps. Reinforcements had arrived. But not for me.

Rajani chuckled. "I don't think you can handle all of us." She flipped me over her shoulder, and I landed on the stairs, flat on my back.

I screamed in agony, my whole body going numb.

Rajani kicked me in the side, over and over. I heard the crack of bones, and the pain of broken ribs was added to my anguish. I tried getting up, but I couldn't get my legs under me.

This was it. It had to be. There was no one around to save me.

The door above me slammed open, and an arrow whizzed through the air, hitting Rajani in the shoulder. Two more followed suit, one lodging in her leg, the other in her abdomen. She shrieked and dropped to the floor, quickly pulling herself down the stairs and out of range of the onslaught.

A cloaked figure secured the bow to their back and descended the steps. They knelt next to me, soaking wet from the rain outside, and dropped their hood.

"Uriel!" I grabbed him, beyond thrilled that he had returned.

He patted my shoulder. "I know, I know, I missed you, too."

I laughed and brushed a tear from my face.

"Please no crying," he whined, lifting me in his arms.

"I'm not," I protested. Then I noticed his clothes. "What are you wearing?"

"Celestial robes. They're not very practical, but we had no time to change."

"*We?*"

He shuffled us through the door and right into Chamuel.

"Chamuel!"

Uriel handed me over to him, and I hugged him fiercely. He returned the gesture.

"Oh, Sophia, I'm so glad you're safe," he whispered.

Then he went to set me down.

"Don't!" Uriel warned. "She's hurt."

"Hurt!" Chamuel's eyebrows rose in worry.

"It's my back," I told him.

"You mean the wings," he said, stunned to see them.

"I don't know. I can't walk, but I'm sure it'll pass."

"We can't take that chance," Uriel said, taking the bow in his hand again. "We have to get you to safety."

"Not yet! We need to find Dafne and Naomi. They were up here with me. I told them to go down another staircase." I paused. "There is another staircase, right?"

"There is," Chamuel assured me. "Zadkiel and Raphael have it covered."

I was glad to hear they were back, too. "What about Michael, Gabriel, and Jophiel?"

"Michael and Gabriel are outside, main entrance," Uriel said.

We creeped down the hall, making our way to the other staircase.

"And Jophiel?"

They were quiet.

"What about Jophiel?" I asked again.

"He is…no longer with us," Chamuel muttered.

A sinking feeling filled me. "How?" I whispered.

Chamuel's jaw tightened. "Lilith."

My eyes welled up. No… This can't be happening. The angels were invincible. They survived everything. I shook my head. There was no adequate response, so I asked, "Where did you go when you disappeared?"

"Heaven," Uriel ground out. "Hence the celestial robes." He raised his arm in the air, and we halted. Nocking an arrow in his bow, Uriel slowly creeped closer to the second staircase door. He opened it and checked inside. It must have been empty because he quickly came back and continued creeping down the hall until he made it to a closet.

I could tell he was listening intently because he had his head cocked to the side. I tried listening, too, and I could hear the murmur of voices.

Uriel banged open the closet door and leveled his bow on whoever was inside.

"Stand down!" Zadkiel shouted. "It's us!"

Chamuel raced over to join everyone.

As soon as I glanced inside the closet, I knew we had a problem.

"I can't stop the bleeding," Raphael said, holding his hands over Naomi's wound. Dafne's were stained red, as well. She must have tried to quench the blood before the angels had arrived.

Naomi looked pale, and her face was strained. She met my eyes. "I," she rasped, "need…to go…outside."

Even now her request seemed ridiculous, but if that was her final wish, then we would make it happen. "Raphael, we have to listen to her."

"Are you sure? It's unsafe."

"Positive."

"We need to regroup anyway," Zadkiel added. "Michael and Gabriel may soon be overwhelmed out there."

"Let's go, then," Uriel said, leading the way.

We followed.

Zadkiel took up arms with Uriel at the front. Raphael and Chamuel carried Naomi and me while Dafne trailed behind.

We made our way down the second staircase without any opposition. When we entered the ER, doctors and nurses hurried about trying to stabilize patients.

Oh no. We had made a mistake coming this way. The adults were in this area. They would be distressed when they saw us.

"Naomi!"

"Sophia!"

"Dafne!"

Each of our names was called by our parents, but the angels didn't stop moving. It wasn't until they moved through the waiting room and reached the entrance that they halted.

Chamuel spied a wheelchair and set me down in it. He turned to Dafne. "Stay here with her."

"Of course." She sat down in a waiting room seat next to me.

The angels went outside, Naomi still in Raphael's arms.

24 GABRIEL

Ithaca, New York, Present Day

Michael and I were drenched from the rain, but it didn't deter us. We fought off Geneloom's assailants, dispatching them quickly. It was astonishing that Geneloom was even launching an assault considering their numbers were small.

Neither of us had encountered Jazema or Penelope yet, which led me to believe that, somehow, a larger attack was coming.

Sure enough, our opponents took off into the trees and all fell quiet. Michael and I analyzed the forest while the others joined us.

Raphael knelt and deposited Naomi on the ground.

"What are you doing?" Michael snapped. "Get her inside!"

"Naomi!" It was Deborah and Peter rushing out in the rain to retrieve their daughter.

The girl gasped and raised her head to the sky, letting the rain pour over her face.

Suddenly, we all heard the resounding click of magazines being snapped into chambers.

"Chamuel!" Michael shouted.

But our brother didn't need the command. He turned and grabbed both Deborah and Peter, who had tried desperately to reach their daughter, and shielded them with his wings.

We all braced ourselves as we heard bullets releasing from their barrels. Raphael grabbed Naomi to protect her, but she broke free from his grasp.

"Naomi!" I yelled.

She stood tall and ran her hands through the air in a semicircle. The bullets dissipated, dissolving into water.

Our foes stepped out from the forest, guns at the ready. Jazema and Penelope were still nowhere to be seen.

Five of us rose from the ground, Chamuel still defending Naomi's parents, to aid the girl, but she gave us a terse warning. "Don't. This is my mission."

Gray-feathered wings unfurled from her back as bullets were unleashed. Every one of them liquefied, as well as whatever remained in their weapons. The Geneloom attackers dropped their guns, but before they could flee, Naomi brought down the storm.

The rain grew into a torrent, then droplets suddenly froze midair, transforming into small shards of ice. Her hands were balled into fists, but she released them, subsequently sending the razor icicles flying toward her enemies. They were fleeing back into the forest, but a few of Naomi's weapons hit their mark.

Everything grew quiet again.

Naomi was neither fazed by her show of skills nor exhausted from their display. She stood confident in what she had done, her injury seemingly healed.

"Did you know she could do that?" I heard Peter ask Deborah.

"Of course not!" her mother exclaimed.

Naomi stepped over to us. "Is everyone all right?"

"Yes," I said. "Thank you."

"Don't mention it."

"You're a Nephilim?" Uriel blurted.

Naomi shook her head. "No, I'm a Supernal."

25

SATAN

Purgatory, Present Day

With the help of the climbing axes, Ariel and I scaled the side of the void and returned to normal ground—or what I now knew were the Wastelands. What I had termed "the void" also wasn't its proper name. It was called the Core.

"What are the bridges for?" I asked her, peering up at the raised structures.

"The bridges allow the lost souls to properly cross over, but when the blood mages feared for their lives, they raised them, just as they sealed the keeps, so nothing and no one could come in or out. They've been this way ever since. Lilith might have found a way to cross the ponds with magic, but that can't lower the bridges. Nothing can, other than a blood mage who was born with their power, and there hasn't been one of those for years."

We left the bridges behind and set out into the Wastelands. Based on Ariel's descriptions, I had been lucky I hadn't encountered any danger on my short trek through the Wastelands to the Core. These lands were filled with unimaginable terrors. I kept my guard up as we crossed the land, especially since many of my enemies lingered here. Unintentional enemies, but enemies all the same.

Ariel and I followed the River of Hate back up to its originating point.

I shouldn't be so shocked that everything here had a name and a purpose. I had done the same for Hell. Except these regions were a land of fables, something angels imagined might exist but could never be certain. I guessed for humans that notion could be applied to Heaven, Hell, and Purgatory. It was astounding to see legends come to life, though, to actually be there and know it existed based on experience and not tall tales.

"We should stop for the night," Ariel said, gazing at the sky.

"Why?"

"Because it's rare to forge the Wastelands without opposition. To do so when light fades and the dark rises is near impossible. Almost pure insanity."

I sighed. "We'll be wasting time if we stop. It's not like we need rest."

"No, we don't. But I'm warning you, danger awaits. It's only a matter of time."

"I say we keep going. It'll allow us to attack Lilith's camp under the shroud of darkness."

"Fair point. Here." She unstrapped a sword from her back. "You can take this now."

She had armed herself for both of us but hadn't let me carry any of the weapons until now. Her complete trust was something to still be gained, but I seemed to be doing it in tiny increments.

Alongside Michael, Ariel and I had trained together as angels of power. Michael and I had certainly been a remarkable duo, but if we ever needed a third, it had always been Ariel who joined us to form a formidable trio.

We had a history, a past, but all the same, I had betrayed her the way

I had betrayed Michael. I just hadn't realized how deep the disloyalty had settled. I understood Michael's resentment. We had been inseparable, and I had ruined everything. But I had never thought the two of us, Ariel and me, had been particularly close. I guessed she had viewed it differently, and perhaps it was worth trying to see her perspective.

"Why do you cover your wings?" I asked her.

At first, I thought I couldn't see them because they were hidden beneath a cloak, but she had actually taken strips of cloth and had woven them meticulously around the feathers so as not to expose them.

"No reason you need to know," she said. "It started as an injury and led to something more."

"You sound like Metatron, speaking in riddles and mystery. Just come out with what you mean."

"And you are awfully hung up on Heaven, referring to our brothers and sisters and speaking about past events. Your regret is plain to see."

"I have no regrets!" I protested. "I stand by my actions."

"So you wouldn't go back?"

"No!" Then I lowered my tone, detecting a change in her demeanor. "This isn't about me, is it? You're projecting your feelings."

She grew defensive. "I'm not!"

"Fine, don't tell me, then." I paused. "You can fly, right? Because if you can't, then I should know that."

Exasperated, she shouted, "I can fly!"

"All right, no need to get feisty. The question was purely for safety reasons. If I need rescuing or if you need to be rescued, it's good to know our limitations and strengths."

"Oh really? And what are yours?" Before I could answer, she said,

"Let me guess. You're insanely talkative and infuriating. Good to know." She smiled sarcastically at me.

"Well you're snarky!" I retaliated, but it sounded lame even to my ears. "All right, that's enough! We sound like children."

She sighed. "Agreed."

We continued in somewhat companionable silence. As darkness fell, I raised my guard, both eyes and ears becoming more attentive to any sight or sound. In the distance, dim firelight could be seen, indicating we were close to Lilith's camp.

"I'll be damned," Ariel whispered.

"What?" I murmured.

"They're moving," she said. "This is the small team that was kept at the ponds. If they're now in the Wastelands, something must be making them leave."

"Or someone," I suggested. "Maybe Lilith commanded them."

Falling quiet again, Ariel crept closer to the group, stopping behind some large boulders to analyze the situation. Whoever these beings were, they must have been some of Lilith's finest assassins. She wouldn't leave a team of misfits to watch over the passageway to Hell, and even now that they were leaving, there had to be an important reason why. All that to say, our fight might be difficult.

"How would you like to proceed?" I whispered to Ariel. None of Lilith's team were angels, so they wouldn't be able to hear our plans. Besides, this was Ariel's territory, not mine. She should take the lead.

"There are ten of them, so we each take five. You go left. I go right. We meet in the middle and deal with whoever's left."

I rose and pulled the sword from my back. "Works for me." It had been the strategy Michael and I had executed during battle, so it had been ingrained in me, possibly all of us, given Ariel's eagerness to use it.

Slinking along the outskirts of their camp, I hid among the shadows like a predator, searching for the moment to strike. I stepped forward, ready to pounce, but pulled back when I heard a whizzing noise.

An arrow shot through the air and ripped through one of the assassin's faces. There was blood and screaming, the rest of the team alerted and on guard.

Several battle cries sounded around us, and a group of Purgatory's denizens attacked the camp. Unlike Lilith's team, though, every one of these assailants had gray-feathered wings.

Shit! These bastards must be the slain angels who wandered Purgatory. And they were savage and fought dirty. I smirked. I admired their tenacity, but they weren't about to steal our opportunity.

I entered the camp calmly, walking through their frenzied ranks and taking out foes in a calculated manner. A slit throat here, a well-placed knife to an artery there. I could meet their violence and dole it out tenfold.

The number of assailants had increased from ten to about thirty. However, it didn't make sense why the angels were attacking. Surely, they encountered Lilith's army all the time, considering they were stuck here and she had pretty much claimed Purgatory as hers. So why now? And why so violent? There had to be something we were missing.

Scanning the camp, I realized there was. A prisoner—bound, hooded, and hidden from sight until now. I approached the two assassins guarding the prisoner and attacked ferociously.

One of them had seen me advancing and met my sword with theirs.

Our blades clanged and then slid apart. The next blow, they went high and I went low, spinning my body and slashing my blade through skin. My opponent could barely let out a shriek of pain before he dropped. The second assassin held her ground in front of the prisoner. Whoever the prisoner was, they must have been important if Lilith's team was willing to die to protect them.

The assassin stepped forward, ready to engage in battle. Her attention was so focused on me that she didn't see another attacker coming from the side, axe in hand and already swinging. The weapon collided with the assassin's chest, sending her sailing through the air and, ultimately, to her doom.

"Look who we have here," the attacker said. "If it isn't Samael."

Oh fu—

I jumped back as Araziel swung his axe at me.

"I forgot," he leered, "you go by Satan now."

"It's been a long time," I said.

"Long time?" he growled. "You let me die!" He swung his axe again.

I sidestepped. "Whoa, whoa, whoa!" I yelled. "You must be misremembering. We were never on the same side. You were doing Lilith's bidding in Heaven, stealing object after object. I was on my own and amassed an army you refused to fight in. As I recall, you used to be a meek angel of music, too scared of your own shadow to resist Lilith's temptation. Unlike me."

He lunged. I dodged his unskilled move and kicked him in the back, sending him sprawling to the ground and landing on his axe.

As Araziel slowly faded, I said, "Even now, I didn't let you die. Your own foolishness caused your demise."

Ariel pounced on another Purgatory angel in front of me, killing him where he stood. "What happened to the plan?" she shouted, breathing heavily.

I took a moment to reply, impressed by her viciousness. "Our plan was blown the second those angels attacked. Besides, we missed the prisoner, who seems far more important than anything else."

Ariel's mouth dropped open, and she gestured to the land behind her, currently filled with slain bodies. "More important than leaving me to deal with all of them?"

I pointed at her. "Not fair. I took some out. Those aren't all yours." Stepping away from her, I approached the prisoner.

I grabbed the hood over their face and tugged it free. The prisoner was smirking and had a gash across his right eye that had healed and scarred. The eye itself seemed to have been blinded from the injury, entirely white and gleaming in the glow of the firelight.

He was no one I knew. But he was an angel, considering he had gray-feathered wings sitting at his back.

"If it isn't the devil himself…"

I ignored him and turned to Ariel, who had drawn closer to my side. "Who is he?"

She shook her head. "It can't be."

"Ariel," I growled.

"It's Kushiel," she whispered.

I still didn't know him.

"You're supposed to be dead. All of you," Ariel said.

Kushiel nodded. "I'm the only survivor among the archangels who were sent here."

"Do you care to explain?" I asked Ariel.

"Right, well, I told you the blood mages were the first to reside here in Purgatory. They manned the bridges, but there were also a group of archangels sent with them to protect the keeps as a way to bring peace to Purgatory."

"Which we brought for many years until Lilith came to claim this place as her own," Kushiel said. "She slaughtered us." He smirked. "Nearly murdered me, but I got away. Not unscathed, as I'm sure you can see." He glanced at Ariel. "Who are you?"

"Ariel, I'm an archangel from Heaven. I discovered a potential way to stop Lilith, which is why I asked Father to send me here, so I could relay the information to you. But when I arrived, the damage was done. None of you were around anymore, and I have been trapped here since."

"Let me guess," Kushiel mocked, "you discovered that bloodstone weakens her."

Ariel was taken aback. "Yes. It was the stone assigned to me on the Council of Archangels. I had to forfeit my position when I left, but I had discovered one of its properties was to weaken a blood mage."

"Correct," Kushiel said, "except she's not a blood mage. She claims to be one, but she wasn't created with that power. She acquired it. Bloodstone will only weaken a *true* blood mage. Ironically, for Lilith, she uses it as the base for all her charms and spells."

"What do you mean?" I asked.

Kushiel nodded to the bodies. "They all wear bloodstone amulets that allow them to forge the rivers into Hell."

That was all I needed to hear. I stalked off to the nearest body I could find, flipped them over, and tore the amulet from their neck. I smiled, finally getting what I wanted, then frowned. The last time I had worn an amulet it had weakened me and led me down a dark path. Did I want to do that again? Bargain with black magic and witches?

I returned to Ariel. "Here," I said, handing the amulet to her. Then I knelt to break Kushiel's bonds. "This might hurt so bear with me." I placed my hands on the shackles and ignited the Hellfire.

He grimaced but was grateful when the metal melted away. "Thanks," he said, rubbing his wrists.

"Wait," Ariel said, "so bloodstone doesn't work against her." She seemed a little defeated, and I didn't blame her. The only reason she had come here and left everything behind was because she'd thought she had found a way to stop Lilith. She had lost her arm and leg over a theory that was debunked in less than a second.

"No," Kushiel said, rubbing his wrists.

Ariel sank to the ground. Kushiel put a hand on her shoulder. "I understand how you feel. We are alone, angels without a home or a purpose."

"Is that why your feathers turned?" I asked him.

He nodded. "And I suspect hers are, as well," he said, tugging on the strips of cloth.

Sure enough, gray feathers peeked through.

Ariel covered her face with her hands. I imagine if she could cry right now, she would.

"It started from an injury," Ariel murmured. "I had traveled to the Eastern Region, hoping to find a way to enter Qliphoth and confront Lilith, but she got to me first. She took my arm and my leg, then threw me in a lava field. I managed to get out before burning my skin, but my wings took the blow. It burned them. They had been white before the injury, but when they grew back in, they were gray. I figured they were still healing after being burned, except they haven't changed back." She stopped. "My faith in Him has been waning, and now it has been severed."

Something about her story had me thinking. "Ariel, you told me the passageways are sealed. Was that true when you went to the Eastern Region?"

She lifted her head. "Yes, I couldn't enter Qliphoth."

"But Lilith managed to come out?" I asked.

Ariel thought it over. "Yes." She raised the amulet. "Maybe this allowed her to do so?"

Kushiel shook his head. "No, those are only for the rivers. Those—" he pointed to a body "—are how they travel between regions."

I followed his direction and picked up a limp wrist. A device, almost like a watch, was strapped to it. I slipped it off and brought it over to them. "What is it?"

"A portal device," Kushiel said. "It's charged by divine light."

I was shocked. I had learned how to manipulate divine light to create portals, barriers, and shields, but Lilith had found a way to mobilize it and take it with her, whereas mine were rooted in place.

"That's why I didn't see you," I said to Kushiel. "They shielded you from sight."

"You're quite perceptive," he said.

I shrugged. "You have to be when you're a king." I turned the device over in my hand. This wasn't powered by magic. This could get me back to Hell.

"Well, I guess you're gone, then," Ariel stated.

I turned my attention to her. "Soon. I still have some questions for our new friend."

"What might those be?" he asked.

"How do you know all this? Why are you Lilith's prisoner in the first place?"

He grinned. "I was wondering when you might ask that."

Kushiel stopped talking, so I said, "Care to elaborate."

His jaw clenched. "Purgatory used to be an orderly place. The keeps were guarded by us, the archangels, and the bridges were protected by the blood mages. No creatures or demons roamed the land, contained as they were to their realms. Some of the slain angels became Guardians of the Lost Souls, assisting them in passing on to a new realm. When Lilith came and claimed this land as hers, when she destroyed us and the blood mages, there was no order anymore. Purgatory was thrown into chaos and has remained that way ever since.

"The blood mages sealed the keeps and raised the bridges before they were killed, subsequently locking all the lost souls here. Creatures, demons, and temptations run free, trying to claim the lost souls for themselves. The Guardians attempt to protect them and have banded together to restore order, but it's an increasingly difficult task as these forces grow stronger the longer they are free. The only way the Guardians can take control is if they regain their corporeal state."

"Their what?" I asked.

"Corporeal state," Kushiel repeated.

"I heard you. What does it mean?"

"Right now, the three of us are angels in a corporeal state. We have physical bodies. If we are slain, we are permanently stuck here, not even able to use that device you have in your hands. We would no longer have a physical body. We would be almost ghostlike in nature. An essence without a shell."

"How can the Guardians reclaim a corporeal state?" Ariel asked.

Kushiel winked. "That's where things start to align. You see, there's a rumor—"

"Oh god, I don't want to hear rumors!" I exclaimed.

"All rumors are based in some truth," Kushiel defended. "Besides, Purgatory is a world full of rumors and fables. You just have to decipher what's truth and what's deceit."

I sighed. "Carry on."

He smiled. "There's a rumor that a blood mage will rise again, and when they do, they will have the ability to not only reopen the passageways but to discover a way to return angels to their corporeal forms."

"For what reason? To leave Purgatory?" Ariel asked.

"No, to remain here and unite it in harmony once again. No matter what, the angels who are here will never be able to go back, unlike us, who still have a chance."

I chuckled. "You want to return to Heaven?"

"Never!" he spat. "I'm going to Hell!"

"Oh really? And you think I'm going to let you in?" I couldn't help but grin at his audacity.

"Of course. Because I'll be indebted to you, ready to commit any favor in return."

"Convincing argument," I said. "You still haven't told us how you know everything and why you're a prisoner."

He pursed his lips. "Still on that? I thought you'd forget by now."

"Never. You're dealing with a devil, not a dumbass."

"I like you!"

"Kushiel!" I growled.

"All right. Well my story of escape isn't as valiant as Ariel's. Lilith took my eye and was about to take my life, but she reconsidered. She needed a sacrifice, and she intended for me to be it. She has bargained with too many dark forces. She united four of God's worst creations to help her destroy the blood mages and archangels, all to possess the blood mage power for herself. Once she had it, she aligned herself with the dark matter of Qliphoth to imprison her allies here in Purgatory. She is indebted to the Dark, has been for centuries, pulling on its power and promising something in return. But she has yet to give it what it wants, and it's only a matter of time before it turns on her."

Ariel crossed her arms. "If you were meant to be a sacrifice, then why weren't you sacrificed?"

"I'm not sure. She's found other things to feed it in the meantime. She's been keeping me for something big. Anyway, that's how I know everything. I've been her captive for years and have perceptive ears." He thought a moment. "I've answered your other question, too. I'm a prisoner because she needs a sacrifice. Anything else?"

"Yes," I jumped in. "Where has she been holding you?"

"I was in Qliphoth, which is where I gained all this information, but she moved me to the Northern Region and clipped my wings so I couldn't escape."

"Each region is linked to an element," Ariel explained to me. "The Northern Region is associated with air, the Southern with water, the

Western with earth, and the Eastern with fire. He could have flown off in the north if she didn't do something."

"It's a spell, though," he assured us. "It's reversible." He stroked the gray feathers.

"And this?" I gestured around me. "Was Lilith moving you?"

Kushiel nodded. "She finally needs to sacrifice me."

"Why?"

He grinned. "Because a blood mage has returned."

26

SATAN

Purgatory, Present Day

"That's the rumor anyway," Kushiel said.

I put a hand to my head.

"You can feel it!" he defended. "Not just in here—" he rubbed at his chest "—but in here." He pounded the ground. "An awakening's coming."

I glanced at Ariel, who met my gaze.

"I know what you're thinking," she said. "He does sound insane, but he believes in the prosperity of this land. I'm skeptical of what he says, too; however, I have been here almost as long as he has and can confirm that a lot of what he says is true."

Kneeling in front of Kushiel, I sized him up. He seemed like he wanted Purgatory to return to its former glory, yet he was ready to leave in an instant.

"I'm not a deserter or a traitor," he said, staring at me. "If I were, I would have left a long time ago. But I held my post and did all I could. I want to leave now because I'm not an angel of Purgatory. That's not to say I'm not concerned about the issues transpiring here, because if they are not reined in, then all of us, the entire world, will face the consequences and it will no longer be one realm's problem."

"Fine," I decided, "you can come to Hell."

Kushiel grinned.

"As can you," I said, standing to face Ariel.

Her eyes went wide. "Wh-what?"

"You want a home? Hell's waiting. I can't guarantee either of you a leadership role since there's no telling who's survived the mutiny, but there might be a chance."

"Mutiny?" Kushiel exclaimed. "You were dethroned?"

"Did I not mention that?"

"No," Ariel said.

I threw my hands in the air. "There were witches and black magic, and Lucifer took over, but I suspect Lilith is now in charge."

They were both dumbfounded.

"Don't worry!" I said. "I'll get it back, and then you'll both have a home again as fallen angels."

Kushiel rose from the ground. "And we're to help you recover it?"

"I'm not asking you to do that. If anything, I'm warning you that I'm not sure what we might be returning to," I said, fiddling with the portal device.

"We should each take one of those," Ariel suggested, pointing at the device.

"Good idea," Kushiel agreed.

They walked over to a couple of the bodies and slipped the bands off their wrists.

"Uh-oh. I think this one is out of power," Kushiel said, inspecting the one he had picked up.

"How can you tell?" Ariel asked.

"It's not lit up. Typically, they glow."

Ariel dropped hers to the ground. "This one is out, then, too."

"As is mine," I stated.

We checked the remaining ones. All of them were out.

Damn it! I needed one of these devices to get back to my kingdom.

"Kushiel, were these assailants here to rescue you?" Ariel asked him, indicating the band of angels.

He shook his head. "No. I think they wanted me dead to piss off Lilith. She has made a lot of enemies here. Many of the occupants despise her, and that animosity leads to frequent attacks."

The two of them conversed, unconcerned about our setback. They had survived here for years, promises of freedom both given and taken many a time. But I was seething. I had a home. I had people waiting for me: Leviathan, Beelzebub, Belphegor, Haborym, Nehema, fallen angels, deceased spirits. The list went on and on. Most importantly, I had Abbadona, who meant more to me than anyone else.

That's a lie.

I turned my head to gaze out through the night. Where had that voice come from?

Stepping away from Ariel and Kushiel, I followed it.

There is another whom you care for more deeply.

I strode past the campfire, abandoning any light that was left, and stared out into the Wastelands.

A figure lounged against a large boulder only a few feet in front of me. *Come closer, my king. I will show you.*

Inching forward, I left the camp and headed for the rock. Without stopping, I came to stand before the mysterious woman.

Look into my eyes.

I did as commanded.

This is the one you seek.

An image of Dane appeared.

He is the one you adore.

The image shifted, and it showed Dane writhing on the ground.

He is your son. He has your power.

My eyes widened.

He needs your help.

Her eyes flashed again, this time showing a large camp.

He's in his mother's clutches, and she has dark intents.

The figure of Lilith emerged, stroking Dane's hair.

You must go before an irreversible deed cannot be undone.

The images receded, and I stared at the boulder. "What—"

A creature sprang from behind it and lashed at my face, coiling around my neck. Two strong hands grabbed my arms and dragged me back. One let go and slashed the air with a sword, severing whatever had latched on to me.

I choked, attempting to breathe.

"Are you insane?" Ariel yelled. "You never listen to a Temptress."

"Those…are…actual…things?" I wheezed.

"Yes! Why do you think I warned you?"

I sucked in a deep breath. "You didn't categorize temptations with creatures and demons. I figured they weren't tangible, in which case I thought I would have more self-control." Gasping, I tried to settle myself.

"What did you see?" Kushiel asked.

I shook my head and didn't speak.

Dane. My son. Lilith, his mother. How? I'd never cavorted with her. I couldn't cavort with anyone! Not with the fire running through my veins.

Oh no…

Blood. I had given her my blood! She probably used it for some spell, and now there was Dane.

Oh, Ace…

I was kidding myself if I didn't admit he had weaseled his way into my cold heart. He had reminded me so much of myself…

I stopped and ran my hands over my face.

You idiot! I should have known, but I hadn't thought it was possible. The poor kid, he had Hellfire. While I enjoyed its strength, I would never wish it on anyone. He must be going through so much.

Holy shit…

Lilith was his mother. Which meant *he* was a blood mage. Which meant a blood mage *had* returned to Purgatory. Which meant…

I held out my arms.

Dane had saved me. He had brought me back to life.

"Whoa! He's not all right," Kushiel said, detecting the hysteria overcoming me.

"Satan, talk to us," Ariel coaxed. "What's going on?"

I stood abruptly. "I need to go."

"Go! There's no way to go back to Hell!" Ariel exclaimed.

"I'm not going to Hell!" I shouted, heading deeper into the Wastelands.

They followed.

"Then where are you going?" Kushiel yelled.

"Qliphoth!"

"You've lost your mind!" Ariel called.

I refused to stop. Dane needed me. I had to find him. I had to save him as he had done for me.

Eventually, Ariel and Kushiel caught up to me.

"Okay, say we're going to Qliphoth," Kushiel proposed. "What is there that can help us? Because I'm meant to be sacrificed there."

"Then don't come," I said.

"I never said I wouldn't come. I would just like to know what we're fighting for." He froze as I turned to face him, my demeanor a little frenzied.

"We're going to rescue my son. Is that enough of a reason for you?"

The two of them looked at each other. Kushiel mouthed, *Son?* to Ariel.

She shrugged, then glanced at me. "We're in. We've come too far to let you go it alone."

I was glad they had agreed because I needed all the help I could get.

27 DANE

Purgatory, Present Day

I didn't know where I was. Moments ago, I had been at the lab with a girl standing before me.

Sophia. Had I done it? Had I killed her?

I couldn't stop thinking about her. I didn't want to hurt her, but something had taken over me.

Someone grabbed hold of my hair and lifted my head.

It was him. Darcel. I couldn't escape him. Not even within the depths of my own mind.

"You've ruined everything! We could have claimed our power."

I had always felt like two different people, and now, after the unbinding, my alter ego had been released. It was weird to have him here in front of me, talking to me like another person outside my body. It was unsettling to see the wicked hatred in his eyes.

Could that be me?

"It almost was."

Darcel vanished, and a woman appeared.

"Holy crap." I had never met her before, but I knew it was Jordan's mother. He looked just like her.

"It's nice to meet you, too, Dane," she said.

Where were my manners? "Sorry, it's crazy how much Jordan looks like you. It's nice to meet you." I put out my hand, then remembered the Hellfire and took it back. "Uh…I can't touch people."

She smiled. "I know. I was unsure why my son had put so much trust in you, but I see I have underestimated your character."

"I'm not him." I pointed behind me. "I don't want to be him."

"You mean Darcel?"

I nodded.

"Jordan asked me to intervene on your behalf, to give you a choice."

"He did?"

"Yes, without asking for anything in return and taking responsibility for the consequences."

"Consequences?"

"He was recaptured and brought back to Hell, which is now under Lilith's rule. She did unimaginable things to me—mind games, emotional trauma. She toys with people. She will toy with him, try to break him."

"What? No, I don't want that." Jordan didn't deserve that. Not for me.

"That is not your choice. The outcome has already been decided. Your choice is deciding between Dane and Darcel. Who you want to be, who can handle the power."

I shook my head. "I want to be Dane."

"But…?"

"But I think Darcel is the one who can handle the power. I mean, I can barely handle the Hellfire, let alone the blood magic. It's strong and consuming."

"Jordan has faith in you. He obviously thought Dane could control the power."

"He sees things in me that I don't."

"Which is why the two of you are the balance."

"I guess. But he doesn't share this power with me."

"No. You are not balanced in that you share things, but rather you equal each other out. Let me ask you something. Have you ever *used* your blood magic?"

"No."

"Then how do you know it's strong and consuming?"

"Because I can feel it—blood pressures, heart beats. I feel like a vampire except I don't have a taste for blood, not in a way that I depend on it and need it to survive."

She smiled. "That's a good comparison. But you wouldn't be feeling the power if you hadn't used it. You needed to claim it."

"Are you saying I killed Sophia?" I was alarmed.

She put her hand on my arm, and I flinched. "No, that's not what I'm saying," she said. "Just think harder. Is there something you did that involved blood?"

"Um… How can you touch me?"

"I'm the holy bloodline. Hellfire does not work on me. Now, is there something you did that involved blood?" she asked again.

I racked my brain. "No." I looked down at my arms. Tattoos covered them. "Oh no."

"What is it?"

"I gave someone a tattoo. Two actually. It was before the unbinding, though. Does that still count?"

"Yes. That act was you claiming your blood magic. Now when you executed those tattoos, were you scared?"

"Of course not. I love tattooing. I love art and artistry." I paused. Those tattoos were meaningful to me. I had thought the man I had given them to was Samuel at the time, a mentor at the gym, not Satan or my father. I had wished he was my father, or rather that my father was someone like him—strong, brave, rugged, cool. Looking back, I guessed I had unintentionally put those emotions into the ink itself. I wondered what it had done to him, if anything, especially since my powers were active now. I wondered if he knew about me, who I was, if he cared. I shook my head. It didn't matter. I would face this without him.

"I've made my choice. I can do this," I said.

"You can do what?"

That voice made me open my eyes.

Lilith.

She stroked my hair. "I was worried about you. You've been unconscious longer than I expected."

My jaw clenched. I hated her. I had to convince her, though, that I was Darcel, not Dane. "Stop." I put steely grit in my voice.

She sneered. "Make me."

My hand flashed out and gripped her wrist. The Hellfire burned her, but she didn't back down. I increased the heat.

Lilith clenched her teeth. "You're too much like him!" she screamed, slapping me across the face with her other hand.

I increased the heat more. "Who? My father! What'd you think would happen? That I'd only be like you? Well, you made this monster!"

"Ah!" she shrieked, pulling her wrist free and cradling it. She bit back the pain. "Darcel," she said calmly, "I wanted you to use your blood magic."

"I don't have it. I didn't claim it."

She rose and kicked a chair, breaking it to pieces. "Try to find it deep within you! Otherwise, I must do something that cannot be undone!"

I didn't have to search deep within for it. It was already lingering at the surface. I could feel the blood running in her veins, hear the beat of her heart. I should just stop it. I wished I could. But I didn't know how. The power played at my fingertips, yet I couldn't release it.

Lilith stepped forward, inching close to my face. "Don't lie to me, Darcel."

My face grew cold. "I'm not, *Mother*."

"You will remain here. If you so much as attempt to leave this tent, the guards will be on you in seconds."

"You're detaining me? How are you any better than Jazema and Penelope?"

She seethed and forcefully pulled her fingers into a fist. My knees rocketed to the ground as my heart squeezed in my chest. "Never compare me to those bitches," she spat.

I breathed heavily.

"Do you feel it yet?" she asked. "Use it," she urged. "Fight back."

"How?" I yelled. "I don't know magic and spells! I can feel the flow of blood, sense heartbeats. What am I to do with it?"

"You move them," she said.

"Move what?" I shouted in rage.

Lilith went sailing back into a wooden table, careening to the floor.

Oh shit!

She scrambled up from the pile of broken wood, dazed. "Of course," she said, "you let your anger control you." Dusting off her sleeve, she crossed her arms. "What are we to do about that?"

"Knowing you, you'll just suck it out of me and feed it to some dark thing."

Lilith grinned. "You're not too far off." She drew closer and brushed a finger along my cheek, despite the burn. "You're everything I wanted you to be." Her hand dropped, and she nudged me back a step. "Except you have too much of Satan in you. We must purge that."

I flipped her my middle finger.

She sighed. "Oh, you angsty teenager. I'll be back soon. Don't leave the tent. I've told them they can do anything but kill you."

Lilith blew a kiss in the air and left.

I *hated* her.

28 SOPHIA

Ithaca, New York, Present Day

I had no choice but to get back surgery. They'd done a second X-ray, and the results showed that Rajani's body slam into the staircase had cause irreversible damage. No amount of flying would heal it. In fact, it would only make it worse. That's what Raphael had said, and he was the only reason I had agreed to the procedure. Because he would be the one performing it.

I trusted him more than anyone right now, certainly more than Penelope's brainwashed lackeys.

When I woke up from surgery, Dafne and Naomi were there to greet me.

"Hey!" they said at the same time, each taking one of my hands and squeezing it. They sat on either side of the bed and must have been watching an HGTV show, since it blared on the TV.

"How do you feel?" Dafne asked.

I stared at my feet. My worst fear was that I wouldn't be able to move them or feel them—or walk for that matter.

"Let me go grab Raphael," Naomi suggested.

She left the room.

"You okay?" I rasped.

"Me?" Dafne waved off my question. "Fine. I should get you some ice chips." She stepped closer to the door.

"Dafne?"

"Hmm."

"Your dad will come around."

She smiled weakly. "I hope so because I've never seen him so disappointed." She slipped through the doorway just before Raphael entered it.

I felt bad for my friend. When Dafne's parents had discovered their daughter at the hospital, her mother was quick to hug her, comfort her, and make sure she was unharmed. Her father, however, remained cold and distant, not even speaking a word to her. It had made both Dafne and her mom very upset. I wasn't sure how it had ended since I had been taken up to surgery, but from Dafne's response and reaction, I guessed not so good.

"I'm glad to see you're awake. How are you?" Raphael asked.

"Okay, actually. I don't feel too bad."

The angel of healing chuckled. "Medicine, my expert surgery skills, or your angelic healing could be the reason for that." He went to the edge of the bed. "Try to wiggle your toes."

I concentrated hard, and they moved instantly.

Raphael smiled and came to my side. "Knees."

I shimmied them.

He grinned. "I think you'll make a full recovery. I'll make sure a nurse gets you ice chips."

"Dafne went to do that," I told him.

"Good. You shouldn't have a problem with liquids or solids, but we'll take it slow for now. Stick to mushy foods."

"Pudding and Jell-O it is," I joked.

"Oh, and you have some visitors." He waved them in.

I figured Naomi or Dafne had returned, but instead, the angels walked in. Chamuel had a bouquet of flowers, Zadkiel a book, Gabriel a thoughtful card signed by all of them, Michael a stack of magazines, and Uriel a balloon.

I smiled. "Thanks, guys."

There was a moment of quiet and then Michael said, "Sophia, I don't want to upset you, but did you have any recollection of who your dad was before today?"

I shook my head. "I didn't know anything about my dad. I still don't, really. The only person I remember is the man who saved me from the lab when I was young, and it turns out it was him. Why?"

"I only ask because he's Allen Clark, the man who came to me in Brazil with information on Geneloom. He was frantic that day when I met him, and then he disappeared. I thought he might be dead. I thought I'd never see him again, but here he is. Although his real identity is Aeron Conway."

"Are you sure?" Uriel asked.

Michael nodded. "Positive. I've been trying to act normal since we're in the thick of a tense situation, but I'll have to mention to him that I know he's Allen."

I fiddled with my fingers. "It's hard to act normal right now when Jordan is still in danger. I'm very concerned about him."

"As are we," Gabriel assured us.

"We were trying not to burden you with the stress of his absence by distracting you a little," Chamuel said, setting down the flowers.

"I know. I appreciate it. What are you going to do, though?"

"We all know he's in Hell," Michael said. "But it's not easy to get there, let alone navigate the place. We'd be going in blind, which is something we've discussed and are prepared for, but we are finalizing our plans as quickly as possible. We hope to commence the rescue within forty-eight hours."

I nodded. "Will I be able to leave soon?"

"Yes, I believe so," Raphael said. "Normally they would keep you, but I can discharge you into my care, as well as Martha's. Between the two of us, it'll be like you're at a hospital anyway." He fell quiet. "Sister Delphine would like to see you. Your parents, too. I said I would ask."

I shook my head. "I don't want to see them. Not now. I just want to go home."

My home had been the orphanage. That was long gone now, but Jordan's house had replaced it, and I couldn't be happier knowing I had someplace where I belonged.

"You can tell them I'm fine," I told Raphael. "And that I'll speak to them soon. Just not today."

"Understood."

Dafne and Naomi came back, the former carrying a cup of ice chips. She handed them to me, and I instantly dug around in the cup to grab a spoonful. My mouth was so dry.

"So are we all going to ignore the surprise in the room?" Uriel asked, staring at Naomi.

She grinned. "If there's something you'd like to ask, just say it."

"Okay. What are you?" Uriel asked.

Chamuel side-eyed Uriel. "Haven't you learned anything?"

Uriel shrugged. "Everyone loves my bluntness. You just refuse to admit it."

Chamuel crossed his arms and sighed, giving up the argument.

Silence filled the room until Naomi said, "I'm a Supernal."

Zadkiel rubbed his forehead. "I've never heard of such a thing."

"Trust me, before Geneloom, I had no idea what I was," Naomi said.

"But how are you what you are?" Dafne asked. "Your parents are humans, right?"

Naomi nodded. "Yes, they are. But I'm adopted."

"You are? Jordan never told us," Michael said.

"That's because I didn't tell him," Naomi confessed.

Dafne met my eyes. Hurt flashed across them. I thought she might have realized that at one point there had been more between Naomi and Jordan than just friendship.

I reached out my hand to comfort her. She took it and squeezed. That small gesture meant we would discuss later. No one had seen our brief interaction, too captivated by Naomi's story.

"My wings came when I turned thirteen," Naomi said, "and I was so scared I didn't tell my parents. I didn't tell anyone. I carried the burden of my secret because I knew I'd be treated like a science experiment if anyone found out. I considered telling my parents, and I'm sure they would have protected me, but I didn't want to endanger them and knowing would endanger them. That's what my gut told me anyway. So I learned how to use my wings, and then I turned sixteen and my powers came."

"Powers?" Gabriel asked. "Like magic?"

"Yes, I have an affinity to water. I was at school one day and I had gotten a simple paper cut. Later that afternoon, when I went to the bathroom, I washed my hands and the cut had healed instantly. I thought I might be imagining things, but I tested it out a few times after that, and it worked every time. Then I discovered I could actually wield water, transform it into ice and manipulate it to do whatever I wanted."

She smiled briefly. "By eighteen, I had mastered my powers. I was also introduced to the Sacrarium. My mom thought I might be a good candidate so she brought me to meet Sister Helen. She was interested, thought I might be a good Novice, but she wanted me to start college first. She knew how important school was to me. If anything, it only helped because I was passionate about science, and when I went to seek an internship, I saw an opportunity at Geneloom. My mom knew what they were and advised against it. Except the more she told me about them, the more I wanted to do it. I needed to know who and what I am."

"I know that feeling," I sympathized.

Naomi nodded. "Except my mom forbade it. Sister Helen didn't, though. She made it my trial of trust. I was never supposed to go as deep as I did. I only stayed on since I knew I hadn't even brushed the surface. When Sister Helen passed and my mom took on the role of Alpha, she stepped in again and tried to get me to stop. I wouldn't. I needed to gain Geneloom's trust to learn any information that was worthwhile, and I was finally making headway. It was there where I learned about the Supernals. Unlike Nephilim who are half-human, half-angel, Supernals are full angel."

"You mean both your biological parents are angels?" Zadkiel asked.

Naomi nodded.

"How?" Michael asked.

Naomi shrugged. "I never found out the specifics. I know angelic bodies cannot carry children so I imagine a human surrogate is needed. It's hard to say, though. Nothing is off-limits with the existence and knowledge of blood magic."

My eyes narrowed. "You know about blood magic?"

"No," Naomi said. "Not how to use it. Each Supernal has elemental magic, not blood magic. But blood magic is connected to the Supernals, and I don't know why."

"You're right," I agreed. "It does have to do with the Supernals because that's what they classified Dane as."

"Dane has blood magic? I thought he had Hellfire," Raphael asked.

"He has both," I said. "Unfortunately, I think he's lost to us. Lilith took him."

"Then we need to find him," Gabriel said. "I didn't realize he was with you at the lab. I thought he was missing and no one knew where he was."

"No, he was there. But I think he made his choice," I said. "Being a blood mage changed him, and it seemed like he succumbed to the power...like he wanted to be with Lilith."

"Oh no," Chamuel gasped.

I nodded and brushed a stray tear from my cheek. "Our attention and resources should be focused on saving Jordan," I said, though it pained me.

Michael moved to the edge of the bed and leaned against the

footboard. "Our priority right now is Jordan because we know where he is. That's not to say we won't be going after Dane. We will find him, whether he wants us to or not, because I refuse to give up on him." He looked over his shoulder. "*We* refuse to give up on him." He turned back and met my eyes. "You shouldn't give up on him, either."

"I don't want to," I said.

But he wanted to kill me.

I was going to add those words, speak them aloud, but I stopped myself. Maybe I was wrong. Maybe there was a chance that Dane was still alive and Darcel hadn't completely taken over.

"For now, just focus on resting," Raphael instructed.

I sunk back into the bed and tried to calm down. It was hard to do when the ones you loved were still in danger, but I did the best I could.

Four hours later, I was discharged from the hospital and into Raphael's care. Naomi had left with her parents and returned home. I'm sure we would be seeing her soon since she lived right next door. Dafne stuck around to assist, pushing me out to the car in a wheelchair.

"Hey, do you mind if I stay with you for a little bit?" she asked.

I went to twist around in the chair to face her but realized I couldn't. "Of course, you can, Dafne. Is everything all right with your grandparents?"

"Yeah, everything's good. I just want to be around. I know I can't help much, but I want to be here when Jordan returns."

"You're more than welcome to stay. In fact, I'm glad you are because we need each other right now."

"Agreed." She sighed, helping me into the car.

When we pulled up to the house, I was eager to get out and go inside, knowing I would feel comforted the moment I stepped in the door. I had just eased out of the car and onto the gravel walkway when Martha came running out.

She ran straight toward me and hugged me gently. "Oh, Sophia." Martha pulled back and touched my cheeks. "You don't need to worry anymore. You're safe, and we'll take care of you." Then she dropped her hands and gave the angels a sharp glance. "You have company."

"Us?" Gabriel asked.

"Uh-huh. She knows how to save Jordan."

The angels raced inside. Martha, Dafne, and I followed them at a slower pace.

Once we entered the house, we headed to the library. All the angels were frozen in place in the doorway.

"Who's here?" I asked. Pushing my way through them, I finally saw our visitor. It was a woman with long black hair and amber eyes. She looked tired, and one of her wings was hunched. I didn't know who she was. From the look of it, the angels didn't, either.

Michael stepped forward, inching closer and closer to the woman until they stood face-to-face. Their eyes locked. The female angel even looked a little flustered.

"I know you," he said. "How do I know you?"

She shook her head. "You don't. We've never met."

"Are you sure? Because I *feel* like I know you."

"Perhaps our souls know each other." She bounced her pointer finger back-and-forth between them. "But we have never met." She faced the entire group. "My name is Katriel. I like to go by Kat. I'm a member of the Triune, and I've been locked in Hell for nineteen years. Jordan and I escaped together, but he ran off to help his friend." She grimaced.

"More like sacrificed himself for his friend... Anyway, they have captured him again. He told me to come here to alert you all; however, I will be doing more than alerting you. I will be helping you save him."

Michael didn't waste any time. He strode over to the table, grabbed a blank piece of paper, and placed it in front of Kat. "Can you draw the layout of Hell?"

Kat sat down. "I can do better than that. I can tell you every in and out."

I hobbled over to the table. "So you're Kat." She seemed amazing and formidable all at once.

She looked up at me. "Yes."

"I'm Sophia. Jordan's cousin. I worked with Aziza and Yadira as part of my trial of trust."

"You're Sacrarium?"

I shook my head. "I never took my vows, but I was training to be."

"Hmm... I heard what happened to Helen. Such a tragedy. Do you know who has taken her place?"

I nodded. "Deborah, she lives next door."

"Really? We'll need her here. She needs to mobilize whoever is left." Kat brought her attention to the paper and began drawing.

"What about Aziza and Yadira?" I asked.

Kat smiled. "I wouldn't worry about them. They're already on the way. They even contacted the Factions of Faith."

"The what?" Dafne asked, coming closer.

Kat stopped. "They're angels from every religion in the world. We often don't work together, but the battle ahead is not just a Christian battle. It's an apocalyptic battle that will decide the fate of the world."

Dafne blanched. "I didn't realize it was that serious. I think we need to talk," she said to me.

"I'll fill you in."

Everyone had come to the table. All except Gabriel.

Kat's hand hovered over the paper. She dropped the pen and turned in her seat. "I thought ignoring you would make it easier. How foolish I was." She rose and walked over to him.

"Why do I feel like I'm looking at myself?" Gabriel asked.

"Because you are in a way," Kat said, holding out her wrist.

Gabriel's eyes widened. He pulled back his robe and held out his arm. "How—" He didn't finish.

"We're twins," Kat whispered. "You and I share energy. Have you ever been in battle and wondered how you inexplicably know what to do?"

"Yes."

"In those moments, you're drawing on my energy. I might be an angel of the Triune, but I was created as an archangel, an angel of power."

"Shouldn't we both be angels of power, then?"

"No, because you have an unexplainable gift for music. Father never anticipated it, but you cannot deny your talent. Before my sojourn to Hell, I used to find solace in music, too. Those were the times when I would draw on your energy."

"You play violin?"

Kat shook her head. "No, piano."

"Why didn't I know about you?"

"Because Father didn't want you to. Father didn't want anyone knowing about me. I was meant to have a different purpose. I was never created to stay in Heaven. That was your role."

"So do you have a sphere? How does it work with the council?"

"Our seat on the council is your responsibility," Kat explained. "I do have a sphere, but it is not needed for the prophecy. It was fashioned to be a prison."

Everything clicked in my mind. "The fourteenth sphere was yours. You trapped Lilith inside it," I said.

Kat smiled. "Indeed. Since I, a blessed angel, imprisoned her, a fallen angel had to be the one to destroy the sphere. Unfortunately, you did not know that," she said, meeting Gabriel's eyes. She took his hands. "Don't blame yourself. The sphere was a temporary fix. It was never meant to hold her forever."

"Nevertheless, I will do whatever I can to help vanquish her," Gabriel said.

Kat nodded and dropped his hands. "There are many stories that need to be told. Many secrets that need to be revealed. But not until the bloodline is secure and all the necessary parties are present. Our attention must be on Jordan now." She returned to her seat and continued drawing. Kat met my gaze. "You, however, need rest. Otherwise, you're going to drop."

I didn't disagree with her. I felt exhausted. Dafne and Martha helped me upstairs, where I sank into bed and closed my eyes.

"One down," Martha whispered. She stroked my hair. "Two more to go."

"Don't worry," Dafne said, "they'll bring the boys home."

29

JORDAN

HELL, PRESENT DAY

I now knew what the consequences were. My punishment was being brought back to Hell, but my torture was fighting the dark matter inside me.

I leaned my head back against the stone prison wall. I shivered and sweated at the same time, hot enough to be soaked through and cold enough for my bones to rattle. I had been sick before but never like this. I felt like I was being eaten from the inside out.

I had my flask of holy water, and I dribbled a few drops on the wound every day. It always stung, and I always shrieked. I didn't use a lot, though. I knew I had to save it. Who knew how long I would be down here? I'm sure Kat and the angels would mobilize as soon as they could. Even then, a plan had to be put in place. Logistics decided. Which was why I was rationing the holy water.

Unfortunately, my wound wasn't far from my heart. Zadkiel had told me the dark matter festers until it makes it to one's heart, in which case it takes over and turns the person into a dark being. I was trying to prevent that from happening. But I didn't have enough holy water to cleanse the wound completely, which is why I fought it off, little by little, every day with a few drops.

I shifted on the ground, and something in my pocket crunched. Rummaging around, I found the roll of crackers I had taken with me. I took them out and opened them, then nibbled on one, grateful the Sentinel hadn't thought to search me when he had captured me.

He had dropped me in here when we had returned and said, "You'll stay here until Lilith arrives."

I hadn't seen him since. Food and water were delivered daily, but I wondered just how many days had gone by because I'd definitely lost track…

Feeling the rest of my pockets, I discovered I still had the dagger from the unbinding on me. I was glad to still have it, but at the same time, it would have been nice to have remembered sooner.

I swallowed, and my entire body stilled. Quickly, I rose and ran to the corner of the cell, vomiting up the cracker and black bile.

Wiping my mouth, I sank to the cold ground. Was this what it felt like to die?

Lying there, I realized the Sentinel hadn't even bothered to chain me up. Just went to show how little a threat I posed to them.

The cell bars clanged.

"Wakey, wakey," the Sentinel said.

He thought I was sleeping. Good. They couldn't see I was sick. If they knew, they would try to heal me. While I wanted to be healthy again, I didn't want to be in their clutches healed and whole. They would just use me for the prophecy and then kill me. I would rather die knowing their chances of supremacy perished with me.

I rose from the ground and followed the Sentinel into the portal room.

"Where is she?" I asked, expecting to see Lilith.

"She's arriving in the Eighth Cavern. We will greet her there."

Confused, I asked, "Where?" I was quickly silenced, though, as we walked through the throne room and stood before a large, deep hole.

"The Pit," the Sentinel said.

"This takes us to the cavern?" I asked.

"Yes," he said. "I'll catch you before you hit the bottom."

"Wha—"

He shoved me off, and I fell through the air.

I yelled, my shouts echoing through the hole. I imagined this was what it was like to skydive, except this was less controlled. I tumbled through the air, not sure how to stop myself from twisting and spinning. After a while, it felt like a bad recurring nightmare where I just kept falling and falling without any hope of an end.

Eventually, I spied a blast of light. As I drew closer, I realized it was a flame.

Oh crap! I was about to dive into a pit of flames and be burned alive!

A force slammed into me and swung me to the left, through a tunnel and into a cavern, where I was then thrown to the ground.

I wanted to vomit again, but there was nothing left in me. Crawling across the stone, I tried to get away from the Sentinel. It was a futile attempt. He took two steps and had me by the hair, lifting me to my feet.

"Enjoy your fall?" he whispered in my ear.

I didn't respond. He threw me to the ground again. This time I lay there, finding comfort in stillness.

Come. Cleanse yourself.

My head bobbed up at the voice. A few feet in front of me were five rivers. The thought of water had me licking my lips.

Just a little sip. That's all you need.

I nodded and crawled closer.

"Stop him!" a woman shrieked.

The Sentinel barreled over to me as I was about to dip my hand in and cup the refreshing drink. The waters rose instead to meet me. I was violently pulled back before they could.

"Shut her up!" the Sentinel shouted.

Who?

I was dragged back, and that's when I saw there was a group of more prisoners, among them a beautiful fallen angel with skin like the night sky. The others were faces I knew well—members of the Six. There were two other females, and I remembered they had assisted Satan at the gala. I guess they were trusted fallen angels of his.

Actually, now that I thought about it, all of them must have been Satan's allies. Why else would they be tied up?

Mammon and Asmodeus were the only two who weren't, which led me to believe they were traitors. It fit both their personalities; they seemed like scum. There was yet another fallen angel present, though I had never seen him before. He was big and strong, even bigger than Beelzebub. He was staring at me with a sour scowl.

"I should kill him for what he did to Murmur," he spat.

"You'll have your chance, Mulciber," the Sentinel assured him. "Not until Lilith is finished with him, though."

He grunted and crossed his arms.

I sank back against the stone wall again, trying to ignore the voice of the rivers. It seemed like they were evil tempters, something I wasn't supposed to indulge, so I did my best to tune them out.

"Stop looking at me," the Sentinel growled.

I glanced around. Who was looking at him? "You mean me?" I asked, pointing to myself.

"Yes, you!" he shouted in my face. "Stop staring at me with those Conway eyes or I'll pry them from your puny head."

Conway eyes? How did he know who I was?

He laughed. "Your bafflement is amusing. I knew many a Conway. I loved one, I envied one, and I killed one."

I sucked in a sharp breath. "I thought Lilith was the one who killed my parents."

He sneered. "You give her too much credit. She killed your mother, but I killed your father. I tried killing your uncle, as well. He knew me too well, though. Knew all my tricks."

"Wh-what? Who are you?"

"Names don't matter. Actions do. All you need to know is I was the one to betray them."

My lip trembled in rage. This man—this *creature*, for he was no man any longer—was the cause of my father's death. A friend turned foe. A deceiver. I wanted to kill him.

Then do it.

It wasn't the rivers speaking to me this time. It was the dark matter. And while it gave me strength, it didn't provide me with a weapon. Otherwise, I didn't think anything would have stood in my way. I would have sliced his throat, watched the blood pour forth, and rejoiced that my dad's killer was dead.

Shaking my head, I pushed out the thoughts. That wasn't me. I might have killed Murmur, but it had been in self-defense. And although I wanted to kill the Sentinel, I wouldn't exult in his death. I would cry and weep, not just for killing a man but for putting an end to my parents' story. Closing the book and leaving it shut for years to come.

Except I had the dagger in my jacket pocket. I could do it...but I was severely outnumbered.

I inhaled and exhaled a few times, hoping to calm myself.

Suddenly, the rivers bubbled and rose, a figure emerging from their watery depths. Her dark hair and snakelike eyes were easily recognizable.

Lilith.

She stepped forth from the water, her eyes searching the cavern and roaming over every being. She smirked when she saw me. "Finally, we meet in person," she exclaimed, striding over. "I know we briefly met in Norway, but now we truly get to know each other." When she was close, she slapped me across the face. "That's for taking my son from me. He tries to hide it, but it's easy to see Darcel does not linger beneath the surface. The boy you love like a brother stays…for now. I have plans to change that. Nonetheless, you had your mother intervene and someone must pay for it." She rubbed my sore cheek, her eyes filled with malice. "What have you done to him?" she screamed at the Sentinel.

"Nothing!" he assured her.

My condition must have been written on my face.

"Have you fed him?" she questioned.

The Sentinel was quick to answer. "Yes."

"Good. We need him alive." She searched my face. "Perhaps your new setting is making you unwell. It takes some time to get used to the Underworld." Lilith turned her attention away from me. "Now where are the hounds? They should be here to greet me."

The Sentinel sighed. "I have not seen them since I arrived."

Lilith focused on Mammon, Asmodeus, and Mulciber. "Well, where are they?"

Asmodeus and Mulciber shrugged. Mammon was the only one brave enough to speak. "Why don't you ask him?" He pointed to Leviathan. "He's the one who trained them."

Oh no… I could tell by her murderous look that someone was not walking away alive.

She sauntered over to the group of prisoners. "I guess it's time to play." She knelt in front of the female fallen angel, the one with dark skin. "It's nice to see you again, Abbadona. Rest assured, the blood I stole from you those many years ago was put to good use."

The female angel fumed. Bound and gagged as she was, there was little else she could do to express her emotion.

Lilith moved on to the two other female angels. "Don't know either of you, so you are of no importance." She waved them off and kept going down the line. "Beelzebub, always an idiot. Belphegor, always a bore. Ah, Leviathan. Where are my hounds?"

He shook his head. "I don't know. They were acting up when Satan fell ill. Lucifer claimed them at that point, but it was short-lived. They disappeared from here and haven't returned since."

"Are they under someone's command?"

"I'm not sure. Certainly not Lucifer's."

"Where is he, by the way?"

No one answered.

Lilith turned to the Sentinel.

"Were you asking me?" he asked.

"Yes," Lilith ground out.

"He wasn't here when I arrived," the Sentinel answered.

"That's because he fled," Mammon said. "We were assisting him in fighting off your scouts coming through the rivers. When the battle became too rough, he escaped and left us. We stopped, knowing you would be a much worthier leader to follow."

Lilith cackled. "Oh, how gallant you three are," she mocked. "Figures Lucifer would bolt. He's more for torturing innocents than fighting valiantly. Now back to you." She returned to Leviathan. "Call forth the hounds."

"What? You think they follow me?"

"They must be following someone."

"Well it's not me. A forceful order must have been given to the Alpha for them all to roam off like this."

A forceful order.

My entire body was covered in goose bumps as I remembered the scene last spring. The hounds had been chasing us. We'd been near the river in New York City. They had been attacking. Dane had commanded them to stop…and they had listened.

The hounds were following Dane. No wonder they weren't in Hell. Their master wasn't here. And whether Dane knew it or not, he had a whole horde of beasts under his control.

Except a small pack had shown up in Africa on our travels. They had chased me over the waterfall. What had that been about?

"What are you thinking, boy? It's so obvious it's like you're screaming it at the top of your lungs," Lilith said.

I came back to the moment. "How did you know?"

"Your face. But I can also feel the blood rushing to your head."

Oh…

"I'm thinking about the last time I saw the hounds. They were chasing me in Africa. I think they were under Lucifer's command, but it was a small pack."

"Just like humans and angels, the hounds vie for power," Leviathan explained. "A small pack could have been following Lucifer while the majority followed another. They would have held out until both Alphas fought. Whichever reigned supreme would be the master they now follow."

"I'm guessing from your story that Lucifer's pack was the small one, eventually beaten out by the larger pack and whoever rules it," Lilith summarized.

"That would be my theory," Leviathan said.

"Hmm…"

The mother of blood magic fell silent.

"He lies to you," Mulciber said.

Lilith's head snapped up. "Excuse me?"

"There is a hound that lingers here," Mulciber elaborated. "The biggest of them all."

"No!" Leviathan yelled.

Mulciber smirked. "Cerberus. He could be yours."

Lilith leered. "Let me guess. He follows Leviathan."

"Always has," Mulciber said. "Even when Satan had a firm hold over the other hounds."

"I guess that'll have to do for now."

It was an unofficial command. Mulciber took it as one, at least, pulling out a dagger and slashing it through the air so fast I wasn't entirely sure what had happened until one of the female fallen angels screamed.

I looked away as Leviathan convulsed, blood streaming from his neck.

"Now I have command over Cerberus," Mulciber said.

Opening my eyes, I saw him kneel before Lilith.

"I shall give rule of the hound to you, so long as you allow me to assume the position as leader of Envy."

A genuine smile crossed Lilith's face. "I like you. You may have your place in Envy, and I shall take the hound."

"Many thanks, Mistress," Mulciber bellowed, striding over to Leviathan's body and prying a ring from one of his fingers.

"You two better start showing your worth like Mulciber," Lilith chided. "Otherwise, I might have to slay you where you stand."

Mammon and Asmodeus blanched.

"We promise we are loyal to you," Asmodeus declared.

"As you told two other rulers, I'm sure," Lilith said. "Words mean nothing. Actions reveal truth. I'm not saying you must prove your fealty now. We don't want to make this a bloodbath," she joked. "You will be tested, though, and if you fail, your life is not guaranteed."

A guttural roar echoed through the cavern. One of the rivers rose, a form taking shape. "I demand what I deserve!" it screeched.

A stream of water lashed out, snaking around Leviathan's almost dead form and dragging it into its watery depths. When the body was fully submerged and had disappeared, the river calmed and returned to normal.

Pure savagery. This place was filled with it. It was frightening to witness.

"Let's go, boy. My work here is done. It's time for me to claim my throne and for us to chat," Lilith said.

"About what?" I asked.

"The past, of course," she stated matter-of-factly. "The truth hurts more than lies, especially in your case, and I think it's time to hurt you."

She made it sound so thrilling when I knew it would be far from it.

On our trip back up to the throne room, the Sentinel grabbed me by the collar of my shirt and lifted me in the air. We followed Lilith and set foot upon the familiar stone ground just seconds after her.

She raised her arms wide. "Finally!" She strolled over to the throne and sat down, sinking back into the seat and crossing her legs.

For the first time in its entire existence, Hell had been claimed by a queen.

30 DANE

PURGATORY, PRESENT DAY

I had to get out of here. Lilith knew Darcel was gone. My hate for her was too apparent. I wasn't about to wait for her return, and I didn't really care what these bastards had been commanded to do. I was breaking out of this tent.

Walking toward the entrance, I saw two figures stood guard. I thought it over, trying to estimate if I could duke it out with these two. Then a better idea came to mind.

I went to the back of the tent, grabbed a fistful of fabric in each hand, and incinerated it to make a new entrance. I sneaked through the hole undetected and found myself facing another tent. Creeping down the small expanse of ground between them, I approached a thoroughfare in the camp. There were people everywhere.

Shit!

I went back the way I had come to check the other side. It was a similar situation. My tent must have been in the middle of the camp for everyone to watch. Glancing to the right, I wondered whose tent stood next to mine. Probably Lilith's, I imagined.

Stepping up to it, I made another hole and peered inside. It was empty. I entered, and sure enough, it was Lilith's tent. The only way I knew was because five sets of keys, my dagger, as well as two of Satan's keys rested along a table.

Inching closer, I realized the weapon I had pulled from the tree for the unbinding must have been taken from me at the lab. I had gone through so much, keeping track of the dagger was the least of my concerns but I was happy to see it. Lilith probably had stolen it when she'd raided the lab, along with Satan's keys, which was how everything was here now.

I had to take it all with me. None of this belonged to her, and even if it had, she wouldn't use them for anything good.

I searched the room for something I could put everything in. There was a large leather sack sitting on the ground. I picked it up and saw that it was empty.

This would do.

I went back over to the keys and inspected them. It was unlikely that Lilith had just left them here without protection. Sure, her followers probably wouldn't take them, but Lilith trusted no one, even the people that were most faithful to her.

Eventually, I spotted the incantation woven around them—a blood magic spell. It was like spotting an iridescent aura. I could *feel* it. She had used someone's blood to bind the keys with a protective ward. Small symbols hovered around them.

I wondered if I was the only one who could see these symbols and detect the aura? It was impossible to say. Either way, I had to break it. But how?

I stuck my hands in the air and traced them to follow the pattern woven around the keys. Instantly, I felt something. It was like a tugging sensation. Was I releasing the spell? Did I have to say something?

I had no idea what I was doing. The only thing I seemed to control at the moment was the Hellfire. So why not use it.

I drew the heat to my hands, and slowly, the symbols around the keys started to fade. I needed to do this faster, though, because someone would surely come looking for me soon.

Increasing the heat, I watched as the auras completely disappeared. I reached out and grabbed a sphere. A searing pain ran up my arm.

"Ah!" I yelled.

I dropped the green-and-red stone, but there was no time to waste. It was like an alarm had sounded the moment my hand touched it. I forced myself to numb the pain as I grabbed the stone again and shoved it in the sack. I took all the other keys, which didn't hurt to hold at all, as well as my dagger, and stuffed them in, too. I pulled the drawstring tight and swung it over my shoulder. Then I hightailed it out of there.

I came to the thoroughfare again and saw that just beyond it lay a wasteland. That was where I had to go, somewhere deserted and faraway. So I raced out into the camp and took off as fast as I could.

But I shouldn't have worried about being chased. Not when the ground beneath my feet gave way and I fell ten feet down.

31

SATAN

Purgatory, Present Day

Our trek to Qliphoth was long. The Wastelands was a vast expanse filled with lost souls and creatures, and we encountered many of each on our journey. None of them were interested in us, far too preoccupied with cowering and hiding in the case of the lost souls and with killing and eating in the case of the creatures. Ariel assured me that not all the creatures here were violent, but the ones running most rampant were. Many of them were demons, and not the type I was familiar with. My demons in Hell were docile beasts compared with these savages.

Ariel had also informed me that it was difficult to fly in the Wastelands since the clouds hung low and visibility was poor. This factor added to the length of our trip.

There was a lava stream that ran from the Core into Qliphoth that we were using as a guide, following close enough to avoid other beings but far enough not to harm ourselves. It seemed most of Purgatory's occupants were afraid of the natural forces that exerted themselves in this land, which gave us easy passage along the lava stream since no one else ventured too close. But we had to watch ourselves since the heat emanating from the molten river was heavy.

There was little conversation, each of us focused on the task ahead, determined to make it to Qliphoth unscathed. Until I thought of something.

"Ariel, you said there are other creatures and Guardians of the Lost Souls here in Purgatory. Why haven't we encountered any yet?"

She shrugged. "The Guardians stick to the regions and only venture out now if they must, since ferrying the souls to the bridges is no longer possible. As for the other creatures I mentioned, I don't know. I guess they're hiding."

"Right," I said, "but where?"

There was nowhere to hide in the Wastelands. Maybe a large boulder here or there, but nothing that would provide long-term sanctuary. I was sure the regions themselves had plenty of places to disappear to but not for creatures who were in direct opposition with the Guardians.

Then another thought struck me. Ariel had found sanctuary in the cave, and from experience, I knew caves could be an underground web of activity. But not everyone would be as risky as Ariel, climbing down the Core. There had to be another entrance.

The keeps.

Structures that heavily guarded would surely warrant an entry point to something important. They weren't guarded anymore, but that only made access easier. If we could get to the Qliphoth Keep and there was an entrance to the caves there, then we might be able to enter Qliphoth underground rather than through the passageway.

Except all this was pure speculation. There was no real way to know if there were more caves and if they connected to one another, let alone how much time this would take since we still had to complete our travel through the Wastelands and then the whole Eastern Region before arriving at the keep.

There had to be a quicker way!

If only those portal devices had been charged…

Kushiel raised his hand, and we halted.

A camp could be seen in the distance.

"What is that?" Ariel asked.

"A prisoner camp," Kushiel said.

"How do you know?" I asked.

"Because I've been held in one before. Lilith doesn't like her prisons to reside in one specific area. She wants them to be mobile, to keep the prisoners moving so as to prevent an attack or an escape."

"We need to infiltrate it," I said.

Outraged, Ariel asked, "Why?"

"Because this is taking too long," I snapped. "If we had a portal device, it would shorten our journey, and if that's a Lilith camp, then one of her lackeys might have what we need."

Horns blared in the distance.

"A prisoner's escaped," Kushiel said.

"How do you know?" Ariel asked.

"Because I have seen many try. Most fail. The ones that succeed, even temporarily, cause pandemonium."

"How difficult will it be to gain entry?"

"Well I wouldn't walk straight through camp, especially now with them on high alert," Kushiel explained. "An attack would be foolish. Lilith is the only one who can use blood magic, but that doesn't mean she hasn't altered some of her troops to be special. A lot of them can regenerate and can't die. Burning their bodies is typically the only way to stop them."

"Or cut off their heads," I mumbled.

Ariel ignored me. "I would advise we skirt the camp for as long as we can, then cut in toward the back."

"I had a similar thought," I said. "Let's go."

We creeped along the outskirts, the camp always within sight. When we neared the back, we started to cross the Wastelands, finally taking cover behind a tent.

In our hiding spot, we overheard the guards talking.

"The boy is gone," one of them said.

"What do you mean?"

"He disappeared. Everyone saw him run right through camp, but then he was swallowed whole into the ground. I've never seen anything like it before. A hole just opened up beneath his feet, and it sealed up once he fell through."

"We have to find him before she comes back! Otherwise, we're all dead!"

"There's no way into the caves! They were sealed long ago!"

"Doesn't matter! We'll dig our way through if need be!"

They retreated into the distance.

My blood boiled. Dane had been here, and now we'd lost him.

Ariel and Kushiel waited for my command.

It was pointless to trek to Qliphoth if Dane wasn't there, but finding a working portal device was still a worthy mission. It could take us to the caves. Those guards had just confirmed their existence, and it seemed like Dane had somehow managed to enter them.

I closed my eyes, giving myself a moment to think of how best we could overtake one of the guards without alerting the whole camp.

That's when I felt it, an energy unlike any other. Opening my eyes,

I tried to pinpoint where it was coming from. I skimmed over tents until I settled on one. It was smaller than the others, set toward the back and off to the side.

"Follow me," I whispered.

Ariel and Kushiel obeyed.

We sneaked over to the tent and stopped outside its entrance.

Ariel sucked in a breath.

"You feel that?" I asked.

She nodded. Kushiel did, too.

The energy was strong and impossible to ignore once you had sensed it.

"Wait here," I said. "I'm going in."

Again, they did as commanded.

Slipping inside, I expected to see some super celestial being, but all that stood before me was Jophiel. He was bound to a chair, his head lowered to his chest.

I went over to him.

He detected my movement, his head rising from its limp position. "Satan," he muttered in surprise.

I knelt and reached for his bonds.

"No, don't," he said. "There is no hope for me if I'm released. Lilith will just find me again and use me to charge her devices until I am no more."

I glanced to the left and saw that there were rows of portal devices set out along a table. Iridescent cords, almost like wires, were connected to each device, all of them snaking to the ground and winding around Jophiel's legs.

"They need to be charged," Jophiel said. "Divine light is preferable. It's much stronger and can last multiple trips. There's not much of that around here, so heavenly light is an acceptable alternative, although the charge is shorter lived and can barely make a round trip. But there's plenty of it here with all the slain angels wandering these parts."

I was horrified, and I wasn't sure at what. The fact Lilith was using my brothers and sisters to charge her vile devices, or that Jophiel had perished. I could tell he had died because there was a hazy glow around him.

My anger had me grabbing the cords from his legs and prying them free. It hurt and stung, almost as if I were reaching into a nest of vipers. I didn't care, though. This wasn't right, and I made sure every last one was gone. "Come on, I'll get you out of here."

"And take me where? The Wastelands?" Jophiel whispered. "She'll only find me again." He paused and took a breath. "There is only one way to end this that will not conclude in suffering." He stared at me.

I lowered my head and shook it. "No. I won't end you forever. I swore to myself I would never…" I couldn't finish.

"Slay us?" Jophiel asked. "You did during the war."

I set my gaze on him. "Says who? I might have incited an army. They might have killed, but I *never* slew a brother or sister. And I won't. Not without a reason."

"Don't you get it? I can't go back. I can't go anywhere. I'm stuck here. Setting me free will only land me back in this chair to be sucked dry."

I focused on the ground again. It was too hard to look at him.

"You still have a chance," he said. "Take the devices and get out of here."

"No, I'm not using them. Not after I know how they are charged."

"Samael, look at me."

I clenched my jaw and glanced up.

"You're running out of time. So make your decision quickly."

Nodding, I stood and found a sack. It must have been used to transport the devices because it was lying on the table like it was meant for them. I gathered them up and closed the sack, swinging it over my head. Then I went back to Jophiel. "I promise you these devices will be destroyed."

"Use them to escape. Then destroy them."

I agreed and braced myself for the inevitable.

Jophiel delayed it by saying, "There is a way to stop her. Bloodstone—"

"It doesn't work," I interrupted.

Jophiel waited. "The mere presence of bloodstone weakens a normal blood mage. Since Lilith is not one, it doesn't work on her. Rather, you must let the stone meet the source."

"Meaning?"

"Meaning the bloodstone must be put *inside* her, not just a cut or wound. It has to hit deep. I didn't know any of this until I was brought here. Not until I saw those devices and interacted with Lilith. I have done what I could. Imparting this wisdom will help defeat her, even if I'm not around to witness it." He met my eyes. "I'm ready."

I sucked in a breath and reached for my knife, prepared to do as he asked.

He stopped me. "Not that." He pointed across the room. "Use that."

A pile of light weapons lay near the tent entrance. I walked over and inspected them. There was a knife, two sai, and a sword. They were his. I couldn't wield light weapons, but I would bear the pain for him. I found a loose cloth on the table with the devices. They probably used it to polish them; the vile things were so bright and shiny. I wrapped the sword and sai in the fabric, then took off the sack. Opening it, I placed the weapons inside. None of them would remain here. Once they were secured, I put the sack back on and picked up the knife.

It burned, more harshly than the Hellfire ever did. It was a biting pain, eating away at my hand. I had to make this quick.

Stepping over to Jophiel, I knelt before him again. I sliced the rope at his hands. He brought them together, his fingers slowly pulling a ring free. "No duty can be left undone," he said. "It is your responsibility to finish what I cannot."

I took the ring, too focused on my task to realize what I had done. Closing my fist around it, I braced my right hand on the chair and used my left hand to sink the blade into Jophiel's abdomen. His figure lit up, the celestial energy glowing around him. He smiled, a look of peace on his face.

"Thank you, Brother," he said. Then the light consumed him whole, his energy returning to the universe in a shock of brightness.

I trembled and dropped the blade. It fell to the wooden chair. I rubbed my hand over my mouth and screamed in mourning.

Ariel and Kushiel came running into the tent.

"What happened?" Ariel demanded.

"You're wounded," Kushiel observed.

"Leave me be!" He was right. The light weapon had done damage to my hand. "It will heal. It will scar. I will survive."

"Satan, we need to go," Ariel said. "Whatever happened here alerted the entire camp. We're running out of time."

I slipped the sack off my back again. Picking up the knife, I placed it safely inside and pulled out three portal devices. "Here. They're charged. We'll portal to the caves."

We all clasped the devices to our wrists. I situated the sack again and stood. Resting my hand on the back of the chair, I said, "You're welcome, Brother. Rest easy now."

Turning to Ariel and Kushiel, I demanded, "The two of you join hands." There was a loud noise outside the tent. They were coming for us.

Ariel grabbed hold of my shirt with her other hand. "We're not getting split up," she explained.

Good point. I twisted the timepiece with my fingers, ready to say the exact location of our destination, but it had already teleported us before I uttered a word.

32

DANE

PURGATORY, PRESENT DAY

"Ah!" I shouted, terrified at the drop. How was I going to make the landing without breaking something?

My wings eased out behind me.

Oh right, I forgot about those.

Gliding safely to the bottom, I let out a sigh of relief. I didn't enjoy flying whenever the angels had taken me. Now I knew it was better to be the one in control rather than the one carried. This experience, while frightening, was much more pleasant. Granted, I really needed to learn how to use my wings and truly fly. I also needed to learn how to hide them. I'm sure I'd get there eventually. Right now, I had to keep moving. Who knew if Lilith's troops could follow me or not?

It was dark in the tunnels. My eyesight adjusted to the dimness quickly to the point that I thought some celestial ability was behind the trick because I felt like I could see normally, even though it was pitch-black down here.

Looking around, it was hard to tell which way to go. There were no signs of light or life. Glancing up from where I had fallen, I wondered what had spurred the hole to open and shut in the first place. I might never find out so there was no point in sticking around. I headed into a tunnel that was straight ahead. Several minutes passed, and it seemed to span for miles without any break in direction. I could stop and turn back, but what good would that do? At least I was making progress. I just didn't know what kind. Was I moving away from the camp? Or was I heading into greater danger?

I had to stop questioning myself. I silenced the voice in my head and carried on.

Farther into the tunnel, my eyesight grew spotty and blurred. Rubbing my forehead, my hand came back with sweat.

Shit! Had the fever returned? That was the last thing I needed.

I shook it off and continued on.

When the whole tunnel tilted before me and I fell to the ground, I knew something was wrong. Disoriented, I crawled along the ground until I could get my feet under me again.

Up ahead, there was an open cavern. I made my way toward it, hoping it would be a place where I could rest. Drawing closer, I saw a heat and glow emitted from the cave. My first thought was that someone had made a fire, except there were no shadows of flames dancing along the walls. My eyes widened when I entered and saw a stream of lava.

Where the hell was I?

It was hot inside the cavern, but I didn't let the temperature dissuade me from sitting down. My body had generated far greater warmth on its own and I had survived it.

Resting against a boulder, I took in the incredible sight of molten lava before closing my eyes. Something brushed my hand, and I swatted it off, trying to drift to sleep. I felt it again, this time in two places. Ignoring it, I started to drift off when I felt a piercing sting. Not once, not twice, but multiple times—everywhere.

Jumping up, I looked down at my clothes. Scorpions had crawled all over me! I shook them off and sought higher ground. A few more stings penetrated my skin. One of them was near my ear. I ran my hands through my hair and jumped up and down, trying to get them off me.

Then I heard a snickering. I slowly turned around to find a gigantic half-demon, half-scorpion creature.

"You've disturbed my nest!" it shrieked.

Great! I had to go piss off the mama scorpion…

We sized each other up, and in that one look, we both knew where this was heading.

Damn it!

I turned tail and bolted into a new tunnel, following the stream of lava. The demon creature was quick to follow, her pincers making scraping noises as she chased after me.

I tripped and caught myself before colliding to the ground, except my balance was off and I felt terribly dizzy. My vision blurred again, but I kept running through the tunnel, the glow of the lava providing me with my only sense of direction.

I was soaked through with sweat, who knew from what—the heat of the tunnel, my own fever, or a mixture of the two.

Up ahead, another scorpion creature blocked my path.

This one must be Daddy.

I kept running toward it until it started running toward me, at which point I jumped into the air, my wings forming a cocoon around me. I twirled and propelled over the top of the male scorpion to the other side of the tunnel.

Landing on my feet, I took a moment to see the demon creatures collide. Then I sucked in a breath and fell to my knees as I was impaled in my hip from behind with a claw.

The creature pulled its talon out, and I dropped to the ground. I pressed my hands against the wound to staunch the bleeding, but it was too deep. The demon lifted a claw again, ready to stab me once more. I rolled out of its path and used the momentum to get to my feet.

Squatting on the ground, I knew I wasn't safe as the other two creatures came barreling down the tunnel to aid their friend in finishing me off.

But then a glow caught my eye. It wasn't the amber glow of molten lava but a silver shimmer of something else. I ambled toward it as fast as I could, thinking I was entering another cavern when I suddenly dropped again, freefalling through the abyss.

I fought to remain conscious. I tried with all my might to summon strength into my wings. "Take me. Just take me," I whispered.

My pleas were for death, not the mysterious angel who swept down and caught me, but I was grateful all the same.

We ascended out of the abyss and into the gray sky.

I was fading fast. There was barely anything left in me.

Gently, I was placed on the ground.

I peered at my rescuer.

"Rest child," he said. "Help will come soon."

"Why…can't…you…help…me?" I managed to get out.

"Because I already have. It is time for your father to assist you."

He disappeared.

I hugged the sack full of keys to my chest. If I was going to die, at least my last act had been bold.

33 SATAN

Purgatory, Present Day

The portal device sent us back to the Wastelands, near the Core and the river where I had first surfaced. I glanced down at my wrist. The charge had been used up. I snatched the thing from my arm and threw it to the ground, watching it smash into pieces.

"Damn it!"

"What happened?" Ariel asked.

"I don't know! When I've used portals in the past, I've had to speak my destination. But I couldn't even get out a word before this thing transported us."

Kushiel analyzed the device. "I don't think it works on verbal commands. It looks like latitude and longitude are what it desires."

"Ugh! Then let's try again," I suggested, grabbing hold of Kushiel's cloak.

We waited for Ariel, who had her hand raised to her forehead to shield the sun from her eyes.

"What are you doing?" Kushiel shouted at her.

Ariel pointed at something in the distance. "There's a body."

Body? Oh no…

I ran in the direction she had indicated. They followed.

As I drew closer, I recognized who it was. *Dane.* I picked up speed until I was at his side.

I collapsed to the ground and pulled him in my arms. "Ace! Ace!" I shouted, grabbing his chin and trying to rouse him.

For once, I had forgotten about the Hellfire, but it didn't matter. As soon as I touched Dane, I knew he had it, too. When I made contact with his skin, there was a pulse of energy, which wasn't the Hellfire's normal reaction. Typically, it ignited right away. Instead, it remained calm.

Kushiel and Ariel dropped to the ground to assist.

"Satan, the bag!" Kushiel said.

Focusing on the sack Dane was hugging to his chest, I detected the energy Kushiel felt. I untied it and peeked inside. My eyes widened. There were so many keys.

What had he done?

Kushiel reached for it and tried pulling it from Dane's grasp. His eyes fluttered, and he stirred awake, tightening his hold on the bag with one hand and using the other to defend himself. He splayed out his hand in the air, and it trembled with power. Kushiel cried out, and his arm twisted into a funny angle.

Blood dripped from Dane's nose, and sweat beaded his brow.

"There's bloodstone in there!" Ariel cautioned. "It's hurting him!"

Grasping the bag, I pried it free and handed it to Ariel. The sudden loss of his prized possession had Dane letting go of Kushiel and lying weak in my arms.

His head fell to my shoulder, and his eyes registered who I was. Tears streamed down his face. "D-Dad?"

"I've got you. You don't have to fight anymore. You're safe," I told him.

He smiled, and then his eyes fluttered shut again.

No, no, no...

I shook him, but he didn't move. "Dane!"

"He's been poisoned," Ariel said, gesturing to the stings and wound.

"By what?" I demanded.

"A demon," Kushiel declared. "There's no hope."

I shook my head. "But he can heal."

"Yes, but the poison needs to be cleared from the wounds. There's no water around here," Ariel explained.

"The river," I stated.

"Won't work," Kushiel said. "Its waters are not pure. It would only contaminate the injury further."

"I won't let him die!" I yelled, rising from the ground with Dane in my arms. I headed toward the river.

"Satan! Don't!"

I wasn't sure which of them had pleaded with me. It didn't matter. I ignored them.

I placed Dane next to the riverbed. I took the sack off my back and emptied it onto the ground. Then I unraveled the piece of cloth from the weapons and set it aside. I dipped the sack in the water, filling it up and then removing it from the river. The water was cloudy and dark. Thankfully, though, the leather held the liquid.

Positioning it in front of me, I did something I have never done, nor will I ever do again.

"Father!" I screamed at the sky. "I know you can hear me! I've never asked you for *anything*, but I'm beseeching you to help! I know I've obeyed you and I've betrayed you, and it seems like I've been punished for both, but I'm not asking you to undo what has been done to me. I'm asking you to purify this water and to heal this boy…my boy. He has done nothing to deserve his fate, and I assure you, if you let him live, he will make you proud and do many good deeds."

The sky overhead turned dark and thunder rumbled.

"I know you're angry! What I did was unforgivable. But I'm not asking for forgiveness. I'm asking for a favor, one I think I deserve considering what I did for you, taking responsibility for the evil you created."

Lightning struck, hitting the ground just to the left of where I was kneeling.

"Fine! Not a favor, then! A bargain!" I looked down at my hand where Jophiel's ring sat and regretted the words I was about to speak. "If you will have me, I will assume Jophiel's seat. I will take his position as the sign of Libra, the sign of balance and justice, and make sure the prophecy is seen through." Thunder rumbled again. I focused on the sack of water. "In exchange," I whispered, "please heal this boy."

A drop of water hit the satchel. Then another and another, until a torrent of water streamed from the sky.

Glancing down at the sack, I saw it was now filled with crystal-clear liquid.

I murmured two words that weren't easy for me to speak. Ever. "Thank you."

The rain soaked me through, as well as Dane, but it didn't stop me from dipping the cloth in the sack, wringing it out, and washing Dane's wounds.

I worked on the large one first, which was near his hip. Then I cleaned every puncture mark I saw while the rain took care of the ones I missed. As soon as the poison was cleared, Dane started to heal and his breathing returned to a normal pattern.

I dropped the cloth to the ground and eased back, taking a moment to relax.

He would survive. I had made sure of it.

A rod of lighting zipped through the sky, came down, and struck me where I stood. I collapsed like a felled tree in a forest.

Dazed, I couldn't help but smirk as I lifted myself up on my elbows. "You bastard," I whispered, "you had to display your dominance."

Thunder boomed.

"Sorry," I muttered.

Glancing beneath my arm, I noticed something that I hadn't seen in a while. A single white feather hidden among the black.

"Isn't that a little premature? I'm doing you one kindness. Nothing more." Then I grinned. That's why it was one feather. Good. I didn't want white wings again anyway.

Ariel and Kushiel finally rejoined me.

"It's not supposed to rain here," Ariel said. "I've never seen it rain here."

Kushiel elbowed her in the side and pointed at Dane.

"You healed him?" she asked. "But how—"

"Many miraculous things occurred today," I said. "Just don't expect them to become a habit."

The two angels were shocked, but they remained silent.

Dane shifted and opened his eyes. "It's really you. I thought I was hallucinating."

"No, I came for you as soon as I knew."

"Knew what?"

"That you were mine."

Dane clenched his jaw. "You didn't know?"

"No, or else I would have come sooner."

He smiled but quickly hid it to conceal his reaction. "Thanks."

"No problem, Ace," I said, matching his vibe and acting like it was nothing.

I emptied the small amount of water remaining in the sack and repacked it with Jophiel's weapons and the portal devices.

"Here," I said, handing the bag to Ariel.

She placed it on her back.

"Where's mine?" Dane asked.

I grabbed it from behind me. "There was bloodstone inside. It weakens you."

"Oh...that must have been what I was feeling, why the one sphere brought me pain." He paused. "You can keep the sack."

"Are you sure?"

He nodded. "I know you'll do the right thing. Besides, we have more keys than you anyway."

I smirked. "Okay, Ace, if you say so."

"I just need something out of it first. It's a dagger."

Searching inside, I rummaged around and drew out the weapon, handing it to him.

"Thanks."

I closed the sack and swung it onto my back. Slapping my hands against my thighs, I announced, "I think it's time we take back Hell."

The three of us put on new portal devices.

I handed one to Dane. "You can choose where you want to go."

He looked up at me and slowly took it.

"You just need the coordinates."

"I don't know the coordinates," he said.

"For where?" Ariel asked. "I might be able to help. All we did was work off coordinates in Heaven."

Dane hesitated. "New York City, I guess. I can fly to my final destination from there."

Smart kid. He didn't want anyone tracking him.

Ariel told him and showed him how to work the device.

"Ready?" Kushiel asked.

"Yeah, I'm coming," I said. "Give me another."

Ariel handed me another portal device, and then they stepped over to the side.

I turned the dial, setting the coordinates for Hell, but didn't push it down. That's what triggered the teleportation.

"Here." I gave it to Dane. "Just in case you change your mind."

I joined my comrades, and we all activated our devices, leaving the godforsaken land of Purgatory behind once and for all.

34 GABRIEL

Ithaca, New York, Present Day

Discovering I had a twin was unanticipated. In a way, I wasn't too stunned because I'd always felt as if I were drawing on something hidden deep inside me. And there was the fact that I had been assigned to the astrological sign of Gemini. At the same time, there was a part of me that felt a little offended that Kat and Father had kept this secret from me. Had they thought I couldn't be trusted with it? And why did her identity have to be so private anyway?

I shook my head. It was never a good thing to question Father's actions. The last time I had doubted myself like this was right before the war.

Wow, I really needed to stop being so nostalgic and get back to the present moment. Our plans had been made. We were attacking Hell today. Jordan would be with us again by day's end, and I couldn't be more relieved. It was odd how attached I had become to him, but he was such a normal part of my life now that his absence felt like a large void.

That's why I was sitting in his room now, hoping to feel connected to him and hear his encouraging voice inside my head, the one that never gave up. I thought being in here would help strengthen my resolve, but all it did was make me more anxious.

I wasn't scared to fight or afraid to go to Hell. No, what I feared most was that something had happened to Jordan. I wished with my entire being that he was unharmed, but I was preparing myself for the worst, knowing how many evil beings he would have encountered in such a short time.

If we hadn't been called back and taken away from them on the night of the unbinding, I wondered if the outcome would have been the same. Would the kids have been separated? Would they have been taken from us and put through so much trauma?

Here I was again, questioning everything. It was no good to dwell on what-if scenarios. What happened, happened. Now it was time to finally remedy it.

The door opened, and Sophia walked in. She startled at the sight of me.

"I'm sorry to frighten you," I said.

"It's fine. I thought no one would be in here."

"I can leave."

"No, please stay."

She sat down on the edge of the bed. I remained in the chair. Sophia fiddled with a box in her hands.

"You know, I went to his room, too," she said.

She didn't have to say who she was talking about. Clearly, it was Dane.

"I felt stupid rummaging in his closet and touching his clothes, but I wanted to because I knew that would be the only way I would ever be close to him again."

"That's not true. We'll find him," I assured her.

"Even if we did, even if he still is the same person, there's no denying he's changed. He has wings and magic and Hellfire. That last fact alone made me realize I couldn't touch him ever again. Not even hold his hand. Which led me wanting to touch his clothes to feel close to him." She set the box down and rubbed her hands over her face. "I feel dumb and crazy."

"You're not," I said. "You love him, and when two people love each other, they sometimes do things that are irrational."

She nodded and chewed her lip. "Then I found that."

"The box?"

"Yeah, it's my birthday gift. The one he never had a chance to give me."

"You should open it. Maybe it will help you feel better."

"I thought about it. But then I worried it might do the opposite."

I was honest with her. "It probably will. But I'm sure the sadness will be replaced with happiness, knowing you have something of him to hold on to."

"I didn't think about it like that." She reached for the box, hesitated, then tore open the wrapping. Sophia popped open the jewelry box, smiled, and then shed a few tears.

"Would you like me to help you put it on?" I asked, sensing it was a necklace. The box had been shaped like a square rather than a long rectangle.

She nodded.

I crossed the room and sat down next to her. She handed me the simple silver necklace, and I fastened it around her neck.

"It's very pretty. Blue lace agate suits you well."

"Is that what the pendant is?" she asked.

"Yes, it matches your eyes. I imagine that's why he picked it."

"Thanks, Gabriel."

"Of course. You never said why you came in *here*."

"Oh." She smiled. "I wanted to feel Jordan's presence. I miss him, and he would have known what to say, just like you did."

I patted her hand. "He'll be back tonight."

"I know. I'm eager to see him."

"Me too. I should go finish preparing."

Sophia took in my attire. "Is that why you're wearing all black?"

I looked down at my black cargo pants, combat boots, and turtle-neck sweater. "Yes, it's for the attack. Michael wants us to blend in. We're even painting our wings black."

"How?"

"Body paint. It was Dafne's idea."

"Really? She didn't tell me."

"I think you were resting at the time. You're more than welcome to assist me with my wings."

She thought about it. "I'd like to, but I'm avoiding people."

"You can't avoid your family forever. Whether you like them or not, you're related to them."

"I know. I just don't think I'm ready to talk to them yet."

Her parents, as well as Sister Delphine, Deborah, Peter, and Naomi had come over to the house. Kat had called in the Sacrarium, and Aziza and Yadira had arrived, too, both just as formidable and amazing as my sister. With the Triune and Sacrarium gathered, we had all been given assignments and were executing them as quickly as possible.

"I wish I could come," Sophia said.

"To Hell?" I shook my head. "You don't want to go there."

"No, I mean, I want to come so I can help. I feel useless here."

I stood. "That's because you're not participating." I left the room and heard her follow. Descending the stairs, I joined the others in the library. Sophia did, too.

I had to do a double take seeing Michael standing before the table with black wings. Kat's map of Hell was spread before him, and it was easy to see he was going over the plan again and again in his head.

Drawing close to his side, I asked, "You ready?"

He sighed. "As I'll ever be. But I'm worried about the portal. There's no guarantee it will open."

We had formulated our plan around opening a portal to descend into Hell. We had sent word to Heaven to sanction our request and had yet to hear back.

"They'll come through. They always do," I said.

I moved to go outside. That's where Dafne had set up her wing camouflage station.

Raphael's arrival had me hanging back. "Look what I found on the porch."

It was a wooden box with angelic script carved into it.

"Is that what we have been waiting for?" Yadira asked. She had a blunt personality similar to Uriel's.

Michael met Raphael and took the box. He set it down next to me and opened it. Inside, there was a letter from Tzaphkiel.

Everyone gathered around. Even those who were outside came in. I picked up the letter and read aloud. *"Dear comrades, I couldn't get Father to sanction the portal. Work is still being done to the Great Tree, and as such, our communing with Him has been spotty. In the meantime, I had our fellow angels of art work on the device found among Lilith's troops. Believe it or not, it's actually a portal device. Our brothers and sisters were able to replicate it—I would go so far as to say perfect it—and I have sent enough for each of you, if not more, for your journey to Hell. You must input coordinates to navigate your way rather than speak a command and destination. I hope this aids your mission, and when you return, make sure to send the devices back so they can be charged for further use. If there's anything else I can assist with, please let me know. We are waiting for your command, as we suspect a larger battle may be imminent, but we stand by for now and await news of the boy. Respectfully, Tzaphkiel."*

Setting the letter aside, I looked in the box. There were at least twenty devices resting inside and we only needed nine of them.

"Are we really going to use them?" Uriel asked. "Tools from the enemy!"

"It doesn't sit well with me, either," Michael said. "But it's all we have to enter Hell."

"All right," Kat announced, "we're an hour from departure. Gabriel, you need to get your wings concealed. Everyone else, make sure you've triple-checked everything—your weapons, your gear. We only have one shot to get this right."

The last thing I heard my sister say before stepping outside was, "Martha, make sure the triage center is ready on the lower level. I know we're all being optimistic, but injuries are expected."

Unfortunately, she was right. Jordan wasn't the only one who might need medical aid. Any of us could come back hurt, or worse. Nothing was guaranteed anymore. Not when Lilith was involved. The loss of Jophiel had taught us that.

Dafne trailed after me, picking up her can of body paint and going to work on my wings. When she was done, I didn't need to look in a mirror to know how unnatural black wings looked on me. It felt uncomfortable.

"I can't wait to take a shower," I muttered.

"I don't blame you. It must be weird," Dafne agreed.

"It's like donning an alter ego," I observed. Glancing at my watch, I realized I had to get inside. We would be departing soon.

I collected my weapons and a portal device, then strapped everything to my body.

"You ready, Brother?" Uriel asked, stepping up behind me.

"As I'll ever be."

"War of the angels, part two," he mused.

"Yes, except this time we're taking it to their turf."

"Exactly," Uriel said with a gleam of anticipation in his eye. "It's time to make them pay, to show them how it feels to be blindsided."

He was right. There was no denying it. Except no one in their right mind would wage war on Hell. Some would say we had all gone insane, but I would say that we were thinking like Jordan. This is something he would have persuaded us to do, so it was only right to do it for him.

Uriel and I joined the others outside. Together, the nine of us flew to a remote area in the nearby forest, close enough to get back to the house quickly on our return but far enough not to leave a trail for the Fallen to track.

We had formed a semicircle, and Kat stood in the middle. "Does everyone have their comms units?" she asked, lifting a finger to her ear.

We all nodded.

My brothers and I had kept them after the gala, uncertain if would we need them again. Fortunately, that decision had worked in our favor.

"Good," Kat said. She held up her hand, tiny bits of paper grasped in it. "Before we leave, I made sure to calculate the proper coordinates for each of you." She walked along the circle, passing out sheets. Once she was done, she strode to the middle again. "As soon as we insert our destinations, the mission will commence. I wish everyone luck, and remember to communicate through the comms. We have a plan, but it can be adjusted if something goes awry." She put her fist to her chest. "For Jordan."

We all repeated the gesture and chanted, "For Jordan."

Then we inputted our locations and disappeared from the forest, well on our way to Hell.

35 SATAN

Hell, Present Day

Who would've known I'd miss the cold caves of Hell? They were a remarkable sight compared with those wretched Wastelands of Purgatory, full of dust and gray skies. I'd take the drafty darkness of my kingdom over that gloom any day.

We arrived in the Eighth Cavern to very little fanfare. Hardly anyone was around except for a few of Lilith's troops who were guarding a group of prisoners that consisted of Abbadona and my other allies. Even with the gag, her face registered shock and relief when she saw me.

One of the guards glanced over to see whatever she was looking at and did a double take. "Who the hell are you?" he asked.

"He's supposed to be dead," Mammon said, stepping from the shadows.

Asmodeus followed.

The two worthless bastards! It was time to make them pay.

Kushiel and Ariel stood at my side. "Free the prisoners and deal with them." I nodded toward the guards. "These two are mine!"

A feral growl vibrated through the entryway cave and only grew louder as the beast clambered into the cavern.

Cerberus.

Leviathan would take care of him. I searched the group.

Shit! Where's Leviathan?

Mammon sprang forward. "He's gone!" He spat in my face, reading it clearly. "Throat slit and blood spilled."

Damn it! Not Leviathan.

I gritted my teeth and clashed weapons with Mammon, shouting to Ariel and Kushiel, "Whatever you do, avoid the dog!" Then I focused on the fight.

Asmodeus joined us, making fancy moves with his rapier as if this was some kind of fencing match. Meanwhile, Mammon was relentless, swinging his war hammer thoughtlessly. His deadly sin was surely consuming him, as was mine, except his greed underestimated my anger.

Our weapons came together in a clang, but rather than battle back and forth for position, I slid my sword along the outer edge of his hammer and struck down on the hilt, disarming him. Shifting around, I parried Asmodeus, grabbed a knife from my belt, and threw it. The blade hit its mark, lodging in Mammon's leg. He pulled it free and advanced.

I stepped on Asmodeus's foot, clubbed free his sword, and took him by the throat, igniting the Hellfire.

He screamed, and I swung him around, right into Mammon who was running with the knife, ready to stab it in my back. The two crashed to the ground, and I took a moment to assess where we were at.

Kushiel and Ariel had slayed the guards, but one was now trying to fend off Cerberus while the other freed the prisoners. They needed help.

Mammon and Asmodeus untangled themselves and let loose war cries, indicating they were resuming the fight until an eerie howl could be heard in the distance.

My two former members of the Six stopped in their tracks. Cerberus hadn't let out the howl. As a matter of fact, the three-headed dog stopped to listen.

Ariel and Kushiel took advantage of the distraction by setting my comrades free.

Everyone was silent.

Then a thundering clamored through the entryway cave, not from the Pit but from the stairs, the domain of the dogs.

"Satan, watch out!" Abbadona yelled.

I twisted to see Mammon's knife mere inches from my neck, but before he could bring it any farther, he froze in place.

"There hasn't been a hound since—" Asmodeus stopped and dropped to his knees.

I smirked. I couldn't say *where* the hounds had been hiding, but I could say *why* they had finally returned.

"Ace," I murmured, turning around.

He stood before the rivers, one hand lowered in a fist, the other raised palm out. Dane swung his hands to the left, and Mammon and Asmodeus went careening into the wall.

I stepped forward to greet him, but a black hound beat me to it. Dane knelt. "I remember you," he whispered, touching heads and looking into his eyes.

A ferocious snarl broke the boy from his dog.

Everyone set their attention on Cerberus, waiting to see what he would do.

There were booms above us, not consistent with the usual rowdy noises of the cities. Something else was taking place.

Dane's hound inched forward, returning Cerberus's snarl.

"Tame him until I can turn him," Dane commanded.

That's all the hound needed to hear. He sprang forward and attacked.

The rest of the masses were about to follow their alpha, but Dane stopped them. "Two of you assist. The others regain control."

Only two of the hounds joined in the bout with Cerberus. The rest ran back to the steps to reclaim Hell.

"Should I be taking orders from you, too?" I asked.

"Never. I don't want your kingdom. I'm just here to help."

"Is that why you came?"

He nodded. "Yeah. I thought going to New York was the right decision, but something called me here. An instinct...a gut feeling."

"That's because you're home," I told him.

Mammon and Asmodeus stirred.

"Tie them up!" I demanded.

"No!" Nehema yelled, Haborym at her side. "Let us handle them."

The two who were always vying for positions wanted a shot at taking them.

"Fine! But make it quick!"

Between the four of them fighting, the hounds running loose, and the taming of Cerberus, a riot ensued.

36 JORDAN

Hell, Present Day

Once again, I was inside the cell left to my own devices. I enjoyed these moments alone, knowing I was out of harm's way and didn't have to witness anymore barbarism. I wondered if Satan's Hell had been this insane or if this was a product of mutiny and two new rulers within a month.

I pulled up my shirt to inspect my wound. Dark lines had spread up my stomach and one was just beginning to reach my chest.

Crap! I had waited too long.

I reached in my pocket and took out the flask, then poured more holy water over it. I did my best to hold back my cries of anguish, knowing that Lilith wasn't far away. As soon as she had sat down in that throne, no one and nothing was going to unseat her for a while. She had worked centuries on gaining power and supremacy, and Hell's throne was just the first reward.

Just thinking about her made me dwell on how vile and cruel she was. I could truthfully say I hated her. She had killed my mother, destroyed my life and my family, and who knew what else? I'm sure there was more. I just didn't know it yet.

I wanted desperately to go home, to sleep in my own bed, to eat a home-cooked meal. I wanted to see Martha and the angels and Sophia and Dane. I wanted to reach out to Dafne, too.

The doors of my cell opened. This dark matter was messing with my body so much, I wasn't even aware of my surroundings.

Lilith stepped inside. "Come, boy. I want to show you something." She stopped and knelt. "What's wrong with you? The Sentinel swore to me he was feeding you."

"He has," I muttered.

She lifted back my head and looked into my eyes. "*No.*" She searched my body, feeling along my arms.

"What are you doing?" I demanded, pulling back.

Her hand brushed my side, and I jumped. "Lift up your shirt," she commanded.

I stood up. "No."

"Do it or I'll make you."

Sighing, I succumbed to the inevitable. I raised my shirt, and she shrieked at the sight.

"Who injured you?"

"Murmur."

"Who?"

"No one you know because he's dead. There's no one you can punish for this."

"Fine. But I must see to fixing it. I need you whole, unscathed."

"Well, unless you can find holy water in this unholy place, there are no chances of fixing it," I proclaimed.

Lilith went rigid. "I see your mother's fiery attitude is coming out."

I frowned. "Don't speak to me about her."

"Or what?"

"Does everything have to be a threat or an ultimatum?" I asked. "Can't people ever speak plainly to you, or do you always find fault in their words."

"Did you get anything from your father? Because your mother was a pacifist, too."

I thought about it. "Actually, yes. I have the Conway trait of making rash decisions. That and my pacifism is what landed me back here, so no one can say I'm just my mother's child."

Lilith smiled. "My mistake. You have the Conway sharp tongue, too. Not to mention the incessant talking." She rolled her eyes. "Never get a Conway talking because they never shut up. Now come."

Lilith escorted me out of the cell and into the throne room. The Sentinel and Mulciber were present, both silently standing there with their ears cocked to the side, listening. Lilith brought me over to the Pit, but I was anxious to get too close, afraid to be pushed over again.

"Do you hear that?" she asked.

I listened closely. Loud howls echoed through the caves.

"The hounds have returned. Everything's going according to—"

Mixed in with the howls, loud booms could be heard below.

The three of them stiffened. Then something was chucked from the Pit into the throne room. It rolled across the cold, stone floor and landed in the center.

"What is that?" Mulciber asked.

I smiled, just as the holy water grenade exploded. Except it was going to hurt me more than them. As the water washed over me, I shrieked.

"Get down there, you fools! We're being attacked!" Lilith screamed.

Just as the Sentinel and Mulciber were ready to dive into the Pit, two figures emerged from it. Gabriel and Raphael were a force to be reckoned with, wearing all-black and armed for battle. And…were their wings black, too?

They engaged the Sentinel and Mulciber midair, sinking backward into the Pit to continue the fight.

Lilith gripped the collar of my shirt and dragged me across the floor. I pried at her hands, trying to set myself free. She was headed to the portal room, and I wasn't about to let her take me anywhere.

I swiped my left leg along the ground and knocked her off her feet.

"You rotten child!" she yelled. She raised her hands in the air and pushed them forcefully toward me.

Nothing happened.

She did it again.

Still nothing.

For once, I smirked and tapped my neck. "Don't you remember? I'm my mother's child."

She let out a piercing howl and launched herself at me. I anticipated her move and rolled to the side, avoiding her. My fleur-de-lis necklace was acting as a ward against her magic, so in a way, she was powerless, left to her own brains and brawn to fight me.

Between the angels' training and growing up with Dane, I had become quite courageous and clever. Now we'd see how it squared up against her.

Lilith and I both rose from the floor and sized each other up. "I got through your ward once! It'll be easy to do again."

This time, instead of waving her hands around, she mumbled incoherent words. I presumed it was a spell to undo my protective ward, but I wasn't about to let her finish. I tackled her to the ground.

It seemed foolish to keep doing this, but she wasn't about to kill me—she still needed me for the prophecy—and I wasn't about to kill her. I had killed enough already, and the memory of it didn't sit well with me. Someone would kill her, but it wouldn't be me. Instead, I would do all I could to trap her, and so far, my efforts were working.

I clamped a hand over her mouth and gently pried the prisoner key free from her belt with the other. Dane had taught me sleight of hand when we were younger, during the phase when he had been obsessed with magic. Who could have known it was his destiny to one day possess it?

I felt victorious until Lilith dug her fingers into my wound. I cried out and jumped back, holding my side. My vision blurred, and I was too dizzy to get to my feet.

Lilith laughed. "You think you can best me?" She went back to mumbling.

Quickly, I lifted my shirt. The black lines were inching toward my heart. I only had one move left in me, and I'd be damned if it was reaching for the flask of holy water.

No, instead I summoned all the energy I had, and roundhouse kicked Lilith back into the prison. She disappeared through the shield, and I followed.

When I met her again, lying before the cell door, it was easy to see she was flustered and dazed. I wasn't about to lose momentum, though, so I made a rash Conway decision and lifted my necklace over my head.

She attempted to rise and take advantage of the opportunity, but I was faster, inching close enough to place the jewelry around her neck.

Lilith froze, eyes wide and mouth open. For a moment, I thought I might have killed her. Then she wheezed in choppy breaths. I shoved her into the cell and locked it with the key I had stolen.

Unlike her, I didn't taunt her for her loss. No, I quietly and calmly returned to the portal room, where I sank to the floor and let the dark take over.

37 GABRIEL

HELL, PRESENT DAY

Raphael and I fought our attackers, him dealing with the burly fallen angel and me taking on the altered man who didn't die.

I rammed my assailant up against the stone wall of the Pit and punched him in the face. He kneed me in the ribs and mimicked my move, ramming me against the opposite wall and leering at me.

Uncharacteristically, I headbutted him and threw him several feet down. I needed to get to Jordan, not fight some insignificant enemy.

Pressing my finger to my ear, I said, "Uriel, Raphael and I need backup!"

The winged man came back at me, slamming into me once more and recommencing our clash.

"Copy," Uriel's voice sounded in my ear. "Anarchy has been brewed in Pride and Envy. I'm heading to the Pit now."

"I'm on my way, too," Chamuel chimed in. "Chaos has ensued in Gluttony and Greed."

"Madness has begun in Lust and Laze," Zadkiel added. "Shall I come to the Pit?"

"Yes!" Raphael yelled. "I can't hold him off by myself!"

The plan had been to incite pandemonium among the cities to

fuel distraction and lack of control. Kat's best suggestion as to how to perform such a task was to literally throw money through the streets of Hell's cities, even if it was fake.

We were skeptical her idea would work, but I guess we shouldn't have underestimated her or the greediness of the spirits.

A glint of silver flashed before my eyes, and I dodged my head to the side. A blade stuck in the rock to the right of my head.

I narrowed my gaze at the man. "Switching to knives, are we?" I shoved him back, swiped my knife from the holster at my leg, and dug it in his shoulder. If I knew he couldn't die, perhaps I wouldn't have been so violent, but it felt nice all the same.

Thankfully, our brothers weren't too far off. They came zipping up through the Pit, zigzagging among our skirmishes, and took the high ground. When they were in position, Uriel shouted, "Fall back!"

Raphael and I broke away from our opponents as our brothers dropped through the air, Uriel diving for the winged man and Chamuel and Zadkiel aiming for the fallen angel. They each collided with their foe, the force of their impact sending them farther down the Pit.

Pressing my finger to my ear again, I said, "We're heading back up for Jordan."

"Copy," Michael said. "Kat and I have finished in Misery. We're heading to the Eighth Cavern. There's lots of unanticipated unrest there. Be prepared for discrepancies in the plan."

"Well, I already have two," Uriel announced. "One's big and the other can't die. We're taking them your way. Maybe the rivers will finish you off, you bloody bastards!"

We had just ascended from the Pit and landed in the throne room when Kat's voice sounded over the comm.

"Ladies, check in!"

"We're here!" Aziza shouted, a loud booming noise in the background. "I've shielded off the fallen angels in Elysium, but it's a matter of seconds before they break through my wards. Be prepared for their vengeance!"

"How's the portal?" Kat asked.

"I'm halfway through it," Yadira huffed. "Breaking this thing and severing its connection won't be easy on my own."

"Chamuel and I can assist you once we lose this fallen angel in the Eighth Cavern," Zadkiel promised. "Should just be a second!"

Everyone waited.

"We're heading back now!"

Then the comms went silent.

38

MICHAEL

Hell, Present Day

When Kat and I had flown into the Eighth Cavern, I had not been prepared to see Satan. Rumors had claimed him dead. There was a part of me that was relieved he hadn't perished. Technically, he was my enemy, but he had been my brother first.

More thrilling was to spot Dane among the ranks of the Fallen. He was alive and in control. Sophia's fears, while warranted, weren't true. I knew Dane had become powerful after the unbinding, adopting both of his parents' abilities, but to actually see him using his gifts before my eyes was extraordinary, especially his sway over the hounds. I knew it hadn't just been a display of dominance last spring. At the time, there had been no logical explanation as to why he was able to call off the hounds. Now it made perfect sense.

Kat and I landed near Satan and his amassing group of followers. Among them was one I recognized. Was that…Ariel? It was hard to say. It looked like her, but a lot had changed.

"What exactly are you trying to do? Bring ruin to my kingdom?" Satan exclaimed before we were even in reach.

"From what we knew," I said, "it wasn't your kingdom anymore."

"It's *always* been my kingdom," Satan growled, pushing through his allies and getting in my face.

"Says the dead man walking," I muttered.

"All right," he conceded. "I'll admit I had a temporary leave of absence, but I'm back now and you're ruining everything."

"Does it look like we care?" Kat said. "We will lay waste to Hell, turn it to rubble, until we complete our mission."

Satan's eyes narrowed. "Hello, Kat. I see you escaped. Can't say I've missed you."

"Don't start with me, Satan," Kat warned.

"You captured her?" I asked, furious.

"She came here on her own accord, and I never let her leave. Capturing is a little harsh," he clarified. "Let me guess. You're here for that bothersome boy."

"Who I view like a brother," Dane said, joining us. He was out of breath after capturing the three-headed hound in a spell. He used his thumb to point over his shoulder. "That's not gonna hold. I barely know what I'm doing. Is Jordan here?"

"Yes," I told him.

"Crap. We need to get him out of here. Fast."

"We have a plan. So far, it's been working, but we weren't anticipating any of this." I gestured to Satan, the hounds, and the fallen angels who were senselessly fighting one another off in the corner. All that aside, I focused on Dane. "It's good to see you."

He smiled. "Same." He turned on Satan. "I'll let the hounds run this place to the ground if you don't give Jordan to us."

Exasperated, Satan said, "I didn't take him! I don't even know where he is!"

"He's in your portal room," Kat explained. "Where I used to be imprisoned."

"Back to that, are we?" Satan jested.

"I've wasted many precious years here, all because of you, so forgive me if I'm not quick to forget," Kat lashed.

Satan lost his temper. "What is it the three of you want from me?"

"Your help," I stated simply.

"I don't know," he said, throwing out his hands, "we said we'd never do that again."

"I conceded to you once. It's your turn to concede to me," I bargained.

"What exactly do you want me to do?" he asked.

"Show the spirits and fallen angels you've returned so this place will return to peace," Kat said.

Satan laughed so loudly that it echoed through the cavern.

Kat crossed her arms.

"You're so naive!" he said. "There's no peace in Hell. Do you really think they care I'm back?"

"Then what can you do to pacify them?" I asked.

He shook his head. "There's no pacifying them. In their eyes I must *fight them* to reclaim my throne. There's no way to end this without battle and bloodshed."

"Fine, then do what you must, but stay out of our way," Kat said, drawing her sword and rushing forward.

She must have heard the comms unit because we had a fight incoming. I already had my weapon unsheathed and was ready to follow her, but I remembered Dane.

"I know things are different now," I said to him, "but please be careful."

"I will," he assured me.

"Am I missing something?" Satan asked.

"They're on a comms unit," Dane said as I went after Kat.

Uriel, Chamuel, and Zadkiel flew into the Eighth Cavern with enemies on their tails, a fallen angel and the man who was Lilith's sidekick. Chamuel and Zadkiel doubled back and exited just as soon as they had arrived to go assist Aziza and Yadira.

Kat took on the big fallen angel, and Uriel had the other. I arrived to aid my brother. "Help her!" he demanded. "I've got him!"

Uriel and the man clashed.

I ran over to Kat and attacked the fallen angel from behind. He swung around and engaged me but not for long as Kat slashed at him from the other side, distracting him once again.

I tried persuading him to surrender. "Just give up! We won't hurt you if you stand aside!"

"Argh!" he shouted. "Never!"

Kat dodged his strike, rolling across the ground and onto her feet. Our swords clanged, and he grinned wickedly. "Cerberus!" he yelled. "Attack!"

Three out-of-sync howls sounded through the cavern.

"Cerberus, don't!" I heard Dane command. He was trying to maintain control over the hound and turn him to his side. From the looks of it, he was having a hard time.

The hound thrashed his head back and forth, trying to shake off Dane's sway.

Kat and I continued to clash with the fallen angel when a loud ruckus could be heard coming from the entryway steps. Suddenly, a group of rowdy fallen angels and demons stormed into the cavern, ready to fight. Satan and his allies attacked them head-on, the king of the Underworld eager to prove his worth among his infernal followers.

Out of the corner of my eye, I saw Uriel under pressure. A full mob had surged in, many of them assailing whomever they could.

"Kat, Uriel needs help!"

"As does Dane!" she replied.

Glancing over my shoulder, I saw Dane's face full of strain as he tried to keep Cerberus tame and hold off a crowd of rebels.

"Go!" Kat said.

Before I could even move, Ariel charged and sank her sword into the big fallen angel's chest. He slumped forward and dropped to his knees.

"Ariel...what have you done?" I asked, astonished.

She faced me. "Picked a side," she said, the feathers on her wings turning black.

Cerberus roared.

"I can't hold everyone!" Dane shouted.

His call for help had me springing into action. I raced over to Dane, ready to fight off those who wished him harm. But I was too late.

Cerberus snarled, his three heads going in every direction. One snagged a fallen angel that Dane had under his spell. Another went for Dane himself, but the boy was quick, escaping the hound's jaws. And the other went for me. I would have evaded the attack, but an arrow hit me in the shoulder. It knocked me to a knee, leaving my other leg vulnerable to Cerberus's bite. The hound sank his teeth into my leg.

"Ah!" I yelled.

Looking across the cavern, I saw Lilith's man had taken Uriel's bow.

Where was my brother?

The hound latched on, cutting through skin and digging in deeper.

I grimaced and tried yanking my leg free.

Now that one head had a victim, the other two were interested in getting a piece of it. Dane wasn't about to let that happen, though. He jumped onto the back of the beast and grabbed hold of the head that had me in its grasp. Dane pulled and yanked until Cerberus let me go.

I gasped at the pain and pulled myself back against the stone wall to assess the damage. There were two large bite holes as well as several small ones. I wasn't too worried about the wound itself. It would heal eventually. Once the poison was cleared.

Except there was no known antidote for a hellhound's venom.

My head sunk back against the wall, and I searched the cavern once more for Uriel. Finally, I found him, helping Satan finish off a horde of demons.

Thank the heavens he was all right.

Next, I checked on Dane, who seemed to have tamed the beast but was still working on the hound's self-control.

Kat appeared before me, taking my face in her hands.

I swore I knew her, but I didn't remember her…couldn't remember her. It's like something in my mind was blocking it.

She searched my eyes, evaluating my condition to see if paranoia might have set in.

I don't think it happened that quickly, but my breathing was ragged and I was starting to feel a little warm in a place that was generally ice cold.

Beyond her, it was utter anarchy. If it was this bad down here, who knew what it was like elsewhere, what my other brothers and comrades were facing. We had to get out. *They* at least had to get out. My chances were slim.

Except we hadn't gotten word that Jordan had been secured. Which meant we had to deal with this mess. We had to keep fighting until he was safe.

I struggled to stand up.

"Stay," Kat commanded. Her face was serious, almost grim. She knew the severity of my injury. "Sometimes even a warrior must know his limits."

I touched her face, my vision beginning to blur. "I know you."

She shook her head, a tortured look donning her face. "No," she whispered.

Dane saw that I was wounded. Rather than let it consume him, he took charge, defending Kat and me from anyone looking for a fight.

Another wave of fallen angels arrived from the Pit. Our good fortune was turning against us, the odds slipping in favor of the enemy. I certainly never thought Hell would be the place where I would fight my last fight.

Grabbing Kat's arm, I tried steadying myself as everything started to shake. She braced herself against the ground by placing out a hand for support.

"You feel that, too?" I asked, unsure if it was just me.

"Yes," she nodded.

Then everything and everyone in the cavern stopped because the shaking only intensified.

All but one figure was unwavering.

It was a female fallen angel. She was kneeling among the rivers with her hands placed on the stone. Her eyes turned white as the waters tossed, mimicking her fury. Then she let it loose. Huge waves rose from the rivers and crashed down among the rebel fallen angels, wiping them clean across the floor. Next, she took out the demons, all of them scrambling for safety.

Whoever this female was, she was powerful. Her attacks were calculated, aimed only at those that posed a threat. Anyone remotely good or on the side of Satan remained free of harm. She wiped out every adversary, leaving the entire cavern soaked through. Then the waters receded back into their beds, and her eyes returned to normal. She rose, evaluating what she had done. Satan met her, smiling proudly.

I focused back on Kat. "You need to go."

"We didn't get a confirmation yet," she said.

"It'll come," I assured her. "But then you need to go."

"No, I'm not leaving you."

"And I'm not arguing about this," I told her. "There's no cure for me. Why bring me back and watch me suffer? All I'll do is deteriorate into a body without a sane soul."

"I'm not leaving you."

"Kat—"

She grabbed my face. *"Michael!"*

That was the first time she had ever spoken my name. It was like smog being lifted. Slowly, images passed through my mind, buried memories suddenly beginning to resurface. It was overwhelming how much was coming through, making it hard to focus on any one thing. Or maybe that was the mind haze from the hellhound venom.

Either way, I stared at Kat and said, "What did you do?"

39 GABRIEL

HELL, PRESENT DAY

Raphael and I unsheathed our weapons and had them at the ready, knowing Lilith lurked within these stone corridors. I prayed she hadn't got away with Jordan through the portal. Aziza and Yadira had been dispatched to dismantle the larger one in Elysium since it would cut the connection to this one. Hopefully, the damage Yadira had done would be enough.

We hadn't encountered any opposition, but we still braced ourselves before rounding the corner into the portal room.

Instantly, both of us put away our weapons and shouted, "Jordan!"

He lay facedown on the floor. Raphael and I dropped to either side of him, and I rolled Jordan over into my brother's arms.

"He's breathing," Raphael assured me, "but shallowly."

I sighed in relief and paused, listening intently. I stood and walked to the wall directly behind me and stepped through. On the other side was a prison, and Lilith was locked inside.

She was wheezing and clawing at her neck. "You'll. . . pay," she choked out.

I placed my hand on my knife and was about to pull it free and end her when I heard Raphael shout, "Gabriel!"

Immediately, I went back into the portal room.

"We have to get him out here!" Raphael said.

"What's wrong?"

He pulled back Jordan's shirt.

I nearly fell over. He had a dark matter wound, and it was almost done festering.

"Portal's down!" Zadkiel yelled in our comms.

"The fallen angels are loose!" Aziza hollered.

"Michael's wounded!" Kat bellowed.

"Satan's back!" Uriel roared.

Things were getting worse by the second, but I pressed my finger to my ear, knowing my report would be sending us all home. "Jordan is secured. He's alive but hurt. Everyone evacuate now!"

Raphael picked up Jordan. I raised an arm around Raphael's left side and brought the other one up to meet it, turning the dial on my portal device and taking us back to safety.

40

DANE

HELL, PRESENT DAY

The cavern was a nightmarish scene, like something you'd see in a Bosch painting. Bodies were everywhere—some dead, some alive, some writhing, some still. There were puddles of water all over, the stone soaked through.

I wiped sweat from my brow, not because I had a fever but because it had taken hard work to subdue Cerberus. The beast had fought me fiercely. Now he lay on the ground, watching everything around him.

"Go back home, Cerberus," I told him.

The hound rose, and I petted his heads as he walked by. Cerberus nuzzled against my hand, then exited the cavern, mounting the steps back to Envy.

Most of the other hounds had returned to the cities and stairways earlier. All that remained was my faithful companion. "You all right, buddy?" I asked, patting his head.

He closed his eyes and pressed his body against my leg.

I glanced around. It didn't seem like I was needed anymore so I figured following the others back to the house was the right thing to do.

I had only lingered because I wanted to make sure my—

I stopped myself. It felt weird to think of Satan as my father. But I wanted to make sure he was unharmed. It was hard to find him among all the chaos and wreckage.

Leaving was probably best. I placed my hand on the portal device.

"Where do you think you're going?"

I turned, and there he was. The Devil back in his full glory, kingdom secured.

"Home," I said.

He placed a hand on my shoulder. The only person in the world who could touch me. "This could be your home."

I sighed. "I don't know. I'm confused. I think the best thing for me right now is to go back, check on my friends, clear the air."

Satan crossed his arms. "Okay."

"I'm not choosing them over you. I just don't want any of this power, but at the same time I know I have to deal with it. And it would be nice to sleep in a bed for a while, and I don't think you have that here—"

"Dane!" he cut me off. "It's fine. Really. I'm not offended. I also don't expect you to accept everything right away. Just know you'll always have a place here."

"No pressure?" I asked.

"None. I want you to be happy."

"Thanks."

"Oh, the only thing I ask is you don't call me Father."

"Okay… So Satan, then?" I asked.

"Yeah, or Dad…whatever works. Just not Father. I have too many issues with mine, and I refuse to be called the same."

"Will do. I better go now." I knelt, wrapping my arm around the hound.

"You're taking him with you?" Satan asked.

"Yeah."

"What about the others?"

"They'll listen to you. I made sure."

"Let me guess. You still have the final sway, though."

I shrugged. "It's kind of inevitable."

"Damn, Ace! Get out of here!"

I smiled and reached for the portal device.

"Wait!" The female fallen angel who had commanded the rivers bounded over to us. "Here," she said, handing me a vial. "Take this. Your friend's going to need it."

"What is it?" I asked.

"The cure for a hellhound bite."

I closed my fist around it and put it in my pocket for safekeeping. "Thank you."

Satan eyed the female fallen angel.

I raised my eyebrows and wagged a finger back and forth. "Are you two a thing?" I only asked because she might be my stepmom or something, if angels let themselves have such relationships. I hoped they were because she was badass and not psychotic like my own mother.

"We were," she said.

"Are," Satan corrected.

Her head turned fast to look at him.

"We just can't touch," he said. "That doesn't change how I feel."

Boy, did that hit home… I hoped Sophia felt that way.

"What's your name?" I asked.

"Abbadona," she said.

"I'm Dane, his son."

Her eyes widened. "Son!"

"There's a lot to explain," Satan said. "But it's time for you to go, Ace."

"I know. I'll see you soon." I reached for the portal device again, this time turning it and leaving Hell.

Instead of going to the city as I had originally planned, I had changed the coordinates to take me to Jordan's house instead. Who cared at this point if Satan followed me? He was my dad, and I think he would find me whether I wanted him to or not. With that said, I had a feeling he wouldn't let anyone come after me. No, I think he would protect me fiercely now that he knew our connection.

41 GABRIEL

Ithaca, New York, Present Day

We teleported back to the rendezvous point, Raphael and I barely taking a second to recover before we took to the air and flew to the house.

We landed in the backyard and rushed toward the house, Jordan in Raphael's arms. I opened the back door, and Raphael raced through.

"Martha!" I shouted, knowing we would need her help.

Footsteps pounded down the stairs, obviously more than just Martha coming to assist.

Raphael took Jordan into a bedroom that he had prepped as a triage room before the battle.

Martha rounded the corner with Sophia, Dafne, Naomi, and Deborah right behind her.

"Deborah, take them upstairs!" I commanded.

"What happened?" Sophia asked, a hint of foreboding in her voice.

"He's hurt, isn't he?" Dafne guessed.

"Martha, Raphael needs you," I said, ignoring them.

She brushed past me into the triage room. Aeron, Emily, and Peter joined us.

"Jordan's in bad shape," I told everyone. "And it's going to be a tough treatment. If you can't handle it, I suggest you leave. Now."

No one moved.

"Fine. You can stay, but you can't get in the way. The others are coming behind us. I'm not sure of their conditions. Would any of you be willing to help?" I asked.

Aeron stepped forward. "Wherever you need me."

"Us too," Naomi said, volunteering herself and her parents.

"Thanks. Wait for the others here. I'm going to see what I can do." I left them and entered the triage room.

"Gabriel, I need more holy water," Raphael said the moment I stepped in.

Martha had gathered all the bottles they had—five in total. Raphael uncorked one, and Martha placed her arms over Jordan's chest. My brother tipped the bottle, and the water hit Jordan's skin.

He shrieked as black lines began to touch his heart. If the dark matter hadn't taken over yet, this was going to be a long, hard battle since the infection had spread so far.

"Did you give him anything?" I asked.

"Morphine," Raphael said. "It's not working."

"Why don't I try?" I suggested, pulling a chair from the corner and sitting directly behind Jordan's head.

"I need more holy water," Raphael urged again.

There was noise in the hallway. The others had arrived.

Zadkiel and Chamuel appeared in the doorway.

"Boys, you can't stay here," Martha said. "We need space to work."

"What do you need?" Chamuel asked.

"Holy water," Raphael repeated, pouring more over the wound.

Jordan writhed.

"On it!" Zadkiel said, leaving with Chamuel.

Placing my hands on either side of Jordan's head, I closed my eyes and tried to calm him.

Raphael poured yet another bottle.

Jordan convulsed but didn't shout.

"What are you doing?" Martha asked me.

"Connecting our energies. Sending him positivity and calm, healing and courage."

More noise from the hallway, this time less rowdy.

Then a knock came at the door. "Can I take some gauze?" Aziza asked, peering in. "Yadira has a deep cut. It's healing already, but it needs to be cleaned up."

"Sure," Martha said. "It's in the right cabinet. Will she be all right?"

"She's fine. I'm fine. Worry about him."

The room fell quiet.

Raphael popped open another bottle.

Jordan's body tensed as the water hit it again, but the pain seemed to be getting more manageable. I could feel his mind reacting less fearfully.

A door banged opened, followed by a lot of cursing and arguing. "Get out of my way! I've just returned from the icy pits of Hell, and I'm in no damn mood to be reasoned with!"

Good ole Uriel.

He must have made it to the triage room because Martha said, "You look atrocious. Are you hurt?"

I kept my eyes closed, refusing to break concentration.

"Not really. A few cuts and scrapes here and there. I broke my arm, but I reset it before I left. Bloody hurt, but I'll survive."

"Excuse us," Zadkiel said, setting another bottle of holy water beside Raphael. "Chamuel is working on more."

"Thank you," he said, opening the last bottle in his stash. "I was just about to run out."

"Any improvement?" Zadkiel asked.

Raphael hesitated. "No."

Zadkiel sighed. "I'll go make more."

"Why don't you go with him, Uriel?" I suggested.

"I'm not leaving," he demanded.

The door outside banged open again.

"Somebody help!" Kat yelled.

My eyes flashed opened.

Michael.

I knew he was hurt before I saw him. I don't think it was because I was connected to Kat. Rather, it was more brotherly instinct.

She walked into the room holding his left side while Aeron supported his right.

"Over here!" Uriel directed.

The two set Michael down on the other bed.

"What happened to—" Uriel stopped. "Oh no."

"What is it?" Aeron asked.

Kat wouldn't answer.

"A hellhound bite," Uriel said.

"What?" I yelled.

Jordan screamed.

"Gabriel, focus!" Raphael instructed.

I settled down.

"There has to be something we can do to help him," Aeron said.

"No," Kat whispered, "there isn't."

Uriel clambered over to the cabinets, searching about and slamming them. Finally, he found what he was looking for.

"What are you doing?" Raphael asked.

"Using the anti-venom kit," Uriel stated.

"That's for poisonous animals," Raphael clarified.

"Precisely, which is what I would classify a hellhound as."

"Uriel if that worked, don't you think it would have been used by now."

He lost it. "I know it probably won't work! But I have to try! He would do the same for us!"

"Fine," Raphael conceded, centering his attention on Jordan.

I lowered my head, trying to do the same.

Uriel injected Michael with the anti-venom, walking across the room to dispose of the needle properly in a sharps container. Then he returned to our brother's side.

Kat hadn't moved from it since she had arrived.

"I'm going to check on the holy water," Aeron said before leaving the room.

Silence filled the air.

I closed my eyes again, clearing the pain from Jordan's mind. But I found something else lingering there.

"No!" I shouted, standing up fast.

Raphael's fingers were at Jordan's neck. "Start compressions!"

Martha had been inspecting Michael's wound and wasn't quick enough.

I stepped forward, placing my hands on Jordan's chest. I pressed down hard repeatedly.

My brother grabbed the defibrillator paddles. "Clear!"

I removed my hands and watched as the shock jolted Jordan's body.

Martha checked for a pulse. "Nothing."

I resumed compressions. "Come on, Jordan! Come on! Come on!"

42 JORDAN

AFTERLIFE, PRESENT DAY

I felt myself leaving. It was too hard to hold on. Too hard to fight.

A part of me was sad. I was so young. I had so many things I wanted to do with my life. I didn't want to die. Yet, when I opened my eyes and found myself in the glen again, I started to rethink matters, especially when my parents were there waiting for me.

Their smiles were radiant and full of happiness at seeing me. They were sitting on a log, and I joined them, settling between them.

They hugged me together. I closed my eyes and cherished the moment.

"Sweetheart," my mom said.

As they let me go, I opened my eyes and looked at her.

"I told you there would be consequences," she said.

I nodded. "I know. But if I get to stay here with you both, then I'm fine with the outcome."

"Are you sure?" my dad asked. His voice was deep and smooth.

"Positive. I've never wanted anything more than to be with you."

"Believe me," my dad said, "we understand that feeling. And while I'd like it to be this way forever, there's a part of me that thinks you should try to fight to return."

"Why? I don't want to leave you. Besides, with me gone, the prophecy can never be fulfilled. It's over."

My mom placed a hand on my shoulder. "We tried so hard to alleviate that burden for you. We never wanted it to come to this. You deserve to live. To have a chance to experience all the world has to offer."

"But you don't understand! It's so hard not to have you around." I inhaled sharply. "You were the one who warned me of the consequences! Now you think I should have done something different?"

My mom pulled me toward her and kissed my head. "Hush," she soothed. "I always wanted you to pick the path of life." She smoothed my hair. "I put my own interests aside, though, to let you choose for yourself. That is what every parent must face: letting their kids make their own decisions. It pains us to see you struggle, which is why we're interceding."

Her tone had changed. I raised my head and followed her gaze. Across from us, I noticed a darkness creeping in on the glen.

"Are you sure you don't want to return?" my dad asked.

Panicked, I said, "Do I have a choice?"

"You do if you fight," he promised me.

"And if I don't?" I wondered aloud, so tired of always being in opposition with something.

My dad took me by the shoulders. "Jordan, if you don't, then your fate is grim. You won't only be taken from us, you'll be taken from everyone who knows and loves you."

His words made me realize what the darkness was. If I let it consume me, I would become a dark being, forfeiting any chance I had of having a happy existence.

I stood. "I won't let that happen." I turned around one last time to get a glimpse of them. I had seen pictures of them before, but having them here right in front of me was better. I heard their voices, felt their touch.

My lip trembled, and I bit back a sob. It hurt to leave them. But I had to.

Facing the darkness, I trudged forth, leaving the glen and hoping to return to the world whole.

43 DANE

Ithaca, New York, Present Day

I arrived in the backyard, hellhound still at my side. "Stay out here, boy. I'll come get you soon."

The hound obeyed, finding a secluded spot on the patio where he wouldn't be detected.

I approached the house and entered through one of the back doors. There was a group of people staring at me as soon as I stepped inside. I barely recognized any of them, other than Sophia and Dafne. Naomi, too, but I didn't think we could trust her, given her connection to Geneloom. Something must have changed.

Sophia rose, face full of worry and tears streaming down her face. "Please be you."

"I am." I spied the necklace she was fiddling with, the blue lace agate one I had bought for her birthday. She must have found it. Maybe there was still hope for us.

"Dane, he's dying!" she sobbed. "You need to help him!"

It was like a bucket of cold water had been splashed in my face. I knew Sophia was referring to Jordan. The news unleashed something inside. The heat from the Hellfire I normally felt beneath my skin cooled while my senses and emotions heightened. I concentrated on everyone, even those in the other room. There were two injured. One alive, but barely. The other…there was no heartbeat.

I raced down the hallway to see what was happening.

Gabriel was doing compressions on Jordan's chest and stopped briefly for Raphael to shock him with the paddles.

"No pulse!" Martha shouted.

My eyes crawled to the other figure. It was Michael. He was the one with the hellhound bite, the wound bleeding and oozing severely.

What was wrong with Jordan, though?

I focused again and heard the whisper. It's what I had felt when trying to fight Darcel. It was the call of the dark, except it wasn't inside me anymore. It was inside Jordan, trying to take over.

My instincts kicked in, moving my feet across the room to where Michael was lying. I placed the vial on a silver medical tray. "That will help him," I said to Uriel.

He was surprised, not only at the vial but at my presence.

I moved over to Jordan.

"Dane, you need to leave!" Martha urged.

I wasn't listening. Not to her. I was listening to the whisper and could see the mark it had left on Jordan, black lines snaking from a deep wound all the way to his heart. It had made it there; except rather than letting it in, Jordan had fought it, fought it so hard that his heart had given out and stopped. He just needed someone to make it beat again. The only way that would happen, though, was if the dark matter was extracted, and there was only one being that could do such a thing.

A blood mage.

I could feel it in my bones, my blood, my heart, my head, my fingertips. My power wanted to spring free the way it had in Hell. This time, however, I somehow knew the words to speak, my voice coming out in a hiss.

Gabriel, Raphael, and Martha stepped back, knowing I was trying to help not hurt.

The words were for a dark spell used to trap dark matter. The incantation was only the beginning. The hand movements were really what made it work. I lifted mine in the air, making shapes and twisting them apart.

Jordan's abdomen rose inches from the bed, his arms and legs staying put. The dark matter was strong; it was fighting back. The black lines along his chest ran together to form one large mass near Jordan's stomach. That was the easy part, consolidating the matter into one location. Now it was time to remove it, and I could feel this is where things would get tricky.

I drew closer to Jordan. Sweeping my hand over the mass, I said, "*Exitus.*"

Jordan tensed. Then convulsed.

The dark matter was resisting the spell.

I swept my hand over the mass again and drew it into a fist, pushing it toward Jordan's head. Slowly, the dark matter moved, creeping up from Jordan's stomach and into his chest.

It stopped and pooled in the area around his heart.

"*Subsisto!*" I commanded.

The dark matter became immobile.

Then I forcefully swooped my hand over Jordan, and the dark matter moved, much faster this time, toward his neck.

"Get a bucket or trash can," I demanded.

Jordan's eyes flashed open, not in consciousness but in survival.

Martha raced over with the trash can and placed it in front of Jordan just as he opened his mouth to vomit the dark matter out of his body.

He sank back to the bed was he was finished.

Martha went to take the trash can, but I stopped her before she could put a hand on it. *"Confinio."*

A small screeching sound came from the trash can, the dark matter angered by its new home.

I moved closer to Jordan's head to inspect him. Small droplets of black spittle still covered his face, but I couldn't start his heart again with any of the toxin still in him. So I hovered my hand over his mouth and turned my palm up very slowly, my fingers tensing and urging the remaining dark matter to rise forth. Whatever was left emerged from his mouth and hung in midair, forming a much tinier mass than the one that had been inside him.

When everything was out and cleared, I let the tiny mass join the rest of the dark matter in the trash with a simple command. *"Exilium."*

The tiny mass lurched in the air and dove to join its counterpart in the trash can. There was still much to do with the dark matter in order to destroy it completely, but right now, bringing Jordan back to life was more important.

Acting on instinct yet again, I brought my hand into a fist and slammed it onto Jordan's chest, yelling, *"Vivo!"*

Jordan jolted and sucked in a breath of air. His eyes opened, a little dazed.

Martha, Gabriel, and Raphael gathered around him, checking his vitals. Once again, I was forgotten as he was doted upon; however, it didn't sting anymore the way it usually did. I finally had someone in my life who would choose me over him.

Picking up the trash can, I intended to go outside to finish off the dark matter, but not before I checked on Michael.

"How is he?" I asked Kat and Uriel.

"Stable," Uriel said.

"We put the antidote on the wound. It cleared up in seconds." Kat drew her attention away from Michael and set it on me. "Thank you."

"Of course," I said.

Then I left them and exited the room with the trash can. I passed by the others out in the hall. I really couldn't put this off any longer, so I said, "They'll be fine," and continued on my way through the doors leading outside.

The cold November air hit my face. It was refreshing after the intense scene inside.

The hound, used to the icy temperature of Hell, was still lying on the patio. His head rose when he saw me, but I told him to stay. He obeyed.

I walked off the patio and into the yard, heading down to the lake's edge. I set the can on the ground and sank to my knees, closing my eyes to concentrate. Just as soon, they flashed open as I noticed someone had followed me.

It was Naomi. She stood before me.

"I'm busy," I said.

"I can see that. But I won't let you do this alone." She sat down on her knees across from me.

"And what am I supposed to be doing exactly?" I asked her.

"You don't know?"

"I know I need to destroy this," I said, indicating the trash can. "I don't know how, though."

"How did you do everything else?"

I shrugged. "Instinct."

"Okay." Naomi sighed. "We need to annihilate the dark matter."

"When did this become a 'we' thing?" I asked. "I barely know you, and the last time you were even mentioned to me, there was talk of you being on Geneloom's side."

"Well, then, you've missed a lot because I'm not. In fact, I'm the one who got Sophia out of there, so maybe save the bullshit for later."

"All right," I said, "no need to get defensive."

"We're wasting time! We need to figure out what to do."

I thought about it. Then my curiosity got the best of me. "What makes you think you can help me?"

She chewed on her lip and threw up her hands. "I have magic. More control than you, but I still don't know everything. When we were at the lab, they classified you as a Supernal, which is what I am, so I think our powers might be connected somehow."

"You're a blood mage?"

"No, I'm not."

"Then we're not the same," I argued.

She huffed. "All right. You're a blood mage, and I'm a Supernal. Either way, I think our powers are connected."

"What can you do?"

"I have an affinity to water."

Weird, given how Abbadona had just given a powerful display of her magic in Hell, which was also connected to water.

"I think whatever the Supernals are," she said, "our magic is linked to the elements."

"Okay, so water, fire, earth, and air. What does that make me?"

"None of those. There's a fifth element. Some call it spirit or ether. I think that's you."

"Why?"

"Because your affinity is to blood. Blood is a life force, similar to spirit or ether."

"I see your point. You think we have to use the elements to destroy the dark matter?"

"Well, we don't have all of them, but I think between the two of us we can do it."

I chuckled. "At least one of us is optimistic."

"Release the dark matter," she told me.

"You sure?"

"Yes." She reached out her hands, and a stream of water shot out from the lake. She formed it into a ball and let it hover in the air. "Put it inside the water. Then you place your hands top to bottom on the ball. My hands will be on the right and left so you won't burn me."

"Will that destroy it, though?"

"Probably not. You need to do the rest."

"Which is?"

"I don't know! Maybe by then your instincts will kick in again. Let's go," she insisted.

Waving my hand over the trash can, I undid the spell and released the dark matter. It shot out and right into Naomi's ball of water, which was floating above it.

I did as Naomi had said, placing my hands on the top and bottom of the water ball. At my touch, the dark matter twisted inside, collapsing into itself, undulating, and then thrashing around again.

The dark matter's fit lasted for a moment before I heard its tantalizing whisper. No words or messages were emitted, just a series of sounds that called to me. I wanted to bring my hands together to smash the ball of water and let the dark matter snake around my arm. The idea was so alluring that my hands inched closer to each other.

Naomi frowned. "Dane, what are you doing?"

I ignored her. The sounds of the dark matter were more musical to my ears than her voice.

"Dane, you have to kill it," she urged.

Did I want to kill it? Its song was irresistible. I wasn't sure I could.

Take it.

My body tensed. Darcel wanted the dark matter. The sound appealed to *him*, and I didn't want to be him.

Somehow, I took the ball of water right out of Naomi's hands and crushed it in my own. The dark matter's song changed from a nice melody to a horrible shrieking, but I didn't stop. I pushed my hands closer together until I was clasping them and there was nothing left. Both the water and the dark matter gone.

Naomi and I remained on our knees across from each other, equally exhausted and stunned. Finally, she said, "I'm not going to ask how you did that because I guarantee you don't know."

She was right. I don't know what I'd done. I didn't know a lot of things about what I was. I did know I had destroyed the dark matter, which was a good thing. But if I didn't learn to control and master my powers, I knew it would be detrimental to my well-being.

We rose from the ground and headed back inside.

On the way in, I waved the hound over, and he joined me. I entered the house, and everyone stared at me.

"What is that?" a woman asked.

"A hellhound," Sister Delphine said. "Why is it inside?"

"He's mine. He's harmless."

I strode over to the stairs, and the hound followed.

"Just give him a bath before you go any farther!" Chamuel yelled.

Smiling, I shouted back, "I will!" Then I paused on the stairs and backtracked until I found Chamuel. "Hey," I said, grabbing his attention.

He turned away from cleaning up a mess of gauze pads and antiseptic. "Is there something you needed?"

"Yeah, I was just wondering, where's Jophiel? I haven't seen him around."

Chamuel's face sank. "I know the two of you were close, so there's no easy way to say this."

A sense of dread overcame me.

"I'm so sorry, Dane, but Jophiel's gone. We lost him during our fight with Lilith in Heaven."

My eyes widened in surprise. That was not the answer I wanted to hear. I figured Jophiel was upstairs in the library. Not dead.

The hound nudged my hand, sensing something was wrong. Numbly, I patted his head.

Chamuel reached out to comfort me but realized he couldn't. "I'm *really* sorry. What can I do?"

I shook my head. "Nothing."

No one could do anything because I was an untouchable freak.

I turned around and raced upstairs before Chamuel could say something else. The hellhound followed me, concerned by my reaction. I intended to head toward my room but decided against it. Instead, I found myself standing in front of Jophiel's door.

I let myself in without knocking since I knew the room would be empty. From the doorway, I could see all that remained of Jophiel were a few belongings: an easel with an unfinished painting, tons and tons of books, and a yoga mat he used for his tai chi exercises.

I closed the door, strode over to the mat, and sat down. The hound joined me.

This was the perfect spot for Jophiel to do tai chi since the window had an amazing view of the lake. He had taught me the martial art and convinced me of its benefits. In fact, I usually joined him whenever he performed the exercises outside. I would miss those moments now.

A sharp pain tore through my chest, but this was no time for tears. I slammed my fists on the floor and expelled my anger. The hellhound pawed at me, and I embraced him, finding some solace in his comforting touch.

I hated my mother more than ever. I had thought playing mind games with me was the worst of it, but nearly harming Sophia and now killing Jophiel were the final offenses. She had to pay. No matter what.

44

GABRIEL

Ithaca, New York, Present Day

I sank into an armchair in the living room, exhausted but relieved. It had been a long day…perhaps a long month. Closing my eyes, I rubbed a hand over my face, the reality of what we had done sinking in. We had breached Hell, caused incredible chaos, and knocked out their portal. The damage was done, let alone the fact that someone had imprisoned Lilith, too.

"Gabriel."

I opened my eyes and raised my head. Deborah stood before me.

"I'm sorry to bother you, but I think it's time we all regrouped and talked."

"About?"

Deborah threw her hands in the air. "Everything. There's a lot you all don't know, and there's a lot we don't know. We should all be on the same page before we make our next move."

"Next move?" I rose to my full height. "There will be no *next move* until Michael and Jordan are recovered. While they are stable, they still have a long road of recovery ahead. Not to mention this is the first time in four weeks that we have all been together, the first time in four weeks that the kids have been safe, at home and in their own beds. Add to that the casualty we faced in Heaven, the death of our brother that none of us has had time to mourn." I gritted my teeth. "Plus, how could I forget the secrecy and deceit on your part and the Conways?" I stepped forward. "We trusted all of you, and none of you had the courtesy to enlighten us of the past, all because of some binding spell." I shook my head. "Don't speak to me of next moves. As far as I'm concerned, you won't be involved in our next moves." I walked away without giving her a chance to respond. I wasn't in a particularly talkative mood, and I wouldn't apologize for it.

I ascended the steps to my room. Raphael had first watch over Jordan, and I figured this would be the best time to wash up before it was my turn to take his place.

The black paint still covered my wings, and the icy chill of Hell had set in my bones. I could use a hot shower right now.

I turned on the water, took off my clothes, and stepped inside the stall shower, immediately sitting on the ground to let the water wash over my wings. I hung my head, elbows braced on my knees. I wanted to weep but angels couldn't shed tears, so I did the next best thing and let out a roar of emotion.

The black paint stained the water, and I vowed that I wouldn't leave until the stream ran clear. Then I would be fully cleansed. My mood would return to normal, and I would be the Gabriel everyone wanted me to be. In the meantime, I would wallow in my thoughts.

At least, they had both survived.

That was what I kept telling myself because it was the only thing that gave me any sort of joy.

Michael and Jordan would be all right. Dane and Sophia were safe, too. We were reunited, though not whole. We never would be again. Not without Jophiel.

He would have loved to breach Hell with us, a sheer thrill to explore a new place, especially one we typically weren't allowed to travel to. His sense of adventure had been such a dominant trait of his personality since he enjoyed gaining knowledge more than anything else. I already missed him dearly.

After my wings were fully cleaned, I left the shower and dressed in my usual garb—full suit and tie. The sweater and combat pants I had worn to Hell were practical, but I had felt weird, almost like a fish out of water.

I exited my room and walked down the hall to Jordan's. We had moved him up here to make him more comfortable and give him privacy. We had done the same with Michael, too. He was conscious, except he had to brave a fever and hallucinations before he was well again. Oppositely, Jordan had yet to wake.

Entering his room, I watched his chest rise and fall as he rested in bed. I strode over to the chair and patted Raphael on the shoulder.

"Time to switch," I told him.

He rose. "I'm going to check on Michael and then take a break."

I nodded. "I'll let you know if anything changes."

Raphael left, and I sat down in the chair, opening the book I had brought with me. I tried focusing on the words, but it was difficult not to worry about Jordan.

At least they'd both survived. It was the mantra I kept repeating to remain hopeful.

45 SOPHIA

Ithaca, New York, Present Day

As soon as I could, I returned to my room and lay down on my bed. Everything was such a roller coaster. We all had been reunited, then Jordan had flatlined. All hope had seemed lost, then Dane had returned and saved everyone. I admired how he had handled the situation, swooping in and fixing everything.

I fiddled with my necklace, thinking about him.

There was a knock at the door.

"Who is it?" I called. I still didn't want to talk to my parents.

"It's me," Dane said. "Can I—"

"Come in!" I shouted before he could finish.

He slowly opened the door and stepped inside, closing it behind him.

"Can I sit?" he asked, pointing at the bed.

I nodded.

He perched on the edge of it, as if he weren't allowed to be there. Meanwhile, all I wanted to do was envelope him in a hug and pull him down next to me so we could lie side by side and snuggle. Except I couldn't. His skin was too hot to touch. And not in a good way.

We had come so far, and now miles spanned between us. There was no denying it. We were both different. Had we changed too much to remain together? Or was our bond strong enough to evolve and weather the storm of our lives?

It was time to find out.

"I'm sorry." He said it to the window, facing it more than me.

"Dane, look at me."

He turned his body and swung his legs onto the bed, finally meeting my eyes.

"What are you sorry for? Telling me you love me?"

His eyebrows shot up. "No! I meant every word I said, and I would never take it back." He reached for my hands and stopped himself. "I'm sorry because I let Darcel take over. If I had fought him a little harder, I could have helped you get out of the lab." His jaw tightened.

"Is that all?" I only asked because I could tell he was holding back.

He ran his hands through his hair and looked away again. "No, that's not all. I'm sorry for scaring you. Even though Darcel had control, I still remember the look on your face. The horrified expression when you thought I would kill you." He swallowed hard. "I'm sorry I'm a monster." He held out his hands. "I'm sorry for what I am." Then he curled them into fists and met my eyes. "You need to know that I would never hurt you. Darcel wanted to, but I wouldn't let him. He's gone now as far as I'm concerned."

Dane sucked in a breath. "And while I never wanted this to be my life, I can't change who I am. For years, I never told you how I felt because I thought I was too damaged for you. Well, it turns out I am, except I'm not going to push you away this time. You should have the choice if you want me to be in your life or not. And I know I have a lot to learn, like limits and controlling my powers, and I know the journey ahead might be rocky, but I'm willing to try if you are. That is…if you want me."

"Of course, I want you!" I exclaimed. "You wouldn't let me get a word in, otherwise I would have told you that several minutes ago," I teased.

He smiled. "Well that's a relief."

"Dane, we're not the only couple in the world who's going through a rough patch. I would actually be worried if we didn't at some point. Granted, I can say for sure our circumstances are unique, but that changes nothing for me. I'm all in."

"God, I love you," he whispered.

I edged closer, as far as I could go without touching, our noses mere inches apart.

"I love you, too," I murmured.

He sucked in a breath. "You're killing me."

Grinning, I said, "I know. I promise we'll figure this out."

"Hopefully fast."

"Hopefully fast," I agreed. We were both trying to be optimistic, even though there was no known "cure" for the Hellfire.

"You found the necklace," he observed.

I drew back slightly, picking up the pendant. "Yes, I love it."

"Happy birthday."

I smiled. "Thank you."

"So I think we need to catch each other up on some things."

"Like?"

"Like the fact that I control all the hellhounds and I brought one home with me."

My eyes widened. "What?"

"Yeah, he's in my bedroom sleeping. Chamuel made me give him a bath, which was not easy."

"I bet."

"What should I name him?" he asked.

"You're naming him?"

"I want to."

"Okay...um..." I thought about it, trying to think of a name. What did you name a hellhound other than Cerberus?

"I was thinking Duke."

"Duke. I like it." I sighed. "My parents are here."

"That's who those people are?"

I nodded. "I haven't spoken to them. I refuse to."

"Rightfully so."

"There was one point where I hugged my dad, but that was after being rescued from the lab so it was just a vulnerable moment. I gave him his necklace back." I paused. "There's not much to say. I'd rather not talk about it."

"Okay, you don't have to. I'm here for you, though. I can talk to them for you if you'd like."

I laughed. "No, absolutely not."

"Fine." He looked me up and down, his gaze piercing. "There's something else. You forget I can sense things now."

"So can I," I reminded him, flexing my wings.

"All right, all right. No need to show off, though they are beautiful. More so than mine."

"I beg to differ. I think yours suit you handsomely."

We both laughed that time.

"Soph, you're diverting."

"I am," I confessed.

"What are you trying to hide?"

"Not hide really. More like forget."

"Care to elaborate?" He played with one of my fallen white feathers that had landed on the bedspread.

"I had back surgery."

His head whipped up. "Why? Are you okay?"

"I will be. Just a little sore and tender still. I'm healing much faster than most. Technically, I should be fully recovered by week's end."

"What happened?"

"I'm still not sure. Jazema did something to me when I was younger, stunted my wing growth or spinal growth." I scratched my head. "It's confusing. All I know is when my wings came out, I was in constant pain, especially during our time at the lab. They wanted to do surgery there to fix it, but I refused because I kind of...hate that I'm a Nephilim. Penelope was going to force me, and then the whole escape happened. Except they brought us all to a hospital afterward, and the conversation came up again since I was in so much pain. I refused, and then we were attacked, and I was fighting Rajani and she body slammed me onto the floor right on my back. I was paralyzed, so I had no choice but to undergo surgery. Thankfully, Raphael had returned by then because I didn't trust anyone else to do it. I have a lot of trust issues, more so now than ever."

I fell quiet.

"Can you walk yet?" he asked, then backtracked. "Obviously you can because you were downstairs."

"My mobility returned immediately, which I'm grateful for."

"But…?"

"But I don't know if I can handle this." I shrugged my shoulders, indicating my wings.

"Well, I can sympathize with you there. It's a weird feeling to suddenly have wings. I just wish—"

"I could hide them," we said at the same time.

"The angels could probably teach us," he assured me.

"Yeah. I just keep wondering if that will be enough."

"You hate it that much?" he asked.

I nodded, a tear falling down my cheek.

"Oh, Soph…please don't cry. Not because I can't handle it but because I can't really comfort you."

I chuckled through my tears and then grew serious. "What am I going to do? I liked the person I was before the unbinding. I don't want to be a Nephilim."

"Try not to look at it that way," Dane said. "Don't label it. It's too new of a change. I get why it's hard. There's a lot of trauma associated with the Nephilim for you, and rightfully so. But like most trauma, I'm sure it'll get easier over time. If you face it and acknowledge it. Hiding it and ignoring it won't help. It'll only makes things worse."

"My parents returning doesn't help. I mean, I think my mom abandoned me, and my dad I didn't even know existed until three days ago."

"I know it's a lot at once, but your real family has returned. The angels are back. I'm here, and we both know Jordan will be joining us any day now."

"I miss him," I murmured.

"Me too," Dane said. "Why don't you relax a little? Lie back and read or something."

I grinned. "Is that really what you think I do all the time?"

"Don't act like I'm wrong!" he declared. "I don't have anything against reading. I just don't call it one of my hobbies."

"Mm-hmm." I brought our faces close together again.

"Making this a habit, I see." His voice was a soft rumble.

"Only if you like it."

"I do, which is a problem."

"Why?"

"Because it makes me ache for you more."

"Is that really a problem?" I teased.

"One day it will be," he said mischievously.

I blushed and pulled back. "Okay, so in the meantime why don't we lie here together and watch a movie instead."

"Sounds perfect."

We settled down, the movie a much-needed distraction for both of us. And as we lay there side by side, I couldn't help but notice how our wings touched, his black leathery ones and my white feathery ones. It seemed the Hellfire didn't extend to that part of him. It only sparked at skin-to-skin contact.

There was no denying our relationship was going to be difficult, but it would be worth it.

Besides, deep down, I knew there was a cure. There had to be. No curse came without a cure. It was only a matter of finding it.

46

LILITH

PURGATORY, PRESENT DAY

I shook with anticipation, knowing this deplorable necklace would be pried free within seconds. It had paralyzed me the moment that boy had put it on me. No magic. No movement. No match against my enemies. Just a useless, ordinary woman. Oh, how I hated that, considering that's what I had been created to be and had been fighting against ever since.

The Sentinel had found a set of pliers in our camp, and he was working at the chain around my neck. When the metal finally broke free, I clutched my throat and sucked in air. I had felt suffocated and submissive, no way to breathe or survive.

I clenched my hands into fists. That boy was dead to me. I needed him for the prophecy, but he was gone the moment it was fulfilled and I had the Sovereign's Orb and Scepter.

Turning to the Sentinel, I said, "Thank you."

He appeared shocked by my gratitude, but I supposed I never had expressed such a thing before. He had done more than pry the necklace free. He had found me in that cell and carried me out of there, whisking me away to safety.

"You're welcome, Mistress."

"I feel ashamed," I admitted, settling on the lounge in my tent.

He sat down on the floor. "Why's that?"

"Because I let my ambition get the best of me. I spread us too thin between Purgatory and Hell, not to mention the attack on Heaven and the rescue of Darcel, which was an utter failure."

"There is still hope for your son," he assured me. "I saw him in Hell. Granted, he had escaped Purgatory without your blessing, but his magic and power are strong."

"I agree, but that doesn't mean he's on our side. I can see it in his eyes. He's *Dane*, a troubled boy raised by a nun whom he views as his real mother." I grew quiet.

"Mistress, you haven't failed."

"I know that, deep down. I'm just letting you see a little glimpse of who I am beneath the hard shell." I grabbed his chin. "Don't forget it because you'll never see it again."

"I assure you, I won't." He paused. "Can I say one more thing?"

"Hmm."

"I understand why you acted quickly, why you let your ambition lead you. There are many things you wish to accomplish, and you've been stopped before from doing them. So it's only natural to want them all while the power is in your lane and you can seize the moment while others are unaware."

My hand dropped from his chin and went to his chest. "What exactly do you gain from telling me this?"

He smirked. "Nothing but your possible affection, Mistress."

I couldn't help but grin and grab the collar of his shirt, pulling him up onto the lounge. Focusing on another task was the perfect distraction. Regrouping and planning could be done later. Now was the time to tend my wounds.

47

SATAN

Hell, Present Day

It had taken three days to fully contain the chaos. Once I had, everything went back to normal—relatively. The remaining members of the Six resumed their posts, along with a few new additions.

Haborym had taken over Greed after striking Mammon with that poisoned knife she had commandeered from me. I had originally been wounded by it after the Sentinel had thrown it into my shoulder at the Empire State Building. When I returned to Hell and extracted it, Haborym was keen on claiming it for herself. The poison did little to me since it was Lilith's and I had grown immune to it, having been bitten once before. Mammon, though, had no tolerance and suffocated until he was blue in the face.

Nehema had acquired her role in Lust by valiantly slaying Asmodeus—or I should say by *viciously* slaying Asmodeus, as she had slit his throat and let him bleed out.

All this had happened in the midst of battle in the Eighth Cavern so it had been hard to witness firsthand, but their accounts were enjoyable to listen to, especially since the two of them regaled all of us—myself as well as Beelzebub, Belphegor, Abbadona, Ariel, and

Kushiel—with their elaborate tales since their versions were much more drawn out than my recap.

Speaking of Ariel and Kushiel, they had decided to stay in Hell, the former claiming a spot in Envy for herself. She had slain Mulciber, who unfortunately had slain Leviathan before that, subsequently seizing the vacant role, unbeknownst to her. She was happy with her new post, though, flawlessly stepping in to round up the spirits and proudly flaunting her black wings.

Leviathan's death was a shame. He had been a good and faithful comrade, cunning and devious when the need arose, certainly a better confidant than others had been. Losing him was a blow to our hellish family, but there was no one better to fill his spot than Ariel.

As for Kushiel, he was content with just residing in my kingdom. I felt like I needed to reward him, though, for all he had done in Purgatory. But I couldn't just hand him the position in Pride. Lucifer was still living, even if he was hiding until the tides settled and he chose who he wanted to align with. My guess was he would go crawling back to Lilith. From what I'd heard, Jazema had taken a severe loss, so she was probably hiding herself and licking her wounds. Lilith, on the other hand, would take the time she needed to recuperate and then come back for more. She and the Sentinel had somehow escaped, the cell attached to my portal room now empty.

No, Pride wasn't an option for Kushiel. Misery, however, was. The ninth level of Hell had no true leader prior to now. Murmur and Mulciber had stayed down there to keep the spirits in line, but neither of them had a formal appointment. It could be time to change that, so I decided Kushiel would be the official leader.

The hounds had returned and aided in suppressing the spirits. They listened to no one now but Dane. Even Cerberus. Dane had commanded them to my care while he was gone, but more than anyone, a king recognized that a power like that should be owned not borrowed. I had no intentions of harming Dane to seize his power. Quite the contrary, actually. I would do everything I could to build him up.

The way I saw it, he was my prince, and all this would be his one day if he wanted it...and I died. I had no plans of returning to Purgatory anytime soon, so my real hope was that he would take over Pride. There were many complications to that plan, though. He would have to kill Lucifer, and I was unsure if he possessed such a capability. He would also have to reside here...I thought. I supposed he could stay on Earth and visit occasionally. The spirits, demons, and fallen angels were too finicky to let that slide, though. They wanted leaders with iron wills and formidable personalities, meaning they most likely needed to be present. The only caveat for Dane was his magic, which could be enough to scare them all into submission.

It would have to be something to dwell on another day. Maybe when I saw him again. There was another angel right now who needed my attention.

Abbadona kept her place in the Eighth Cavern, maintaining the rivers, though they had become much calmer since the battle. I wonder if whatever creature lurking in the River of Hate had finally been satisfied. As for our relationship, it was the opposite—unsatisfying. We hadn't talked much after Dane had left since everything around us was in shambles and needed fixing. I had hoped to speak with her once Hell had settled, except it had taken longer than expected.

What I had said was true. Nothing had changed for me, other than the small issue of us not being able to touch. A relationship could be more than touch, though, right? I hoped so, but it was time to see what she thought.

I returned to the Eighth Cavern, cautious of the rivers' tantalizing whispers. None came. Relaxing, I walked over the cold stone ground to Abbadona's hut.

It was hard to knock since there was no solid door, so I cleared my throat instead.

"You can come in," she said, her back turned to me and seemingly unsurprised by my presence.

I joined her at the table and sat on a stool across from her. She had books spread out everywhere, her focus currently on one that she was reading.

"Might I ask what you're doing?"

"Trying to find a cure," she said without taking her eyes away from the page.

"A cure for what?"

She looked at me. "Hellfire."

"There is no cure. That's why it's my punishment. It's not meant to be fixed or reversed."

"A punishment is just a curse, and every curse has a cure," she assured me, returning to the book.

I fiddled with my hands. "What if I don't want to be cured?"

Her head came up again. "What do you mean?"

I shrugged. "I like Hellfire. Initially, it sucked. Now, though, it's incredible. I'm not sure I want to give it up."

Abbadona slammed the book shut. "If you don't give it up, then you're giving me up."

I shook my head. "Not necessarily. We can figure this out without a cure."

"How?"

"I don't know."

"Exactly. So we go back to the way it was." She stood abruptly from the table and started picking herbs from the bushels hanging from the ceiling.

"No, nothing's changed," I said adamantly.

"But it has!" she yelled, slamming her hands on the table.

Herbs went flying and hit me in the face. I couldn't help but think I had pissed off another witch, which was a thought that scared me considering the sentence I had been dealt by the last one.

Abbadona wouldn't hurt me. That's what I kept telling myself anyway.

"Are you listening?" she shouted.

"Yes. You think there's no hope for us."

"I do, seeing as you don't want a cure to exist!"

"I never said that. A cure can exist. But if it does, I'm unsure if I would take it."

"Because power is more precious than love."

I stood. "You're being unreasonable. We'll talk about this another time." I strode to the exit.

"Now you're running because I used the L-word."

"Excuse me!" I roared, turning back. "I'm not some pathetic male human who can't hear the word *love*, or express it for that matter, without balking."

"Then say it," she commanded.

"No."

"Why not?"

"Because I refuse to be bossed about. Not to mention it's what you want to hear to reassure yourself rather than genuinely caring how I feel. I will say it when—"

"You mean it." She put words in my mouth.

My jaw clenched. "Abbadona, this is childish. Do I love you? Yes."

"But?" she insisted. "Just admit it."

"What?" I growled.

She drew close to my face, as close as she could come without touching me. "You know what."

I did know what. I just didn't want to crush her by saying it. If that's what she wanted, though, then it's what I would give her.

"But power is more precious," I whispered against her lips, stepping back and retreating the way I had come.

48 MICHAEL

Ithaca, New York, Present Day

I went from an icy chill to a scorching heat. My entire body was sweltering, and if you told me I had Hellfire running through my veins, I would believe you.

Except my body was the least of my concerns. Right now, my mind had me in its grasp. Flashes of memories played before my eyes like a movie.

Swords clashing.

A horse rearing.

A crusade cross.

A girl who needed saving.

And Kat.

She was the lead actress in every scene. We had been close. Certainly not strangers. Why had she tried to hide our history?

My mind took hold of me again…

A searing pain in my forehead.

The need to track the Sacrarium all over the world for centuries.

A war gone wrong.

A battle won.

And Kat. Again.

And the searing pain. Again.

What had she done?

Someone dabbed a cloth against my forehead, and my eyelids lifted. A figure shifted in and out of focus. I latched on to their wrist.

"Don't worry, Brother. Raphael and I are here." It was Zadkiel.

I tried sitting up.

"You're not ready for that," Raphael said, pushing me back down. "Fever's too strong." He checked my eyes. "And from the looks of it, you're hallucinating."

I shook my head. "No…I'm not." It sounded forced even to my ears. "I'm r-remembering."

They glanced at each other, concern written across their faces.

Raphael stepped away from my side to examine my leg. Cerberus had bit me in the shin. It was hard to say right now, but it felt like he had pierced the bone.

"Almost healed," my brother declared.

Well…maybe I was hallucinating, then, because it felt much worse. My head sank to the bed.

"Just relax," Zadkiel urged.

How? There were too many questions, too many worries. We had to keep moving…or fighting…or…

I ran my hands over my face. We had to do *something*. I just didn't know what.

"Stop thinking," Zadkiel demanded. "Just give in to it. It'll be over soon."

I listened to him. I shut my eyes. Not to fall asleep, as angels couldn't do that, but it was still nice to close them and feel like I was drifting off for a moment, away from reality.

When I opened them again, morning light bathed the room in a cheerful glow. I sat up, this time successfully, and peered around the room. It was empty. I was alone.

Thank goodness. I could use the privacy to pull myself together. I swung my legs over the edge of the bed and sat for a minute.

The hellhound toxin had worked its way through my system. I could tell because I could think clearly again, and I felt like all my other senses had returned.

I pushed myself off the bed, stood, and went to walk, but when I put weight on my injured leg, I nearly collapsed. Careening into the end table, I hit the lamp, and it went flying to the floor, shattering and emitting a loud noise.

Footsteps thudded from the hall. It sounded like all five of my brothers were coming to my rescue.

The door burst open, and sure enough, there they were, ready to fight whomever they thought might be threatening me.

"Back in bed," Raphael ordered.

"Not happening," I said, rising from the floor. I braced myself against the end table, using it as leverage to push myself up. I rose to my feet again but didn't attempt to walk.

"Thank the heavens, you're back," Chamuel said, striding across the room and embracing me in a hug.

I patted his back. "Thanks, Chamuel."

"Do you need some help?" he asked, pulling away.

I sighed. "I guess so. I just wanted to take a shower. It seems my body won't let me get to the bathroom, though."

"What do you expect?" Uriel huffed, coming to brace my right side.

"A full recovery? That's near impossible. You're lucky you're alive. Be grateful it's just impaired mobility."

Chamuel stayed on the left, the two of them assisting me across the room.

"Thanks, Uriel. Your pep talks are always so reassuring."

He smacked me on the shoulder. "I tell it like it is, and you all love me for it."

I grinned. He was right.

They got me to the shower when I realized something. "Who's watching Jordan?" I figured Martha, or maybe even Dafne, might be taking a turn.

They all froze briefly, then raced out of the room and down the hall.

I guessed no one.

Wobbling into the shower, I sat down on the seat inside, undressed, and then let the warm water rush over me and rinse away the grime from Hell.

49 JORDAN

Ithaca, New York, Present Day

I had died. That was something I would never forget. I had met my parents—not just my mom again but both of them. That was something I would cherish. I had returned thanks to Dane wielding his magic. That was something I would always be amazed by.

I opened my eyes and stared at the ceiling of my room. *My room.* I was home. Thank goodness. I couldn't handle being in Hell—being in a villain's clutches, being separated—anymore. I sat up, surprised no one was lurking around watching over me. That was unusual behavior for the angels. I hoped no one else was hurt. That would be the only thing that would take their attention off me, especially if their injuries were serious.

Calm down. You're jumping to conclusions.

Taking a deep breath, I climbed out of bed and headed straight for the shower. When I walked into the bathroom, I took a glimpse at myself. I definitely wasn't the picture of health. I had lost a lot of weight. Too much. It made sense, since I had small meals for the past four weeks. The crazy thing was, I wasn't even hungry anymore. It was like the sensation had been completely wiped from my memory. I'm sure as soon as I was faced with an appealing dish of food, it would kick into overdrive and my next worry would be overeating or eating too quickly, which would surely make me sick.

I paused. Obviously, I had to be hungry if all I could think about was food and eating. I'm sure Chamuel would help ease things back into my diet.

Pushing back my hair, I looked at my face. Pale. Shadows beneath my eyes. Turning sideways, I saw the remains of the dark matter wound. It was red and irritated, the cut itself shallow and already scabbed over. I'm sure it would leave a nasty scar. Something to remind me of the life I had taken.

I stopped my examination and stepped into the shower, hoping the water would wash away the haunted memory of Murmur.

Once I was clean, I dressed myself in sweats, a T-shirt, and a hoodie. I figured the best thing would be to go downstairs to find someone. Maybe Sophia and Dane were around. It would be nice to see them... Actually, it would be nice to see anybody, but I wanted to make sure they were okay.

I went down the short steps attached to my room and entered the hallway. Looking out the window, I saw it was cloudy outside. I peered closer and noticed two figures were out there sitting on the dock. I smiled. It was Dane and Sophia.

Trudging back upstairs I found some shoes and a coat, knowing it was probably freezing outside. Then I continued my journey down, all the way to the lower level, without being detected.

Where was everyone?

Opening the back door, I stepped outside, and sure enough, a blast of cold air hit me. I shook it off and strode through the yard all the way to the dock.

Dane and Sophia were too caught up in what they were doing to notice me.

"It won't work!" Sophia laughed.

"Yes, it will. Eventually," Dane chuckled, throwing a rock onto the frozen lake. He had a pile stacked next to him.

The rock hit the ice, causing small crystals of frost to fly in the air, but then it skidded across without breaking the surface.

"I told you! The ice is too thick. You're never going to break it," Sophia assured him.

"I could just heat it up," Dane said, holding another rock in his hand. "Then it would work."

Sophia disapproved. "That would be cheating."

"No, it wouldn't."

"Yes, it would. If Jordan were here, he would agree," she pointed out.

"Actually," I said, "it would be pretty cool."

They both whipped around and sprang to their feet.

I smiled as they careened into me, each of them grabbing me in a hug, Sophia squeezing my abdomen and Dane clutching my shoulder.

Suddenly he pulled back. "Shit! Did I hurt you?"

Sophia did, too, alarmed.

I shook my head. "No. Why would you?"

"My hand touched your skin. The Hellfire…" he trailed off.

"I don't think it works on me," I told him.

His eyes widened. "You might be right. Can we test it?"

I held out my hand.

"Wait!" Sophia exclaimed. "That's absurd to just try it. Besides, what are you even doing out here? You should be inside where it's warm."

I shrugged off her concern. "No one was around when I woke up, and I wanted to see you both. You're the crazies for being out here in December."

"Let's go inside," Sophia urged.

"Wait!" Dane was the one to say it now.

"Yes?" I asked, my hand still out.

"Can I try?" he wondered.

"Of course."

He pulled his hand from his pocket.

"This is such a bad idea!" Sophia cried.

Too late. His palm was already clasping mine.

"Told you," I said.

Shocked, Dane muttered, "She was right."

I didn't know who he was talking about, but Sophia distracted me by asking, "How is that possible?"

"I think it's the holy blood."

"It is. I think it's time we get you inside, though" Dane finally agreed.

"Fine," I said, turning to walk down the dock. I stopped in my tracks, my heart jumping into my throat. "Is that…"

"Dafne," Sophia supplied.

She was standing by the back door, frozen on the patio. Eventually, she inched forward, as did I until we were both walking quick toward each other.

When we finally met in the yard, we enveloped each other, fitting perfectly together. She pressed her face against my neck and wept. I stroked her hair and brought my mouth close to her ear. "I'm sorry," I murmured.

Dafne shook her head. "Don't be sorry," she whispered into my neck. "These are happy tears." She pulled back to wipe her cheeks, but I still encircled her with my arms. Our eyes met, and we stared at each other. Then we both leaned in, her hands going to the back of my neck, to rest our foreheads together. We closed our eyes, content in each other's presence.

I don't know how long we stood like that. Surely a minute or two.

"Jordan," Dafne said, "I think it's time we get you inside. Yours lips are turning blue."

Opening my eyes, I felt a weakness enter my body. I nodded against her forehead.

She grabbed my arm to balance me and drew back.

Dane stepped forward, swinging my arm around him. "Typical Jordan," he muttered. "You're back for two seconds and you're already doing something irrational."

We started walking to the house.

"Says the guy who was trying to crack frozen ice with a rock," I mumbled.

"Boys," Sophia and Dafne sighed behind us.

When we entered the house, there was full hysteria going on. Everyone was shouting, "Jordan! Jordan!" searching for me everywhere.

Uriel stepped out from the swim room. "He didn't fall in the pool!" he shouted, knowing his brothers would hear him. Then he saw us. "Crap! What were you thinking?"

"This wasn't our idea," Sophia explained. "He came to find us."

"Of course, he did," Uriel sighed. "I found him!" he yelled for everyone to hear. Before they all could clamber downstairs, we ascended them and decided to meet the crew in the living room.

Dane deposited me on the couch, and I appreciatively sank into the cushions. Clearly, my stroll outside was taking a greater toll than I'd thought it would.

The angels gathered around, as well as Martha, my aunt Delphine, and Kat. There were also two other female angels I had yet to meet, a woman I didn't recognize, and a man who had me doing a double take because he looked like my father.

Then I did a quick count and realized we were missing someone. "Where's Jophiel?"

There was silence, and it seemed like everyone was suddenly more interested in their feet than in me.

I found Gabriel and searched his face. He was the only one willing to look at me.

All it took was one glance to know the truth. My eyes welled, and my lip trembled. Dafne sat down next to me and took my hand. I wouldn't pry my eyes away from Gabriel, though.

"No," I whispered.

He stepped forward and knelt in front of me.

"Yes," he confirmed.

I broke down, falling into him. He knew I would. That's why he had come close, to support me. I sobbed into his finely pressed dress shirt and vest, but he didn't care. He held on and let me get out my grief.

Eventually, I quieted and righted myself. Pulling back, I said, "How?"

"Lilith."

That was all the explanation I needed.

I regretted not killing her when I had the chance, but the memory of Murmur flashed in my mind again. The vision of him wheezing for breath—for life—would haunt me forever. I wasn't a killer. At least, not a natural-born one. Murmur's death had been self-defense, instinctual, purely for survival.

Wouldn't Lilith's have been, too? Would she have hurt me, though? I was too precious to her alive right now.

"Ugh," I said, rubbing my hands over my head.

"Stop," Gabriel warned.

"What?" I grunted.

"Blaming yourself," he clarified. "I know you're the one who locked her in that cell. I don't know how, but I saw your necklace around her neck. That was enough to infer it was you." He placed a hand on my shoulder. "You couldn't have done anything more. Not in your condition. When Raphael and I found you, you were barely alive."

I nodded, unsatisfied with the explanation but unsure of what to say.

Looking past Gabriel, I set my sights on the man who looked like my father. "Who are you?" I demanded. His green eyes matched my father's and mine too much not to notice the resemblance.

"Your uncle." He scooched forward in his seat and crossed his arms. "I guess I can finally talk."

Sister Delphine rolled her eyes. "Aeron, don't play the martyr. Just be happy they're finally speaking to you." She thought about it. "Us, really."

"Well maybe I don't want to speak to them now and answer their questions," Aeron said defiantly.

He was a Conway all right. Stubborn pride.

"Aeron be reasonable," the woman I didn't know suggested.

"I can be reasonable, Emily. I'm just choosing not to be."

"Like you've done for nearly twenty years," Sophia jabbed.

Battle lines were drawn, and the flood gates opened.

"How dare you assume that?" he yelled.

"Oh please! Don't act like what you've done has been logical," Sophia snapped.

"All right, all right," Chamuel said, waving his arms in the air.

It didn't work. They kept at it.

"And what do you think I've done?" he asked her.

"Abandoned me, killed dozens of innocent people," she elaborated.

Those were some harsh accusations. I just kept wondering why they were fighting and how they knew each other. It was almost like they were…

I glanced between them. Sophia had crystal-clear blue eyes, but she had Aeron's blond hair and fair skin. Was this her dad? But if he was her dad, that meant she was my cousin…

"*Enough!*" Chamuel bellowed.

They finally fell silent.

"Bickering is not how this will go down," he demanded.

Aeron and Sophia sank to their seats.

"It's more than time for everyone to share their story," Chamuel went on. "Especially now that everyone is healed and conscious." He eyed Michael and me. We happened to be sitting next to each other, the angel resting his foot on the coffee table, which wasn't normal behavior. He must have been injured.

"However, we will not argue with one another. Right now, we need to be united, not divided," Chamuel continued.

Almost everyone shook their heads in agreement.

"But first, Jordan needs sustenance. Then we can begin our chat." Chamuel whisked away to the kitchen to prepare me something.

"It's a good time for me to take a look at you," Raphael said, stepping over to me and taking Gabriel's place. "You had us all frightened when we found your room empty," the angel of healing stated, inspecting my face.

"No one was around," I said.

Michael gently elbowed me. "That's because they were checking on me."

"What happened?"

"Hellhound bite."

I blanched. "I thought those were fatal."

"They are, but Dane brought some cure back from Hell," Michael said.

"Abbadona gave it to me," Dane explained, though none of us knew who she was.

"Anyway," Michael continued, "it helped me survive. Gave me a bout of bad hallucinations, but it saved me." I couldn't help but notice he directed that last part at Kat. She seemed unfazed by the comment.

"How's the cut?" Raphael asked me.

"Fine. A little irritated."

"I'll give you something to calm it. In the meantime, rest is what you need. You're too fatigued and starved. We'll see how Chamuel's food goes down. If it's too much, I might have to put you on an IV to get you some nutrients."

"I hate needles," I complained.

"I know," Raphael said, standing. "That's why I haven't done it yet, but we might not have a choice."

Sighing, I brought my attention to Dafne, who still held my hand. She squeezed it once she noticed me looking at her and smiled.

I interlaced our fingers, feeling comforted by her presence. It was surreal to think that we were all here together. The angels minus Jophiel. Sophia, Dane, Dafne, Martha. My uncle and aunt, for that matter since Sister Delphine had revealed as much to us several months ago before the unbinding. Kat and what I assumed to be the Triune. The only one I couldn't figure out was the woman named Emily.

"She's Sophia's mom," Dafne whispered in my ear. "The one who abandoned her."

I was surprised, both at how Dafne knew what I was thinking and the fact that the woman sitting across from me was the cause of Sophia's trauma. No wonder no one was talking to them and Sophia was being defensive. She had every right.

The doorbell rang, and Martha rose from her seat. "I'll get that."

"It's Deborah, Peter, and Naomi," Chamuel said, returning with a mug. "I invited them over since I think they need to be here, too." He handed me the cup.

Reluctantly, I took it. "They're involved?" I asked, glancing down to see a hot liquid. From the smell of it, it was chicken broth.

"Yes, they're Sacrarium," Sophia said.

"And Naomi is badass," Dane added.

Dafne nodded. "I would agree with him. I saw her in action."

In action? What had I missed?

"Hello, everyone," Deborah said, entering the room with Peter, Naomi, and Martha.

We all returned their greeting, and they settled in.

"Oh my goodness! Jordan, you're awake!" Naomi exclaimed, noticing me on the couch.

I set down my broth and rose briefly to give her a hug. "I guess I don't have to worry about you and Geneloom anymore."

"No. You never did. I wasn't on their side."

"I was concerned. You're my friend. I didn't want to see you get hurt."

"I understand. Now sit back down before you fall over."

I laughed and sank to the couch.

Dafne handed me the broth. "You haven't had any yet."

"Because I don't want to."

"Just sip it," she urged. "Please."

I took the mug and sighed.

"Don't be stubborn like your uncle," she said.

I grinned. She was right, so I brought the cup close to my mouth and took a few sips. It was warm, which was nice since the air outside had set a chill in my bones. It tasted good, too. Everything Chamuel made did. The only problem was that I was hungry, and I knew this would barely hold me over. I kept sipping, though, thinking of the broth as one step closer to a juicy burger.

"All right!" Chamuel called out. "We're all here. Who wants to go first?"

Everyone looked around the room, waiting for someone to start spilling secrets.

50 JORDAN

Ithaca, New York, Present Day

"That can't happen yet," Michael stated before anyone could speak. "You said we have to be united, not divided, and without him, we're missing an important side of the story. I think he should be here if we truly want all the answers."

"Are you seriously suggesting what I think you are suggesting?" Gabriel asked, outraged. "It'll compromise our location."

"Is that even a worry anymore?" Uriel wondered aloud. "Especially with him here." He gestured at Dane. "I'm sure he's keeping tabs on his son."

I finally realized who they were talking about. "You want *Satan* to be here?"

"Absolutely not!" Deborah said, rising from her seat.

"No offense, Deborah, but it's not your call," Uriel said.

"He's right," Michael agreed. "It's your house, Jordan. You should be the one to decide."

I didn't need time to think it over. "I'm fine with it. I just don't know how to send him a message."

"I think I might be able to," Dane said, bending over to scratch the hellhound's head. The creature rested at his feet like a house pet.

Dane placed his forehead on the hound. "Call him," he whispered. "Get one of them to bring him here."

Dane backed off, and the hellhound howled.

When he stopped, the room was silent.

"Now we wait," Dane announced.

"How long?" Uriel asked.

Dane shrugged. "Not sure. It could be seconds or hours."

Chamuel patted his thighs and stood up. "In that case, let me go get some snacks for everyone."

We all talked among ourselves. Eventually, Chamuel returned with a giant charcuterie board, which he placed on the coffee table. Everyone picked and munched on nuts, fruit, veggies, cheese, crackers, and deli meats.

I refrained and kept sipping my broth. I knew it was the best thing for me right now.

Footsteps thudded down the hall, and everyone went quiet as the king of the Underworld entered the room.

"What the hell is this?" he demanded.

Dane stood up. "Let me explain."

"Please do, Ace, because here I thought you were in trouble, and now I find I've been summoned for trial."

"No, that's not what this is," Dane assured him. "We're sharing stories about the past to get everyone on the same page."

Satan smirked. "Oh, we're spilling secrets."

"Uh…you could call it that," Dane said.

Satan stepped farther into the room. "And there's snacks." He clapped his hands together. "There must be a lot to say."

"Are you staying or not?" Michael asked.

"I guess so, since I was kindly invited." He strode over to the kitchen and pulled a stool from the island, then brought it over and sat next to Dane.

With everyone present and settled, the conversation began.

"Perhaps I should start," Aeron said. "A lot of what I know will piece things together."

He paused for a minute. I imagine he was figuring out where to start. If I were him, I knew I would need a moment to gather my thoughts.

"My brother, Arthur, knew Evangeline throughout grade school and middle school. It wasn't until high school, though, that they got to know each other. Once they did, they were inseparable."

Looking around the room, I could see Martha, Deborah, Peter, and Sister Delphine agreed, smiles on their faces at the memory of my parents.

"Soon after, it was off to college, and that's where things started to get interesting. They went to separate schools and wanted to try the long-distance thing. Our mother was hopeful the match wouldn't last. She knew the Sinclair family, their ancestry, and she didn't want to be involved in the burden that was the holy bloodline, knowing a lot of responsibility and strife came with it. No, she wanted her family to be the best and greatest, otherwise our seat among the Ishim would be compromised."

Dafne sat up straight next to me. "Wait, you're the Conway family connected to the Ishim?"

"Yes," Delphine said. "Are you familiar?"

Dafne nodded. "I'm a Delucci. My ancestors have held their seat for years. There's always been talk and whispers about the Conways." She looked to me. "I never realized you were them."

"What kind of talk?" Sophia asked.

Dafne hesitated. "Well, mostly of ruination and disgrace. The Conways have always been the chief of the Ten Families, and all the children refused to carry on that legacy."

Aeron scoffed.

"At least, that's the rumor," Dafne amended.

"Is that true?" Sophia demanded.

Delphine sighed. "Partly."

"How it works," Aeron explained, "is that the seat gets passed on to the eldest of the family, which is me, except I don't have the Conway gift, making me my mother's greatest disappointment. So then it gets passed on to the next child, if there is one."

"Which would be Delphine," Sophia stated, trying to understand this.

"Yes, and unlike my brother, I do have the gift," she said. "But I was already committed to becoming a nun and taking my vows, which disqualified me from assuming the seat, making me our mother's next greatest disappointment."

"Why would that disqualify you?" Zadkiel asked.

"Because the whole point of the seat and the Ishim's teachings is the ability to pass them on to your ancestors, and the assumption was that I would have none since my holy vows would prevent me from having a family of my own."

"That's ridiculous!" Sophia exclaimed. "I mean, you might not have children, but you have two siblings who then went on to have children."

Delphine shrugged. "I don't make the rules, and the Ten Families love rules. They also love avoiding conflict, which is why involving myself with the Church, or my brother involving himself with the Sinclairs, was frowned upon."

"Pause," Satan interrupted. "Let me get this straight. The Sinclairs are the holy bloodline?" He turned to me. "And you're the remaining descendant?"

"Yeah," I said.

"Well, shit. I almost killed you. A few times."

I nodded. "I'm well aware."

"Hmm." He didn't apologize. All he said was, "Continue."

Sophia jumped in. "So Arthur didn't get the seat, either."

"Actually," Aeron said, "he did. Since Delphine and I were unworthy, the seat fell to Arthur, who had the gift more so than even Delphine. He was powerful, and he was our mother's pride and joy."

"Until he met Evangeline," Delphine added.

"Exactly. Which brings us back on track," Aeron said. "Arthur loved Evangeline and refused to let her go, no matter how much our mother begged him. They fought and argued ruthlessly over the matter until Arthur was done. After having the seat for four years, he relinquished his claim to it, disowned the entire family other than the two of us, since we were already rejects, and married Evangeline to live a happy life together.

"Our mother didn't attend Arthur and Evangeline's wedding, but she did have parting words for them later that night over the phone. She warned them that any child of theirs would have too much ancient blood, meaning they would be gifted more than the Ten Families had ever seen. Something so powerful would not just break their rules; it would break all the rules in the universe."

"Which is why Jordan was our sign," Gabriel concluded. The angels nodded in understanding.

"You're jumping ahead," Dane complained.

"Sorry," Gabriel smiled. "We just always wondered. Continue on."

"Wait," I said. This was hard for me to comprehend. I didn't see myself as that special. "Why would Conway and Sinclair blood be so powerful? I know the holy bloodline is extraordinary and the Conway gift is an outlier, but why should it matter when they come together?"

"Because both are lines of prophets," Delphine explained. "The ability to prophesize is a remarkable gift. A prophet's actions, as well as their words, can inspire people to do the unthinkable, to believe in things that aren't even tangible. The fact that it's Conway and Sinclair *is* symbolic. It's a union of pagan and Christian beliefs."

"Okay then. No pressure," I stated, feeling overwhelmed.

"Thus, the rumors of ruination and disgrace," Delphine supplied, "as none of us were able to, or quite frankly didn't want to, hold the seat. Not with our mother's constant judgment."

"What happened to the Conway seat, then?" I asked.

"She still holds it," Dafne said.

Sophia was shocked. "Who? Our grandmother?"

"Yes," Aeron and Delphine said together.

"She's alive?" I asked.

"Very much so," Delphine confirmed. "We don't speak to her, and she doesn't know about either of you. She wouldn't approve."

"Sounds like she doesn't approve of anything," Uriel muttered.

Aeron nodded. "You're right about that."

"Why wouldn't she approve of us?" Sophia asked.

"Soph," I said, "I'm the embodiment of exactly what she didn't want to happen. In her eyes, I'm sure I'm a reminder of everything she lost."

"No offense, Jordan, but you're right," Aeron agreed.

"And what about me?" Sophia prodded.

Aeron chewed his lip. "You're a Nephilim."

"That's new, right?" Satan asked. "Because I distinctly remember you didn't have wings when I chased you through the church."

"Yes," Sophia snapped, "it's new. Aren't you going to apologize?"

Satan chuckled. "For chasing you? No. I don't apologize for anything." He stood. "Let's get one thing straight. I'm here as an ally because the enemy has bested both of us and we only stand a chance if we work together. That doesn't mean I've turned over a new leaf or that I regret my past decisions. This relationship is a means to an end. Once it ends, it's over. Granted, I won't be as terrorizing as I have been, but I certainly won't remain friendly. Got it?"

"We got it!" Uriel yelled. "Now sit down!"

Satan flipped him off but obeyed.

Sophia picked up where we had left off. "And why does it matter if I'm a Nephilim?" she insisted.

Aeron didn't answer her.

"The Ten Families hate Nephilim," Dafne said quietly.

Sophia met her gaze. "What?"

"Not my family," Dafne corrected. "The Ten Families are complicated, and they're not our current problem, but I will say that when they were founded, one of their main principles was that they would be enemies of the Nephilim, because the Ishim are good Watchers and what broke the Watchers apart was essentially the creation of Nephilim. I'm not condoning the idea, just explaining how it works. There are a few families currently who wish to change that outlook, mine being one of them, but Delphine was right in what she said. The Ten Families love rules and tradition, and to break or adapt them is something that simply does not occur easily." Dafne sighed. "They're an issue for another day."

"She's right," Delphine said. "We should move on."

"Getting back to your parents," Aeron said. "They acknowledged our mother's warning, and while they wanted to have children, they did not worry because it was difficult for them to have any."

"Your mother struggled with that a lot," Deborah confirmed, taking over the conversation. "Your father did, too, but for your mother, it was a greater sadness. They did their best to distract themselves, traveling all over the world, teaching in your father's case, and painting for your mother. But nothing could truly divert their attention from what was really going on."

"Which was?" Sophia asked.

"Evangeline wanted children, but she knew if she were to have a child, the responsibility to fulfill the Union of the Spheres would fall to them. Those were the rules. She was hesitant to hand off that burden, especially to her child, whom she felt should have a choice. Essentially, she was uncertain if having children was a good idea, not without ensuring there was a way to make their part easier."

"Was there?" Raphael asked.

Deborah nodded. "At the time, Evangeline thought you were the enemy." She pointed to Satan. "Her plan was to retrieve your keys—classic, gemstone, and sphere. She knew the other keys for the Union were safe since they were hidden and guarded—only the bloodline or the angel the key belonged to could unlock it. She figured eventually you all would show up with the rest when the time arose. Evangeline believed that if Satan's keys were in her possession, it would make the Union easier for her child since nothing would fall into the wrong hands."

"She was trying to avoid a conflict," Michael stated. "Neutralize the enemy before they were a threat."

"Precisely. That is what she wanted, not just for her child but for herself and Arthur, too," Deborah said.

"You don't need me to tell you why that was a bad idea," Satan commented.

"Why is he here again?" Aeron demanded.

"Because he needs to share his side of the story so we understand everything," Michael insisted. "Why don't you enlighten us, Brother."

Satan laughed. "Trying to win me with endearing terms won't work. Besides, right now there's not much I can offer to the story. By this point, I knew about my keys. Lilith had planted the idea of their existence, and one of my fallen angels of teaching had instructed me further about them and their purpose. I wanted to find them, but I didn't know where they were located."

"That makes sense since Seraphiel didn't tell us the locations of ours until we were sent down to Earth, which was after the Fall," Gabriel said.

"Exactly. So I wasn't after the bloodline. I was after the keys, and I had no leads during that time. My path hadn't crossed with any of yours yet," Satan said.

"Anyway," Aeron continued, "we made plans to collect Satan's keys. Everything was in place."

"Wait," Satan said, outraged. "You knew the locations of my keys?"

Aeron nodded. "Yes, the bloodline knew the locations of all the keys."

"Damn, that stings," Satan commented, then fell quiet.

Deborah picked up the story again. "And then Lilith struck. Evangeline went to bed one night and didn't wake up the next day. She was gravely ill, and no one knew why, not even the doctor. So Helen called in the Triune."

"I was wondering when you'd get to us," Kat said, stepping forward with the other two female angels. "Hello, everyone. I'm Kat. These are my comrades, Aziza and Yadira."

"Before we go further," Aziza added, "I'd like to clarify something. Many think the Triune is meant to protect the holy bloodline and anything pertaining to it, but that's not our job. That's Kat's job. My and Yadira's jobs are to protect that which is sacred to our religions. We come together to form the Triune when there is an issue we cannot face alone. I only say this because the Christian problems we assist with tend to be the only thing we're known for, when in reality, Yadira and I are dealing with conflicts that are just as important."

"Thank you, Aziza. I forget that many misinterpret our purpose," Kat acknowledged.

Aziza nodded and motioned for Kat to resume.

"When Helen called on me to help Evangeline," Kat continued, "I came straightaway. I had my suspicions Lilith was behind the attack. She is the biggest threat to the bloodline because she wants to complete the prophecy, so I was aware of her antics. Her first assault is always mental, trying to weaken the heir from the inside."

Wow, Kat really knew her stuff. That was exactly what Lilith had tried to do to me.

"Sure enough," Kat continued, "as soon as I saw Evangeline, I knew exactly what had happened. Lilith had trapped her in one of her dreams. I pressed my thumb to her forehead…"

I couldn't help but notice that Michael, who was sitting next to me, also rubbed his.

"She woke up instantly," Kat said. "From the look on her face, I knew she was scared. I also knew that this had been going on for quite some time. This was the only instance that had gotten out of hand, though. She confessed as much."

"It was then that we all realized Satan wasn't the true threat. It was Lilith," Aeron elaborated.

Satan scoffed. "I get blamed for everything, even when I do nothing."

"You're not exactly someone we can trust," Aziza said. "You said as much yourself."

"Right, but that doesn't mean every bad thing to happen in the world is my fault," Satan defended.

"I beg to differ," Yadira commented.

"Moving on," Kat interjected. "Evangeline said Lilith intended to go after Satan's keys since they were the least protected."

"That bitch," Satan muttered.

Kat leveled him a razor-sharp look.

"Fine, I'll shut up," he said.

"Evangeline wanted to stop Lilith before she could get the keys so no future heir would have to suffer the consequences," Kat went on. "I knew she needed a protective ward, but they're not easy to come by, so I called upon Sandalphon to help."

"You know Sandalphon?" Gabriel asked.

"Yes," Kat said. "We were introduced a long time ago. For those of you that don't know him, Sandalphon is an archangel who formerly served on the Council of Archangels in Heaven. Now he resides in Purgatory, and when I met him, he had been given new duties by Father, ones that came with more power, which is why I thought he could help with the protective ward. Sure enough, he did. He created the necklace, and I gave it to Evangeline to wear to guard her from Lilith."

"And the necklace was all that was needed to stop her?" Dafne asked.

Kat shook her head. "Unfortunately not. It slowed down her attacks, but she still got to Evangeline every now and then. Nothing nearly as bad as trapping her in a dream, though."

"What did she want?" I cut in. "I only ask because she did the same to me. She wanted me to set her free from the fourteenth sphere, so there's always a reason."

"You're right. She wanted Evangeline to give her a page from *The Book of Prophecies*," Kat admitted.

The angels and I froze.

"What did you just say?" Zadkiel asked.

"She wanted a page from *The Book of Prophecies*," Kat repeated.

My eyes widened. "My mom had *The Book of Prophecies*?"

"Actually," Kat said, "it was given to the Conways and was passed down through generations ever since. So, technically, it's your dad's."

"Do you know what page Lilith wanted?" Zadkiel pressed.

"Mm-hmm. It was the spell to create him," Kat said, pointing at Dane.

Everyone looked at him.

"Shit," he whispered under his breath.

51 JORDAN

ITHACA, NEW YORK, PRESENT DAY

"So she must have gotten what she wanted," Sophia inferred.

"Yes," Kat said. "Evangeline wouldn't give it to her, though." Kat settled her sights on me. "Your mother was strong, with an iron will. She fought off Lilith's advances and mastered her skills so expertly that she gave Lilith a taste of her own medicine."

"At what expense?" Satan asked. "There's always a price."

"The price was her inability to conceive," Kat said. "Evangeline's greatest fear was bringing a child into this world while the bloodline's fiercest enemies still existed. As Delphine said, she wanted children more than anything, but she wouldn't consider it until she knew they would be safe."

"Obviously, something went wrong because here I am, dealing with those enemies," I stated.

Kat crossed her arms. "It did. Your father decided to intervene, mainly because he couldn't stand seeing Evangeline the way she was. She developed insomnia and was always fatigued. Her positive and happy nature was nowhere to be found. He knew the toll Lilith was taking, and he couldn't stand for it. He ripped out the page from *The Book of Prophecies* and delivered it to Lilith."

"Face-to-face?" Dane asked. "That's ballsy."

Kat grinned. "It was. He decided to give her the page on one condition: she had to leave Evangeline alone."

"And an ultimatum," Dane said. "Oof."

"How do you know?" Dafne asked him.

"Because I've done both those things, and she doesn't take either well. Mommy Dearest is a bit psychotic when it comes to threats… Come to think of it, she's a bit psychotic, period. Threats and displays of superiority are definitely triggers, though," Dane explained.

"Arthur walked away unscathed because Lilith knows when and when not to react. The page was more important than hurting him so she agreed to his ultimatum. But all it did was ignite a simmering rage that would come back to burn them later," Kat said.

"But it worked," Deborah acknowledged. "Lilith did back off. That's how you're here."

"I'm curious to know how *I'm* here," Dane said, looking to Satan.

"Don't ask me, Ace," he said. "I don't go around cavorting with women. I'm not a lustful being, and even if I were, it's near impossible with Hellfire running through my veins. Lilith's not my type anyway. All I know is I gave her a vial of my blood long ago in exchange for information. I'll admit it was a dumb decision on my part, but I didn't know she would come to possess a blood mage's powers. Nor did I know what she intended to do with it. If you want more answers, I'm afraid you'll have to ask her…or find the page she used."

Dane sighed. "Figures. I'll be the one walking away with more questions than answers while everyone else gets what they want."

"Hey," I said, sitting forward to look at him. "That's not true. You're probably right that by the end of this conversation we won't know a lot about your origin or your powers, but that doesn't mean we'll quit searching."

"Jordan's right," Sophia agreed. "We won't stop until you know everything."

A soft smile played at Dane's lips. "Thanks."

"Some things are being left out of the story," Aeron said a moment later. "Arthur only ripped out the page because he foresaw the outcome—Lilith would use it to create Dane, but Dane would be brought up with Jordan, establishing a bond between them that would never let the other falter. Arthur never would have done it if he knew Dane would become Jordan's enemy. Trust me, he meditated for days trying to spark a vision."

"Oh, I had no idea," Kat said.

Aeron didn't acknowledge her. He just kept going. "Yes, Lilith did back off and Evangeline was able to heal and eventually become pregnant. It was a pleasant surprise for Evangeline and Arthur. But our plans to retrieve Satan's keys were back on the table, now spurred by Arthur, who wanted his family to be at peace once and for all. Except unbeknownst to us, there was a betrayer in our midst who told Lilith everything we intended to do."

"Before we go on," I interrupted, "can you tell me who, at that time, were members of the Sacrarium?"

I remembered what the Sentinel had said to me in Hell. That he had been the one to betray my parents. He hadn't told me his real name, but he must have been close to them to know their plans or be trusted.

"I was," Deborah said. "I rose through the ranks the traditional way, starting out when I was eighteen, completing my trial of trust at twenty, and taking my vows thereafter. I quickly became a Beta, one position below the Alpha."

"And Sister Helen was the Alpha, right?" Dane asked.

"Yes," Deborah confirmed.

Peter cleared his throat. "I, too, followed the traditional path to becoming a Sacrarium member. That's actually how Deborah and I met. Unlike her, though, I wasn't nearly as skilled and to this day remain a Gamma, which is the lowest classification."

Aeron sighed. "I guess it's my turn. I didn't enter the Sacrarium the traditional way. I was an honorary member. When Arthur married Evangeline, they told us about the Sacrarium—" he turned to Delphine "—because we were very close."

"Yes," Delphine said. "Evangeline was like a sister. They trusted us, so they felt it was best to tell us. They treated Aeron and me like Betas."

When Delphine finished speaking, everyone's attention fixed on Martha.

She grew serious and looked me straight in the face. "Jordan, I'm terribly sorry, but I've been lying to you. All of you," she said, including the angels. "I am a member of the Sacrarium, Gamma classification. I told you otherwise when you first arrived. I also told you as little as possible about your family because I was concerned about what I could or could not say without the unbinding spell harming Delphine." She took a breath. "It was so hard! You kept asking me questions. Some things I genuinely didn't know and am only just learning about now. I was just so worried!"

Every time Martha got worked up it was hard not to smile. She became so flustered and her sense of humor was unleashed without any inhibitions. "I forgive you, Martha," I said. "That's why we're all coming clean."

She nodded. "Thank you. Helen and I followed the traditional path to becoming Sacrarium members. We entered together. She outshined me, though, and rightfully so. She was exceptional."

"That she was," Emily said. Everyone's attention turned to her. "Right," she said, scooching forward. "For those of you that don't know me, I'm Emily. I became a Sacrarium member the traditional way, although I will admit it was something my parents wanted, not me. I'm a Gamma classification." She sank back in her seat.

Emily. Why did that name sound familiar? I couldn't remember.

"Was there anyone else?" Raphael asked.

"Yes," Aeron said. "There was Theo, Evangeline's brother. Technically, he wasn't Sacrarium since he was the bloodline, but he was involved in everything we did. There was also Silas Sharp, who Arthur and I grew up with. He was like our other brother and was training to become a member but never had a chance to take his vows." He paused. "And then there was Cecil Wallace, a Beta."

"Wallace?" Dafne asked. "Some say the Wallaces are the eleventh family of the Ishim, or rather, that they should have been the chief family if the Conways hadn't stolen it from them."

Delphine smirked. "The families still tell these old wives' tales?"

Dafne nodded. "Unfortunately. Also, your mother is very keen to mention the story whenever the name Wallace is uttered."

"I bet," Delphine said.

"What's the deal with Cecil?" Dane asked. "You made it sound like he was trouble."

"All Wallaces are," Aeron said. "Cecil especially since he betrayed us."

They knew the betrayer? But that didn't make any sense. If they knew him, why did he go around hiding his face under a hood whenever he was in public? There must be more to the story.

"You're sure Cecil Wallace was the betrayer?" I asked.

Aeron nodded. "Yes. Why?"

"Do you have a picture of him?" I asked instead of answering.

"*Why?*" Aeron demanded again.

"Because there's this guy called the Sentinel who works for Lilith and he keeps attacking us, but every time his face is hidden—"

"By a hood," Satan cut in. "I'm familiar."

"As am I," Aeron commented.

"Okay, except when I was alone in Hell, I finally saw his face and he admitted to me that he was the betrayer. He confessed that he killed my father and tried to do the same to my..." I trailed off, putting pieces of information together. "My uncle...meaning you," I said to Aeron.

"Yes," Aeron acknowledged. "Theo, Arthur, and I traveled to Stonehenge to extract the first key. We were successful and met no opposition. We then carried on to Giant's Causeway. After collecting the key there, the Sentinel arrived, shooting Arthur in the head. He went down before I even knew what was happening. Theo was a pilot, and he had flown the helicopter we had taken there. We were under fire, but I got Theo back to the helicopter and urged him on to New York where the final key resided.

"I stayed back, refusing to leave my brother, but I was shot, too. Twice. He was going for the third and final shot when I decided to jump off the cliffs into the ocean, abandoning Arthur. I'm sorry for being so blunt, but I refuse to skip over or sugarcoat this part since it shows how serious of a fight we're involved in."

The whole house was quiet.

His story made my chest hurt, my heart breaking into tiny pieces the more he talked. My father hadn't just been killed. He had been brutally murdered.

"Theo made it to New York," Kat continued, detecting how hard it was for Aeron to finish. "He went to the Empire State Building and unlocked the last key. As he was returning to the helicopter, the Sentinel arrived and killed him, too."

First my father and then my maternal uncle. I'd had no idea.

"Theo's death triggered me into action," Kat said. "I'm linked to the bloodline, so I can feel them. I called Aziza and Yadira immediately."

"Why weren't you with them to begin with?" I asked. It came out sounding more defensive than I'd intended.

"Because your uncle's skipping parts," Kat admonished. "They never told anyone what they were doing."

"Hence the years of trauma and survivor's guilt," Aeron snapped.

I rubbed a hand over my face. "What happened next?"

"We engaged the Sentinel at the Empire State Building," Aziza said. "He had stolen the keys from Theo, but Yadira managed to reclaim Satan's sphere. We would have gotten the Sentinel, but the police were alerted to our presence and all of us had to flee. The Sentinel got away with two keys."

"I would have preferred to lock the sphere back up," Kat added, "but its location was compromised. So I gave it to Helen."

I was bewildered. "That's how she got it?"

"Yes," Kat said. "After that, funerals were held, and Aeron was found. Evangeline was consumed by grief."

"We all were," Martha admitted.

"I see now why you wanted me here," Satan said.

Michael perked up. "Why?"

"Because there are gaps in your story that I can fill," Satan confessed.

"Please do," Deborah urged. "We'd like to know."

"The Sentinel isn't the only one who works for Lilith. Lucifer does, too. Or did," Satan said. "He's been causing mutiny and changing sides, and not just with me. When you all were trying to stop me—when I posed no threat, might I add—" he glared at everyone around the room "—Lucifer was aware that my sphere had been taken by the Sacrarium, putting me on their trail and"—he winced—"starting my obsession with tracking them. Except I was stuck in Hell so I sent the Six to do much of my bidding."

"Which is why I was chased by them through the subway when I had the sphere in the backpack," I guessed.

"Correct," Satan confirmed.

I turned my attention back to my uncle. "I still don't understand why you think the Sentinel is Cecil Wallace."

Aeron reached into the pocket of his flannel shirt and pulled out a picture. "The son of a bitch had the decency to leave me this. I found it my mailbox." He slid it over to me.

I peered at it. The picture was a group of people. Along the bottom, written in marker, it read *Which one betrayed you?*

"This is the Sacrarium," I said, glancing up. "All of you when you were younger."

"Just about," Aeron stated. "Silas is in there, too."

I looked closer, recognizing my mom and dad, even Sister Helen.

I was able to identify everyone except three men. One of them was Theo, my uncle, and even though I'd never met him, he looked so much like my mom that it was easy to rule him out.

Placing the picture back on the coffee table, I faced it toward Aeron and pointed. "That's him. That's the Sentinel."

His eyes widened. "No, you're wrong."

"I'm not," I assured him. "I've seen him close up. Trust me."

"Jordan, you don't understand," Delphine intervened. "That man, Silas Sharp, is dead. He died of cancer."

"That's impossible. I know it's him!"

"Let me see," Satan demanded.

I slid the photo over to him. He looked at it but didn't pick it up.

"Kid's right. That's the Sentinel," Satan agreed. "I've never seen his face, but I've fought him before. His height and build match perfectly."

"It can't be!" Aeron shouted, rising from the couch.

"Aeron, calm down," Emily soothed.

"No! Not when they're accusing my best friend!" Aeron ran a hand through his hair. "Silas would never do this to me. He would never kill Arthur, and I would have recognized his voice during our encounters. Besides, he's dead and has been for years."

"I'm not so sure," Delphine said.

Aeron raged. "About what? You think he's alive?"

Delphine shrugged. "I can't comment on whether he's dead or alive. But say he is living… I can see why he might turn on you. He was always jealous of you."

"That's bullshit, Delphine, and you know it. You're only saying that because you never liked Silas and were friends with Cecil. That always blinded you from seeing who he truly was," Aeron accused.

Delphine laid a hand on her chest. "You don't know the half of it, Aeron, and the fact that you would even go there is low." She stood and left the living room.

Sophia turned on her father. "What's wrong with you?"

"Sophia, don't make me the bad guy," Aeron said. "You don't know everything."

"*Then tell us everything!*" she screamed. "Go apologize to my aunt and come back together to finish the damn story!"

Aeron's jaw tightened. "Fine." He strode past us.

"You sure?" Satan called. "I like that I'm not the bad guy for once!"

I glared at him.

He smirked. "What? It's hard to be the villain all the time, especially when I'm not that evil compared with others inside and outside this room."

"Is anyone else sensing this Cecil guy and Delphine had a thing?" Dane asked.

Dafne raised her hand. "Me! There's something definitely going on there."

"Stop," I said. "Both of you. She's a holy Sister. That can't happen."

"Doesn't mean it didn't before she took her vows," Dafne pointed out.

"And it doesn't mean it won't since she recently left the order," Peter added.

"Dad!" Naomi chastised. "Now is not the time to be playing matchmaker."

He hunched his shoulders. "Sorry! I personally liked Cecil."

They all quieted down when footsteps could be heard from the hall. Aeron and Delphine were back, although they looked like they hadn't really mended things. Delphine had her arms crossed, and Aeron's jaw was still clenched.

"Where were we?" Aeron asked.

"We were talking about Silas Sharp, and I'd like to stay on that topic before we get to my mother's death." All eyes were on me. "I know it's coming. It's inevitable."

Aeron sighed. "Right. Silas and I are the same age. We went to school together since kindergarten. When we graduated high school, Silas enlisted and eventually became a Marine. I joined with him but got out as soon as I could, while Silas stayed. Eventually I worked my way into the CIA. I can't talk much about my job, but Silas and I crossed paths many times in our lines of work, so we always remained friends.

"Since he was always around, Silas knew my entire family. When I got involved in Sacrarium matters, it was hard to keep things from him. He knew me too well. I encouraged him to join because I trusted him and knew he would be a good candidate, especially when it came to more covert situations.

"He was a Novice, in the process of completing his trial of trust, when he was diagnosed with terminal cancer. It wasn't long after he found out—maybe a couple months—that he died. That's how I know he wasn't the betrayer. He never got far enough within the Sacrarium to even know what we were doing. Whereas Cecil had followed the traditional path and took his oath at the age of twenty and was very much involved in everything." Aeron sank to the couch, his story over.

"And what do you have to say about Cecil?" Sophia asked Delphine.

Now it was her turn to sigh. "Cecil grew up much like we did." Delphine motioned between her and Aeron. "His family knew about

Nephilim, Watchers, Ishim, the Sacrarium. Essentially, he was trained in the old ways, much like we were. The difference was that his family never turned on him the way our mother did to us. And even though the Wallaces were never accepted into the Ten Families, they still remained current in whatever situations were happening, just from afar.

"Cecil wanted more, though, and since he couldn't be part of the Ten Families, he joined the Sacrarium. When you grow up in these circles, it's hard to stand by and watch things happen rather than act. The Sacrarium had no big prejudices as to who you were or where you came from, as long as you were ready to face the initiation path and willing to protect the bloodline."

"You make him sound like a hero," Aeron grumbled.

Delphine rolled her eyes. "You didn't know him like I did. However, I'm the first to admit that Cecil isn't easy to be around. He's stubborn, argumentative, and a bit brash." A soft smile played at her lips. Then it vanished, and she grew serious. "But he's not a traitor. Too many criticized him and his family. He wasn't looking to make those rumors reality. He joined the Sacrarium to bring new honor to the Wallace name." Delphine chuckled. "I know it sounds ancient, but it's the truth."

"And what were they accused of again?" Naomi asked.

"The tales say the Wallaces stole power to gain the approval of the Ishim," Delphine said, shaking her head. "But you must realize, if this happened, it was centuries ago." She waved it off. "Like Dafne said, it's a story for another day."

"Where's Cecil now?" Michael asked.

Delphine shrugged. "I'm not sure. We lost touch. He had left the

Sacrarium before we decided to retrieve Satan's keys. He needed to return home and take care of family, and none of us have heard from him since. But I can assure you, he wasn't around when we were making our plans, so I don't know how he could have betrayed us."

"Just because he was an inactive member doesn't erase his Beta status," Aeron defended. "He could have found ways."

"As could Silas," Delphine sparred. "He might have been a Novice, but he was expertly trained in covert arts. There's no telling what means he had to infiltrate and gain information."

"All right, all right," Chamuel said. "Let's not have another feud. You both have made your cases."

"The remaining question," Gabriel said, "is how could either of them have built an acquaintance with Lilith?"

The room was silent as we all thought.

"Well, there might have been a way," Naomi said. "And it's probably Geneloom."

52

JORDAN

Ithaca, New York, Present Day

"Lucifer and the Sentinel aren't the only ones working for Lilith," Naomi elaborated. "When I was at Geneloom, I uncovered a lot of information, mainly that the whole operation was Lilith's brainchild."

"What? You didn't report that," Deborah said, outraged by her daughter's secrecy.

Naomi was offended. "I wasn't keeping it from you."

It was easy to detect the tension between her and her parents. She hadn't told them about her wings and abilities for years. I guessed they were questioning everything now.

"I only discovered this information the morning of the rescue," Naomi explained.

"It's been a few days since the rescue," Deborah said. "You could have mentioned it."

Naomi opened her mouth to protest, but Satan beat her to it. "Oh, get over it, Deborah, and let her speak!"

Now it was Deborah who looked offended.

"Thank…you," Naomi said hesitantly.

"No problem. Continue," Satan urged.

"As I was saying, Lilith created Geneloom, not the Watchers. They took it over once Lilith was captured. Before Lilith partnered with the Watchers, she needed to experiment with her powers. I can't say how many there were, but I found records of patients she specifically recruited to use as tests. All of them had been diagnosed with terminal cancer."

"No." Aeron shook his head. "I refuse to believe it's him."

"Then you're ignoring facts," Uriel said.

"Why use cancer patients?" Dafne asked.

Naomi shrugged. "I can't say concretely, only guess that she used them because they were near death and she wanted to see if she could revive them."

"Was she successful?" Martha asked.

"Yes," Michael answered. "I've had to fight the Sentinel. We all have," he amended, glancing at his brothers. "He's impossible to defeat. Inhuman. Definitely altered unnaturally in some way."

"Actually, I'd like to somewhat disagree," Naomi said. "From what I saw, she wasn't successful in reviving them with her powers. She needed more patients to truly get the results she wanted. When she finally found more, she had one that survived. They're unnamed, though, so I have no idea if it's Silas Sharp, but there are a lot of similarities. And you're right that the Sentinel is unnatural because whatever magic she used was dark."

"So she has the Sentinel and Lucifer. Now what?" Dane asked.

"She kept assembling her group of allies, which consisted of the Sentinel, Lucifer, and the Watchers. There were more than just Jazema and Penelope. They were just the only ones who either survived or were brave enough to take over Lilith's operation."

"Was Lilith's vision of Geneloom the same as Jazema's?" Gabriel asked.

"Not exactly," Naomi said. "Lilith never wanted to make Geneloom as public as it is today. It was supposed to remain a secret operation. The intents were similar. Lilith wanted to make hybrid celestial beings, but not Nephilim. She wanted to mix DNA and create beings that were more powerful than anything that had ever existed. Her purpose was to essentially create enough of these hybrids to take over the world, much like the Watchers want, except it wouldn't be a Nephilim nation. It would be an apocalyptic awakening."

"And this information was just lying around in files?" Satan asked, disbelieving.

Naomi shook her head. "No. It was classified information, locked deep inside the lab."

"You mentioned borrowed magic," Delphine said. "What do you mean by that?"

"Her blood mage powers aren't natural," Naomi said. "They're stolen from actual blood mages. She did that so she could create her hybrid beings. I believe the Sentinel was her first successful experiment with her new magic. But he was just a test, not celestial in any way, so she kept going." She stopped briefly, seeming to summon more courage from deep within. "The next step was her hybrids. Supernals, she deemed them."

"Wait, that's what you are," Dafne said.

Naomi nodded. "Yes. I don't know who my biological parents are, but I was indeed one of Lilith's creations. I went to Geneloom hoping I would discover information about what I was, and I got more than I bargained for. Anyway, I was one of four before she attempted her final creation." Her eyes landed on Dane.

He grimaced. "Me? And what does she want me to do exactly?"

Naomi shrugged. "It's hard to say, but it seemed like you were supposed to lead the awakening."

Dane's eyes widened. "You mean start an apocalypse?"

"It makes sense," Zadkiel interjected, speaking more aloud to himself then to the room. "Lilith created an anti-Christ figure, giving you godlike powers. The mixture of blood magic and Hellfire doesn't just allow you to control or kill." Zadkiel seemed to return to the room and stared at Dane. "I bet you can create, as well."

"Create what?" Dane asked, an edge of hysteria in his voice.

"Life," Zadkiel said. "With nothing more than a snap of a finger."

Dane was silent, fear and insecurity lurking beneath his eyes.

"All right," Satan said. "No need to scare him. What you're saying is purely speculation."

"It is," Zadkiel confirmed.

Dane sighed in relief.

"But I believe it's a strong speculation," Zadkiel continued.

Dane's shoulders sagged.

"Why?" Chamuel asked him.

"Because Lilith obviously doesn't have the ability to do it herself. She tried and failed. And stealing magic isn't the same as possessing it. Sure, her newfound abilities gave her enough power to create hybrids, but I'm sure there was a price to pay. Lilith needs Dane to start her awakening since he truly possesses the magic she requires. She essentially equipped him with powers that can match those of her true enemy."

"Which is?" Emily asked.

"Father," the angels said at the same time Satan pointed upward and said, "Him."

"Great," Dane said. "I was brought to this world to destroy it."

"That won't happen," Sophia assured him. "You're meant for more than that."

"She's right," Raphael said.

"Damn straight she's right!" Satan concurred. "You might have power running through your veins, but it doesn't control you. You control it. Remember that."

"Okay, Papa, settle down now so they can continue the story," Uriel taunted.

Satan stood, ready to fight. Uriel rose, too, equally prepared to spar with the Devil.

Before either of them could do anything, I said, "Uriel, don't be mean. Satan's advice is actually helpful."

The two of them eyed each other. Then Uriel sat down. "Fine."

Satan sank into his seat.

"Getting back on track," Chamuel said, "it's safe to say Silas is the Sentinel, correct?"

"I'm afraid so," Michael said. He focused on Aeron. "The evidence so far points in his direction, not Cecil's."

"I know you all think Silas is the Sentinel, but I won't believe it until I see him with my own eyes," Aeron stated.

"Moving on, then," Deborah intervened. "I think it's time for Emily to share a little."

Sophia fidgeted in her chair.

Emily nodded. "About a month after the funerals and Aeron was found, Sophia was born." She beamed. "It was the happiest day of my life, even though there was so much sadness and grief around us. It was a long journey, though, getting to that point of holding her in my arms." She took a deep breath. "Aeron and I got married, and we tried having a child for five years but nothing we did was working. It put a lot of strain on our relationship."

Aeron was squirming in his seat, obviously uncomfortable having everyone hear this.

"For those five years, we had been doing IVF with Geneloom. I had no idea that Jazema and Penelope were frauds, or that the company itself was a front. If I had known, I never would have gone there. I was tricked, just like everyone else, except Penelope took her deceit one step further when it came to me.

"After all those years of failed IVF attempts, it was time for me to realize that if I really wanted a child, I would need an egg donor. So Geneloom provided options, and I chose one. I never told Aeron. By this point, we were estranged, and this was something I wanted more than he did. Except it wasn't until I was about six months along that Penelope cornered me and told me the truth. That she didn't respect my wishes and didn't use the egg donor I had chosen. She used herself instead." Emily met Sophia's eyes. "She threatened to take you away as soon as you were born. I didn't know what to do or where to go to, so I confided in Helen and she became my rock…the mother I never had myself since my own had died when I was very young. She stepped in and made sure I was protected, cutting any remaining ties I had to Geneloom altogether, even seeking legal action on my behalf." Emily motioned toward Deborah.

"Oh, I was ready to fight them, too, but they agreed to a settlement," Deborah acknowledged.

"You have to understand," Emily said. "None of us knew Jazema and Penelope were Watchers or that they were creating Nephilim. We only had the facts in front of us, and Penelope interfering the way she did was enough to settle our legal dispute. So by the time you were born, I was able to rest easy, thinking Geneloom and Penelope posed no threat. I named you Sophia after my mother and wanted your middle name to be Helene since Helen had essentially saved us both." Emily turned to Aeron. "Would you like to share your side of the story?"

Aeron sighed. "I'll admit I had been distant, initially because of my job." He looked at Sophia. "But don't think I never wanted you. At the time, after so many years of trying, I was ready to give up. Then Silas got sick and died—at least I thought he had—and once that happened, I completely checked out, which is why Emily went along with the egg donor without telling me. She never gave up even though I had.

"When I learned it had worked, I was ecstatic, and there was a period of time where everything seemed normal and we seemed on the right path of moving forward. But that was right around the time when Lilith started attacking Evangeline and Arthur was ready to confront her. So I started growing distant again, trying to help them as best I could. Delphine, Deborah, and Helen were all involved, yet they managed to help Emily at the same time, too, whereas I hadn't."

"You can't blame yourself for that," Emily said. "I didn't want you to know, and I made sure none of them told you what was happening with Penelope. You already had enough on your plate, and you didn't need more. In a way, we were both at fault for our lack of communication and not relying on each other."

"You're right, but I still feel bad about it," Aeron confessed. "And then, of course, everything went wrong. I was injured, and there was more death on my hands, not to mention tons of survivor's guilt. I fell into a deep depression that not even your birth could pull me out of. I was hell-bent on revenge, on finding the man who had killed two of my brothers, since Theo and I had been just as close as me and Arthur. Then, that picture—" he pointed to the one still resting on the coffee table "—showed up in our mailbox, and I knew we were in danger because the enemy was a friend not a foe. So I made sure Emily moved and took Sophia, and I officially pulled away, leaving them together.

"There were several reasons I left: I was no use to either of them, they didn't deserve the man I had become, and I knew this enemy was after me, not them. I was the one that got away, and that picture was a clear sign the Sentinel wasn't going to stop until I was in a grave. I tried investigating the whole incident at work, but they never let me on the case because I was too close to it. I still accessed all their files anyway and knew they were getting nowhere. It was inevitable that they were going to close the case, but then Evangeline passed and her death was suspicious, too."

"How was it suspicious?" I asked. "She died giving birth to me."

Delphine shook her head. "That's not completely true. We told you that to make things easier."

"You mean so I wouldn't ask questions," I said, angry.

"That's exactly why we did it," Delphine acknowledged. "It's why we did everything, and I'm sure I'm one among many who regret it. But we thought these secrets would protect you. Instead, it made an elaborate web of lies that got more and more tangled as you grew up. All of you."

Sophia and Dane nodded.

"Well I want to know how my mother really died," I said adamantly.

"This is where I jump in," Deborah said. "After the funerals for Arthur and Theo, everyone was cast into grief, and while Aeron tried to find the man behind the murders, Evangeline locked herself away in this house, completely scared and heartbroken. She was pregnant and worried that whoever had come for Arthur and Theo would come for her, too. Evangeline admitted that she believed Lilith was behind the attack and that she merely had someone doing her dirty work for her.

"Helen, Martha, Peter, and I took turns watching over Evangeline. She only left the house to go to her grief group meetings. Her doctor suggested them, and they seemed to help. Evangeline had made a friend in the group, another pregnant woman named Tamar. She had no family or close friends and had just left a tough relationship. I only mention her because this woman was Naomi's mother."

"What? You know my biological mother?" Naomi asked.

Deborah shook her head. "I didn't. Evangeline did."

"Unfortunately, neither of us had a chance to meet her," Peter added.

"You were born in February," Deborah told Naomi. "Evangeline insisted she had to be there, even though she was nearly nine months along herself. I took her to the hospital and had dropped her off so I could park the car. When I met her inside, she was white as a ghost. She told me Tamar had died, and she swore Lilith was behind it, that she had poisoned Tamar. I wasn't sure what she was talking about. All I knew was that Tamar had died, and I figured her death had thrown Evangeline into a setback.

"They brought you out to Evangeline, and it was then I found out that Tamar had asked her to take you if something bad happened. Almost as if she had known it might. Evangeline was in shock from Tamar's death, so I took you and held you in my arms and I couldn't let go. I fell in love the moment I saw you. You were discharged, and I brought you home. I did my best to explain everything to Peter, and he couldn't say no, either. So we treated you like our own, and your sisters were overjoyed to have another girl in the house. The whole incident was strange, especially the way Evangeline was acting, but we all wrote it off since she hadn't been the same since Arthur and Theo died.

"Helen had returned from a trip and questioned Evangeline about what had happened, and she stuck to her story: that Lilith was the one Tamar was running away from and that you had to be protected. It didn't make sense, it never did—until now when you tell me that you're a Supernal, a creation of Lilith's. No wonder she wanted you. But thankfully, she never got you."

"So Tamar most likely wasn't my biological mom," Naomi said.

"Why do you think that?" Peter asked.

"Because I'm not part-celestial like a Nephilim. I'm all celestial," Naomi explained. "Both of my parents are angels. That's what makes Supernals different. Tamar must have been a surrogate since angels can't have children."

"And then?" Dafne urged, eager to know more.

"And then March came," Kat picked up. "As did Jordan. You and your mother were both healthy, and might I say *happy* since Evangeline now had a bright light shining in her life." She paused and took a deep breath. "You had three months together...until Lilith started mentally attacking Evangeline again. She refused to let it consume her life, so she demanded a confrontation. Lilith agreed, always up for a challenge. Except it was more like a trap. It was June thirtieth in the late hours of the night."

"Oh no," Dane said.

"What?" Satan asked.

"I was born July first, and I have an ominous feeling this is leading to me somehow," he answered.

Kat nodded. "You're right. Evangeline met Lilith in the designated spot, a place in Central Park. When Evangeline arrived, she was expecting a fight. Instead, Lilith was in labor and needed help. All her so-called allies had abandoned her, and she had nowhere else to turn. She couldn't go to a hospital. There would have been too much paperwork. Evangeline thought of leaving her to let her suffer and potentially let her child die. Two lives—that of hers and her child's—for the two lives she had stolen from Evangeline—her husband's and brother's. But there wasn't a malevolent bone in her body.

"Lilith's call for help rang louder for Evangeline than any warning. So she helped her, and for once, Lilith was telling the truth. She was desperate and weak, and knew the good in Evangeline would outweigh anything she had ever done. Lilith also confessed that she believed her child might be born with Hellfire and knew Evangeline was immune to its heat with holy blood running through her veins. And that's how Dane was born.

"Evangeline wrapped him in a blanket that Lilith had brought and handed him to his mother so she could hold him without facing the burn of Hellfire. As soon as Dane was in her arms, Lilith struck like the snake she truly is, burying a dagger deep in Evangeline's stomach. The Sentinel stepped out from the shadows, and Lilith gave him Dane, bidding him to bring Dane to Purgatory. He insisted on taking her, too, but she was too weak and was sacrificing herself to buy them time since she knew I would arrive.

"I was alerted yet again that the bloodline was in danger, and when I arrived, I was too late. Evangeline had told no one of her plans, and Lilith was still there when I showed up. She had stayed and watched Evangeline bleed out. I hated that Lilith put up no fight, but I wasn't about to let her go free. She had caused too much death, pain, and hardship. And now she had taken Evangeline.

"I captured her in the fourteenth sphere, right there on the spot. Then I pressed my hand to Evangeline's forehead and witnessed everything that had occurred before I had arrived, which is how I know to tell this story." Kat shrugged. "It was a trait I was created with, much like Gabriel.

"After I knew what had happened, Helen suddenly showed up, distraught and holding a note in her hand. When she saw Evangeline, she sank to the ground and cried. I pried the paper from her grasp and read Evangeline's last words. She had known why Lilith needed her as she had come to Evangeline in her dreams. She also knew there was a chance she wouldn't return, which is why she left the note. She wanted to make sure we followed her wishes.

"And they were as follows: Delphine would be Jordan's guardian.

He would live at the orphanage in both her and Helen's care. The house was left to Martha until Jordan was old enough to do with it as he pleased. Satan's sphere was already in Helen's possession, but she informed us she had gone back and locked *The Book of Prophecies* inside the backpack, as well, because it couldn't be left unguarded at the house. Her most urgent demand was that by no means could Lilith's child fall into the wrong hands. He had to be taken to the orphanage and raised there, too.

"Evangeline didn't have visions like Arthur, but she was a powerful prophet in her own right and knew the three of you—Jordan, Dane, and Sophia—were special. So special that enemies would come knocking. Her main goal in life was to neutralize anyone who might cause you harm, and she was never able to complete it. So she gave Delphine a task to create a tapestry and bind the three of you as a way to keep you from your legacies, subsequently keeping you from harm's way. She had planted the daggers at the trees herself, knowing there had to be a way to undo the binding but hoping it never came to that. You cannot create something and have nothing to balance it out. That's what she said. Do you still have the daggers?"

"Yes," I said, looking over at Sophia and Dane. They nodded.

"Good. We'll need them to retrieve the scepter pieces," Kat revealed.

"My mom had the daggers?" I asked.

"Yes, they were passed on to the Sinclairs much as the book was given to the Conways," Kat said.

"Who separated the scepter?" Zadkiel asked.

"We did," Michael answered, his focus on Kat.

Everyone was surprised.

"What? You decide to tell us this now?" Gabriel demanded.

"I didn't know," Michael confessed. "Someone stole my memories." The words were an accusation thrown at Kat, but she didn't take the bait.

"Returning to the story," she continued, "I quickly realized that one of Evangeline's wishes had not been fulfilled. Dane had been taken by the Sentinel. In that moment, I knew I had to rescue him, but I also knew the fourteenth sphere had to be hidden before I traversed the depths of Hell. So I called upon Sandalphon to meet me there since he was close and could get there before me. I left Helen to attend to Evangeline and flew straightaway to the only place that is nearly uninhabited—Antarctica. Once the sphere was hidden, I went to assist Sandalphon.

"Sandalphon had arrived just in time, before the Sentinel could cross over to Purgatory with Dane. Lucifer had held him up, trying to take Dane himself. At this point, Lucifer had turned on Lilith and was fully allied with Jazema. Lucifer's interest in Dane had nothing to do with protecting him. If anything, it was to deliver him to Jazema for testing, or even worse, potentially ending his life before it started since Lucifer knew Dane was Satan's child, a potential threat to his rank.

"I joined the battle and commanded Sandalphon to secure Dane and bring him to Helen immediately. Lucifer and the Sentinel were too focused on slaying each other that their interest in Dane dwindled, allowing Sandalphon to complete his task quickly. He left as soon as he had him. I faced off with the other two, but the Sentinel took the first opportunity he could and fled into the rivers, essentially escaping to Purgatory. I was fighting Lucifer, and the rivers distracted me, giving him the chance to use his weapon and slam it into my wing, shattering the bones.

"He called reinforcements, other fallen angels and demons, and

I was swiftly overcome. I knew there was no way out for me, but I felt good knowing Dane was safe. Lucifer brought me to Satan. He questioned me for many years. I refused to talk so he stopped trying and kept me as his prisoner. My wing healed, but it hasn't been the same since. I can't use it anymore. I was down there for two decades until Jordan came and saved me."

It was hard not to look at the Devil sitting next to me with some animosity.

"All right," Satan said. "Everyone back down. I can feel your hatred like an inferno."

"You're lucky I practice forgiveness," Aziza said. "Otherwise, you wouldn't be sitting here right now."

"Are you threatening me, Aziza?" Satan asked. "Your words of peace are hidden beneath a veil of fury."

"Don't play games with me, Satan," Aziza warned. "Your foolish behavior and wisecracks add nothing to the conversation."

"They don't," Satan admitted. "Other than a little humor. Such heavy topics require a bit of lightheartedness."

"Cool it, you two," Kat said.

"I have a question," Dane interrupted. "Who named me? Obviously not Lilith because she calls me Darcel."

Delphine nodded. "Sandalphon deposited you at the orphanage. When Helen and I found you, you had a piece of paper tucked in your blanket. It had the name Daniel Samael Cross written on it. Knowing your lineage, we told you your name was Daniel Cross, and you were the one who shortened it to Dane. So I surmise Sandalphon was the one who named you."

"Really?" Dane pondered aloud. "That's interesting."

"Is there more?" Dafne asked.

"There is," Aeron said. "Evangeline's death kept the investigation going, but only for a short while. There were no leads so they closed the case, but it didn't stop me. I became brazen—obsessed, really—to the point where it got me fired. It was a dark time for me. Delphine, Helen, and even Emily tried to pull me out, tried to involve me in the kids' lives. It didn't work. If anything, I only grew more enraged when I learned they had been bound. I was rash and cut the tapestry apart, hiding a piece in this house and locking it away in the hopes only Jordan would find it one day."

"Aeron's actions didn't break the binding, but it made it unsteady," Delphine said. "When Sophia was five, her wings appeared for the first time, and when Jordan was six, he had his first vision. In Sophia's case, everything went horribly wrong before it went right. In Jordan's case, luckily I was there to pull him out. Helen gave Jordan his mother's necklace to protect him after that. Dane had no apparent problems."

Delphine fell quiet and looked to Emily.

Sophia's mother sighed. "This is the story I hate to tell." She mustered up the courage and forged ahead into the tale. "It was my birthday. Sophia and I had a wonderful day."

Glancing over, I saw Sophia brush a tear from her eye and pull her knees to her chest.

"We returned home after a long day out. My boyfriend at the time was coming over with his mom to celebrate. About a week prior, Sophia's wings had come out and he had been there, but he swore he wouldn't tell a soul. I believed him because I trusted him. When they showed up, something was off. I had never met his mom prior, and the way they acted toward one another wasn't friendly, let alone a mother-son relationship. It was then that I realized I shouldn't have trusted him. The woman pulled out a gun and leveled it at me. I imagined their plan was to kill me and take Sophia.

"But the woman turned and shot Preston instead. The shock was plastered across his face, even in death. As soon as the gun was away from me, I didn't wait to see what happened next. I ran from the kitchen and scooped you up. I took you to the library, thinking a public place was the best idea until I could regroup and find help. I was watching you pick out books when I decided to pull out my phone to call Helen, except my phone wasn't in my purse. Before I could move to find a phone, a woman passed by me and puffed something in my face. I felt I was about to fall to the ground, but someone caught me, entwining our arms and leading me out. I couldn't fight or struggle. I could barely remain conscious.

"I was brought outside and shoved into a taxi. At some point, I lost consciousness. When I woke again, I was in an alley with Preston's body, the gun lying beside me. Whoever was behind this, they were trying to frame me. I rose to flee, but cop cars pulled up before I could. I surrendered, thinking it was better to cooperate than not. I was pressed against the car and handcuffed.

"That's when I saw her in the distance—Penelope. Watching. Smiling at her victory. I wondered how long she had been watching, not just in that moment but in the years since Sophia was born. I had thought I didn't need to worry about her, but all I had done was become complacent, letting her pick up our routine, the people we let into our lives. And then she struck, manipulating even those I thought I could trust."

Emily's eyes were downcast, a clear sign of sadness and defeat. Then she suddenly looked up and gazed at Sophia. "I never meant to leave you!" she sobbed. "I never meant for her to take you!" She took a deep breath. "I know you think I abandoned you." She shook her head. "But I would never do that. You were the one and only thing I wanted in my entire life. Once I was arrested, there was too much evidence against me. There was no way I could save you myself. So I made sure someone else did." She turned to Aeron. "I used my only phone call to reach out to Aeron. He came straightaway. Did his best to persuade them to release me, but there was no way out for me. Instead, he promised to find you.

"It took a few months, but eventually you were found. Helen came to tell me to put my mind at ease. She assured me that you were safe in her care, reunited with Jordan, although the two of you could never know you were related because of the binding. Helen also told me you were given a similar token to wear to reinforce the binding spell and hide your wings. I believe it was Aeron's St. Michael medallion. I asked her why Aeron hadn't taken you himself, and Helen told me he had some issues to deal with, that you were safer with her and Delphine. I didn't push the issue. I was just happy you were protected.

"I wanted so bad for Helen to bring you to see me, but she told me how much the trauma was affecting you and I didn't want to make it worse. A suitable substitute was for her to write me letters with updates about you. I would always write back."

That's how I had known the name Emily. It was the correspondence Michael had found in the Geneloom files "Allen Clark" had given him. Sure enough, I remembered the subject of the letter was about

Sophia. At the time, it had scared me, but now it seemed so innocent.

"Helen would sometimes visit me, too, when she could," Emily said. "It was a hard experience being in prison, but the thought of you was what got me through."

Emily and Sophia locked eyes. Sophia stood and crossed the distance between them, enveloping her mother in a hug. The two cried in each other's arms, finally able to make amends.

Their reunion was touching, affecting almost everyone in the room. The angels, Naomi, and I had wide grins on our faces, happy for Sophia. Delphine, Martha, Dafne, Deborah, and Peter all were wiping tears from their faces. Dane smiled softly, the look in his eyes more expressive than his actual face. You could tell how much he loved Sophia and how pleased he was to see her reconnect with her mother.

Satan was the only one with no outward emotion, but he was the Devil after all, so even if he did feel the tenderness of the moment, he clearly wasn't going to show it.

Emily and Sophia pulled apart, wiping their faces.

"When did you get out?" Sophia asked, her voice shaky.

"At the beginning of November. They reduced my sentence for good behavior. I came to find you right away, but Delphine told me you were missing. I was heartbroken, so I did everything I could to help rescue you."

They hugged again.

"It makes sense now why Emily's letters were in the Geneloom files," Gabriel said, looking at Michael.

"It does," he answered. "Penelope must have been intercepting your messages somehow. Which brings me to our last point of contention."

He set his eyes on Aeron. "How exactly did the persona of Allen Clark come to be?"

"I was wondering when we might hash this out," Aeron said.

"Seems like now would be the perfect time, given it's the only mystery left in the story," Michael said.

Aeron nodded. "All right. Let's get this over with."

53 JORDAN

Ithaca, New York, Present Day

"After I had left Emily and Sophia, I started working for myself," Aeron began. "I wasn't an official private investigator, but that's what many people believed I was. I went by the name Allen Clark so no one from my past would recognize me. I needed a fresh start, and the first thing I did was try to find Cecil Wallace. I firmly believed he was the Sentinel, but none of my searches for him came up with anything. So I took a lot of odd jobs, some of them immoral. I wanted so bad to find the Sentinel, and I figured, whoever he was, he would be involved in hidden arenas, ones that involved dirty work. The only way to make your way into those places was to embrace such nefarious ways and earn the trust of those involved.

"Many of my clients didn't ask a lot of questions; they just wanted answers. I did this for years, and made good money doing it, too, but I never found the Sentinel. Actually, all I was doing was chipping away at my integrity. Then Emily called and told me she was in trouble. I went down to the station where they were holding her and did all I could to try to get her released, but they wouldn't budge. Instead, I focused on finding Sophia. Like Emily said, it took me a few months, but I did have two leads: Penelope and Geneloom. Emily knew Penelope had taken you, and she knew the company had to be crooked after what they had done, so I threw myself into researching everything about them.

"I found a few others who had been mistreated by them, too. Their testimonials did nothing but solidify Geneloom's unlawful ways. Eventually, I disguised myself and broke into their main public facility. It was there that I found a schematic of their underground labs. They were relatively undocumented and off-radar since they held their special patients there. Essentially, it was very similar to where Penelope had just taken you recently." He looked at Sophia but continued.

"Immediately, I went to search the facilities for the patients. At first, I thought I might have misread the schematic since there was nothing there. Then I found a concealed door. My initial thought was to call the authorities. It would take too much time for them to show up, though, so I notified Helen and the Sacrarium, knowing they would send reinforcements. But I wasn't going to wait for them. The risk of Penelope finding out and moving Sophia was too high, so I acted.

"I entered the lab and searched every level. For a place full of special patients, it was relatively unguarded. It just goes to show how confident Jazema and Penelope were at the time, thinking no one would be smart enough or brave enough to challenge them and discover their hidden secrets. Each level contained about twenty patients. My estimate was that they were all underage. Some looked like teens, but it was hard to tell their actual ages. I realize now they were all Nephilim.

"I desperately wanted to release each of them, but I still hadn't found Sophia, and I knew if I started setting patients free, Penelope would be alerted to my presence." He turned to Sophia again. "I needed you in my care before I did anything too rash. Finally, I found you. The room you were in was like all the others, except you shared it with another girl. She looked about your age."

"Really?" Sophia interrupted. "Was she blond like me?"

"No," Aeron said. "She was Asian and had black hair."

Sophia frowned. "Oh...that must have been Moriko. Jazema mentioned her, but I don't remember."

Emily patted her hand. "It's understandable. The trauma could still be blocking your memories, if you still even have them."

"You seem like you have some professional training in how the mind works," Zadkiel said to Emily.

She nodded. "I do. I'm a psychologist. Or I was until I was convicted of a murder I didn't commit." Her eyes were downcast. "Anyway, Aeron should finish his story."

"I'm almost done," he assured us. "When I found Sophia, I knew I had to take the girl with us, too. You two were inseparable, and besides, it would have been unfair taking one and leaving the other, especially when I had every intention of setting everyone free. So I got you both out of there. As we exited the building, I met no guards yet again. This time, though, a warning bell went off in my head. I rushed to the exterior door and ran into none other than the Sentinel himself. We each shocked the other with our presence, both of us freezing for a brief moment until I set you two down and told you to run outside.

"You listened while I engaged the Sentinel in a fight. When I had first met him, he wore a fedora hat and face mask to hide his identity. Now he had donned the unmistakable hood we all know him to wear. The only two similarities from our first encounter were the gold-plated gun and the double helix ring. During our fight, he never pulled his gun on me. I guessed he wanted to hurt me more than a simple gunshot would. And trust me when I say he beat me so badly I could hardly move.

"Whoever the man was, he had changed, growing so strong it seemed inhuman. I stood no chance and accepted that fate, knowing I had saved you. I figured he would leave me for dead again, but he didn't. I remembered he stumbled on his feet, holding a hand to his head. Once he righted himself, he looked at me as if a fog had lifted, a new sense of clarity in his eyes. Then he dragged me outside. He was about to pull off his hood when he faltered again, suddenly becoming the treacherous killer once more. Before he did anything to me, he pulled out a detonator and pressed it. The lab exploded behind him. I let out a horrific scream, knowing there were still so many children inside.

"He kicked me across the face, ready to pummel me again, but he was deterred by a buzzing phone. He answered it. The person on the other end was panicked. You could hear the shrillness in their voice. Then the Sentinel said, 'I know you're upset, Jazema. You have every right to be, but I'm looking at the culprit right now. It's Conway. He came searching for his daughter.' There was a brief pause, and then he finished by saying, 'I'll finish him and then check to see if there are any survivors.' The bastard had blamed what he had done on me. At the time, I figured he was just covering his tracks, but now I understand.

"He had always been working for Lilith, even when he'd sworn allegiance to Jazema. He sabotaged her and her work any chance he could get, and covered it up in a believable way that allowed her to still trust him. I came to learn this wasn't the first time, and it wouldn't be the last. Anyway, he was going to kill me, but the Sacrarium arrived. He was outnumbered, and his head seemed to start aching again, so he jumped on his motorbike and fled.

"Helen rushed over to me to make sure I was all right, but I insisted they search the area for Sophia and the other girl. I also begged them to see if there were any survivors inside. She assured me they would take care of it. Fortunately, they found Sophia and her friend. Unfortunately, everyone inside had perished either in the explosion or beforehand at the hands of the Sentinel himself, which explained why there had been no guards. Afterward, Helen brought Sophia to the orphanage. She thought the best thing for you was to hide your wings, so I gave her my St. Michael medallion to use as a protective ward. She told me she would take care of it. It's hard to say how, but I imagine she might have asked Sandalphon, too, if he did Jordan's.

He swallowed and met Sophia's gaze. "I thought you were finally settled, but then the lawyers on Emily's case tried to get you to be a witness. Helen and I protested fiercely, but you said you wanted to. Except they tried to discount everything you said, and it made the situation worse, so we pulled you from the trial."

"And the other girl? What happened to her?" Sophia asked.

"I'm not sure," Aeron confessed. "Helen promised she would take care of that, too. If she wasn't at the orphanage with you, I guess Helen sent her somewhere else."

I couldn't recall a girl who fit the description, or one that Sophia had been close to.

"Why would she do that?" Sophia demanded.

"She did it," Delphine said, "because she wanted you to heal. You all seem to forget that I ran that orphanage alongside Helen. She had to make so many difficult choices, and I was her sounding board for most of them. It crushed us both to separate you two, but it was for the best. You both needed to forget."

Emily disagreed. "Forcing them to forget is worse. They need to acknowledge what happened. That's the only way they can heal."

Delphine sighed. "What's done is done. It might not have been right, but we can't go back and undo it."

Sophia shook her head. "Fine. You're right that we can't change the past, but it doesn't mean I have to forgive you for what you did." She looked at her father. "And why didn't you stay around?"

"I didn't stay because once Jazema thought I blew up her lab and subsequently got away, she wouldn't let it go," Aeron explained. "Staying would have put you in danger. She didn't know where we had taken you. She knew nothing about Holy Trinity, and it had to remain that way. Besides, I pretty much was on the run. I couldn't settle down anywhere for lengthy periods. I couldn't make connections with anyone. I destroyed my phone and anything that linked me to my life as Aeron Conway. I fully became Allen Clark.

"For a while, I played into their game of cat and mouse, letting them chase me everywhere. But once I realized the Sentinel was trying to destroy Geneloom and was blaming all his vile acts on me, I couldn't stand to be his prey anymore. I decided to fight back. I lay low for months, letting them think I was gone. I changed my appearance—dyed my hair, grew a beard—and went undercover. I was hired at Geneloom as one of their lab technicians. They had no idea Allen Clark was Aeron Conway. They essentially let me walk right in their front door. While I was there, I dug into their files and amassed all that I could. Until one day, when the Sentinel discovered me."

"I was at the lab in São Paulo when it happened, so I fled with the files. Miraculously, I stumbled upon a private investigator's office, and that's how I met you." Aeron pointed at Michael. "I told you what I knew, gave you everything I had, and left. The Sentinel started chasing me again. We had another encounter, which we both walked away from, except this time there were no blips in his behavior. Whatever had been going on with his head and his judgment must have been addressed because it hasn't happened again in the times I've seen him since." Aeron sighed and ran a hand through his hair. "If the Sentinel is Silas, those blips make a little more sense. It shows that he hesitated or rescued me because he was my friend and had some remorse or relapse. But it also demonstrates that the Silas I knew slowly lost himself to the dark because he has no qualms about what he's doing anymore.

"And while he has never confessed his identity to me, the Sentinel did tell me I had fallen into their elaborate trap. I should have known they were playing me. I was so confident, though, I detected no suspicion. Looking back, it makes sense now."

"What does?" Michael asked.

Aeron crossed his arms. "I had worked at Geneloom for about a year, floating from lab to lab without any encounter with the Sentinel, and then one day he magically appeared. They let me in their doors. They planted information for me to take. Here I thought I was doing something brilliant, while all I was doing was feeding into their schemes."

"I anonymously sent the files to the authorities like you'd asked, but they either disappeared or wouldn't take it seriously," Michael explained. "And I tried a few times."

"Makes sense since all of it was a hoax," Aeron said. "Giant Heart Healing Center doesn't exist. It was something Jazema made up because she knew I would latch on to it as a way to convict them, as a way to get me to come out of hiding and into the public eye where she could catch me."

"But there was evidence in there about Geneloom's secret experiments, which is true. And you told me there was some kind of lab accident that resulted in the death of a doctor," Michael said.

Aeron shrugged. "I can't say now if the death of the doctor was fact or fiction. They could have made up people, given them names. What was true was the information about Geneloom's secret experiments, but it was buried in so much untruth and speculation that the authorities probably thought it the rantings of some irate person, which is why they never took it seriously and never investigated them. I'm sorry I roped you in. I thought I was doing the right thing."

"There's no need to apologize," Michael assured him. "I'm just sorry for all that they've put you through."

"What about Geneloom and Jazema and Penelope now?" Dane asked.

"We seized all their assets," Deborah said. "The Sacrarium has confiscated all their facilities. We're working with trusted authorities to make convictions, and we're attending to the legal matters. Geneloom essentially has been taken down once and for all."

"No, it isn't," Sophia assured her. "Not if Jazema and Penelope are still out there."

"I beg to differ," Deborah challenged. "They might have disappeared, but they have no access to their operation anymore."

Sophia shrugged. "Believe what you will."

"Wait...how exactly are you here now?" Satan asked Aeron suddenly. "You've done all this running, abandoning your daughter in the process, and now you sit here on this couch like you haven't a worry in the world."

Leave it to the Devil to make a bad situation worse.

Aeron leaped from his seat. "How dare you judge me, when you did the same to your son?"

Satan remained seated, straddling his chair. He wagged his finger back and forth. "Not quite the same. You see, I had no idea he existed, whereas you witnessed her birth." He slowly rose to his full height and stepped closer to Aeron. "And as soon as I knew Dane was mine, I saved him from danger and haven't let him out of my sight since."

His words were a warning, and the tension in the room skyrocketed.

"Fine," Aeron said, jaw tight. "You want to know how I'm here? Well, after São Paulo, I had no choice but to admit defeat, so I went to Helen and she secured me in a safehouse and made sure both Aeron Conway and Allen Clark were erased from the world. The only way I'm here is because I'm a ghost. I don't exist. The Sacrarium called upon me when Helen died because when an Alpha perishes all must be notified, but I had to remain in the safehouse for my safety. Deborah made sure of it. I only surfaced because my daughter was in Penelope's clutches yet again, and Deborah knew there was no stopping me from saving her. So she included me in their plans instead of leaving me out of them." He stopped, then threw down his own challenge. "And why exactly are you here? Because you've contributed nothing of worth to this conversation."

Satan smirked. "That's only because you all have gone on and on with these long sob stories, which I'll admit contain some heavy shit, whereas what I have to say is far less dramatic. If you would sit down and let me speak, then we can finish this chat and I'll be on my merry way back to Hell."

They sized each other up.

"Aeron," Emily pleaded.

He conceded and sank down.

Satan clapped his hands together. "All right, so we left off with me sharing how I became obsessed with finding my sphere, thanks to Lucifer planting the idea in my head. However, what I have yet to tell you is that once Lilith was captured, Jazema came to me with a proposition. She would give me technology in exchange for her precious bullets made from the river water in Hell. I was trapped in Hell at the time, subsequently forcing me to send Lucifer in my stead to meet with her. I started sending him for everything after that, thinking I could trust him."

"That's why they hurt us," Zadkiel said. "They're essentially dark matter bullets."

"Yes," Satan said.

"And that's how you got those trackers," Gabriel said.

"Yes, again," Satan confirmed.

"And what trapped you in Hell to begin with?" Uriel asked.

"The bloodline," Satan said, giving me an annoyed look.

"Wrong bloodline," Kat said.

"Excuse me? I think I would know," Satan defended.

"Really?" Kat argued. "I was there for Astrid's divination, too, and your interpretation was severely wrong. But that's only because you didn't have all the facts. It was *your* bloodline that trapped you in Hell, not the holy bloodline. The moment Dane was born, you were stuck down there. And the part of the prophecy about you being bound to *her* didn't mean the *heir* was a girl. The *her* it referenced was Lilith. The real question is how you're here, walking on Earth without an amulet and with your son still living."

Satan sank down to his chair. "Probably because I died, severing my connection to her."

"Wait...did you say died?" Chamuel asked.

"Yes, he did," Aziza confirmed. "Except why aren't you still dead?"

Satan fumed. "You'd like that, wouldn't you, Aziza?"

"She's not the only one," Uriel and Aeron said together.

"Maybe I should just leave, then," Satan said.

"No," Michael commanded. "You will remain and finish."

"Like I listen to you," Satan growled. "Kings take no commands."

"Dad," Dane said.

That got Satan's attention.

"How are you alive?" he asked, a look of knowing in his eye.

Satan crossed his arms. "Your tattoos. They revived me. It must have been a blood magic spell. You did them before you were unbound so you didn't know what you were doing. But they saved me."

"That's how you had your powers right away," Sophia said. "Lilith kept saying you had to use your powers before midnight, that you had to kill, but you had already used them, which is how you still have them."

"Sorry to backtrack," Naomi said, "but what happened to your keys? I know the Sacrarium has the sphere, but what happened to the ones the Sentinel stole?"

"Well, I retrieved them over the summer, which makes me think they somehow got returned. I'm not sure by who, though," Satan said.

"You have your keys?" Raphael asked.

"I had two of them, but then Jazema took them, and then Lilith stole them, and then Dane recovered them, ultimately giving them back to me. So the long answer is yes," Satan said. He stopped and stared at the cuff of his sleeve. "I have more than that, though. Lilith had five sets of keys in her possession, which Dane gave to me."

"You did what?" Zadkiel asked.

"I gave them to him because the only way we'll win this is if we trust one another," Dane explained. "Lilith is nearly unstoppable. We need every asset we can get. Besides, you'll have seven sets when we finish collecting your keys, and you have my dad's sphere, so technically, you'll have the advantage when it comes to the prophecy."

"Speaking of seven," Satan said, "we need to finish this conversation outside."

"Why?" Michael asked.

Satan didn't answer. He just stood and left the room.

Everyone was surprised. The angels were the first to react, rising and following. The rest of us humans had to bundle ourselves in coats—some of us even needed shoes—before we could rush outside.

We found them all gathered in the dormant garden in the backyard. I noticed Satan had some sort of sack on his back that he hadn't had in the house. He must have stashed it outside before entering.

"We're all here now," Aziza said. "Talk."

"I think you all need to speak first and share how Jophiel perished," Satan urged.

"He's right. They deserve to know," Michael agreed, then dove right in. "We were called back to Heaven by Seraphiel, the Head Seraphim." He looked at me, then Sophia, then Dane. "Which is why you three were captured and we were unable to help. Lilith was about to attack Heaven, and Seraphiel wanted us to protect the five sets of keys that were there at the time. We did as she asked, except we had never faced Lilith's power before and when she attacked, we were drastically overwhelmed.

"There was a moment where she was distracted, though, and Jophiel tried to take the chest of keys and run, but she struck him down before any of us could act. Except when she struck him down, we realized the whole situation was a trap. There were no keys; the chest was empty. Lilith had already taken them. She had turned Seraphiel to her side and essentially derailed us on purpose. No matter what her ruse was, though, we lost our brother in the fight."

"But you didn't," Satan said, reaching into his sack and drawing out a sword. He pulled it free and stuck it in the cold, hard ground.

It was a samurai sword. Jophiel's sword.

Everyone was silent as Satan reached into the bag again, lower this time, drawing out two more weapons from each side of the sack.

It was a pair of sai, three-pronged blades that had been Jophiel's preferred weapon.

Satan stuck them in the ground on either side of the sword.

"You might not know this," he said, "because I never did, but when angels perish—either blessed or fallen—their energies don't return to the universe. They go to Purgatory."

Zadkiel dropped to his knees and reached for the sword hilt. He gripped it hard. "That's why she said it."

"Why who said what?" I asked, stepping forward away from the group.

"Why Lilith said she would see him again," Zadkiel explained.

Satan nodded. "And she did see Jophiel again."

The six angels were hooked on his words.

"As did I," Satan continued. "When I came back to life, I was in one of Hell's rivers and it spit me out in Purgatory, where I eventually came to find Lilith's camp. She was holding Dane there, and I went to rescue him, but he had already rescued himself. I was going to leave to find him, but a powerful energy called to me. When I followed it into a tent, I found Jophiel there, tied up and being used as a freaking battery for Lilith's portal devices. I rushed over to free him, but he stopped me. He told me there was no use. Lilith would only find him again because he could never leave that forsaken land. Then he looked me hard in the eye and said there's only one way to help me."

Satan looked down and curled his hands into fists. "Contrary to what many of you believe, I'm not one who kills for pleasure. There needs to be a purpose. And at that, I've never killed one of my brothers or sisters. I incited a war in Heaven, but no blood was on my hands. Until now." He sighed. "Jophiel was the first, but only because he asked me to. There have been a few fallen angels since, but only because they had wanted me dead. And I'm afraid to say there's a chance it could happen again as another war lies ahead.

"I didn't come here to listen to your stories. I came to tell you how our brother died, and I stayed because you all need to hear what he had to say." Satan took a deep breath. "There is a way to stop Lilith. It won't destroy her, but it will impair her magic and make her vulnerable. We need bloodstone, and we need it to penetrate her skin. Jophiel made sure to tell me it couldn't just scratch the surface. It needed to be planted deep, somewhere on her person that she couldn't easily dislodge it. As angels, I think we all know which place is best."

"Center of the back, between the wings," Michael murmured.

The others nodded.

Satan unbuttoned his right cuff and rolled up his sleeve. "He also asked me to finish what he couldn't."

The angels gasped when they saw Satan's wrist. The sign of Libra was branded there.

"I have his ring, too," Satan said, reaching for a chain around his neck. "But I refuse to wear it on my hand because it's not rightfully mine." He showed them the citrine ring.

"What does this mean exactly?" Chamuel asked.

"It means," Satan said, "Jophiel would like me to assist you when you go to collect the spheres. Now, I know Jordan can do it for him, but he granted the responsibility to me, and I would like to fulfill it."

"Why?" Uriel demanded.

"Because he's the balance," I said. "Because we need him. Because united we stand, divided we fall." I dropped to my knees like Zadkiel. "Jophiel wanted it this way."

Dane and Sophia knelt on either side of me. Dafne stood behind me, hands on my shoulders. As one, Satan and his brothers knelt, too.

"For Jophiel," they said in unison.

"For Jophiel," we all repeated.

In a way, it was nice to have this memorial for him. It helped give closure to his death, although his absence would always be felt, especially as we moved forward.

Satan stood. "Call me when you're ready to travel."

Michael rose. "And what will you be doing in the meantime?"

"Preparing an army," Satan said. "We'll need more than just Heaven's."

Michael nodded.

"Take care, Ace," Satan said to Dane. "I'll see you soon."

With that, he launched into the air and disappeared from sight, his regal black wings glistening in the sun.

I looked around at our group. We had some healing to do, and not just physically. There had been too much trauma, too many secrets, for everything to be forgiven and erased overnight. But with time, we would be a force to be reckoned with.

54

LILITH

Purgatory, Present Day

It was time to spill some blood. After the loss I had taken, I needed to feel in control again.

I sharpened my rondel dagger, the point of the blade already piercing.

"Mistress," the Sentinel said.

"Hmm?"

"Your armies have reassembled. We're stronger than we were before. You've got angels on your side now."

"Purgatory angels?" I asked.

"Yes."

I checked the point of the blade against my finger. A small bead of blood rose to the surface. "Excellent."

"There are some new demons, too. A winged one in particular has surfaced from the caves. It's quite large."

Smiling, I said, "It's about time the residents here joined our ranks."

"Our only remaining obstacle is how we move the army. Most cannot traverse to Earth as they are unliving."

"I know. I have plans to fix that." I finally took my attention away from the weapon and faced him. "Is the sacrifice ready?"

"Indeed."

"Good. Once I complete it, be ready for an attack."

"Who are we attacking?"

"Hell. I need to test the powers I receive from the sacrifice. It won't be a large fight." I rose and stroked a finger along his cheek. "I can't wait to share victory with you."

"I'll be waiting," he assured me.

I pulled away.

"There is one more thing," he said.

"What?"

"Lucifer's back. He wishes to see you."

My hands curled into fists, and my fury ignited. "Bring him to me at once."

He motioned for the guards to enter the tent. They carried in Lucifer and deposited him at my feet. I ripped off the hood covering his head and smacked him across the face.

"Ow!" he shouted, hands tied behind his back.

My hand whipped out to seize his throat. "You are brave to come here."

He opened his mouth, but no sound came since my hand quenched his words.

I threw him down to the floor. "Why have you returned?"

"I want to help you," he rasped.

I sneered. "You think I'll trust you again?"

"No, but I'm an asset."

"Oh really? Convince me."

He thought it over. "Fine, I might not bring much to the table, but I can offer a distraction. Satan is obsessed with killing me right now."

"As am I, but continue," I urged.

"So if you plant me in the right place, I can lure Satan away and sever the bond between him and the boy."

"You couldn't kill him before," I stated. "Why should I think you can now?"

"Fine!" Lucifer shouted, dropping to his knees. "I can't offer anything, but I'm begging you to spare me. I'll do whatever you want. I just can't keep hiding anymore."

I pondered his plea. I wanted nothing more than to kill him, but I already had a sacrifice. While I could keep him as my prisoner, he was far too tiresome. I supposed he could offer a distraction, especially as the spheres were unlocked, but there had to be more.

"Listen to me," I said. He stared up at me. "I'll send you out to distract Satan and the others, but you must return with a sphere. If you don't, you're as good as dead."

"Of course! Whatever you ask!" Lucifer said.

"Guards! Take him away, bring him to a tent, and don't let him out of your sight."

They obeyed and left with the fallen angel.

"Are you really going to use him?" the Sentinel wondered aloud.

"Probably. I want to play with the angels and Satan as they retrieve their keys, and Lucifer is good at being annoying."

"What about the sphere you asked him to get?"

Laughing, I said, "That was just a threat. We'll see what he can do."

I exited my tent, leaving the Sentinel behind. We had moved our encampment closer to the Core, as I would be offering the sacrifice there, knowing placement and intention meant everything when dealing with dark forces.

Taking to the sky, I flew low through the clouds. Most winged beings didn't fly here, but I had gained enough clout to know how to navigate Purgatory's meticulous ways.

I landed right at the edge of the Core, where the River of Hate tapered off into an impressive waterfall. A group of guards stood waiting, holding a prisoner.

Approaching them, I said, "I can handle it from here, boys."

They stepped away and retreated.

I grasped the hood around the prisoner's head and pulled it free.

Seraphiel squinted against the muted daylight.

"It's a shame," I said. "I had wanted to hold on to you longer. Torture you a bit before eliminating you."

"What changed?" she asked.

"My other sacrifice escaped."

"You tricked me and killed me once already. Wasn't that satisfaction enough? Must I be killed again at your hand."

"Yes. You're the last being of worth I have lying around, and the dark demands a desirable prize."

I strode behind her and took her robes in my hand, lifting both of us into the sky again. I flew to the center of the Core, wind lashing at my wings. I fought against it and eventually settled myself in the air so I was hovering directly over the middle of the abyss.

"Please," Seraphiel begged.

"Your words are wasted on my ears. I'm not merciful like your God," I said.

Ignoring her, I raised my dagger above my head. "I summon thee, O dark forces, to grant me power and passage."

The air stilled around me.

"I call upon thee to give me strength to move my army through the realms."

The waterfall, the lava, the mudslide, and the wind tunnel all ceased flowing into the Core.

"I ask of thee to place your powers in my blade."

A mass rose from the abyss. It was a tall tower of rock upon which was a platform. It came to settle beneath my feet, and I eased my wings down. As soon as my boots touched the platform, the elemental forces commenced yet again.

I kept my dagger above me, but nothing else seemed to be happening.

"Please, O dark forces, I seek your aid."

The elemental forces increased, attacking me from every side with wind, rain, fire, and air. I took it as a sign the dark was willing to comply, so long as I gave it something in return.

Without hesitation, I slit Seraphiel's throat and tipped her over the side.

Blood poured down her white-and-gold robes, and her eyes were wide in shock as she fell into the Core.

I raised the dagger once more, blood soaking the steel, and a rush of power flowed into it, the likes of which knocked me to my knees. Except the dark was unpredictable, and when the dagger was filled, the remaining power flowed into me.

My body tensed and convulsed.

I hadn't anticipated something like this would happen, but I didn't resist.

When the forces finally settled, I fell forward, catching myself with my hands. Around me, there was a creaking noise. Then the bridges turned, a single raised arm from each one coming down to rest along the platform, creating a clear path to cross.

The Core hadn't been connected since the blood mages ruled these lands. I must finally have been powerful enough to spark such a change.

I grinned.

This was only the beginning.

55

Sophia

Ithaca, New York, Present Day

The winter months zoomed by, along with all the holiday festivities. I had more presents to buy than I ever had before, and it had been really nice to feel like I had a big family. It had been wonderful to spend New Year's with Dane also. We hadn't done much other than stay at the house and pass the time in each other's presence. The "no touching" rule was a definite problem, but I didn't want to cut him out of my life.

Besides celebrating, Dane, Jordan, and I had taken the time to relax a little and give ourselves some much-needed rest and healing. We had all gotten past the worst of our injuries and were now in the strengthening phase, as I liked to call it.

"I finally caught up with you," my mom huffed, her breath easily visible in the brisk morning air.

I stopped jogging and slowed to a walk. She joined me, smiling in relief.

"I'd say those Nephilim skills are kicking in. You've gotten faster and faster ever since we started running every morning," she said. "I've barely been able to keep up. But I enjoy the time with you." She shrugged. "And I suppose the exercise is good for me."

I laughed, putting my arm around her and drawing her close in a side hug. More than anything, I was thrilled to have my mom back. Our reconnection hadn't been instant, but I warmed up to her sooner than to my dad when I realized just how much she loved me and everything she had gone through.

My relationship with my dad was still a bit icy. It was hard to forgive him when he willingly walked away from me, unlike my mom. I kept teetering, knowing he had rescued me several times, but if he could only show up for the big moments and not the small ones, then I wasn't sure if I should give him my attention, let alone my love.

Then there was Aunt Delphine. It was weird to think of her as my aunt rather than a Sister, but that's what she was now. I had connected with her before the unbinding when she had taught me to weave and mend the tapestry. I'd felt bonded with her, and then she'd admitted everything she had done, and that bond wasn't stable anymore. I had a feeling I would forgive her before my dad, only because I knew she had good intentions, many of them the same as Sister Helen's, and I don't think I would ever be mad at her for anything she did, so why not extend the courtesy to Delphine?

My mom wrapped her arm around me. "What are you thinking about?"

I sighed. "Forgiveness."

She smoothed my hair back. "It'll come." She pulled away. "Don't you have an important day today?"

"Yes, I learn to fly today," I said, not so enthusiastically.

"Don't do it if you're not ready," she told me.

"I'm ready… I'm just still coming to terms with the whole wing thing. I mean, I'd rather learn how to hide them so we didn't have to run in the woods every morning rather than out on the street in public," I said.

My mom chuckled. "That would be nice. You'll be with Dane, right?"

I smiled. "Yes."

"Good. Then you'll be fine," she assured me.

It was hard not to hide my grin. My mom loved Dane, and she made every effort to show it. My dad, on the other hand, hated him and also made every effort to show it. I thought his animosity was more toward Satan rather than Dane, but he saw them as an extension of each other. As far as I was concerned, it was another reason to distance myself from my dad. If he couldn't accept Dane, then I wouldn't accept him.

"Stop thinking about your father," Mom said.

I stopped walking. "How do you know these things?"

"Well, I'm your mother, but I'm also a psychologist, so it's pretty easy to read your thoughts since you wear them so clearly on your face. Must be a Conway thing since Jordan does it, too."

We entered the house through the front door, heading toward the kitchen for some water.

"I think I do a better job at concealing my thoughts than Jordan does," I argued.

"I would have to agree," Jordan said.

We looked down.

"Sweetheart, what are you doing on the floor?" my mom asked him.

Jordan sat up. "Nothing to worry about, Aunt Emily. Just searching for keys."

"How exactly are you going to find the key to Uncle Arthur's office by staring at the turret?" I asked. He had been exploring the house all winter without luck.

"He's not," Dane said, coming downstairs.

My heart fluttered, and an immediate smile broke across my face. Every time I saw him, I had the same reaction. You'd think I'd have been used to the sight of him by now.

"I'm embracing Martha's tactics," Jordan said.

Dane stood above him and crossed his tattooed arms. "You're avoiding the e-mail you got from Cornell."

"Hey! You promised you wouldn't say anything," Jordan whined.

Dane scoffed. "Yeah, like a week ago. Besides, if you knew how many promises of mine you broke…"

Jordan thought about it. "I guess you're right. But they were all broken with your best interest in mind."

"Just answer the damn e-mail," Dane said. He focused on me. My heart fluttered again. "You ready?"

"As I'll ever be," I sighed. Looking down at Jordan, I asked, "Do I want to know what this e-mail is about?"

"They're just asking about my two-year deferral since it's coming up soon," he said nonchalantly.

"Jordan! You have to e-mail them back!"

"I know! I'm just trying to figure things out," he admitted.

"Like what?" I asked. "Don't you want to go? I made sure Harvard knew I'd be coming back in the fall."

He grew serious. "I know I need to notify them to secure my place. And I will. We can talk about this later, though. Otherwise, you'll be late."

"Fine, but we will talk," I said, stepping over to Dane and striding down the hall together.

"Good luck!" my mom shouted.

We went downstairs and exited the house through the lower doors.

"I know you're genuinely concerned about Jordan," Dane said, "but you were also stalling."

I frowned. "Was it that obvious?"

Dane laughed, the sound sweet to my ears. "Maybe not to him, but I know you better."

I stopped in my tracks and closed my eyes. "I'm nervous."

Dane stepped closer.

I relished in the heat his body emitted.

"It's okay to be nervous," he whispered.

"You're not nervous."

"Not necessarily," he confessed. "When the angels used to pick us up and fly around with us, I hated the experience. So I can't say I'm thrilled to be flying, either. The only comforting thing I keep telling myself is at least I'm in control, considering I don't have control of most things in my life anymore."

I looked up at him. "We'll find out how to control those other things. I promise."

He leaned in close. I met him halfway.

The tension rose between us.

I pulled back. "Okay, we're never going to learn how to fly if we linger here."

He smirked. "That was *my* attempt at stalling."

I grinned and started walking. "Your tactic was much better than mine."

"I would have to agree," he said, following me.

We walked through the woods together until we reached the nearest hill, where Chamuel stood waiting for us.

"There you are!" he said. "I thought you might have decided to bail."

A blush rose to my cheeks. "No, we just got a little distracted."

"Well, you better focus now," Uriel commanded.

I let out a groan. "You're here?"

"What's that supposed to mean?" Uriel asked. "You were happy with my presence when I saved you at the hospital."

"Yes because you're one of the best fighters I know, but when it comes to teaching, you lack a…gentle touch," I said. "And I'm nervous."

"There can't be any nerves involved in flying or you'll crash," Uriel said.

My eyes widened.

"Uh, Uriel, I think that's what she meant by you not having a gentle touch," Dane remarked.

"Sorry not sorry that I'm brutally honest," he said.

"How about we start with some simple warm-ups?" Chamuel suggested.

"Like?" Uriel asked.

"Wing flexes," Chamuel said.

Uriel scrunched his face in confusion. "What in Heaven's name are those?"

"These," Chamuel said, stretching out his wings and drawing them close again.

Dane and I mimicked Chamuel's moves.

"See, a nice warm-up," the angel of the home said after a few minutes. "Now let's analyze our summit."

He stepped closer to the hill's edge. The three of us followed.

I peeked over. I wasn't afraid of heights. I was more scared of falling.

Someone's hand connected with my shoulder and gave me a good shove. I screamed as I went over the hill, too freaked to do anything to save myself. I landed in Chamuel's solid arms before hitting the ground.

He flew us back to the top and gently set me down.

"Are you insane?" he yelled at Uriel.

"Don't worry. The boyfriend over here already chewed me out," Uriel grumbled.

Dane came over and sat down next to me.

"Uriel, just go back to the house!" Chamuel shouted.

"You're kidding, right?" he asked, bewildered. "I'm just trying to teach them like any bird would their young."

"They're not birds!" Chamuel screamed. "They're people!"

"Fine!" Uriel roared in return, taking flight and leaving like a wounded puppy.

Chamuel joined us. "I'm sorry he did that. Maybe we should do this another time."

"No," I gasped out. Placing a hand on my chest, I tried to calm my heart. "I have to face this."

I stood and went over to the hill's edge again. "What were you going to say?"

"I was going to tell you," Chamuel said, "to picture what it would feel like to coast through the air. Imagine your wings undulating and flowing. When you feel ready, make an attempt. I'll be there if you fall or lose control."

Dane was the first to go over. Effortlessly, he soared into the sky, embodying exactly what Chamuel had just told us to visualize. He was graceful and strong in the way he flew. Returning to us, he landed on his feet with a heavy thud.

"Landing could use some practice," Chamuel evaluated, "but overall great job."

Dane smiled. "That was kind of exhilarating!"

"It really is once you get the hang of it," Chamuel agreed.

"I noticed the wind snaps hard at my wings," Dane commented, "but I think that's only because they're leathery. The feathers probably help."

I nodded, taking in all their observations. I sucked in a deep breath.

You're in control.

Stepping off the hill, I closed my eyes and fell through the air, hoping to feel some sort of instinct or urge. Nothing happened. My eyes flashed open, and the ground was barreling toward me. A small breeze swept hair into my panicked face, but it also ruffled my feathers. Suddenly, something clicked and I pulled up, easing away from the ground and into the sky.

I rose higher than Dane had gone, probably much higher than Chamuel ever intended for us to go, but it was hard to stop. It *was* exhilarating. It was also freeing. It felt like every worry in the world melted away, carried off by the wind. I spiraled through the air, caught myself, and launched high again. It was silly to think I was scared of this…scared of being a Nephilim. All that truly made me different were my wings, and look what amazing things I could do with them. Who I was wasn't something to fear. It was something to celebrate. I was extraordinary.

"Hey!" Dane shouted, joining me. "You're having too much fun without me!"

"Sorry!" I smiled.

"No need to be sorry! I'm just glad you're happy!"

"Happy is an understatement! I'm ecstatic!"

We glided and spun, twisted and danced through the air together.

It was a moment made better by experiencing it with Dane. Accepting myself filled me with confidence, and knowing he was at my side gave me strength. I felt ready to take on any obstacle, and I guess that's what these months of reprieve had been for—not just healing but preparedness and control.

After a long while of flying, Dane and I finally decided to land back where we had left Chamuel. Both of us touched the ground, steady on our feet.

Chamuel clapped. "Nice job!"

"We had a good teacher," I told him.

"Thank you," he said. "Unfortunately, you're not going to like what I have to say."

"Which is?" I asked.

"Now it's time to show you how to hide them."

Dane and I glanced at each other. I didn't want to do that yet, not when I had just found the joy of using them, and Dane seemed to be feeling the same way. But realistically, if we wanted to journey out in the world again, it was important we could hide them when we needed to.

So we followed Chamuel over to a grassy area where he sat down cross-legged and closed his eyes. We mimicked his stance and shut our eyes, too.

"This is all about energy," Chamuel said. "You need to feel the force of your wings. Once you find it, it's easy to manipulate and control. Silence and meditation will help you to focus."

He stopped speaking.

I concentrated on my wings, gently shifting them up and down.

Their power was easy to feel, as it extended from my back and into each feather, but what about the other way? My wings connected to my spine, the main structure of my bones, which inevitably meant I should feel the energy of my wings through my entire body, all the way down to the marrow.

As soon as I thought it, my eyes opened. I twisted to look at my back. My wings had disappeared, even though I could still feel them rising from my body. I turned to Chamuel and beamed.

"You two are making this look easy," Chamuel said.

"I think it came naturally to us because it's who we're meant to be," Dane said.

"And we're not hiding anymore," I added with a self-assuredness I'd never felt before.

56 JORDAN

Ithaca, New York, Present Day

I closed my laptop and set it aside. I had e-mailed Cornell back. I had made a choice. Hopefully, it was the right one.

I stared out the window. Spring was starting to make its first appearance, small buds blooming on the tips of frosty trees. Someone knocked on my door.

"Come in," I said, pulling my attention away from the view outside.

Dafne peeked her head in. "Hey! Am I bothering you?"

I smiled. "You never bother me." Then I thought it over. "On second thought, maybe you used to a little bit."

She entered the room and sat down in my lap. "Are you teasing me?" she asked with a sly grin on her face.

"Definitely," I said.

We each leaned closer. My right hand came up to cup her cheek, and just as I was about to kiss her, my eye caught the ring on my hand.

Pulling back, I slid it from my finger and inspected it.

"Is something wrong?" Dafne asked.

I met her eyes. "This was my dad's. It's the only thing I have of his."

"Okay," Dafne said. "And why is that relevant in this moment?"

I frowned.

"Don't do that!" she chided.

"Do what?"

"Pout in frustration because I don't know where your mind went. You have a very erratic, imaginative mind that thinks of things no one else would dream of, so bear with me while I catch up."

I furrowed my brow. "I don't know if I should be offended or touched that you know me so well."

Her mouth dropped open. "I was going for touched."

I grinned. "I know. I just like it when your temper flares."

She shoved me in the shoulder. "I like when you pout and furrow your brow, too, because you look cute, but you don't see me egging you on."

This time I let out a big belly laugh. "Gosh, you're amazing, you know that?"

"I do, actually. Now do you care to explain why your dad's ring is so important?"

"Well, I just wondered if it's the key," I said.

Dafne jumped up. "We have to try it!"

"Okay." I rose from my desk chair, and she grabbed my hand, then pulled me from the room.

It was hard not to enjoy her enthusiasm, but there was a part of me that didn't want to get my hopes up.

Dafne guided me all the way to the library and didn't stop until we were standing in front of my dad's office. "Now what?" she asked.

I shrugged. "I don't know."

"Looking for something?" Zadkiel asked, popping his head out from around a bookshelf.

"No, I just have another crazy hunch," I told him.

He set down whatever he was holding and came closer. "What are you thinking this time?"

"I've been trying to find the key to unlock my dad's office, but I've had no luck. Then I remembered I have his ring." I held out my hand to Zadkiel. He took the ring from my palm and analyzed it.

"Not a bad thought," the angel of teaching mused.

"Thanks, but I have no idea how that—" I pointed toward the ring "—could fit in there." I shifted my hand to indicate the doorknob.

"Wilder things have happened in this house," he assured me.

"True. I wish they would get easier," I said.

Zadkiel nudged me. "Where's the fun in that?"

Focusing my attention back on the ring, I turned it around, searching for a hidden button or something that would transform it into another shape, similar to my mom's necklace.

I found nothing, though, so I guessed it wasn't the same. Sliding the ring back on my hand, I set my sights on the doorknob instead. Was there some hidden hole or loop, someplace the ring could fit?

I inspected it, pulled it, practically dislodged it from the door.

"I think my idea was a bad one," I said. I set my hand on the knob as if I was about to turn it, except my thumb rested on the circular keyhole. There was a sudden heat against the pad of my finger. Then a keyhole popped out and inside rested a perfectly circular indent where the ring could be placed.

"Oh...my...god," Dafne said, shocked.

"Now that might have been the most impressive of all," Zadkiel commented.

I nodded. "I agree." Meeting Dafne's eyes, I said, "A thermal fingerprint scan."

"It's like your dad was some sort of spy," Dafne joked.

"At this rate, who knows," I said. "Anything could be possible." Although, I highly doubted he was a spy. At least, I hoped he wasn't a spy. That would have been a true curveball.

Shaking my head, I tore myself from my erratic thoughts and took the ring from my hand and placed it in the circular indent. Once the ring was inside, the keyhole slid shut, returning the doorknob to its normal appearance, only this time when I tried opening the door, it moved.

I swung the door open wide and gazed into my dad's office. It was covered in dust, much like my mom's studio had been. Floor-to-ceiling built-ins lined the walls, consisting of cabinets, bookshelves, and other unique compartments for storing things. For example, he had a whole row of open rectangular compartments that were typically used to organize envelopes, but instead, he used it as a place to put his pocket journals. There was a special place set within the overall shelving where he had a book displayed to a particular passage. His desk was covered in papers and notebooks. A briefcase was sitting beside the door. The most wonderful thing, though, was the enormous maps on the right-hand wall. There was one of the present world, but then there were a few depicting what the world had looked like during ancient times.

Stepping inside, I drew closer and peered at them intently, seeing that he had marked particular locations. "Zadkiel?" I asked.

"Yes," he said.

"Are these the wonders of the world?"

He joined me, taking a closer look. "Seems like it. Although some aren't."

"Hmm…I guess he was tracking the keys," I said.

"He was tracking something," Zadkiel agreed. "Maybe more than one thing."

Dafne had come in the room, too, exploring the other side of the office. "Look at this," she said.

I turned around and joined her. She was pointing at a bookshelf full of tiny cassette tapes. I picked one up. "What are these?"

"Tape recorder cassettes," Zadkiel said, picking up the dusty device on my dad's desk.

I rushed to his side. "Are you serious?"

"Yes, why?"

I grabbed the recorder and whispered, "I can hear his voice again."

Dafne came to my side and handed me a cassette. "You can hear both of them."

I looked at the tape she held out. It had my name on it with a heart and the words *Mom and Dad.* I took it from her and held it in my hand.

I had heard their voices before. My mom's many a time, as she spoke to me and came to me in visions. My dad was just the once when I had died, and they had both came to guide me back. But it wasn't the same. Their voices were already distant memories, something I had to recall and hope it sounded like before, while what I held in my hand could be played whenever I wanted or needed to hear them.

Sliding the tape into the recorder, I closed it and hit "play."

"Evie!" my dad's voice called.

I smiled.

"Evangeline!"

My mom huffed. "What is it, Arthur?"

"Nothing. I'm making a tape for Jordan, and I wanted your voice on it."

My mom laughed. "You could have just said so!"

"Where's the fun in that? Anyway, you have any advice for him?"

"Tons!" my mom exclaimed.

"Any that comes to mind in this moment?"

"Always be kind and stay true to yourself. You?"

"Hmm..." My dad thought it over. "Imagine the impossible and one day it will be possible."

"No riddles!" my mom chided.

"That wasn't a riddle," he protested.

"It sounded like one."

"Fine. How about...follow your compass. It'll never steer you wrong."

My mom laughed again. "Now you're just being silly!"

"All right, all right! I guess I don't have great advice today, but I do have one thing to say that will always be true."

"What's that?"

"I love you, Jordan."

"Arthur! You're going to make me cry."

"I expected as much. Anything else you'd like to say?"

"I love you, Jordan," my mom murmured.

The tape stopped.

I sank into my dad's chair and sobbed. My chest hurt at how much I missed them. A part of me couldn't help but think about how unfair it was that Sophia and Dane came out of this with parents—imperfect but living—while mine were still gone.

I almost didn't return to my body, my life, because I hadn't wanted to leave them. I'd wanted to stay. It had been one of the toughest decisions I'd ever had to make. And since I came back, I wasn't the same. I acted normal, played if off like nothing had happened, but on the inside, I was struggling. Every night I was either haunted by Murmur's bulging eyes as he suffocated to death or a voice that tried to tempt me the way the dark matter had.

Every day I tried to occupy my mind so none of it would come through while I was awake, which is part of the reason I started the search for the key to unlock my dad's office, but even that was over now. When I wasn't searching, I was training, trying to get my body back to the way it was. In actuality, I was probably stronger than I had ever been. It didn't matter, though, not when I could still feel my heart stop, hear its beat go quiet.

Ultimately, I guessed I understood how a vampire felt. Unnatural and like I didn't fit in.

Dafne rubbed my back as I sucked in a few breaths to calm myself. She had been a shining light in all this, except I felt myself pulling away from her, too, afraid to get too close.

What was wrong with me? Would I ever feel the same again?

I wished I had the fleur-de-lis necklace. It would have at least helped soothe my anxiety and protect me from my mind.

"You all right?" Dafne asked.

I nodded. "I'll be fine."

"You should digitize that," Zadkiel said, pointing at the tape recorder. "You won't want to lose something that precious."

I already had, but I knew what he meant. "You're right."

"Would you like a moment alone?" he asked.

I looked at Dafne. "Do you mind?"

"Of course not," she said, stepping over to Zadkiel. The two of them left the office together.

Gazing around the room, I realized how much stuff my dad had amassed. It would take weeks to go through everything. The first thing I had to do was clean, but even though the desk was dusty, I laid my head down and closed my eyes.

"I was wondering when you'd arrive," someone said.

My eyes snapped open. I wasn't in my dad's office anymore. I was outside in a glade with a roaring waterfall that cascaded into a basin of clear water. There was a man, an angel, sitting upon the basin, floating just above the surface.

"Who are you?" I asked.

"Someone you'll soon meet," he answered.

He had long, straight black hair and smooth, russet-brown skin.

I rose from the grass and stepped over to the basin's edge. "I've done this before."

"What?" he asked.

"Communed with supernatural beings in my sleep," I explained. "I just need to know if you're friend or foe."

He glanced over his shoulder, spying a look at his wings, which were pure white. He returned his gaze to me. "I would say friend."

I had been tricked so many times before that I was wary, but then again, no one had ever presented themselves with massive white wings so that had to be a good omen.

"What do you want?" I asked bluntly.

The angel grinned. "I see you are annoyed by my presence. Perhaps I should go."

"No, wait!" I shouted, eager for his help. If he was coming to me in a vision, he had to be offering help, right? And I could desperately use some. "I'm sorry. You caught me at a bad time. I'm not in a very welcoming mood."

"I know. That's why I came," he said.

"So you are here to help me?"

He nodded.

I waited for him to say something more. He didn't.

"What are you here to help me with?" I asked, trying to pull information from him.

He rose and crossed the water to stand in front of me. "Your mind." He clasped his hands behind my head and slowly brought them forward.

I felt a soft heat along my neck. Glancing down, I saw he was creating me a necklace.

"Not creating," he said, as if he'd read my mind. "Returning and repairing. You'll need it in the days ahead."

Sure enough, my fleur-de-lis necklace hung around my neck once again.

"You're Sandalphon, aren't you?" I guessed.

"Your mother was an astute pupil," he said, ignoring my declaration. "I have great expectations you'll follow in her footsteps."

"I'll try," I said, eyes wide.

"Go. We shall meet soon. In the meantime, heed your father's advice," he suggested.

"What advice—"

I couldn't finish. Sandalphon pressed his thumb to my forehead, and the next thing I knew, I was waking up on my dad's desk. I lifted my head and immediately felt for the necklace. It was still around my neck. I rubbed my head. My dad's advice?

I peered at the tape recorder still clutched in my hand.

"Imagine the impossible and one day it will be possible," I said aloud.

I had to agree with my mom. Something about that one didn't sound right.

"Follow your compass. It'll never steer you wrong," I said, testing it out.

The center of the desk moved. I grabbed the papers and calendar my dad had on top and looked underneath. A compass met my gaze, one carved into the wood. It was descending into the remainder of the desk until it slowly spun and spread apart. An object rose from the middle. It was hard to see what it was because the desk kept moving. Once it finally stilled, I saw a real, metal compass sitting before me.

What the...

Maybe my dad was a spy after all.

I reached for the compass and picked it up. As soon as it was freed, the desk moved again, closing and returning to its normal form.

The compass was made of different metallic materials, as it was gold, silver, blue, and black. Each direction was inscribed on the face, but it was missing the needle that swung between them.

I strode to the door to go show the others when I heard the doorbell ring. I walked through the library, noticing Dafne and Zadkiel had left it entirely, since it was deserted. Entering the hall, I saw pretty much everyone was gathered around in the turret. I wondered who was on the other side of the entranceway.

Gabriel broke away from the group and reached for the door. When he opened it, his eyes widened, and his mouth lifted in a grin. "Sandalphon!"

An odd sensation overwhelmed me when I heard the name.

I crept down the hall and joined Gabriel at the door. The angel I had just seen in my dream stood before me.

"I told you we'd meet soon," he said.

"And I listened to my dad's advice," I told him, holding out the compass for him to see.

He smiled. "You're already turning out to be a good student."

57 DANE

Ithaca, New York, Present Day

When Chamuel, Sophia, and I came back from our flying lesson, everyone was gathered around at the front door.

"What's going on?" I asked.

The angels parted to let me through, and I froze when I saw the figure standing at the door. "It's you," I said.

Jordan focused his attention on me. "You know Sandalphon?"

I teetered my hand in the air. "Sort of. He helped me get out of Lilith's camp."

"Which brings me to why I'm here," he said.

"Why's that?" I asked.

"She's reassembled her army. It's stronger than before. She's stronger than before, and she must be stopped," Sandalphon explained.

"How is she stronger?" Gabriel asked.

"She did the sacrifice, didn't she?" I guessed.

Sandalphon nodded. "We need to rally. The Heavenly army must be summoned. The Factions of Faith must be called. The rebels in Hell must be ready to fight on our side." He scrutinized each of us. "We need to collect the remaining spheres as well as the scepter pieces. War is brewing, and it will be on our doorstep within five months' time."

"Five months?" Naomi asked. "That's awfully specific."

"It is," Sandalphon agreed. "Because by then, these two"—he looked from me to Jordan—"shall be twenty, and the prophecy cannot be completed until you are that age."

Jordan and I looked at each other.

"*Thirteen bound in blood by two from ancient lines born anew,*" Zadkiel whispered. "He's right. You're the two."

"Who's the thirteen?" Dafne asked.

"Not who," Sandalphon said. "What. The thirteen are the stones."

"Let's go to the library," Michael suggested. "We have maps in there. We can strategize and make a plan."

All the angels and adults moved down the hall.

The rest of us were about to follow when I noticed Jordan staring at the floor.

"What's wrong?"

His brow was furrowed, and he knelt to the ground like something was wrong with the floor.

"Jordan?" Sophia asked.

He glanced up at us with a crazed look in his eye. "It's a complete compass."

I shifted my gaze to the marble floor. "Yeah, and?"

He held up something in his hand. I knelt to get a closer look. Oddly, it was an actual compass, one that resembled the one set into the floor.

"Where did you find that?" I asked him.

"My dad's office." He explained how they opened it and what he found inside. Then he told us about the dream with Sandalphon and his dad's insane desk.

"I have to find the needle," he said, "and I think it's here."

"Why?" Sophia asked. She had joined us on the floor along with Naomi and Dafne.

"Because—" Jordan ran his hand over the floor "—it's the exact same compass but this one has the needle."

We all inspected the marble compass. Jordan was right. This one did have a needle, each end tapering off into a feather—one black, one white.

"I got it!" Naomi said. "It's a compass, so maybe we have to stand on each cardinal direction."

"What about the fifth person?" Jordan asked.

"They should wait to see what happens," Sophia said. "Maybe they'll need to stand in the middle, though, since that's where a compass needle usually goes."

"All right," he said.

Naomi, Sophia, Dafne, and I moved to stand on each direction. Suddenly, my feet sunk a few inches into the ground.

"Whoa!" I exclaimed. "Did you feel that?"

The others nodded.

Jordan stretched between Sophia and me, stepping on the center of the compass. We sank lower, and he rose higher. Bending down, Jordan inspected the stone he was standing on. He reached down and fumbled around underneath it until he latched on to something. His eyes widened, and he grinned.

Bringing his hand up, he showed us the needle. It matched the marble one perfectly. He stepped down from the stone, and it sunk back into the floor. Ours rose until the surface was smooth again.

We all gathered around as Jordan placed the needle in the compass. It spun around…and around.

"Shouldn't it find north?" I asked.

"Typically," Sophia said.

Jordan sighed. "All that and it's broken."

"Not necessarily," Dafne pointed out. "Maybe it just needs more time to calibrate."

"Yeah," Naomi agreed. "Or you might not be close to what it needs to point to."

"I guess so," he said, clearly disappointed.

The situation was a little unsatisfying even for me. It had been fun to work together to solve the puzzle, so to speak, even though it was short-lived. The fact that the result was kind of nothing left a sour feeling behind.

"We should join the others," Sophia suggested.

"You're right," I said. "They're probably making plans without us."

We all went down the hall to the library. It seemed they were, in fact, already planning, since a large map was spread across the long table, but they were arguing over something. I spied a small easel set up on the table with a whiteboard sitting on it. There were three groups of names.

"What's going on?" I asked.

"Sandalphon wants us to split up into groups," Raphael said.

I examined the board and saw that Jordan, Sophia, and I were each in a different group. My chest squeezed. The thought of being separated from them again threw me into a panic.

I couldn't be alone. Not again.

Jordan and Sophia balanced me out. They settled the urges of power that tried to sneak to the surface. Their presence offered a sense of control that I didn't have on my own, and I didn't want to hurt anyone.

Sure, in the months since we had returned, I had tried to understand my power, but every time I used it, nothing good came of it. The only decent things I had ever done were resurrect Jordan and help Satan take back Hell. I figured conditioning my body might help, but that did nothing other than make me feel good physically. Jordan and Sophia were the only ones who silenced the call of blood.

Of course, as I thought about it, I became keenly aware of the heartbeats in the room, the rush of blood through veins. The sounds were a summons, an invitation. Except they never quite indicated what they wanted me to do. There had to be a use, a reason, for this power. One that wasn't dark and evil.

"Ah!" I shouted.

Everyone turned to look at me.

"You all right?" Jordan asked, concern furrowing his brow.

I nodded. "Yeah, I'm fine."

The conversation resumed.

Sophia searched my eyes. "You're lying."

She was right.

"You know what," I said loudly. "I'm not fine. We can't split up."

"Thank you," Gabriel said. "At least I have someone on my side."

"Well…not completely," I amended. "It's a good thought. There's a lot of ground to cover, and if Lilith attacks, we won't want all the spheres together. What I meant to say was I'm not fine with splitting the three of us up." I gestured to Jordan, Sophia, and myself.

"Seriously?" Uriel pointed to the board. "The teams are literally centered on each of you. If we put you all together, it ruins the whole plan."

"Who cares?" I said.

"I do," Sandalphon stated. "It must be this way. We are not just going for the spheres. We're going for the scepter pieces, too. Those need to be unearthed one at a time, in a certain order. That's why I split you up."

"Well can't someone else do that part?" I tried.

Sandalphon crossed his arms. "Are you really asking me that question, considering the daggers have been bound to each of you?"

"It was worth a shot," I said, defeated.

Then I realized I could request others to be on my team, people who didn't necessarily balance me the way Jordan and Sophia did but who did make me feel secure.

"Can I at least have Satan and Naomi?" I asked.

"Thank the heavens someone took him," Uriel said.

"I don't want to be on Dane's team," Aziza commented. "Not if Satan's there."

"Me either," Aeron said.

"Everyone, stop!" Sandalphon bellowed. "This is not going to turn into some human game where you pick members of your team and hope you're not the last one remaining. I thought we could handle this civilly, but since we cannot, I will decide."

He grabbed the board and vigorously wrote down names.

"What gives you the authority?" Uriel asked. "Last I checked, you were just an angel of nature like me, an archangel on the council."

Sandalphon raised his eyes to his brother. "Those titles are in my past, along with many others. The duties I have now go beyond anything you know because you have been absent from our home for many centuries."

"Meaning?" Uriel asked.

"Meaning be quiet and take his command," Michael urged.

Uriel was compelled into silence.

Satisfied, Sandalphon showed us the board. My group consisted of Michael, Satan, Kat, Naomi, and Aeron. Jordan had Gabriel, Raphael, Yadira, Dafne, and Zadkiel. Sophia had Uriel, Chamuel, Aziza, Deborah, and Delphine.

"Where will you be?" Jordan asked Sandalphon.

"I need to assist each of you with obtaining the scepter pieces so I'll be moving among the groups on the journey."

"And what should I do?" Martha asked.

"Martha, you will stay here with Peter and Emily. Our forces will start to arrive, and they need a place to assemble."

"You mean angels," Peter said.

Sandalphon nodded. "Correct."

"Why are they coming here?" Naomi asked.

"It's the most secure location on Earth in terms of privacy," Sandalphon explained. "The battle will take place somewhere in this realm so it's best to gather everyone ahead of the attack." He scanned the room. "Any other questions?"

"I have one," Michael chimed in. "You have us in teams, but what's the order of how we extract the keys?"

Sandalphon approached the map. "Dane's team will start at Angkor Wat and then travel to the Colosseum. Jordan's team will start at the Taj Mahal and go on to La Sagrada Familia. Sophia's team will start at the Great Wall of China and move to the Acropolis. All the teams will finish in Europe, where we will join to get the last sphere."

"Where's that?" Dafne asked.

"Paris," Zadkiel said. "The Eiffel Tower."

The mention of Paris made her eyes fill with stars.

"The order for the scepter pieces must go Dane, Sophia, and then Jordan," Sandalphon said. "As we collect the scepter and spheres, we must secure them immediately, so I will be going back and forth to bring them here, and then will return straightaway to our mission."

"When do we leave?" Kat asked.

"As soon as we can," Sandalphon answered.

I crossed my arms and braced myself for the journey ahead. It would be a long one, full of who knew how many surprises.

58

SATAN

Hell, Present Day

“Haborym, report on the portal devices,” I said, sitting around the large table I had erected in the former portal room.

I now used it as my council room, since the portal no longer worked, and I was trying to restructure the way things were done in Hell. It was about time I met with my leaders more regularly in a setting that didn’t always remind them of my superiority.

“Right. I met with an angel of art on Earth. They showed me how the devices are crafted and charged. It’s simple to recreate, but we would have to find a source in Hell that could replace the divine light charge they use in Heaven.”

“There might be something in Misery,” Kushiel said. “I haven’t been there long, but I discovered one section where the flames burn black instead of orange. It might be something worth investigating.”

“Please do,” I said. “For various reasons.”

“Yes, sir.”

“As for you, Haborym, keep at it. I would like to *not* be indebted to Heaven every time we want to travel to Earth. Right now, they’re playing nice because they need us, but once this battle is over, I assure you their resources will go with it."

"Of course, sir. We could always go back to the old way if something doesn't pan out."

"True. But I like the devices better. What of the weapons and armor?" I asked, changing subjects.

"We're still forging every day, preparing for battle. We will be ready," she assured me.

"And the bullets?"

"We aren't making them anymore, as you asked," she said. "And we've destroyed whatever was left."

"Excellent. Ariel, where are we with training everyone?"

Ariel looked to Haborym, and they shared a smile.

Hmm…I wondered what was going on there.

"With Haborym's help, we've been able to equip everyone and get them practicing. I'm confident they will be ready."

"And the battle plans?"

"I'm still working on arranging our troops into formations based on their skills," Ariel said.

"All right. But pick up the pace. I need something soon. Otherwise I'll start making plans myself."

"Yes, sir."

"Nehema, how are your ventures coming along?" I asked, moving to the next order of business.

"Well, with Dane's permission, I've been working with the hounds to prep them for battle. Obviously, they heed his command, but we thought it would be a fine idea to train them a bit to know some basic attacks and defensive maneuvers," she told me.

I nodded and grinned, happy to know Ace was involved, even if remotely.

"Keep up the good work," I said. "Beelzebub, Belphegor, how is your work with the demons and spirits?"

"The demons are raring for a fight," Beelzebub reported. "They can't wait to clash with their counterparts from Purgatory, so morale is up. I've been training with them to try to hone their skills and make their attacks less erratic. Overall, it's working."

"I'm glad to hear that," I said. "The demons have always been finicky."

"Well the spirits continue to be so, as always," Belphegor interjected. "Some fear war, thinking it will be fought in our domain. I assured them otherwise, but they don't listen. Some want to fight, but it's difficult to wrangle them together. I think some need to hear from you, while others need to feel like they have a purpose. Maybe you can address them directly."

"Sure, I can arrange that," I told him.

I glanced around the table. There were only two seats left that needed to report. One was entirely empty, given that Pride had no one at its helm at the moment, which left Abbadona.

We'd only talked formally since our argument. She clearly was still mad at me.

"Abbadona, any updates?"

She looked at me. "Nothing new to note. I'm still devising a way to freeze the rivers. The potion should be operational within the next day. Since I cannot always be there watching the waters, I've entrusted a small team to assist. I made them amulets that allow them to withstand the allure, and I put up simple wards to alert me of any activity."

"Great," I said.

A howl echoed through the room, and I paused. That was how Dane had summoned me last time. I had heard a familiar sound two days prior, as well, but I hadn't been able to act on it since it had been my day to visit the cities and spread good will among the denizens of Hell.

Such a thing couldn't be missed, otherwise they thought I was slighting them.

To hear the howl again meant he needed me…now.

"If we're done here, I think we can adjourn," I said.

Abbadona gasped and raced from the room.

Those that remained, me included, knew whatever had triggered that reaction wasn't good. Her wards must have been breached.

We all sprang up and exited the council room, heading for the Pit. We dove down together and approached the Eighth Cavern.

Lilith rose from the river, along with other figures, presumably some of her soldiers.

Abbadona raced from her hut with bottles of liquid. She threw one my way. "Pour it in the river! It'll start to freeze!"

I caught it and followed her instructions, as did the others. The liquid inside must have been some sort of potion she'd concocted. Once it hit the waters, it *did* solidify the element in the riverbed.

We had frozen three of the five rivers. The remaining two were the ones Lilith and her team were ascending from. Kushiel poured the liquid into one, freezing Lilith's companions. Nehema followed behind and slashed their frozen bodies to pieces.

Which left the she-devil herself all alone.

She emerged from the water, setting foot into the cavern.

Ariel threw the potion in the river behind Lilith, blocking her escape.

With all the rivers now frozen, it was time to set our attention on her. But something didn't seem quite right. Why would she expose herself like this with hardly any protection or backup? Something was amiss.

Before we could engage her, Dane's hound came barreling through our ranks and launched at her, aiming for the throat.

Shit!

Dane was attached to that dog. If something happened to it, I didn't think he would be able to handle it.

I bounded after it just as Lilith stopped it with her magic. The hound froze and lay down, belly exposed. Lilith placed her foot on the dog and drew a knife.

I dove and careened into the creature, pushing him out of Lilith's way. I managed to slide along the stone floor with it, barely evading her weapon.

She laughed maniacally. "What a shame! I would have loved to see Darcel's reaction." Lilith waved her fingers and disappeared.

I was shocked by the strange encounter.

"What the hell was that?" Nehema asked.

"It was a test," Abbadona said, kneeling to check the rivers.

"Of what?" I asked.

She stood. "Did you not notice she wasn't wearing a portal device?"

"So?" Beelzebub wondered aloud.

"So she somehow got enough power to open portals herself," Abbadona enlightened.

"Meaning?" Belphegor asked.

I swallowed. "Meaning she has the ability to move her army, whether living or dead."

59 DANE

Ithaca, New York, Present Day

It took everyone two days to prepare. We all had to pack, Deborah had to call out from work, and the angels had to request new portal devices from Heaven. At least they had found a way to charge the devices much more ethically than Lilith did.

Now, with everything ready, we all gathered in the library again, prepared to depart.

Except Satan hadn't showed up. As soon as our plans were settled, I made sure to summon him as I had done before, by giving Duke the order. After day one with no answer, I'd sent Duke to Hell, and now he and my dad were both MIA.

I hoped nothing was wrong.

A hand rested on my shoulder, and I jumped, not because the gesture scared me but because I was afraid of hurting whoever it was.

"It's just me," Jordan said.

I sighed in relief.

"You could give me some warning," I said.

"I did. I was calling your name for nearly a minute," he told me.

"Oh…sorry."

"You ready for this?"

I shrugged. "Yeah. I just wish I knew where I was going. Sandalphon has yet to tell me where the first scepter piece is." I grabbed the dagger from the holster at my waist and twirled it in my hands. "Can't say I'll miss this thing."

"Me either." Jordan paused. "I'll miss you, though."

"You had to say it!" I exclaimed.

"Well, that's part of the reason I came over. To say—"

"No!" I cut him off. "You won't say goodbye because we'll see each other again." I stuck out my hand. "Promise?"

He grabbed it. "Promise."

I let go. "I'll see you in Paris."

"I'll be waiting," he said, shuffling over to his group.

Just like I was waiting for my dad now.

"He'll turn up," Sophia said.

I met her eyes. "I hope so."

She sat next to me. "I'm sure he'll be strutting in any minute."

I leaned over. "Please don't tell me you came over to say goodbye, too," I whispered.

She sighed. "We have to get going."

I raised my head.

"But I'm not saying goodbye," she assured me. "I'm saying I love you."

Smiling, I said, "Love you, too."

Footsteps thudded from the hall. Everyone went quiet and turned to the door.

"Look who decided to show up," Uriel said.

Satan entered the library with Duke at his side. Without stopping, he gave Uriel the finger and kept walking over to me.

"Don't send the hound anymore," he said.

"Why?" I asked, growing defensive. This was the first time he had ever been even a little abrasive with me.

"Because she nearly slaughtered it," he confessed.

Duke came close and rubbed his head against my leg. I cradled him tightly. "Did she hurt him?"

"Almost. I made sure he was unscathed." He glanced at us. "I know how fond you are of him."

"I am," I admitted. "But he's tough."

"He is. He tried to rip out her throat."

"Good boy," I said, patting his head. I brought my attention to Satan. "Did she attack you?"

He sighed. "Sort of. She used the rivers to enter Hell, but she remained only for a second. She was testing her powers. We've got the rivers under control now, though."

"How?" Sandalphon asked.

Satan turned. "What the hell brought you here?"

"Lilith."

"I see." He paused before continuing. "We froze the rivers. It's working. We'll see if it lasts. The problem is she found another way to get around."

"You mean the portal devices?" Sophia asked.

Satan shook his head. "No. She teleported herself. She must have gained some new power. All I know is she can move her army now."

"Which is why we need to leave," Sandalphon urged. "Has everyone calibrated their devices with their locations?"

"No," Satan growled. "I didn't realize we were so organized."

"Here," Michael said, handing him a portal device. "It's ready to go. I can fill you in on the details later. All you need to know is you're up first."

He rolled his eyes. "Of course, I am. And who exactly am I traveling with?"

"You're on Dane's team so most of us are friendly toward you," Michael said.

"I'm not," Aeron barked.

Satan chuckled. "Me and Uncle Aeron traveling together. Someone has a sick sense of humor." He slipped the portal device on his wrist. "I guess I'm as ready as I'll ever be."

I stood and clamped a hand on his shoulder. "I have a task to complete first, so I'll be joining you soon."

"What? I thought I was on your team," Satan said.

"You are."

"Then shouldn't I be going where you're going?" he asked.

I sighed. "It's a long story. Michael will explain. I won't be gone long, so just be good until I come back." I knelt and took Duke's head in my hands. "You stay here with Martha. You've had enough adventure for one day."

He whined.

"You can fight in the war when I get back," I assured him.

He rubbed his head against mine.

"But we'll have to make you some armor."

Hmm...I'd have to sketch something.

I returned to Sophia. "See you soon."

She winked. "I'm counting on it."

Stepping over to Sandalphon, I said, "Let's get this show on the road."

"Here." He handed me a portal device.

I slipped it on my wrist and turned the dial without hesitation.

60 DANE

Near Ein Gedi, Israel, Present Day

My feet landed on thin dirt, two small clouds of dust rising into the air next to my shoes. An azure sea spanned before me, the deepest parts a dark lapis while the shallow parts had hints of turquoise and aquamarine.

"The Dead Sea," Sandalphon said.

His sudden appearance made me jump. He hadn't made a single sound, and still didn't even now as he trod along the ground.

I followed him over the mixed terrain consisting of smooth dirt and hard rocks. The ground swirled in a gradient of brown, and it was safe to say this was one of the most incredible places I had ever been. Certainly in my top three favorites.

I stood next to Sandalphon and gazed out at the horizon that spanned miles.

"You have the dagger?" he asked.

I drew it from my holster.

"Empty your pockets," Sandalphon commanded.

"Why?" I asked.

He met my eyes. "You're going to get wet."

"Really? You could have given me some warning," I complained.

"I did. I told you not to bring anything," he stated rather seriously.

I rolled my eyes and handed him the sketch pad I always kept with me.

He slipped it in his pocket. "Come."

We walked to the edge of the water where I slipped my shoes and socks off, knowing it would suck to have them soaked, and slid my phone out of my pocket.

"Return the dagger to the Earth," Sandalphon instructed.

I pursed my lips, confused. I had taken the dagger from a tree, and there were none of those in sight. I glanced at Sandalphon. I got the feeling I couldn't ask questions from the way he was staring at me so I unsheathed the dagger, bent over, and stuck it in the ground in a shallow part of water.

As soon as the blade met the Earth, it sent a shock across the sea.

"Enter the water," Sandalphon directed.

Sucking in a deep breath, I strode forward into the Dead Sea until the water was nearly to my chest.

"Breathe," Sandalphon said from behind me.

I glanced over to see how he had appeared so quickly and quietly once more, and was amazed that he hovered over the water, so close it looked like he was walking on it.

He placed his hand behind my head and gently dipped it forward.

Crap! I'd forgotten to breathe.

My head went under, and I closed my mouth so I wouldn't inhale any water. As my head came up, I drew in a deep breath of air before I was submerged again.

Sandalphon kept repeating the gesture, and I started to wonder how many times we would do this.

The truth resides inside.

The words whispered through my ear while my head was in the water. When it surfaced, I peered through the droplets along my lashes and saw a figure in the distance. A horseman. Sandalphon dipped my head again. This time there were four figures assembled. Once more I went down and came up, only to see a lone figure holding out a card. I was dunked yet again before I could get a better glimpse, except when I surfaced, there was no hand holding my head.

I wheezed in air, needing more than I was able to get between submersions. I turned to find Sandalphon and fell back into the water when I noticed he was sitting cross-legged behind me.

"Geez! Will you stop doing that?" I asked.

He smiled. "I'm not doing anything other than being myself." He stared at me for a few seconds. "Whatever you saw were glimpses of the future."

"How'd you know I saw something?" I wondered aloud.

"Everyone does when they're cleansed," he explained.

"Okay…and what about the scepter?" I asked.

"You have it."

"No, I don't," I said, lifting my hands to show him.

Except that was a lie. Instead of holding the dagger sheath, I now had a black rod in my left hand. It was engraved with feathers.

"What the—" I looked around and saw the dagger itself had disappeared.

"It's gone forever, its purpose fulfilled."

I set my eyes on Sandalphon. I didn't know what he was, but he was more than an angel. I could feel it in his presence. He acted like a wise sage, knew more than any celestial being I had ever met.

"Now what?" I asked.

"You dry off and return to the group," he said matter-of-factly, rising from his position and then crossing back to land.

I trudged out of the sea, sopping wet, still holding the scepter piece. "I think you need this," I told him.

He nodded. "Yes, I'll take it to the house. Hopefully, reinforcements have started to arrive. Shall I set the coordinates for you?" he offered, gesturing to my portal device.

"Oh…sure." I held out my wrist.

He fiddled with the dial. "They're still at Angkor Wat, so you haven't missed out on anything."

"Okay, thanks." I handed over the black rod.

He took it. "Godspeed."

"Uh…good luck to you, too," I said, turning the dial.

61 SATAN

Siem Reap, Cambodia, Present Day

We arrived on the bridge that connected Angkor Wat to the surrounding area. In front of us, the temple loomed large. Behind us, a sea of tourists gathered, phones and cameras at the ready, waiting for their guided tours.

"I hate humans," I said bluntly.

"Hey!" Aeron said, offended.

I ignored him.

"What makes this site a modern wonder?" the girl asked. I thought her name was Naomi.

"Good question," Kat said. "Many of what are considered modern wonders were actually built long ago; however, the fact that their ingenuity and genius is still standing to this day is what classifies them as modern."

"I see. So the ones designated ancient wonders no longer exist," Naomi clarified.

"That's correct for most of them. Only the pyramids remain, and they're severely damaged," Kat explained.

"Now that the history lesson is over," I said, "why don't we get started?"

"Okay, lead the way," Michael urged.

I chuckled. "You expect me to know where the sphere is?"

"Jophiel would have," he said.

I clenched my jaw. "Well I'm not Jophiel."

"No, you're not," Michael snapped. "But you said he bestowed his duties to you."

"He did!"

"Then you should know where the sphere is," he chastised.

I crossed my arms. "He never told me."

Michael sighed. "That makes this harder."

"Harder?" Kat repeated. "It makes it nearly impossible."

"Okay, Miss Dramatic, no need to exaggerate," I said.

"She's not," Michael defended.

I stopped. "You mean to tell me that only Jophiel knew the exact location of the sphere?"

Michael nodded. "That's how it works."

"How *what* works?" I asked.

Michael threw up his hands. "We were given the sites of the keys before we left Heaven!"

"I know that! But you were given the *exact* spot of where they would be hidden?"

"Not exactly. We were just told the overall location, and once that happened, we just knew," Michael explained.

I stared at him in disbelief.

"It's a feeling," he continued.

"A feeling…that only Jophiel could feel," I said.

Michael tensed. "There's no need to be sarcastic."

"I'm not," I assured him.

He shrugged. "Jophiel would have felt it, but Jordan might have the ability, too."

Then where the hell was Jordan? is what I wanted to say, but I settled for silence.

"How about we split up and start searching?" Naomi suggested. "Maybe something will come, then."

"Fine," I said.

We all walked down the bridge together toward the temple. When we stood in front of Angkor Wat, we decided to break off into two groups: Kat and Aeron took the right-hand side while Michael, Naomi, and I searched the left.

Without Dane, I felt outnumbered. It was crazy how attached I had become to him, but I thought it was because I could relate to him more than anyone else.

I shook my head. No need to worry about the kid now. We had to find this sphere so we could keep moving.

As we searched the temple, the complex felt like a maze. Every piece of stone looked the same on the outside, and every corridor on the inside was similar. Occasionally, there was a carving or a statue that stood out, but nothing called to me.

"Maybe you need to wear the ring," Naomi said.

Michael and I stopped in our tracks.

"Just a thought," she elaborated.

"A good one," Michael stated. He turned to me. "Put it on."

I slipped the chain from my neck and slid off the ring. I held it in front of my finger, hesitant.

"This seems right, yet so wrong," I confessed.

"He wanted you to do this," Michael encouraged.

"Yeah, yeah," I said, putting on the ring.

A jolt of energy rushed through me. My head tipped back, and my eyes sank shut. I breathed deeply, steadying myself. It was strange, but I felt an urge...a feeling of certainty, a sudden shock of purpose.

My eyes flashed open. "Dear God, this self-assuredness is going to make me vomit."

"We can't vomit," Michael said seriously.

"Do you all walk around like this?" I asked, ignoring him and grabbing my chest.

Michael clenched his jaw. "Very funny."

I smiled and straightened up. Of course, I knew this was how they were. I used to feel the same way all the time. Michael just couldn't take a joke.

"All right," I said, "let's go."

"Where?" Naomi asked.

"To the Northern Thousand God Library." I strode off in the direction we had come, my feet leading me with a newfound sureness and urgency. Michael and Naomi followed.

When we arrived at the designated building within the temple, it was hard not to marvel at the architecture and the fact that it was still intact. It was a real masterpiece—the intricately carved steps, the columns, the figures portrayed in stone.

I climbed the stairs and entered the small space of the library—small compared with the large complex surrounding me, at least. It was dark inside, but the hot, afternoon sun was enough to illuminate the way, shining effortlessly through the open windows and doorways.

I searched the room for the spot where the sphere was hidden. I halted, feeling a thrum beneath my feet. I knelt and swiped the floor with my right hand, clearing away the dirt, then set it against the stone.

The key-retrieval process wasn't new to me. I had done it for my own keys. Except with mine I had felt the item calling to me in a way that ached, almost like a part of me was hidden away. Whereas this wasn't as strong. More a slight tingle or sensation.

I stared at my hand. "Nothing's happening."

"Is it the right spot?" Michael asked.

"I think so."

"Call it," Naomi instructed.

I glanced over my shoulder. "I've never had to do that before."

"Of course not," she berated. "This is another angel's key. It doesn't matter how much Jophiel bestowed upon you. That stone is bound to him, and while it might recognize that you now have some authority over it, it's certainly not going to just rise for you the way it would have for him. You need to put in some effort!"

Normally, I would have lost my temper if someone criticized me in such a way. But Naomi's lack of fear reminded me of the only other being who treated me that way—Abbadona.

I rose and stepped over to her. "You aren't scared of me."

She crossed her arms and met my challenge. "You underestimate me." She waited. I said nothing. "Are we done with this masculine need to display your power?"

I grinned. She was strong, fierce…and two steps away from crossing over to the dark side. Ariel had. Dane was fighting it. Naomi was considering it…weighing her options as I was sure she felt obligated to uphold a moral standard for her "parents." But I could see she was hiding her true self behind a wall. We all hit that point eventually. It was a matter of what would be the trigger to push her over the edge.

For now, I ignored her and asked, "How do you suggest I summon the stone?"

"With Hellfire," she answered. "Like calls to like. Your heat will attract the sphere's energy."

I nodded and turned around, striding back to the middle of the room and kneeling. I placed my hand on the ground again and ignited the fire running through my veins.

The entire room shook.

"Oh dear, he's going to destroy everything," Michael muttered.

"Have faith in him," Naomi whispered.

Damn, I was becoming a mush, letting these kids weasel their way into my heart.

I shook my head and focused. The Hellfire had found the sphere. It was now just a matter of commanding it to rise. *"Ascensio."* The Latin word spilled out before I knew what I was saying. That was what happened when you did good deeds. You started to revert. I couldn't wait to hold this sphere so I could take the ring off and fulfill whatever promise I'd agreed to.

I increased the heat, and finally, the sphere broke through the ground, the yellow citrine stone peeking out. It ascended and kept rising until it was freed.

The Hellfire receded, and I reached out to pick up the sphere. Holding it in my hand, I could see why combining thirteen of them was a tantalizing deed, as just one of them made you feel significant.

I had been lured by that notion in the past. I'd been quite obsessed to fulfill the prophecy myself. But I already had a crown, a necessary one that no one else could wear, and I'd rather exult in that than borrow one that could be destroyed.

"Let's go," I said, standing and reaching for my portal device.

"We have to find the others," Michael reminded me.

I rolled my eyes. "Right. I'm new to this teamwork thing."

We exited the structure.

"You have a whole crew of fallen angels," Michael pointed out.

"Yes, but teamwork isn't at the front of my mind. The mission usually is our priority, and once that starts going batshit sideways is when we start to care for one another."

"Then this situation should work well for you," Naomi stated.

I brought my attention to what she was staring at. The bridge where we had entered was swarmed with a demon horde, the Sentinel front and center at command.

"Shit! Already?" I yelled.

Michael drew his sword.

"That's a little premature," I said.

He shook his head. "Not when they have *them*." He launched into the air to meet the enemy.

"Them who?"

"Kat and Aeron!" Naomi chided, taking to the air.

Right. I'd forgotten about them. Again.

I spread my wings to follow, but what the hell was I going to do with the sphere? I couldn't just bring it over there and flaunt it. And it definitely wasn't going to fit in a pocket. Wasn't Sandalphon supposed to collect these or something? I thought that's what Michael had told me.

A snickering came from my left. I didn't need to look to know it was one of those scorpion-like demons from Purgatory. They were the only ones that made such a noise.

I shot into the sky with the sphere, figuring that was better than a confrontation. I whizzed over the bridge, inspecting the battle below me.

Michael was efficiently slaying demons, but there were too many of them for him to take alone. There had to be fifty or so, and to my knowledge, the Sentinel was unkillable. The best course of action would be to get Aeron and Kat, then hightail it out of there. I was about to go assist, even though I had no idea what to do with the sphere, when movement from the water on either side of the bridge caught my attention.

It lurched, swayed, and then quickly rose from the riverbed, slamming into assailants on the bridge.

What the…

Water didn't just move like that. Maybe a sea, but not a river.

For a moment, my hopes soared thinking Abbadona had followed me, but my eyes did not detect her on the bridge. Instead, I saw Naomi weaving her hands through the air, the water mimicking her commands.

She was controlling it…just like Abbadona.

My eyes widened. What had Naomi called herself? A Supernal…a being not part-celestial but full celestial.

Shit! Could she…

I had to speak with Abbadona when I saw her again before I jumped to any conclusions. Besides, Michael still needed help.

I flew down and joined him on the bridge. He had just freed Kat when I arrived.

"About time!" she shouted.

"How long were you captured?" Michael asked.

"Long enough that *that* should have triggered a warning," she demanded, reaching a finger out to poke Michael's forehead.

He sidestepped before she could touch him. "You're not doing that again."

"If you're blocking me, that's probably why my warning didn't work," she explained.

"Sorry, but I prefer my memories to remain intact," he snapped.

"Are we really going to chat about this now?" Kat asked. "Aeron needs us."

"As does Naomi," I said, handing the sphere to Michael.

The Sentinel was inching closer to her, and she wasn't aware, given that she was surrounded by demons.

Icicles sprayed from her fingertips, hitting every opponent around her. But the Sentinel kept moving forward. And now he raised his gun.

A group of demons came at me.

Damn it! She needed help.

I grabbed a knife from my belt and gutted one of the demons. Another I took by the throat, its teeth gnawing at nothing but air, and incinerated it with Hellfire. The others went down easy, one stabbed in the back through his chest, another straight in its heart, and the final one through the head.

In the seconds it took for me to vanquish them, Naomi had disintegrated the Sentinel's bullets. They must have been the ones made from the river water. I had seen Abbadona herself perform a similar trick.

Except all that did was force the Sentinel to holster his gun. It didn't stop him from moving forward, closer to Naomi.

She backed up, her energy clearly draining.

I raced forward as two demons sprang from the water on either side of her. Their appearance distracted her, giving the Sentinel the moment of opportunity he needed to bring down his knife. But suddenly he froze mid-action, the blade mere inches from Naomi's heart.

Glancing around, I noticed every other demon had frozen, too.

I saw Michael and Kat manage to free Aeron from their grasp, but my eyes kept moving.

Where was Dane? He had to be around given everyone had stopped in their tracks against their own accord.

Sure enough, I finally spotted him on one knee behind the Sentinel, his arms out in front of him, tense and full of power. His entire body shaking.

He barely had control, which meant only one thing.

"Set your devices!" I shouted. "And get the hell out of here!"

Michael, Kat, and Aeron heeded my command.

I brushed past Naomi to help Dane. She followed. I spun around to face her. "You did enough. Follow the others."

She glanced at Dane.

"I got him. Go!"

She nodded and twisted the dial on her device, disappearing before my eyes in a burst of light.

Stepping around the Sentinel, I held out my arm. "Grab hold."

Dane side-eyed me. "Like…I…can…do…that…right…now."

The Sentinel started to slowly turn toward us as Dane shifted focus.

"Quick, Ace!" I shouted.

He brought his left hand down on my arm and kept his right one up, holding off the Sentinel whose range of motion grew before my eyes.

I brought my right hand closer to my left and turned the dial, getting us both out of there.

62 JORDAN

Agra, India, Present Day

The Taj Mahal was absolutely breathtaking. I stood on the path beside the beautifully crafted pond of water and just admired the white marble structure.

"Magnificent, isn't it?" Gabriel said next to me.

I nodded. "Uh-huh."

"Reminds me of Heaven," he remarked. "Our castle is made of white marble just like this."

"Are you allowed to spill those kinds of details?" I teased. "Isn't it supposed to be a mystery?"

"There are no mysteries between us." He met my eyes. "Not anymore." He shook his head. "To think of where we started and where we stand now." He paused. "You're not that naive boy anymore."

I laughed. "Are you sure? Because all I can think about right now is that monkey behind you."

Gabriel turned and smiled at the primate. "Nice try," he said. "I know you're just diverting attention so you don't get too sentimental."

"Me, sentimental?" I waved him off.

He continued. "I also know you've been through a lot and aren't sleeping again. Care to talk about it?"

I shook my head. "Not really. I just keep seeing Murmur's eyes before he…" I shrugged it off. "It doesn't matter. I have this again." I lifted my necklace.

"You can't rely on that forever," Gabriel said.

"I know. I just really haven't had time to focus on finding a teacher. Every moment of rest I get is usually because I've just suffered some injury, so I'm recovering rather than ready to learn how to master my mind."

"I understand. I think Sandalphon can help, though," Gabriel said. "You should ask him."

"I'll give it a try after all this is over," I assured Gabriel. "You should go get the sphere."

"Would you like to come with me?" he asked.

My head snapped in his direction. "Really?"

He nodded. "I was being overly cautious trying to protect you before, but what I've come to realize is you're capable of taking care of yourself. Besides, now I know you can touch the keys, too, without being harmed."

I smiled. "Thanks, Gabriel." I touched his arm. "But there will always be a point where I'll need you."

"And I'll always be there," he said. "We should get moving."

We rejoined the others.

"Okay, team, are we ready?" I asked.

"Yes," Raphael said. "Gabriel, where is the sphere?"

"In one of the minarets," he told us, pointing to the four towers that flanked the Taj Mahal. "That one to be precise." He indicated the one in the far right back corner. "Everyone's attention will be up here in the front. It's the most picturesque. But I think we all should head that way, just in case there's an attack."

"The children will go with you," Yadira said. "Raphael, Zadkiel, and I will stand watch at the bottom."

I guessed Dafne and I where the "children" she referred to.

"Works for me," Gabriel agreed.

Together, we headed toward the Taj Mahal. As we got closer, it only became more amazing to see. There were so many details cut, set, and carved in the marble. We skirted the right-hand side, walking toward the back corner. When we were behind the marvelous structure, I saw a large river that meandered for several miles.

Dafne, Gabriel, and I split away from the others, moving closer to the minaret. There were a few short steps leading to a double door. Gabriel ascended them while Dafne and I stood in front of them to try to block anyone's view.

Gabriel touched the door, and it opened.

"How did you do that?" Dafne wondered aloud, shuffling inside.

"A celestial touch," he said, waving his fingers.

I entered the minaret, and Gabriel followed, shutting the door behind him.

I looked up, shocked by all the stairs we had to climb. "Who's ready for a workout?"

Rather than using words, they answered by beginning the trek up them.

Just like the mausoleum itself, the minarets were crafted from white marble, too. I was glad we were inside the tower during the day because the only light we had was from the sun shining in. If it had been night, we probably could have lit torches or something, but that would have added an extra thing to worry about, especially as we climbed the stairs.

I didn't think I could manage to hold a torch right now. I kept having to bend over and wheeze in air.

Eventually, we made it to the top. I glanced at my watch. Almost thirty minutes had gone by. We approached another door, which Gabriel also opened. We stepped through it and walked out onto a balcony.

Wow, the view was incredible. India stretched out for miles before us.

Dafne grabbed my arm and pulled me down to the floor of the balcony.

"What's wrong?" I asked.

"I don't want anyone to see us up here," she said.

"She's right. You two should stay low," Gabriel stated.

He was standing tall, and I wondered why he wasn't crouching. In fact, his wings unfurled, and he gently rose a few feet in the air so he could reach the top of the minaret.

It didn't take long for him to retrieve the sphere. As soon as his fingers touched the marble roof, it seemed as though the sphere couldn't wait to be extracted. It slowly came way in his hand, and once it was fully freed, he returned to the ground and bent low, showing us the golden-orange sphere.

"What type of stone is it?" Dafne asked.

"Danburite," Gabriel said. "It comes in many colors, but this one in particular is rare." He held on to the sphere tightly and said, "Let's head back before we're seen."

I knew the return trip would be easier since going down was always more leisurely than up. But there were so many steps that my knees were aching by the time we reached the bottom.

We eased through the doorway and returned to the others who were waiting outside.

"Any activity?" I asked.

"None," Zadkiel said. "Other than Sandalphon showing up." He gestured to the angel.

"I was happy to hear you've faced no opposition," Sandalphon said.

"Has that been the case for everyone?" Yadira asked.

"Not sure. You're the first group I've checked in with. Dane and I retrieved the first scepter piece, and I returned to the house to secure it, but there were some new arrivals there so I had to settle matters."

"New arrivals? Who?" Raphael asked.

"Tzaphkiel has come down from Heaven with a small contingency from the army. They're trying to see how many we can house without drawing too much attention. There is not enough room for everyone—our numbers are far too big—but they will remain and call upon the others closer to battle."

"That's good to hear," I said. "I was worried about keeping Martha, Emily, and Peter alone at the house with the keys. I mean, I know you're going back and forth, but Martha and Peter are trouble by themselves with all their silly schemes, let alone together."

"They were certainly in good spirits when I arrived," Sandalphon said. "Did the sphere retrieval go well?"

Gabriel handed him the sphere.

Sandalphon took it. "Thank you. I'll bring this back right away and then check on the others."

"Sandalphon, there's something I'd like to ask you before you go," I said.

"Yes?" he wondered aloud.

"It's about my visions. You said you could help."

He nodded. "Indeed. I'd like you to start meditating when you have time. Perhaps when all this is over. Nothing too difficult. Just sit, close your eyes, and breathe. Don't think about anything."

"Okay, I can do that," I said.

"Godspeed, friends," he said before departing.

"I guess we're off to the next location," Raphael said.

Which meant we were one step closer to reuniting with everyone. When we had been forcefully separated, everything had gone wrong. This time I hoped things worked in our favor.

63 SOPHIA

Huairou District, Beijing, China, Present Day

"Are you ever going to talk to us?" I asked Uriel.

He ignored me.

"Aziza," I pleaded.

"Uriel," she said, "what seems to be the problem? You've hardly spoken to any of us, and there's no clear sense of where you're leading us."

"Well maybe that's because I wanted to be on Jordan's team. He never yells at me like they do," he said, indicating Chamuel and me.

"What? I never yelled at you," I told him.

He thought about it. "I guess you didn't, considering the circumstances. But he did."

Chamuel shook his head. "You pushed her off a hill! I have every right to yell at you, especially since she's too nice to do it."

Uriel shrugged. "Perhaps my method was a little extreme. But she's flying, isn't she?"

Chamuel nodded. "She is. I'm sorry for yelling. We've been through too much to let this small thing get between us."

They hugged it out.

"All right," Uriel said. "The Great Wall has many sections, but we're headed for Mutianyu. It's the most restored part."

"Are we close?" Deborah asked.

"That structure up ahead is where we need to be," Uriel indicated.

It looked like a large watchtower along the wall. All around us were tons of budding trees and rolling mountains. The wall itself looked to be made of stacked bricks, a simple material yet so magnificent when used to craft something of this scale.

We were alone on the wall, and as we neared Mutianyu, a lone figure stood in our path.

Uriel, Chamuel, and I halted. We were at the front of the group, and I didn't like the sight of who blocked our way.

Uriel drew his bow, and Chamuel pulled free a knife. I spread my feet, positioning myself for a fight. That's what Rajani had taught me to do when faced with an opponent.

"What deep part of Hell did you come from?" Uriel asked.

Lucifer smirked. "I fled the Underworld as soon as Lilith arrived."

"Seems like you've done a lot of fleeing lately," Chamuel said. "Lilith, Satan, Jazema. Whose side are you really on?"

"My own," the fallen angel confessed. "But I'll align myself whichever way the wind blows."

"And whose direction is it blowing in now?" I asked.

"Lilith's," Lucifer answered. "But my allegiance hangs by a thread. I need to prove myself to her again. Otherwise, I'm dead."

"Let me guess," Chamuel said, "she told you to come back with a sphere or don't come back at all."

Lucifer nodded. "Pretty much."

"Like hell you're getting mine!" Uriel shouted, letting loose his arrows.

Out of the corner of my eye, a black figure crawled over the wall. I turned to look at it. It was a monster, a horrendous demon. "Chamuel," I said cautiously.

"I see them," he responded.

Them?

I glanced down the wall. Several other demons were scaling up it.

Aziza, Delphine, and Deborah were armed and ready with knives and swords.

"Fly up to the roof," Chamuel told me.

"What?" I asked.

"The watchtower! Get on the roof! You'll be safer there!" Chamuel urged, jumping into the fray.

I spread my wings and swiftly flew to the roof. When I landed, I noticed it wasn't a roof in the traditional sense but more like a barracks as there were places where soldiers could have attacked, as well as stairs leading down. I hoped no creature made its way over here, but I tried preparing myself for the worst.

Watching the battle from above, I felt guilty not helping. I had picked up some training from the angels and Rajani, but none of it was with weapons. The only weapons training I'd had was the archery class I had taken as a kid, and I hadn't held a bow in years.

Uriel burst into the air in front of me, also seeking refuge on the tower. I backed up as Lucifer followed him, the two duking it out.

My cover had been blown, so I vaulted over the other side and landed on the wall again. Looking through the watchtower, I spotted Uriel's bow lying unattended on the ground.

I walked into the tower and found stray arrows. I picked them up, easing past the stairs I was sure led to the top barracks where I'd just been. Striding out the other side, I discovered the battle with the demons was no better, so I grabbed Uriel's bow and loaded it.

I stepped back a few paces to get Lucifer in my line of sight. He was still fighting Uriel on top of the barracks.

A moving target was certainly harder than a sedentary one, but I had to try. My eyes narrowed, Nephilim senses kicking in. Based off their movements and fight patterns, I adjusted my arrow to the left and let it fly, even though Lucifer wasn't in reach quite yet. But in the seconds my arrow sailed through the air, he dodged backward, right into the arrow's path.

"Ah!" he shouted as it planted in his shoulder. He fell to one knee.

I launched into the air and nocked another arrow, using the moment of opportunity. I loosed the next one, and it hit him in the back. He shrieked as it lodged between his wings.

My feet found the short pillars atop the watchtower, holding me steady as I took the bow and smacked Lucifer across the face with it. He fell to the floor of the barracks, and I took my last arrow, driving it into his wing and tearing through his feathers.

He roared and reached out to grab my foot. I drove the arrow into his hand, then released the bow and grabbed his wrist, flinging him over the wall. He tumbled down the mountainside, probably still alive but definitely injured.

My chest was heaving from the exertion.

"What in heaven's name was that?" Uriel yelled.

"Vengeance for Sister Helen," I said. Bringing my attention to him, I added, "And loads of Nephilim instincts."

He raised his hand in the air for a high-five.

I smacked it.

"It's always the quiet ones that are deadly!" He grinned.

I shrugged. "Thanks… Maybe you should get the sphere, though, so we can get out of here."

"Oh, right!" He grew serious, stepping over to the middle of the barracks. He placed his hand on a small section of brick wall and called forth the sphere. Uriel drew it from among the bricks and held it out for me to see.

It was a glorious ruby orb.

He pulled back. "Admiration time is over. We have to help the others and get out of here."

We flew down to the wall and raced toward the battle. "It's time to go!" I yelled as we approached, Uriel taking out a few demons on our way to the group.

"Ready!" I shouted. "Set!" I placed my hand on my dial. "Go!"

The flashes of light from our devices had the demons withdrawing, but they were a complete afterthought as we traveled to the next site.

64 SOPHIA

Tiberias, Israel, Present Day

I landed, very ungracefully, in a marsh of reeds. Getting to my feet, I scanned my surroundings and had the sneaking suspicion that I wasn't in Greece, which had been our next location. In fact, I was entirely alone, not a single member of my group with me.

I glanced at my device, finding it hard to believe that Sandalphon had calibrated it wrong. I went to fiddle with the coordinate dials when someone said, "You're in the right spot."

I dropped my hand and stepped out from the reeds to find Sandalphon himself waiting for me. That's when I realized what we were doing here. There must have been a scepter piece hidden here.

I reached for the holster at my waist and pulled out the dagger. I hadn't used it in our battle on the wall since I figured I shouldn't be fighting with it. It was too precious an object to be exploiting mindlessly. Besides, I really wasn't skilled in using any type of sword.

"I see you're ready," he observed.

I nodded. "Yes." There was a part of me that hoped I would never see this dagger again. It was a symbol of severe change, an item that had driven us all apart. Luckily, we had made our way back to one another.

"Follow me," Sandalphon said.

There was a large body of water sprawled before us. Sandalphon walked toward where the water lapped the ground. I followed.

"Where are we?" I asked.

"Israel. This is the Sea of Galilee."

My eyes widened. This place had a lot of biblical significance. No wonder a scepter piece had been placed here.

"Return the dagger to the Earth," Sandalphon instructed.

I looked at my feet. Did he mean the ground? Technically, we were surrounded by the Earth. My eyes focused on the water. That must have been it. He wouldn't have brought me here if the water itself wasn't significant.

Slipping off my shoes and socks, and adding my phone to the pile, I walked to the sea's edge. I unsheathed the dagger and plunged it into the ground, right where the water met the Earth. A shock rippled across the surface.

"Enter the water," Sandalphon directed.

Without hesitation, I stepped forward into the Sea of Galilee, letting the water hit up to my chest.

"Breathe," Sandalphon said from behind me.

I breathed in and out calmly.

He placed his hand behind my head and gently dipped it forward.

The water rushed over me, relatively warm, soaking my hair and spanning it loosely around my head.

Sandalphon drew my head back, I breathed again, and then was submerged once more. He kept repeating the action.

The next time my head was underwater, I heard a voice whisper,

"Deceit lies without."

As I broke the surface, I squinted through tendrils of hair stuck to my face and saw a figure in the distance. A young man holding a large bird. I was dunked again and brought back up. Then I saw the silhouettes of five angels. I went under one more time. When I came up, those five were replaced by ten, two of which held out books.

I took another breath as I felt myself go back down. This time, there was no hand holding my head when I re-emerged.

I turned around. "What was that?"

"Whatever you saw were glimpses of the future," Sandalphon said, sitting cross-legged over the water.

I recalled the different figures in my mind. What did they mean?

"You're not supposed to know their significance. Otherwise they wouldn't be your future."

"How did you know I was thinking that?" I asked.

"You look confused," Sandalphon explained.

I nodded, lifting my hands to push the hair from my face. I froze when I saw I wasn't holding the dagger sheath anymore. Instead, I was holding something else. "What is this?"

"That's the top of the scepter," Sandalphon explained. "It sits on the rod and holds the Sovereign's Orb once it's created."

My jaw dropped open in shock. The item was made of two pairs of silvery-gray angel wings intersecting to form a place where the orb would rest. Right on the tips of each wing.

I handed it to him without saying a word.

He took it and rose to his full height, crossing the water and returning to land.

Finally, I pushed the hair from my face and joined him back on solid ground, noticing the dagger was gone now, too.

Thank the heavens I'd never have to see that thing again. It was like closing a chapter of my life I never wanted to relive. I was much more satisfied with the current me rather than the old one.

"Is that it?" I asked Sandalphon, ringing water from my hair.

"Yes. You may return to your group now."

I reached for my portal device.

"Sophia," he said.

I looked up at him.

"You might not be at the crux of this prophecy—the Union of the Spheres—but you are important. Dane, while good in nature, symbolizes the dark, whereas Jordan is the light. The two of them are in a constant struggle to maintain the balance. You, as a Nephilim, embody both the dark and the light, and rather than fight for balance, you already *are* balanced. Equal parts of light and dark that come together to make gray. That is why the blade of your dagger was that color." He paused. "I thought you might want to know your role in this journey."

I was grateful for his explanation. I sometimes wondered why I wasn't needed for the prophecy but still seemed an integral part. His words helped to alleviate my doubts and questions.

"Thank you, Sandalphon. From the beginning, I knew this wasn't my journey. If this is anyone's journey, it's Jordan's, and he's my family, so I'd never let him do this alone." I took a breath and looked out at the horizon. "I also know that my journey is out there, waiting for me. Those figures I saw were a sign of it."

"Indeed."

I sighed. "Well, I might not know what's to come, but I do know where I have to be now. I'll see you soon."

"Godspeed."

As I was whisked off to Greece, I knew I could add hopefulness and confidence to the ever-growing list of things I had regained. The trauma from my childhood had torn me down, but I was building myself back up.

65

DANE

ROME, ITALY, PRESENT DAY

I fell onto a cobblestone walkway, completely jarred. I was breathing heavy and squeezed my eyes shut to regain some control. All that did, however, was make me focus on the heartbeats around me. The urge to pull at them increased.

A hand touched my shoulder, and my eyes flew open, a surge of power compelling me to raise my hands in the air, ready to attack.

"Ace, it's me!" Satan shouted.

I dropped my hands, and I crumbled, my head sinking to my knees.

"What the hell happened to you?" Satan asked. "Your hair's full of salt. Your clothes are stiff as a board. Where did Sandalphon take you?"

"I can't do this," I whispered.

Satan sat down on the cobblestone before me. "What can't you do?"

My head whipped up, and I held out my hands. "I can't take this power!" I screamed, body shaking.

"All right," he said. "Just stop for a second. Don't move, close your eyes, and breathe."

I followed his advice.

"What do you feel?"

I started to open my eyes.

"Don't open your eyes," he chided. "Don't think. Just say whatever comes to mind when I ask you." He waited. "What do you feel?"

"I feel...like I'm being suffocated, constricted. There's always this rush in my head, and I want to just grab it and..." I trailed off.

"Anything else?" Satan asked.

"No."

"No numbness, no pain, no ache?"

I shook my head.

"Hmm...do you have Hellfire?"

"Yes, I had uncontrollable fevers at the lab, and I burned Sophia," I told him.

"Anything since?"

I thought about it. "I used it in Purgatory, but after I brought Jordan back to life, I haven't tried again. I'm too scared to touch anyone, and when I touch inanimate things—" I reached over and pulled at some blades of grass that flanked the walkway "—it doesn't work."

"That's because you need to ignite it when you touch inanimate things," he said, taking the grass from me. He held it briefly, and then the green blades slowly crumbled. "We only have control over the fire when it comes to the unliving. The Hellfire feeds off anything with a heartbeat, which is why it burns immediately."

I pulled out some more grass to give it a try.

Nothing.

I focused harder, my brow furrowing in concentration. "It's not working," I said.

"I know," Satan said. "That's because your pilot light is out, so to speak."

"What do you mean?"

"I'm starting to see why Lilith created you. Zadkiel's explanation at the house was accurate, but combining blood magic and Hellfire is lethal. You see, for me, the Hellfire is pain, aching, numbness. I had to learn to live with those feelings constantly. That's the only way I control it. But you don't just have Hellfire. You have blood magic, too, and that's all emotion. Our blood is reactive to our moods and situations. It boils when we're angry and flows smoothly when we're calm.

"That's why it's more of a roller coaster for you because you're not only riding your emotions but you can also feel everyone else's. Essentially, your body feeds off heartbeats and blood. It needs them to regulate itself. But what I've learned is you can't always be feeding off heartbeats, so I had to manage the power without nourishing it."

"How?" I asked.

"You cage it like an animal. Turn those feelings of suffocation and constriction into the power rather than let them consume you."

"That doesn't sound easy," I acknowledged.

"It's not. I nearly succumbed after the Fall and let it take me."

"What changed?"

He grinned. "My stubbornness. I remembered that this was something done *to* me, not something I asked for, and succumbing was what they wanted. So I fought it to defy them."

That definitely resonated with me. Lilith was the one who wanted this, wanted me to possess these powers. Succumbing to them would fulfill her will. Not succumbing to them would destroy me. I had a tougher choice than Satan because defiance in my case meant insanity.

"I know what you're thinking," Satan said.

"Do you?"

He nodded. "Your immediate thought was to deny your powers. To never learn control. The expense being your entire self. Am I right?"

"Yeah," I murmured.

"That's what *not* to do," he said.

I rolled my eyes. "Then what *am* I supposed to do?"

Satan smirked. "I guess you have my anger after all."

I sighed. "Sorry."

He grabbed me by the collar. "Never apologize for who or what you are."

Those words were what I needed to hear—a balm to my broken mind.

Satan let me go. "Blood magic is all about emotion," he said again. He raised his hand, palm flat. "Hellfire is all about numbness." He raised his other hand, palm flat. "Right now, the blood magic is drowning the Hellfire to the point that it's blown out your flame." He placed his right hand over his left, almost like the two were eating each other. "That's what Lilith wants. She gave you the Hellfire as a way to intensify your blood magic, never intending for you to use it on its own. What you need to do is the opposite." He flipped his hands so the left was eating the right. "You need to master the Hellfire so the numbness drowns out the emotion. Only then will you be able to use both your powers without either consuming you."

"Easier said than done," I said, daunted by the task.

"Yes," Satan admitted. "Except you have the one thing Lilith never wanted you to have."

"Which is?"

"Me. I'll help you. We'll work on this together."

"Really?"

Satan stood. "You're stuck with me, Ace." He reached out his hand.

I grabbed it, and he helped me up. "Whether you like it or not," he added.

I laughed. "Leave it to the Devil to force me into his company."

He slapped my back. "That bastard. How dare he," Satan joked. "Now let's go see what these mightier-than-thou angels are up to. Which reminds me…" He took off the chain around his neck, slipped a ring off his finger, then looped it on the necklace. He hooked it back around his neck. "I don't want to wear that ring anymore," he said.

We strode over to the rest of the group, who looked to be huddled up and strategizing.

Naomi noticed us and pulled away from the others. "Are you okay?" she asked me.

I nodded. "Yeah, I'll be fine."

"Thanks for the save. I owe you one," she said.

I waved it off, settling the matter without words. "What are we up to?"

"They're trying to make a plan to get the sphere. It's directly in the floor of the Colosseum," Naomi explained.

"Figures," Satan scoffed.

I glanced at the building. It was crazy to think we were standing where Roman soldiers once walked, where gladiators once fought.

"Can't you just fly down and extract it?" Satan suggested. "Easy in, easy out."

"Except there are people everyone," Aeron pointed out. "We're trying to err on the side of caution."

Satan sauntered over to him. "You and I have different philosophies. Who the hell cares about caution? Just do it! We need to get to Paris, and these people will make up mindless excuses anyway."

Michael and Kat stared at him.

"Fine," Satan conceded. "Do it your way. We already made a scene at Angkor Wat, and I'm sure Paris will be a shitshow, but let's stop now and err on the side of caution."

"You don't have to come if you're so against our methods," Michael said, heading toward the entrance with Kat and Aeron.

Satan crossed his arms and glanced at Naomi and me. "When did this become his team?"

Naomi and I remained silent, following after the others. Satan trailed behind us.

"Michael," I said once I caught up to him.

"Hmm?"

"What did you do with the other sphere?" I asked him.

"We put it in Aeron's backpack," he said. "Hopefully, Sandalphon will come soon."

When we finally got through the line to get inside, Michael said, "Find a tour group and follow them down to the floor."

"Like that one," Satan indicated.

Michael rushed down the uneven steps. We all followed after him.

"This is ridiculous!" Satan shouted. "We look desperate!"

"Aren't we?" Naomi asked cynically.

At the bottom, we blended into the tour group as best we could.

"Pull out your phones and take some pictures," Satan demanded.

We reached into our pockets.

"You too, Uncle Aeron," he said.

Aeron tensed. "Must you call me that?"

"Just take out your damn phone," Satan snarled.

"I don't have one," Aeron bit out. "I'm not supposed to exist."

"Oh, right. I forgot because you're currently existing where I am and it's incredibly annoying," Satan barked.

I grabbed his arm and pulled him back. "Smile," I said, snapping a selfie.

"What the hell, Ace!" he yelled.

"You're making too much of a scene, so kindly shut up and play along," I told him.

He sighed. My words compelled him into silence.

Eventually, the tour group was led through a gate and onto the floor of the Colosseum. It was a shame that only select people could experience this because it changed the entire experience of visiting the ancient stadium. Everyone got to roam the arena and the outer halls, but this was roaming in a gladiator's footsteps, a true walk through history.

Since the group was relatively big, no one noticed when Michael knelt, pretending to tie his shoe. The five of us surrounded him, hoping to hide him and what he was doing.

Placing his hand to the floor, he summoned the sphere. As it rose from the ground, I could see it was a deep-blue stone. Lapis lazuli, I guessed.

Kat unzipped Aeron's backpack, reaching inside to grab a water bottle, which she handed to me while Michael stood and slipped the sphere inside, zipping it shut. The two of them worked together so fast that no one around us noticed anything.

When the tour guide brought us lower to the underground tunnels, we broke away from the group and secluded ourselves in an alcove.

"To Paris," Michael said.

"Hold on, Brother," Sandalphon said, appearing out of nowhere.

"Where the hell have you been?" Satan asked.

Sandalphon grew serious. "Securing spheres, retrieving scepter pieces, and arranging an army at the house. You?"

"Fighting demons and the Sentinel," Satan threw back.

Sandalphon turned to Michael. "You were attacked?"

Satan huffed, clearly frustrated that he had no authority.

"Yes," Michael said.

"This doesn't bode well," Sandalphon mused. "You're the first to report such an occurrence, but I have one more group to check on. Hopefully, they've been faring all right."

Kat took the spheres out of Aeron's backpack and handed them to Sandalphon.

"I'll secure these, then go check on the final group," he assured us. "I'll see you all in Paris."

Once he vanished, everyone focused their attention on their portal device, knowing exactly what to do.

66 JORDAN

Barcelona, Spain, Present Day

"I don't think this works," I said to Dafne.

We were standing across the street from La Sagrada Familia in front of a large park full of green trees.

She looked down at my dad's compass, which I was holding in my hand.

"All it does is keep spinning. It can't even find north." I sighed. "It must be broken."

"Let me see," she said.

I handed her the compass. As soon as she was holding it, the needle steadied and pointed north.

"What the… How did you do that?" I asked.

She shrugged. "I'm not doing anything other than holding it." She passed it back to me.

It started spinning endlessly again, and I frowned.

She patted my cheek. "I'm sorry. You're obviously meant to do something with it, but I'm not sure what."

I sighed again. "My life used to be full of secrets. Now it's puzzles."

"Puzzles are better than secrets," Dafne said.

"How?" I huffed.

"Because puzzles can be fun while secrets never are."

I noticed her tone of voice had changed. Slipping the compass in my pocket, I asked, "Everything okay?"

She smiled. "Yeah."

Except her answer seemed forced.

"Dafne, are *you* keeping a secret?"

She sighed. "Sort of."

I waited.

She bit her lip. "I'm going to Paris in the fall."

"Okay," I said.

"For school. I'm attending Parsons in Paris."

"And what's the problem with that? Isn't that a good thing?"

"Yes, it's exactly what I wanted."

"But?"

"But I'll be gone for three years," she said. "I mean, there are breaks and stuff, of course."

It finally dawned on me what she was getting it. "You're worried about not seeing me?"

"Yes!" she shouted. "Shouldn't I be?"

"Well, I don't know. I wasn't sure what we were doing," I confessed.

She raised a hand to her forehead.

I gently touched her wrist and lowered her arm. "Dafne, I've never done dating and girlfriends before."

"Neither have I!" she admitted. "And you seem like you like me, but you're also very distant."

"I do like you! So much. But I've been distant because I don't know how this ends for me," I said. "I already nearly died, and—"

"Stop," she said.

But I kept going. "And I don't want you to feel the pain of losing me if we were to get closer."

She met my eyes. I couldn't help but notice hers were full of tears. "You're not dying."

My heart squeezed, and I grabbed her in a hug.

"Besides, I already had to feel that pain," she mumbled.

I drew back. "You were there?"

She nodded. "I saw you flatline."

A tear fell down her cheek. I brushed it away with my hand.

"I already feel close to you, Jordan," she said and laughed. "Which is crazy because we hardly know each other. But I feel like I know enough…like I know the best parts of you, which makes me want to know everything else about you."

I smiled. "I know what you mean. Since the day I met you, I haven't been able to stop thinking about you. And at first, I kept wondering why you were so cold to me." She grinned. "And then you opened up in New York when we were getting ready for the gala, and something clicked."

"I was only cold to you because that's how I always am around boys, which is probably why I've never gotten close to anyone. But you're different, easy to talk to. You don't judge people."

I leaned my forehead against hers. "Okay, so I think we can safely say that we're officially dating."

She smiled and rubbed her nose against mine. "I would agree with that statement."

"Then we'll make long-distance work," I said, "and enjoy every moment we have until you leave."

She looked into my eyes. "Promise?"

"Promise," I assured her.

Without saying a word, we leaned toward each other for our first kiss.

Someone cleared their throat.

I sighed and turned to face Gabriel. "Yes?"

He pointed at his watch. "We have to get inside."

I let go of Dafne and grabbed his arm, pulling him to the side. "You couldn't have waited just a few minutes. Our lips hadn't even touched," I said, outraged.

Gabriel looked at me sternly. "This is one topic I refuse to discuss." He pressed the crosswalk button and waited for traffic to change. "Besides," he added, "you can kiss in Paris. It's more romantic."

The light changed, and the crosswalk turned green. He strode forward toward the church.

Crap, why hadn't I thought of that?

The rest of the group came forward and followed Gabriel. Dafne grabbed my hand, and we trailed after them.

La Sagrada Familia was beautiful. There were so many intricate details carved into the stone façade, and the structure itself soared into the sky. We gathered around the doors and entered the church together. Once we passed through the doorway, my mouth dropped open and I was speechless.

I had never seen a church like this. The ceilings were enormously high, and there were so many decorative elements, it was hard to fixate on one. Stained glass windows were everywhere, and as the sun shone through them, a rainbow of light reflected along the interior white walls.

It was like we had walked into a jewel box.

"You see those four pillars in the middle?" Raphael said.

I nodded. Each had some sort of oval at the top with artwork on it.

"Those represent the four Evangelists," Raphael continued. "The sphere is inside Matthew's pillar. It should have an angel depicted in the oval."

Dafne and I strode over to the pillars with Raphael. We angled our heads up and analyzed the ovals.

"It's the yellow one," Dafne said, pointing.

Raphael nodded and waved the others over. They joined us around the pillar. Zadkiel sat down in the pew directly next to it, Yadira in the one in front, and Gabriel directly behind. Dafne and I flanked Raphael as he knelt on the floor, all of us trying to hide him from sight so no one would take interest. The church surrounding us was much more interesting anyway, so I didn't think we had much to worry about.

I watched Raphael place his hand on the pillar. Slowly, he drew out an emerald sphere, the green color so spectacular it was hard to miss.

"What do you feel when you do that?" I asked.

"Warmth," Raphael said. "My energy connecting to the energy of the sphere. In a way, each key is part of the angel who protects it, so it's an exciting feeling, almost like a homecoming or reunion." He passed the sphere to me. "Here."

My eyes widened. "I can take it?"

He nodded. "Bring it to Sandalphon."

"But I don't know where he is," I said.

"I know," Raphael answered. "But I imagine you'll be meeting him after this to retrieve a scepter piece. He wanted everything secure before the last location, and you have yet to leave us."

I reached out and took the sphere. A surge of energy rushed through me. I understood now why this could harm people. It was strong, overwhelming, but at the same time calming and serene. For me, when I looked at the sphere and held it in my hand, I could hear choirs of angels singing.

In that moment, I finally felt as though we were going to win.

67 SOPHIA

Athens, Greece, Present Day

By the time I arrived in Athens, the sun was beginning to set. I had dried off from my excursion in the Sea of Galilee, but I rubbed my arms to get out the chill that the cool evening air blew over me.

"Oh, thank the heavens!" Chamuel shouted, racing over to me. He enveloped me in a hug.

Once he pulled away, Delphine took me in her arms. "I'm so happy you're all right!"

"Where did you think I went?" I asked.

She eased back. "We weren't sure."

"But the last time this happened," Chamuel added, "we were separated for weeks, so don't blame us for being worried."

I smiled. "I would never blame any of you for worrying. If anything, I'm sorry I worried you."

Deborah pulled off her windbreaker and draped it around my shoulders.

"Did you get the sphere?" I asked.

"No," Uriel said. "He was too distraught about you." He pointed to Chamuel.

"I only went to meet Sandalphon and collect the scepter." I held out my wrist. "I guess these are programmed because I had no idea I would be leaving you all; otherwise I would have said something."

"I told you that's where she went," Aziza chided.

"All right. I'll admit I might have overreacted," Chamuel said. "But it was warranted given everything we've already been through the past few months. Anyway, now that you're back, let's get the sphere."

Chamuel headed for a flagpole in the distance.

"Isn't that the Acropolis?" Uriel said, going after him and pointing to the large structure behind us on the rocky hill.

Chamuel shook his head. "Not exactly. The whole rock we're standing on is considered the Acropolis. Technically, this entire place is a modern wonder. What you're pointing at is the Parthenon."

"Well, shouldn't it be there? It seems more important," Uriel commented.

Chamuel stopped. "Did I question you when we were gathering your sphere?"

"No," Uriel muttered.

"Exactly. So trust me."

I figured Chamuel would know best so I strolled after him, taking my time and gazing at the splendid view. It was as if I could see the entire country from here as it spanned across the horizon. The gorgeous sunset made it a million times more beautiful, and it was hard not to stop for a moment and revel in the scenery.

"It's glorious, isn't it?" Delphine said.

I nodded.

She crossed her arms against the wind. "I'm sorry."

I glanced at her. "Don't be sorry. I've realized that who I am right now in this moment is the best version of myself I've come to know so far, and that wouldn't be possible without the things you did. Sure, some of your decisions still leave me a little sour, but I know you had good intentions."

"Am I forgiven, then?" she asked.

I wrapped my arm around her and pulled her close. "Yes. Although, I'm not sure I can let my father off as easily. At least you cared for me. All he did was dump me and leave."

"I'm not going to defend your father because I'm not happy with the choices he made, either," Delphine said. "All I can say on his behalf is that he struggled more than anyone with the circumstances we were dealt."

"And perhaps someday I'll be able to accept that as enough," I said. "But today's not that day." I left her side and went to find Chamuel.

"Sophia," she said, catching up to me.

"Yeah?"

"I'm very proud of who you have become."

I hugged her again. "Thank you."

When we found Chamuel and the others, they were all standing beneath the flagpole. Delphine and I mounted the short steps to join them.

"What did we miss?" Delphine asked.

Deborah shrugged. "Not much. We're waiting for this couple to clear out, and then Chamuel is going to retrieve the sphere."

There weren't too many people around at this time of day. At least, not near the flagpole. Most were more intrigued by the temples and structures behind us.

Once the couple walked down the steps, Chamuel stooped and placed his hand against the smooth ground.

"I see I arrived just in time," Sandalphon said.

Uriel jumped on him. "Where have you been? We were attacked and have been carrying around this sphere." He walked over to Deborah and took the sphere from the backpack she was wearing. "Here." Uriel gave it to Sandalphon.

"You were confronted, too?" Sandalphon asked, taking the sphere.

"Yes, by Lucifer and some demons," Aziza said.

"Hmm." Sandalphon pondered her words.

"Who else was attacked?" I asked, concerned.

"Dane's group. But no one was harmed," Sandalphon assured us.

"And Jordan?" I asked, curious for information.

"They've had no issues," he said.

"Here you go," Chamuel said, coming over with his rose quartz sphere.

Sandalphon took it. "Thank you."

"Is it off to Paris now?" Delphine asked.

"For you all," Sandalphon said. "I have one last scepter piece to get with Jordan, but we shouldn't be far behind."

"Sandalphon, what should we expect next?" I asked.

"In Paris?" He sighed. "A full-on assault. I think the two minor attacks were purposeful to gain intelligence on our plans."

"Wouldn't Lilith wait for the war to do that?" I wondered aloud.

"She'll use every asset she has for the war," Sandalphon said. "But for Paris, I'm sure she'll show up herself, along with Lucifer and the Sentinel. Possibly some demons."

"She has more than that?" Deborah asked.

"Much more," Sandalphon said. "She has all of Purgatory on her side."

I gulped at the daunting fight ahead.

"You all should go. Get to safety and rest for the night," Sandalphon said.

He didn't have to tell any of us twice. We all were exhausted, and I was sure us humans couldn't wait for some warm food and a pillow to rest our heads on.

68 Jordan

Near Degania Bet, Israel, Present Day

When I had used my portal device at the church in Spain, I knew I wouldn't be going to Paris right away. Yet, I didn't expect to be dropped into the middle of some countryside. Before me was a stream of water. Around me were plants, palms, and other trees. Behind me, it looked like there might be a road, but it didn't sound like a busy one.

It was almost dark, and Sandalphon was nowhere in sight. For a brief moment, I worried for my safety, but I tried to remain calm.

Maybe I should practice some meditation.

I sat on the ground, still holding Raphael's emerald sphere. I closed my eyes and breathed deeply, inhaling through my nose and exhaling through my mouth, trying not to think.

A few moments went by before I opened my eyes again. It was pitch-dark around me, bugs buzzing in the moonlight.

"That was some good meditation," Sandalphon said.

I glanced over and saw him sitting next to me. "How long have you been here?"

"About an hour and a half," he answered. "I didn't want to disturb you."

"I wouldn't have minded," I said. "Actually, I would have preferred it. I'm getting hungry."

Sandalphon grinned. "Then let's begin."

"Wait. You should take this," I said, handing over Raphael's sphere.

He took it from me and placed it in the large pocket of his cloak. Then we stood together. He approached the stream's edge, and I followed.

"Do you know what this is?" Sandalphon asked.

"A stream," I said.

He shook his head. "It's a river."

"A river?" I repeated. Then I stopped when I thought it over. "You mean…" I pointed to myself.

"Your namesake."

Wow, I was standing before the River Jordan. Which meant I was in Israel.

Goose bumps prickled along my arms.

"Return the dagger to the Earth," Sandalphon instructed.

I pulled it free from the holster at my belt. Taking the blade from its sheath, I bent over to stick it in the ground, but Sandalphon tsk-tsked.

I guessed the placement wasn't right. I stepped closer to the river and decided to insert the blade where the water met the shore.

He didn't stop me that time, and a shock rippled across the river.

"Enter the water," Sandalphon directed.

I grinned. This was awesome! I was going in the river!

I slipped off my shoes and socks, and emptied my pockets, taking out my phone and the compass. I walked to the center of the river, the water fairly shallow, coming close to my waist.

"Kneel," Sandalphon said from behind me.

I did as I'd been told, the water rising to my chest.

"Breathe," he said.

I sucked in air.

He placed his hand behind my head and gently dipped it forward.

The waters washed over my head and then receded as I was pulled up by Sandalphon. He kept repeating the action, and I figured this was all that would happen, which was fine with me.

Then I heard words whispered.

The journey to both is obscure.

My head rose from the waters, and all I saw was death. Sophia with blood spilling from her abdomen. I went under and came up. Gabriel with a wound in his chest. I was dunked and reemerged, only to be presented with the winged angel of death himself—Azrael. I gasped as I went forward once more, this time choking on water when I surfaced. There was no longer a hand holding my head.

I pushed my hair back with my hand and whipped around to find Sandalphon. "What was that?" I demanded.

"Whatever you saw were glimpses of the future," he said solemnly. "Yours were more distinct than the others because of your gift."

"Gift!" I shouted, outraged. "What gift? All this has been is a curse!"

Sandalphon didn't speak.

"How soon?" I whispered, hysteria setting in.

"I don't know."

I smacked my hands against the water in frustration, sending up a splash. "I hate this! I just want answers!" I opened my mouth to yell some more when I noticed I wasn't holding the dagger sheath anymore. It had been replaced with a white rod engraved with feathers.

I walked out of the water and handed to him. "Here." I pretty much dropped it at his feet, but he caught it before it could hit the ground.

"Where are you going?" he asked.

"To Paris," I said, collecting my things. I couldn't help but notice the dagger was no longer in the ground. It had completely disappeared.

"Jordan, I'm sor—"

I didn't wait for him to finish.

69

JORDAN

Paris, France, Present Day

"Surprise!" everyone shouted.

My head was too bogged down from what I had seen at the river that I didn't even register where I was or why everyone was so celebratory.

"Wh-what's all this?" I asked.

"It's your birthday, silly," Naomi said.

Birthday? Was it March twenty-fifth already?

I glanced at the phone in my hand. Sure enough, it was past midnight so it was officially my birthday.

"Jordan, are you okay?" Dafne asked.

I nodded. "Yeah…I just need a shower and some food." I turned away from everyone to walk down the hallway, but I realized I had no idea where anything was. We seemed to be in an apartment, but I didn't care about details right now. I was sure I would get them later.

"Last door on the right," Dane said.

"Thanks." I could hear them start to whisper as I headed away.

I entered a bedroom that had two twin beds in it. Dane must have claimed one already because his clothes were resting on the edge.

I grabbed the sweats and T-shirt off the other and headed to the shower.

Once I was washed up and changed, I went back out to the kitchen and pasted a smile on my face. "Sorry, everyone! I feel much better now."

"There's the Jordan we all know," Delphine said.

I inspected the food they had set out for the small celebration and saw fruit and cheese, quiche and croissants. I filled up a plate and dug in, needing some nourishment after a long day.

We reveled in one another's company, and then a cake was brought out and everyone sang "Happy Birthday."

"Make a wish!" Dafne said.

I didn't hesitate.

I wish no one dies.

I blew out the candles and ate a huge slice of chocolate cake, thinking that would be the end of the festivities for the night. But then Sophia shouted, "Time for gifts!"

"Gifts?" I asked. "I don't need any gifts."

"Well, too bad," Dane said, giving me his first.

It was a magnificent drawing of New York. "I love it. Thank you."

Uncle Aeron gave me a pocketknife, Aunt Delphine a really nice watch.

"You didn't have to do this," I said.

"It wasn't just me. It's from Martha and Emily, too," Delphine stated.

Next up was Deborah and Peter, who gave me a set of framed photos of my parents. Then Naomi gave me a flask.

"Naomi!" her mom chastised.

"I know what you're all thinking," she defended. "He's not legal yet. But it's not for alcohol; it's for holy water."

"Mine next," Sophia said. "They let me do it." She gestured to the angels.

I ripped the wrapping paper and pulled it back. It was a framed photo of me and the angels. All of them. Even Jophiel. "When did you take this?"

"On our trip last spring," Sophia said. "I wasn't going to do anything with it, but then I thought it would be a great gift. I asked them if it was all right."

"I thought photos were forbidden," I said.

"They are," Gabriel stated.

"Which is why you only get the one," Uriel finished.

"Now here's our gift," Michael said, handing me a heavy, rectangular box.

I set the frame aside and flipped open the latches. Inside was a short sword, the blade a shiny silver, the hilt a gilded gold.

"We don't usually go around handing out celestial weapons," Chamuel said.

"But we thought you were an exception," Raphael replied.

I was shocked and honored. "Wow...this is amazing. Thank you."

Dafne stepped forward with her gift next, but Satan cut her off. "All right, so I'll just come out and say I don't have a gift for you because I had no idea it was your birthday. But—" he slapped his hands down on top of my shoulders "—think of me not killing you in Tokyo as my gift."

I glanced up at him. "You infected me with dark matter."

He scrunched his face. "Maybe not the best gift, but you're still alive."

I frowned but couldn't help but begin to smile as Dafne stepped forward again.

Yet, once more she was interrupted. This time by a sudden burst of light. Sandalphon had returned.

"How did everything go?" Michael asked.

"Spheres and scepter are secured," he said. "I thought I'd find you all resting."

"It's Jordan's birthday," Gabriel said.

Sandalphon grimaced. "Oh…I had no idea."

"It's okay. Our trip was already a gift," I said, a touch of venom in my tone.

He ignored it and changed the subject. "Whose apartment is this?"

"It's a Sacrarium safehouse," Deborah said.

"It's the perfect location," Sandalphon remarked, glancing out the window at the Eiffel Tower.

That launched a lengthy discussion about tomorrow and strategy.

"Can I talk to you?" Dafne whispered.

I nodded.

"In private."

"Oh…sure."

We stood and went out to the balcony, closing the door behind us. There wasn't any furniture so I sat on the ground, and Dafne joined me.

"What happened with you and Sandalphon?"

"You promise you won't tell anyone?" I asked.

She extended her hand, pinkie finger raised.

I smiled and wrapped my pinkie around hers. Then I told her what had happened and what I'd seen.

"You've had strange visions before that never came to fruition," she said. "Are you sure it wasn't one of those?"

I hugged my knees to my chest. "Sandalphon sure made it sound like it wasn't."

"Well what does he know?" Dafne raged.

"I don't want it to be true, either," I said.

We sat in silence, holding hands.

"I never had a chance to give you this." She passed me a square box.

I untwined our fingers and opened it. It was a brown leather bracelet with a braided design. I picked it up and unbuckled the clasp.

"Wait," she said before I slid it on my wrist. "Look on the inside."

There was a fancy *DD* inscribed in gold lettering. "You made this?"

She nodded.

"I love it!"

Our eyes met, and we reached for each other. The first kiss was slow, our lips meeting and lingering. The second was full of desire, my hands tangling in her hair, hers roaming my chest. The last was deep, both of us drinking in the other like we were each other's last breath.

I pulled back, resting my forehead against hers, before it could go any further.

She lightly touched my lips. "Happy birthday," she whispered.

I smiled, snuggling closer, our noses touching.

Eventually, we drew back, and she helped me put on the bracelet.

"We should get some sleep," Dafne said.

The very thing I was trying to avoid, knowing I would be plagued with nightmares of Sophia and Gabriel dying.

Dafne leaned back against the wall of the building, making herself comfortable. "Lie down."

"We can't stay out here."

"Says who?"

I supposed she was right. I listened to her and laid down. She coaxed me to put my head in her lap and stroked my hair.

"Sleep," she instructed.

And just like that, I fell asleep without any hesitation.

70

JORDAN

Paris, France, Present Day

The next morning, we all ate a quick breakfast—minus the angels—and walked over to the Eiffel Tower.

When we were about a block away, we had a team huddle.

"Okay, everyone, we have new groups," Michael said. "There's the Tower Group, consisting of Zadkiel, Jordan, Satan, and Sandalphon. There's the Air Group, consisting of Sophia, Dane, Uriel, Chamuel, and myself. And there's the Ground Group, consisting of Kat, Gabriel, Yadira, Aziza, Aeron, Delphine, Deborah, Naomi, Dafne, and Raphael, which will break into sub-teams depending upon what we're up against.

"Tower Group, your goal is the sphere. Find it, retrieve it, and secure it—meaning you all go back to the house with it, except for Satan. He'll notify everyone else that we've accomplished our mission. The rest of us are your defense. Any questions?"

No one had any.

"All right. Then here we go," Michael said.

The Air Group launched into the sky, doing recon overhead while everyone else continued our walk to the tower.

We just reached our destination when trouble started brewing.

A crack of lightning pierced the sky, even though it was a dry spring day, leaving a jagged streak of light over the gardens of the Eiffel Tower. Suddenly, the streak of light elongated, and a massive horde of demons came swarming through.

Kat, Yadira, and Aziza stepped forward, ready to fight.

"Get to the tower," Gabriel said to me, drawing his weapon.

"On it," I assured him as Sandalphon, Zadkiel, and Satan headed for the entrance.

I grabbed Dafne's arm. "Be careful."

"You too," she urged.

I ran after the others toward the entrance and spied an onslaught of demons arriving from the other side near the River Seine.

"Uncle Aeron!" I called.

He turned around.

I pointed to the hooded figure walking down the middle of the nearest bridge.

"On it!" he shouted, assembling a team.

Finally, I regrouped with the others by the entrance.

"We need to go to the second floor," Zadkiel said. "Typically, I would try to take the elevator or stairs—"

"Screw that!" Satan roared.

"We must conform to humanity's ways when we're among them," Sandalphon chided.

"But in this case—" Zadkiel started.

"Not when *that's* heading our way!" Satan barked, grabbing me by the shirt and rising into the air.

Zadkiel and Sandalphon blanched at the sight of the huge demon that was barreling toward them.

"I'll take it!" Sandalphon said. "You go!" He drew two hatchets from his cloak and engaged the monster.

I squirmed in Satan's grasp.

"Stop wiggling!" he yelled at me.

"You're...choking...me," I wheezed. He still had me by the back collar.

"Shit!" He flung me high, and I free-fell for a second before he caught me around the waist.

My stomach churned. "Never do that again," I said.

"Don't tell me you get motion sickness!"

"Sometimes," I admitted. "It's gotten much better, but you throwing me around isn't helping."

Zadkiel flew by us, leading the way to the second floor.

At this point, everyone on the ground was screaming and running so there was no point trying to hide what we were doing.

We landed on the second-floor viewing deck, and I couldn't help to take a minute to look at what was happening below.

71

GABRIEL

PARIS, FRANCE, PRESENT DAY

I could feel something approaching from behind. I grabbed a knife from my vest and flung it, anticipating a spray of gore, but none came. Instead, I slashed through the underbelly of a demon creeping up on Kat.

So that's how our shared senses worked.

Michael, Uriel, and Chamuel swooped down from the sky and landed next to me.

"There's not much activity in the air," Michael reported. "Lucifer is nowhere to be found."

"Probably because Sophia bashed him good on the head," Uriel commented.

"So we're leaving the kids in the air and coming down to help," Michael finished.

"Be my guest," I said. "I wish Jophiel was here. We need to come up with a way to take out that portal."

"That crack of lightning was a portal?" Chamuel asked.

I nodded. "Lilith's gotten stronger, but she refuses to show herself."

"Their attacks have been strange this entire time," Michael said. "But we can't dwell on that now. We'll focus on the portal."

"No," Uriel said. "You'll fight the demons. Yadira and I will focus on the portal." Without another word, he raced over to her.

"Where are our other human friends?" Michael asked.

"They went with Aeron to fight the Sentinel. Raphael's with them," I told him.

"All right. You stay here. Chamuel and I will go help them," Michael commanded.

72 MICHAEL

PARIS, FRANCE, PRESENT DAY

Chamuel and I quickly zoomed through the air over to the river. Why Aeron had thought it was a good idea to take Delphine, Deborah, and Dafne to fight the Sentinel was beyond me. Naomi would've been a much better choice, considering there was water on either side of the bridge.

When we arrived, I was surprised to see the trio of women holding their own against a small group of demons. Perhaps I shouldn't have underestimated them. Two of them were Sacrarium members, and Dafne had Tony as a grandfather.

Aeron was fighting the Sentinel one-on-one. Somehow, he had unhooded the monster so I figured it was best for them to hash it out for now since Aeron could plainly see that the Sentinel was really Silas.

"Chamuel, stay with Delphine, Deborah, and Dafne. I'm going to find Raphael," I said.

I searched the area, but there was no sign of him or Naomi. A sense of foreboding kicked in. I glanced over the bridge and finally found them along the riverbank. I jumped over the side and landed on the walkway beneath.

There was a trail of blood.

"Who's hurt?" I demanded.

"Me," Raphael said.

Well, that was a first.

I rushed to his side to see what was wrong.

"The Sentinel shot him," Naomi said. She was pulling water from the river to create an orb in her hand. She brought it close to Raphael's shoulder and cleansed the wound.

"I got the bullet out," he said. "But it's one of those Geneloom ones, so it won't heal as quickly."

I pulled off my Henley, since I was wearing a tank underneath, and tore it in two, using one half to put pressure on the wound.

When Naomi was done, I wound the other half around his shoulder to hold the makeshift dressing in place.

"You need to go back," I said.

"No, I can fight," he assured me.

"Raphael, this isn't a discussion. Go back to the house and let Martha help you bandage this properly. I won't lose another brother."

"Fine." He sighed, turning the dial on his wrist.

He disappeared.

"Are you hurt?" I asked Naomi.

"No."

"Good. I need you to drown these demons."

73

JORDAN

Paris, France, Present Day

I looked over at Zadkiel, who was kneeling on the floor of the viewing deck, hand placed flat against the metal. Satan stood watch over him, making sure he wasn't attacked.

My hands gripped the safety gate, and I was about to let go, intending to cross the distance between them and me, when Satan tensed and reached for me.

Unsure why he was rescuing me, I glanced over my shoulder and saw a large, winged demon coming from the sky. Dane was behind it, chasing the creature and trying to control it, as its wing was wounded, but it was no use. It was coming down, and I was in its crash path.

The monster narrowly missed the tower itself. Instead, he careened into the silver gate, taking me over the edge with it.

I fell through the air, hands still gripping the gate as it was my only defense against the chomping teeth of the demon that now wanted to eat me since I was easy prey.

The ground grew closer and closer.

I pushed the gate down and used the momentum to jump higher, trying to extend the length of my fall. I saw the demon and the gate hit the ground and knew I wouldn't be too far off.

Until someone slammed into me, grabbing me under the arms and pulling up.

I fully expected Satan or Dane, but when I glanced behind me, I saw Sophia.

"I've got you, cuz," she said, bringing me safely to the ground.

The gardens surrounding us were a mess. Hedges had been broken, plants had been trampled, and there was black gore everywhere. There didn't seem to be a flux of demons anymore, though.

Satan and Dane landed behind us.

"You're fast," Satan said to Sophia.

"I know," she said.

Satan was offended.

"Dad, you can't expect her to thank you when you had a hound chase her around the city, scaring her senseless," Dane reminded him.

"Oh, right. That was you," the Devil remembered.

"Yeah, that was me," Sophia snapped.

"Is Zadkiel all right?" I asked.

"Yes," Satan said. "We were ambushed once that winged thing went crashing down, but Zadkiel and the sphere are safe and back at the house."

"Which means we can go," Sophia said.

Dane nodded. "Yeah."

"You three leave," Satan said. "I'll tell the others."

"I'm not leaving without everyone. The fighting's almost over anyway. We're not in any harm," I said. "Besides, I need to find Dafne."

Dark clouds brewed thick overhead, a torrent of rain coming down immediately.

"Was this in the forecast?" Deborah asked, joining us along with Delphine, Aeron, Sandalphon, and Dafne.

"No, I think your daughter has something to do with it," Sandalphon said.

Dafne rushed over to me and squeezed me tight. "I saw you fall and was so worried."

"I'm fine," I assured her. "Are you?"

She nodded.

I pulled back when I saw Aeron staring at me.

"You were right," he said. "The Sentinel is Silas." He looked shaken and unsteady.

"Are we clear?" Uriel shouted, striding over with Kat, Aziza, Yadira, and Gabriel.

"Yes," Dane answered as they got closer.

Gabriel put a hand on my shoulder. "Why is it that you're always falling or jumping from something extremely high?"

"It wasn't intentional! Trust me, I could have done without soaring through the sky today."

He grinned. "It's never truly intentional, is it?"

The rain intensified, soaking us through and cleaning the ground.

Michael, Chamuel, and Naomi appeared in the distance, eventually drawing close.

"Is this everyone?" Uriel asked.

"Zadkiel left with the sphere," Satan said.

"And Raphael left because he was injured," Michael said. "But he should be just fine."

"Good, then let's head back to the apartment and go home," Uriel concluded.

"I'll be leaving from here," Satan said.

Almost everyone kept walking, uninterested if Satan was leaving. Dane, Sophia, Dafne, Naomi, Michael, Gabriel, and I stayed put.

"Thank you," I said.

"Yeah, yeah." Satan waved off my words. "I'll be back for the war. I just have to check on my kingdom and prepare the Fallen."

"How should we call you?" Dane asked.

"I'll know to come," he said.

Dane tilted his head. "What? How?"

"Don't worry, Ace. I won't let you down." Satan turned the dial on his portal device and vanished.

The rest of us walked back to the apartment before teleporting to the house since police sirens blared in the rain.

Finally, we were ready to fulfill the prophecy and go to war.

74

LILITH

Purgatory, Present Day

"Your plan worked," the Sentinel said.

"I knew it would," I told him. "After what happened in Hell, there was no way I was exhausting my resources again."

"You certainly exhausted me," Lucifer said, holding ice to his head.

I rolled my eyes. "You aren't a resource. You're a nuisance. I'm only keeping you around to distract Satan; otherwise you'd be dead."

"Then why did you send me to a location he wasn't at?" he demanded.

My eyes narrowed, and he dropped to his knees, clutching at his throat. No more hand maneuvers and spells for me. All I had to do was think it, and I could make everyone suffer.

I rose from my seat and strolled around him as he struggled. "Because I didn't know their groupings. And then you had to go and get injured by the girl."

"Which provided us with useful information," the Sentinel added.

"Yes. Those small attacks were a way to get insight, and this last one in Paris was to test my new powers further."

Lucifer turned blue. I released him, and he choked in air.

"The girl grows stronger as she becomes more confident," I mused.

"And the Supernal who got away has grown to be quite talented. They both must die in battle."

"Noted," the Sentinel said. "As must Aeron."

I flicked my hand. "He's your problem."

"He knows who I am," the Sentinel confessed.

I laughed. "What a miracle it's taken this long! If he was keener, he'd have discovered that long before now. All you do to hide your identity from him is change your voice."

"Aren't you disappointed we don't have any of the keys?" Lucifer asked tentatively, rubbing his throat.

"Whether I have the keys or not truly doesn't matter. They have to be used to complete the prophecy, so the most important thing is showing up when they are," I said.

"Then why steal them from Heaven in the first place?" he asked.

I sighed. "My pet, you've done so much double-crossing that you have no idea what our purpose is: inflicting pain. Attacking them in their paradise was the best way to do that." Returning to my seat, I inspected my nails. "What of the bloodstone?"

"From what I gathered," the Sentinel said, "they aren't using it."

"Good."

"Would you like to hear of Darcel?" he asked.

I dropped my hands, my gaze turning venomous. "Why mention *him*? He is my biggest mistake and disappointment!"

"I only bring him up because I thought you'd like to know he's failing miserably," the Sentinel reported. "He has no control."

I sneered. "That's all fine and good, but he's with Satan."

"Why should that be a problem?" he asked.

Lucifer chuckled. "I, at least, know the answer to that one."

"Which is?" the Sentinel asked.

"Satan is always a problem," Lucifer answered. "Even when you think he can't be."

"You're right, Lucifer," I agreed.

His pride inflated like a balloon.

"Darcel is also too much like Satan. If they attach themselves to each other, there is a risk of Darcel gaining control over his own magic," I stated.

"Then he must be a casualty, too," the Sentinel remarked.

I nodded, adjusting the cuffs of my shirt. "Indeed."

75

SATAN

HELL, PRESENT DAY

The cold, dark caves of Hell were a welcome sight. I exited my council room and headed for the throne. I lounged in my seat, knowing I had many responsibilities to tend to but just needing a moment for myself.

"I see you're back."

I straightened up as Abbadona came up from the Pit. She sauntered across the room, heading for the rooms beyond the throne.

I waited for her, knowing she would have to come back this way.

Sure enough, she did.

"Are you still mad at me?" I asked.

She stopped and crossed her arms, holding a dagger in her hand. "If you have something to say, I will stay and talk."

I sighed. She was still mad at me. "What do you need that for?"

She held up the dagger. "If you don't want me to have it, I'll put it back."

"That's not what I said. You can have it. I was just curious why."

"Because I don't want to take supplies from Haborym who needs them for the troops," she explained. "You never use everything on that weapons wall anyway."

"Fair enough," I said.

She stepped over to the Pit.

I gritted my teeth. "I was wrong."

She stopped in her tracks and turned around. "About?"

"Power isn't more precious," I said. "Not when that's all I had with me on my trip, and I couldn't stop thinking about you." I played with the skull ring on my finger. "I don't want to fight with you."

Her steps echoed on the stone floor as she came back to stand before me. "I don't want to, either." Her hand came up to caress my cheek.

I flinched and grabbed her wrist, noticing she was wearing gloves. Not just any gloves. They were made from Lilith's snakeskin, a material we no longer had since most of it had been used up.

"How did you…" I trailed off.

"She left them behind when she fled."

I sighed and entwined our fingers, bringing our hands to my cheek and enjoying the sense of touch. Her other hand came up to rest on my head.

"Did you really think I'd give up on you?" she asked.

"I wasn't sure. What I said was hurtful."

She nodded. "It was, but I understand why you said it. You were created with a purpose, and that was stripped from you. And then you discovered this power you have, and that became your new purpose, and it has remained that way for centuries. Even suggesting the idea of a cure was an attack to your purpose, which is why you lashed out. It was wrong of me to do that."

I looked at her and noticed all the things she had done to make anything between us even possible. The gloves. The long-sleeved, high-necked dress. She even wore tights, covering every bare inch of skin on her legs.

Pulling her to my lap, I asked, "Is there even a cure?"

"I believe so, but it involves a ritual, recorded in a book that has been lost to the world for centuries."

I leaned forward and placed a kiss on her clothed shoulder. "And if we could find the book?"

She placed her hand under my chin and tilted my head up. "I would perform the ritual on myself in a second."

Her breath rushed overs my lips, distracting me for a moment. "Wait…*you* have to do the ritual?"

She nodded. "I learned that there is no cure for the Hellfire. The only semblance of a cure is becoming immune to its heat. I would have to do the ritual." She placed her hand on my chest. "If it were the other way, I would never consider it."

I grabbed her hand. "Well maybe I don't want you playing with magic on my behalf."

"Are you trying to tell me what to do?"

"Yes, but only because I know the consequences of ancient, dark magic and I don't want to see you suffer."

"No one's suffering," she assured me. "We don't even have the book."

"But if we did?"

"It would be my choice."

I sighed. She was right. I couldn't decide for her or force her not to do something. I had chosen the path of dark magic. She had a right to choose that, too, if she desired.

"All those warnings against black magic," I said, finding it hard to let it go, "and you would throw them to the wayside for me?"

"Yes, but only for you."

"I don't deserve you."

"You deserve everything," she said.

"Can I ask you something?"

"Anything."

"You won't get mad?" I asked.

She pulled back. "Possibly."

I was too curious not to ask, so I came out with it. "What's your history with Lilith?"

She put her hands in her lap. "Brief. We met long ago on one of my excursions to Earth. I fell for her charms much like everyone else, as she promised she could teach me how to hone my craft. She was assembling disciples at the time."

"And?"

"And while most of the knowledge I know today is owed to her, I realized what she was doing and what she aspired to do was wrong."

"What was she doing?"

Abbadona shook her head. "She wanted to create beings. Powerful, celestial beings that had no right to exist. She was stealing blood magic, slaughtering people for it. She was appropriating a collection of blood to mutate genes." She looked at me. "She obviously was successful if Dane exists."

"She was."

Abbadona smiled. "He reminds me of you. I enjoyed meeting him."

I shared a smiled with her. "He liked you."

She grew serious. "Why bring this up? Is it because of Dane? You told me there was nothing between you and Lilith, and I believe you. I know what she's capable of when it comes to creating offspring unknowingly."

"Actually," I said, "this conversation has to do with you. Did *you* ever give her your blood?"

"Yes, why?"

"Because I met this girl. She's one of Dane's friends. She calls herself a Supernal, not part-celestial like a Nephilim but *full* celestial. She discovered Lilith's past history, her dealings with creating unnatural beings. She thinks she's one of them."

"Okay, but what does this have to do with me?"

"Well, she has magic and can command water in a way I have only seen you do." I paused. "And she looks like you. She has lighter skin, but her face is the same…her personality."

Abbadona frowned. "If she is mine, I had no idea she existed." She thought it over. "I need to meet her."

I nodded. "I had a feeling you would say that, and you'll have the opportunity to meet her soon when we assemble for battle. But I think I should prepare her first. Or I should let Dane say something. She's guarded, and the last thing I want is to screw this up and force her away. At least, for your sake."

"Let Dane mention it," Abbadona agreed. "She trusts him?"

"More than she would you or me."

"Let Dane do it," she repeated.

I couldn't help but notice she had drawn in on herself, her mind clearly racing over how this might have happened.

"Hey," I said. Our eyes met. "We face everything together now."

She pressed her lips to my shirt, right over my heart. "Always."

76

DANE

Ithaca, New York, Present Day

When we returned home, we all rested for a week. Then April was upon us and we had two months to prepare.

We all knew when the battle would take place: July first. I was going to have a terrible birthday, but at least last year's was incredible when I'd spent it at the aurora borealis in Norway.

Jordan's backyard, as well as Naomi's, had become training areas used by humans and angels alike. Anyone who wasn't battle ready became battle ready, and the ones who already were practiced their skills. I fell into the not-battle-ready category, unlike most of my friends.

I had hand-to-hand combat skills but very poor weapon skills. And my magic prowess was nonexistent.

"Not too low," Michael instructed as Jordan and I clashed swords. "Bring your knee in. Now you're swinging too high."

"That's it!" I shouted, frustrated. "I need a break." I dropped the loaner sword and sank to the ground.

"You'll get better," Jordan assured me, sitting down next to me and sipping water.

"When did you become so athletic?" I asked.

He thought about it. "The day I was chased by the Fallen on the subway. It hasn't stopped since, and it's been two years."

I lay back on the grass. "I wasn't being literal."

"Oh..." Jordan said.

"Dane?" Michael called to me.

"Yeah!"

"Can you come here?"

Jordan's eyes widened. "Michael never does that."

"Does what?" I asked, rising.

"Calls someone over privately during training. It must be serious," Jordan said.

"Calm down, Sherlock Holmes. There's nothing to investigate here," I stated, striding over to Michael.

"What's up?" I asked him.

"I think your training is suffering because you don't have the right weapon," he said.

Gosh, talk about blunt.

"All right, so no swords?" I asked.

He shook his head. "You'll do fine with a sword—so long as it's the *perfect* sword."

I sighed. "How do I find that?"

"You don't," Michael said, heaving a box onto the patio table. "Because I'm going to give it to you."

This weapons box was much larger than the one Jordan had gotten for his birthday.

"Okay," I said, a little excited at the thought of getting my own sword.

"I never thought I would part with this," Michael explained, unlatching the box. "Not because I have any sentimental attachment to it but because there is no one who should wield it. Or so I thought."

He drew the sword from the box and handed it to me. It was long, with a silver blade and a gilded gold hilt, much like Jordan's. Except this hilt spanned into two wings.

I took it and gripped the hilt in my hand, testing out a few swipes through the air. It felt a million times better than the loner had.

"That was your father's broadsword," Michael stated.

I froze and turned to look at him.

"When he fell, it was left behind in Heaven. Seraphiel was going to destroy it, but I couldn't let that happen. So I kept it, thinking it would never be used again." Michael paused. "You're the only one I considered giving it to, and I think that might have been wise."

I glanced down at the sword, noticing an engraving on the handgrip between my fingers.

"This is angelic script?" I asked.

Michael nodded.

"What does it say?"

"Samael."

I focused on the sword. "That's my middle name."

"Which is why I would only give it to you. You're his namesake."

I rubbed my fingers over the letters. This battle was coming, whether I wanted it to or not, and I had to be ready.

"Practice some more with the sword on your own," Michael said. "Get used it to it before you start sparring." He closed the box. "We'll resume tomorrow."

Gabriel came outside. "Are you ready?"

"Yes," Michael said.

The two donned sparring gloves.

"Don't go easy on me," Michael told him. "I need to strengthen my leg."

"I won't," Gabriel promised.

They went down to the grass and began their training for the day. You knew what lay ahead was serious if Michael felt he needed extra practice.

A raven alighted from the sky and came to land on my shoulder. I froze, shocked by the bird's boldness.

A note was attached to its foot. I untied it, and the raven took off.

I skimmed the short message. It was from Satan. He believed Abbadona might have been Naomi's biological mother. Abbadona wanted to meet her, their first encounter most likely to come during the war, but they wanted me to prepare Naomi beforehand.

I immediately went to find my friend, who was sitting at the lake's edge practicing her magic.

"Hey!" I said.

"Hey! What's up?"

I sat down next to her. "I have something to tell you."

She focused on me. "Okay. Spill."

"Satan thinks he might know your biological mother," I told her.

Her face lit up. "Really?"

"Yeah, one of the fallen angels in Hell… He's really close to her, and he thinks you might be related because she has water magic, too."

"Wow…I'd love to meet her," Naomi said.

I smiled. "Turns out you will. She's coming for the war. I know our priority is fighting, but you might find time to chat with her."

"That would be amazing! Thanks for telling me, Dane!"

"No problem," I said.

She went back to practicing magic with a radiant grin on her face.

I wished my relationship with my power were like that.

77

Jordan

Ithaca, New York, Present Day

After spending a month training with Dane, I knew it was time to get serious about using the compass. It was mid-May, and I was running out of time, so I went to the library to get *The Book of Prophecies*. I wanted to look over the Union of the Spheres again. Maybe there was something in it that would help me find the location of where the ceremony needed to take place.

As I walked inside, I noticed there were more beings in here than usual. With all the new arrivals from Heaven, the house was getting packed, so much so that we had started filling up Naomi's place, too. And this wasn't even the army. It was Michael's team of lieutenants, significant members from each council in Heaven, as well as healers. Raphael had requested a team be sent down ahead of time to begin preparations.

On the left-hand wall of the library, directly next to the doors, was a floor-to-ceiling display cabinet. My parents had kept artwork and rare books in it, but we had vacated a section for the keys, scepter pieces, and *The Book of Prophecies* since it was under lock and key, in addition to an alarm system. Sophia had helped find a new home for the items we moved, her knowledge in art history and preservation playing a big role in relocating them to my mother's studio. Eventually, everything would return to its rightful place, but at the moment, adjustments had to be made.

I just wasn't sure how many more I could handle.

Going over to the cabinet, I inputted the code to disarm the alarm, then drew the key from my pocket and opened the door.

"What are you doing?"

I glanced over my shoulder. An angel had asked me the question, one I wasn't familiar with. "Taking out the book," I said, returning to my task and reaching inside for it.

"You can't do that." She raced over and held out her hands, expecting me to give it to her.

"Says who?" I asked, locking the cabinet and rearming it.

"Says me!" she shouted.

"Chastity!" a voice boomed from across the library. "Leave him be!"

"He's taking the book," she protested.

The angel who had chided her strode over to us. "That's because it's his book, and this is his house."

"Oh," she muttered. "I didn't know. There are so many humans here with special abilities, I figured you were one of them, not the bloodline. I'm terribly sorry." She left us, going back to whatever she was doing.

"I don't think we've met," the angel said, extending his hand. "I'm Cassiel."

"Jordan," I said, shaking it. I liked him a lot more than Chastity.

"Good to meet you." He elbowed me. "If anyone gives you a hard time, just tell them they should come talk to me."

I smiled. "Will do."

Cassiel went back to his table.

I guessed he was one of Michael's lieutenants, not only because he had a warrior's commanding presence but because he was sketching out armed maneuvers as I passed by him to go into my dad's office.

Closing the door behind me, I sat down in the peace and quiet and flipped open the book to the correct page. I translated the angelic script as I read and recorded it on a separate sheet of paper:

The Union of the Spheres
Grants power to the one who commandeers.
Sovereign's Orb and Scepter in hand,
They can dominate any land.

For thirteen spheres to unite
Components must be brought to light.

According to an angel's vision,
The Union must follow this precision.
Sphere in circle, circle in sphere,
Placed together during the twentieth year.

Only the river can locate
The depths where the rocks await.
Stone in stone they become one,
The place hidden for all time by the Sun.

Thirteen bound in blood by two

From ancient lines born anew.
Both must live until blood is spilt,
Afterward fighting hilt to hilt.

Time will tell how events come to be,
As the route to the spheres is hard to foresee.
No matter the path, the Union is completed
Since the Orb and Scepter must be defeated.

The first, second, and last stanzas I crossed out. We already knew the information within those lines. I read what was left one paragraph at a time:

According to an angel's vision,
The Union must follow this precision.
Sphere in circle, circle in sphere,
Placed together during the twentieth year.

So the angel's vision was Metatron's Cube, an intricate placement of circles that connected to one another. I sketched that out on my sheet of paper. The spheres had to be placed in this shape. I put *X's* on each circle. The twentieth year was this year, as I had just turned that age.

Next paragraph:

Only the river can locate
The depths where the rocks await.
Stone in stone they become one,

The place hidden for all time by the Sun.

I stared at this section. It was hinting to the location. I set it aside for a minute and looked at the last:

Thirteen bound in blood by two
From ancient lines born anew.
Both must live until blood is spilt,
Afterward fighting hilt to hilt.

That was me and Dane. But it seemed like we had to combine our blood for the Union to even work, at which point the battle commenced because everyone would be fighting for what was created—the Sovereign's Orb.

All right. So I had a good handle on this after all. Now it was time to go back.

Only the river can locate
The depths where the rocks await.
Stone in stone they become one,
The place hidden for all time by the Sun.

The location had something to do with water between the mention of a river and the use of the word *depths*.

As had the scepter pieces, I realized.

I stood and went over to the map on the wall. There were tons of lakes, rivers, even waterfalls in Ithaca, let alone the entire world.

Only the river can locate.

Wait…I was the river. I was literally named after one. Only I could locate where the Union would occur, and if the spheres had to be placed in rocks that were hidden by water, then the location had to be deep.

The place hidden for all time by the Sun.

I went back to the desk. There was a capital *S* on *Sun* but nothing else jumped out to me. Almost the way *Son* was capitalized when referring to the Father, the Son, and the Holy Spirit, which in a way could signify the bloodline—meaning me.

I rewrote the line with my idea.

The place hidden for all time by the Son.

It didn't make sense. I went back to thinking of the sun. The location was hidden by the sun?

Glancing down, I saw the compass engraving peeking out from my dad's desk.

Oh my…

The compass had been hidden from the sun inside the desk. It kept spinning every time I pulled it out because it had been daylight.

I rushed over to the window and fumbled with the shade. I tried pulling it down, but it wouldn't budge.

What the…

My hand brushed a button on the wall, and the shade moved, coming down along with an entire black-out curtain.

The room went pitch-dark, and I pulled the compass from my pocket. It glowed in the darkness, the needle steady and pointing west.

The sun clue wasn't just darkness, I realized. It also was talking about me because the desk had opened to my voice.

Wow, my parents were clever about hiding the compass.

But they weren't around to hear my voice so that meant Sister Helen and Delphine must have had a part in securing the compass. Except Delphine hadn't mentioned anything, and I don't remember ever recording my voice.

There was a knock at the door.

I slipped the compass in my pocket. "Come in!"

It opened, and Peter stuck his head inside. "No one told me you had unlocked your father's office."

"It happened right before we left," I said.

He stepped inside and shrugged it off. "It's fine. I'm a Gamma. I'm used to being told on a need-to-know basis." He looked around. "Well, if you're sitting in the dark, I see you found the compass."

He couldn't see my face, but my mouth dropped open. The compass wasn't a secret, but the fact he knew why I was sitting in the dark was. Then I remembered he was an engineer. "Peter, did you do all this?"

He crossed his arms and leaned back against a bookcase. "Your mother hid the compass in the desk. It's a celestial object so I couldn't touch it. But the rest was your father's idea. I just executed it. The fingerprint and voice command I programmed recently, after you came over to the house for the first time."

I stood and hit the button on the wall to bring the shades up. Daylight filled the room again.

"Are you telling me you recorded my voice and copied my fingerprint during a casual dinner?"

He nodded. "You forgot to mention that I had to piece together recordings to get the right phrasing."

"And why aren't you a Beta?"

He laughed. "Because I don't want to be one. Because this was something only your parents and I knew about. I would have helped you figure it all out, but you beat me to it. I'm sorry for invading your privacy and not telling you sooner."

"Honestly, it's fine. I kind of had fun doing it," I said.

"Good. How are you otherwise?"

I sighed and threw my hands in the air. "Who knows anymore?" I went over to the map again.

"Are you sleeping?"

I nodded. "Yeah. That's gotten better because I meditate every night before bed. It seems to keep the dreams and the visions at bay. I haven't had one for a while."

"Your father used to do that," Peter said. "He didn't have visions much once he started meditating."

"That's good to hear. I wonder if it's the meditating or this, though," I said, picking up my necklace.

"It's not that," Sandalphon said from the open doorway.

I tensed. "Come in, Sandalphon."

"Sorry to intrude," he said. "I wanted to apologize to you, and Cassiel said you were in here. I happened to hear you were talking about your visions. The necklace is a protective ward, but it won't stop the visions, only guard you from any harm they might pose."

"Oh…then I guess the meditation is working," I acknowledged.

He nodded. "I'm sorry, Jordan. I cannot control what the scepter showed you, nor can I explain what you saw because I don't know what it means myself. I merely was doing my job as a messenger."

The images of death I had seen at the river didn't haunt my dreams, but it was hard to shake from my mind, especially knowing a war was imminent. It was wrong of me to blame Sandalphon. He hadn't done anything.

"I forgive you, Sandalphon," I said. "It was just hard… It's still hard to think about."

"I know," he said. "All I can say is that, sometimes, what you see isn't the literal truth. I'm sure you've experienced that with your visions before."

He was right. That had happened before, things playing out differently from what I'd seen. Those moments of death were that. Brief flashes. It didn't mean it would happen.

My eyes focused on the map before me. "Peter," I said.

"Yeah?"

"Did my dad hike a lot?"

He chuckled. "Very much. Especially all the parks and trails around here."

I knew it. The location for the Union was close. I could feel it.

78 SOPHIA

Ithaca, New York, Present Day

I loaded the bow I was holding and shot the arrow at a target far out in the lake. From here, I could see it was a bull's-eye. I reached for another arrow.

"You've gotten good at that," Uriel said. "Or maybe you were good all along. I'm not sure."

Glancing at him, I smiled and let the bowstring go.

We both turned our heads back toward the target.

Another bull's-eye.

"All right, Miss Show-Off," he said. "I want you to look at this."

I set the bow down and took the arrow he offered. It seemed normal, but the tip felt different, like it was made from another material.

"It's bloodstone," he told me. "The Forge in Heaven is making these arrows. I want you to practice with them."

"Okay," I said.

He looked as if he wanted to say something else.

"Was that everything?"

"Listen, between you and me, I believe it's our responsibility to take down Lilith," he confessed. "We need to plant the stone in her back to weaken her. The whole battle hinges on it, and there's no way it'll happen in a short-range fight. It needs to be us. Are you okay with that?"

"Yes," I said.

"Then get practicing," he commanded.

I notched the bloodstone arrow and let it loose. It hit the target, but it wasn't a bull's-eye. The stone was heavier than an average arrowhead.

I loaded another and drowned out the sound around me, of Naomi and Dafne training, as well as Deborah and Delphine. They all were honing their swordsmanship skills, practicing just as much as I was.

Then I realized something. How was Dane going to fight with bloodstone around him? Unlike Lilith, the mere presence of the stone affected him, and he was still struggling with his powers.

I lowered the arrow and looked across the lawn. He was sparring with a dummy and had gotten very skilled using the sword Michael had given him.

Putting the bow down, I started walking over to him when Jordan burst from the house with determination.

"Where are you going?" I asked him as he passed me.

"On a hike," he said.

"Now?" I looked at the sky. It was almost sunset.

"Yes!" he shouted, not stopping.

"Jordan, you can't go alone!" I yelled, grabbing my jacket from the chair I had discarded it on and chasing after him. Once I caught up to him, I grabbed his arm and forced him to stop.

"What's all this about?" I asked.

Dane, Naomi, and Dafne joined us.

"I know how to find the location for the Union. But I have to go there in the dark." He pulled the compass from his pocket. It spun wildly.

"It doesn't seem like anything's changed," Naomi pointed out.

"Because it's not dark yet," Jordan said, adamant. "Trust me."

"We trust you," Dafne assured him. "But shouldn't we just wait until it gets dark *before* we venture into the wilderness, so the compass can guide us."

Jordan's face fell. "Good point."

"We probably should tell someone where we're going," Dafne suggested.

We all agreed and went back to the house to let everyone know. Gabriel insisted on coming with us just in case there was any danger.

When night fell, Jordan pulled out the compass again. It glowed, and the needle was steady.

"Holy crap!" Dane exclaimed.

"Told you," Jordan said.

"Let's follow it," I told him.

We headed west as the compass indicated. We trudged through woods for several hours until we saw a sign for Taughannock Falls State Park.

"We're getting close," Jordan said.

"How do you know?" Gabriel asked.

I shrugged. "Just a feeling. I think we're looking for some kind of water element. A waterfall maybe."

We continued, our hike becoming a little easier once we entered the park and headed onto the clear, paved trails. All the signs we passed showed that we were going toward the waterfall.

Jordan picked up the pace as the needle on the compass started twitching faster. He ran ahead, and we followed, bursting through a span of trees and over a bridge.

I froze. The waterfall was magnificent. My heightened vision allowed me to see it clearly, even though it was pitch-dark out. It was tall with large rocky cliffs on either side of it. You could hear the rush of water.

I joined the others and could feel the waterfall's spray against my face.

"This is it!" Jordan shouted. His spun around with his arms in the air.

I couldn't blame him for the excitement. It had not only been a lot of pressure to find the waterfall but it was so sublime to stand before it.

Except, Jordan being Jordan, he took it too far.

"What are you doing?" I asked.

He was taking off his backpack, his shoes, even his jacket. He climbed atop the short partition between the falls and the walkway and jumped. It wasn't far down, but I didn't expect the journey tonight to turn into a rescue mission.

Jordan trudged through the water, still holding the compass.

He was looking for something, but I had no idea what. I thought finding the waterfall was enough.

When he got to the deeper part of the waterfall basin, he dove underwater.

Dane started stripping off his jacket and shoes.

"Not you, too!" Naomi shouted.

Over he went, disappearing into the water.

The three of us waited. Too long in my opinion.

"That's it," Gabriel said, unbuttoning his vest.

Then suddenly, a rocky platform rose from the water.

Jordan and Dane surfaced on the outer edge of the waterfall and swam to shore. They came out of the water, completely soaked, and rejoined us.

"I knew there had to be more!" Jordan shouted in excitement.

Finally, the platform stilled. Tall pillars, thirteen in total, rose out of the rocky platform and stood before the waterfall.

"Stone in stone they become one," Jordan whispered.

"Wait," Dafne said. "The spheres go in those pillars?"

He nodded, growing serious. "Yep."

Gabriel put his arm around Jordan. "It's time."

79

JORDAN

ITHACA, NEW YORK, PRESENT DAY

Once we found the waterfall, time sped up. We'd had five weeks to prepare, and now we had a mere hour until the war began.

Uriel had stepped in right away to get the park closed. He'd flashed his credentials as a wildlife research specialist and had gone on and on about how an endangered bird species had appeared at the park. I didn't know the specifics, but he'd said the right things to get it shut down.

It was easier that way. We didn't need human causalities on top of what we were already expecting. It was inevitable that everyone wouldn't survive.

As for our numbers, between Hell and the Heavenly Army we were ten thousand strong. The Factions of Faith had yet to respond to the summons we had sent several months ago, so we weren't counting on them joining our ranks.

At the moment, I was at the house getting ready to embark to the waterfall for battle. I glanced at myself in the hallway mirror. At one point I would have thought it weird to wear a leather breastplate, but I had been training in it for weeks now.

Gabriel appeared behind me, tugging at my straps and readjusting.

He was decked out for war, too, leather lining almost the entirety of his body. The most impressive part of his regalia was the huge scythe he had strapped to his back.

He saw me looking. "Just a little something I pulled out of my storage chest."

"And dusted off since your last war," I added.

"Something like that," he said.

My eyes trailed over to the triage room that had been set up on the lower floor. "Is Raphael staying here?"

Gabriel shook his head. "No. He will assess injuries on the battlefield and send anyone who needs care here. There are plenty of angels of healing on-hand, and Martha, Emily, and Peter will be assisting them."

"Good. Even with training, Martha, Emily, and Peter aren't the strongest fighters."

"I agree," Gabriel said.

I sighed. "I wished we could have talked Deborah, Aeron, and Delphine into staying, too, but they're eager to fight."

"Unlike the others they are well-trained, high-ranking Sacrarium members," Gabriel justified.

"True. But I would still feel better if they were out of harm's way. I have enough beings to worry about."

He patted my shoulder. "We'll be fine. You ready?"

I nodded and reached for the small gift I had set down. It was Dane's birthday today and, even though a war was brewing, I still felt the need to give him something to show him I remembered.

We went outside, and Gabriel grabbed me under the arms. Then he launched us both into the air and took us to the waterfall.

In minutes, we landed on the paved walkway in front of the falls.

I saw a lone figure sitting before the rushing water and headed over to him.

"Happy birthday," I said, handing him his gift.

"Thanks. What's this?"

"Open it."

He tugged the string and the wrapping fell back. It was a medium-sized black jasper gemstone.

"It's meant to bring protection and grounding," I said. "Thought you might like it."

He smiled. "I do. Thank you." Then he slipped it in his pocket.

It was 11 AM. We were planning to be assembled by noon.

"Are you nervous?" I asked.

"Yeah." He crossed his arms. "I came early to get ready mentally."

Sophia joined us. "It's strange to think this will all be over today."

I nodded. "By the end of the day, everything will change."

Sophia and Dane leaned forward.

"What?" I asked.

"Just checking," Dane said.

"That sounded like your vision voice," Sophia elaborated.

I shrugged. For all I knew, it could have been.

As the sun grew higher in the sky, the others arrived one by one.

Michael, Gabriel, Uriel, Raphael, Chamuel, and Zadkiel waded into the water, taking their positions in front of one of the pillars.

"That's our cue," I said, jumping off the partition and into the water.

"I'll be right there," Dane told me, lingering with Sophia for a moment.

80 DANE

Ithaca, New York, Present Day

We sat in silence.

"Are you okay?" Sophia asked.

I shook my head, unable to vocalize how I felt. Now that the battle was here, I was worried. Not about myself, but about her. Nothing could happen to her. I couldn't bear it if something happened to her…

"Dane, look at me," Sophia urged.

I turned and faced her.

Her brow was furrowed in concern. "What's going on?"

"I'm nervous," I said, which wasn't a complete lie.

"I get it. I can't help but be nervous, too."

I shook my head again and sighed. I had to be more honest. "Sophia, just promise me you'll be careful."

"Of course I'll be careful, but the same goes for you," she said. She inched closer until our noses were inches apart.

"I love you. So much," I whispered.

"I love you, too. Nothing is going to happen to *either* of us. We're going to make it out of this."

I nodded and took a few deep breaths. "You're right. We're going to be fine."

Overhead, angels swooped down and began gathering on the cliffside.

I let go of her wrist. "You should join them."

She nodded, stretching her wings and taking her place with the archers.

Meanwhile, I jumped down into the water to join Jordan. Swimming over to the platform, I took my place next to him at the tallest pillar in the center.

Sandalphon came down the path with three other angels—two males and one female. I thought the female had been at the house for a while now, but I didn't remember her name. They took their places among the pillars while Sandalphon came over to Jordan and me, holding the scepter pieces.

"Once we assemble the scepter, the Union begins," he told us.

"Aren't we missing someone?" Jordan asked.

A steady, rhythmic beat filled the air.

The denizens of Hell appeared one by one via their portal devices and amassed in the shallow water. They seemed to be exulting in their freedom and the impending war, slamming swords against shields and forming a thick sea of black wings.

Satan arrived in the middle of their ranks. He was dressed in black armor from head to toe. Even his sword had a jet-black blade. The other leaders of Hell materialized next to him, most of them directing the fallen angels and demons into legions and formations.

The Devil broke away from the group with Ariel, the two coming over to the platform.

“I can’t believe we’re doing this,” one of the angels I didn’t know muttered.

“What’s that, Metatron? I think you need to speak up,” Satan taunted. “Shouldn’t be a problem for you.”

“Sandalphon, I gave up my seat and its responsibilities when I moved into the Seraphim ranks,” Metatron explained. “I shouldn’t have to do this.”

“Nor should I,” the other unknown angel said.

“I did, too, but you don’t see me complaining,” Ariel stated.

“Stop!” Sandalphon shouted. “All of you. You might have given up your seats, or in my case were called elsewhere, but it doesn’t matter. The original thirteen on the Council of Archangels who were assigned the duty of protecting the spheres must complete the prophecy. That cannot be passed on except in the case of death.”

His words were a stark reminder of the loss of Jophiel.

“Are we ready?” Sandalphon asked. “Once we begin, there’s no going back.”

Everyone nodded, though some reluctantly.

“Hold on,” Satan said, looking to Sandalphon. “Where’s your army?”

Michael signaled to the top of the waterfall and shouted, “Wings up!”

In seconds, the Heavenly Army glided over the waterfall, their white wings catching the midday sun. They flew through the mist, rainbows dancing along their feathers. Others appeared from the trees at the top of the cliffs, mainly archers and a second aerial team. Any currently flying in landed across from the fallen army.

Seeing the two armies next to each other revealed their stark differences, regal magnificence in the case of the Blessed and rugged debauchery in the case of the Fallen.

"Satisfied?" Michael asked.

"Very much so," Satan said.

"This is how we shall proceed," Sandalphon announced. "I will assemble the scepter and place it in the pillar. Satan, you will set your keys into the same pillar and then take up Jophiel's position. Once you are situated, the rest of us will each position our keys in the proper stones. At that point, Jordan and Dane will add their blood, and the Union will be complete."

"And then all hell breaks loose," I added.

"Most likely, depending on Lilith's arrival," Sandalphon stated.

"And what's the plan to destroy the Sovereign's Orb and Scepter?" Jordan asked.

Sandalphon gulped. "It'll be incinerated."

"You can't be serious!" Metatron yelled.

"Get over it, Metatron," Satan barked. "Times are changing."

"That might be so, but we are doomed if we're to place our faith in you destroying the object for which you started this battle in the first place," Metatron snapped.

"I'm not that same being anymore," Satan said. "I'm a new devil."

"For heaven's sake!" Uriel exclaimed. "Just start already!"

Sandalphon nodded, taking the two scepter rods and screwing them together. Then he placed the winged topper on the staff and inserted the entire scepter into the stone pillar.

A beam of light shot into the sky, and the surface of each pillar shifted, revealing three spaces for the keys to be placed—a keyhole, an engraved shape cut to each gemstone, and a rounded basin where the spheres would sit.

Jordan and I looked at each other. There was no going back. This was happening.

Sandalphon reached into his cloak pocket and pulled out Satan's sphere. He handed it to the Devil and then stepped down and found his place among the others.

Satan pulled out his classic key and inserted it in the keyhole. He then placed his gemstone key in its rightful spot and, lastly, set down the sphere.

The beam of light grew larger and brighter.

Satan left the center pillar and took Jophiel's vacant position on the outer rim. As soon as he was settled, the twelve angels around us deposited their sets of keys into the pillars in tandem. Everyone knew when the spheres had been placed because the beam of light intensified, sending a powerful shock into the air that made everyone sway on their feet.

I met Jordan's eyes, and he nodded.

Together, we pulled knives from our belts and raised them to our hands, Jordan gently slicing his right palm and me gently slicing my left.

We grabbed each other's hand, our blood mixing and running down our arms to slowly drip atop Satan's black onyx sphere.

The whole world jolted around us, sending us flying backward, but we held on to each other, digging our heels into the ground to steady ourselves.

Streaks of white light appeared, twisting and turning, creating the shape of Metatron's Cube and connecting each set of keys to the other. They looped around us and spun incessantly, much like the compass had done during daylight.

I could hear the sizzle of energy, feel its heat along my skin. Jordan and I watched as Satan's classic key and gemstone key disintegrated into the air while the sphere turned to pure molten liquid. The friction from the light force pulverized the keys in each pillar into a similar state. Then there was a *boom* that sent us flying back to the ground as the light pulled the molten liquids toward the scepter and infused them into one.

I rolled over, disoriented, squinting through the bright streak of light. I saw Jordan across from me doing the same. As my eyes adjusted, I spotted the fully formed Sovereign's Orb sitting atop the Sovereign's Scepter.

Everything was quiet. Everyone was still.

And then the hounds, dressed in the armor I had created for them, lifted their heads and let out a collective howl.

Together, every angel—Fallen and Blessed—drew their weapons and waited as one.

Jordan and I stood, and I couldn't help but notice the water at my feet had switched directions and was now flowing upstream.

"She's coming," I said in shock, knowing instinctually what was happening. Then I shouted, "She's coming!"

I seized the scepter from the stone, and a jolt of energy coursed through my arm just as my mother and her demon horde came streaming through the waterfall.

81 JORDAN

Ithaca, New York, Present Day

I drew my sword and ducked low as our opponents came forth. Lilith must have opened her dark hole to Purgatory within the cliffside, directly behind the waterfall itself.

The hounds raced forward behind me, tearing into the demons while the Fallen and Heavenly armies met Lilith's ragtag host of lost souls head-on. The archers atop the cliffs rained down a deluge of arrows, hitting their marks and felling beings.

Lilith must have persuaded a mass of Purgatory's angels to join her side because fighting soon commenced in the air in addition to on the ground.

The she-devil herself wasted no time in using her powers to attack Dane.

I sprang to my feet and slashed my sword through the air, grazing one of her gargoyle-like wings.

She hissed and whipped around like the snake she was, smirking at the sight of me. "Well, well, well. It seems we meet again." Her eyes narrowed on me. "You'll be my first kill," she purred.

An arrow suddenly lodged in her shoulder. She shrieked, stepping back.

"Dane, get out of here!" I shouted. "Find Satan!"

He nodded and launched into the air with the scepter.

I sideswiped Lilith's feet, bringing her to the ground as she struggled to pry the arrow free. I jumped on her, digging it in deeper.

She cried out in pain.

I was about to break the arrow shaft so she couldn't pull it free, when I saw a shadow behind me. I reached up to grab their arm as they brought it down, intending to hit me in the head. I flung them forward, and the Sentinel landed splayed out before me. That move had been used on me too many times, and I had trained relentlessly on overcoming it.

The Sentinel rose on his elbow, his face unhooded and his red eyes like daggers. He had a gun strapped to his hip while his sword lay mere inches from his reach. Swiftly, he seized the weapon and sprang up. Our blades crashed together. I twisted, unlocking our swords, and executed a sequence of blows, alternating directions and striking him from different angles. He parried my attacks and then performed a combination of his own, putting me on the defensive. I blocked his last strike and ducked as he swung his blade overhead and brought it down, hitting a rock instead of my head. Sidestepping, we circled each other.

82 SATAN

Ithaca, New York, Present Day

After the Sovereign's Orb and Scepter had united, I barely had time to ease up from the ground before Lilith's demons were on me.

I slashed my way through five of them and sent them sprawling off the platform into the water. I turned to see another creature looming over Metatron so I reached for a knife and threw it through the air. The weapon hit its target, lodging in the demon's head.

"I suggest you get out of here," I said to Metatron, who looked ashen.

He nodded but didn't move. Raziel grabbed Metatron's arm and rose into the air, the two of them fleeing without any words of gratitude.

An icicle whizzed past my head and hit a being behind me.

"Thanks," I said as Abbadona approached.

She shrugged. "Of course. Where's Dane?"

I glanced around the platform, which was now deserted. Once Lilith's army came spilling from the waterfall, everyone had sprung into action. Even Dane, who had taken the scepter. Now he was nowhere to be found.

"I don't know, but I have to find him," I told her.

I scanned the battlefield hoping to see some sign of him. Instead, I saw Lucifer. He was taunting a blessed angel midair, whom he slayed with a brutal strike to the abdomen. He delighted in the kill with a sick smile.

The sight of him ignited the fire inside me. It was time for a rematch.

"Abbadona—" I was going to tell her to find Dane, but she was fixated on something else.

Several feet ahead of us, Naomi commanded the water and used it as her weapon. She was dispatching demons and lost souls with frozen icicles while trapping some angels from Purgatory in a watery prison. Deborah, Delphine, and Gabriel were fighting alongside her, trying to protect the girl from surrounding threats. Her power made her a target. And they could use some help.

"Abbadona," I said again.

This time she focused on me.

"Go assist them," I urged.

"Are you sure?" she asked.

I nodded. "Positive." My attention returned to Lucifer. He noticed me and grinned, beckoning me with a hand gesture. "I'm going to take care of an old enemy. Then I'll find Dane."

"All right." Abbadona followed my gaze, then grabbed my arm. "Just make sure it's him that dies this time."

I placed my hand over her gloved one. "I will." Then I rocketed into the sky to chase after Lucifer.

83 GABRIEL

Ithaca, New York, Present Day

I never thought this battle would be easy, but I didn't expect to feel so overwhelmed. Deborah, Delphine, and I were doing our best to aid Naomi as she took out assailants. Her power was drawing much attention, though, and soon we were swarmed.

Seven opponents circled me—none of them angels—so I lifted into the air and swung my scythe. It took out all of them, but it didn't stop more enemies from coming. I had slayed seven, yet it felt as if fourteen more had taken their place.

If only we could get Lilith's portal closed. That would finally stop them. Except I feared our attempt at shutting it would be futile. The portal was too large and Lilith's power too strong. There was only one force that could shut it: Father. But Lilith had severed our connection to Him when she destroyed the Great Tree, and there had been no reports from Heaven stating that it had been restored.

We were on our own.

Gritting my teeth, I focused on my current opponents. I sidestepped a demon's attack, allowing me a small moment of reprieve, which is when I saw one of us go down.

"Deborah!" I yelled.

A demon had nicked her leg and was going in for the final blow. I tried to intercede but I was overpowered myself.

"Mom!" I heard Naomi cry.

Then I was engulfed in a powerful wave that came out of nowhere. The water latched on to the demons and caged them in while I broke through the deluge unscathed.

I choked up some water and brushed the hair from my eyes, expecting to see that Naomi had saved her mother. Except she was surfacing from a wave that had taken out her opponents, too. My eyes trailed over to Deborah, who was wincing in pain but otherwise alive.

Above her stood Abbadona, staff in one hand and an ice spear in the other. I couldn't help but notice the ice spear was caked with black demon gore. She must have sliced the creature in two.

Naomi jumped to her feet and raced to her mother's side. "Mom, are you okay?"

I stood and joined them since Abbadona's attack had slayed our remaining threats for the time being. Delphine hobbled over, too, and I reached out to steady her.

"Thanks," she said, leaning on me.

"What happened?" I asked her.

"I twisted my ankle. Nothing serious," Delphine assured me. "I'm more worried about her."

"I'm fine," Deborah insisted.

"You're not fine, Mom," Naomi sobbed as she inspected the wound on her mother's leg. "You're infected with demon venom."

Deborah froze, a touch of panic settling in her face.

Abbadona set down her weapons and knelt before Deborah. Gently, she examined her leg. "This is curable."

Deborah sighed in relief.

"But you must be treated right away," Abbadona said.

"I can take her to the healers at the house," Delphine offered. "I have my portal device." She showed us the object on her wrist.

I sighed. "All right, but don't return."

"Why not?" Delphine asked.

"Because you're not in good shape, either," I said. "Your injury might not be as serious as Deborah's but it's still an injury."

Delphine clenched her jaw. "Fine. There's no time to argue over the matter anyway." She looped Deborah's arm over her shoulder.

"Before you leave," Abbadona added, "take this." She reached into a pouch buckled to her waist. "It's a potion for demon venom. It'll heal the infection."

Deborah took the small bottle. "Thank you." She turned to Naomi. "Don't worry about me. I'll be fine. Just take care of yourself."

Naomi grabbed her mom's hand and squeezed it. "I love you."

"I love you, too." Deborah let go, and Delphine turned the dial on her portal device, both of them disappearing to safety.

Naomi brushed the tears from her cheeks and looked at Abbadona. "You saved her."

Abbadona nodded.

"Thank you." Naomi paused. "Dane told me about you."

"Did he?" Abbadona asked.

Naomi nodded. "Not much. Just that you have magic and can control water."

My eyes widened. Could Abbadona be Naomi's biological mother? I remained silent and continued to watch the interaction.

"I'm Abbadona."

"Naomi."

They shook hands.

"I know this isn't the best time," Abbadona said, "but I would enjoy getting to know you more. I'm confident we have a connection."

"As would I."

Both of them smiled.

"How about we show them what we can do together?" Abbadona asked.

Naomi dipped her hands in the water, drawing out icicles. "It would be my pleasure."

Abbadona picked up her staff and spear, and the two of them returned to the fray.

I was about to join them, except my chest felt heavy all of a sudden.

That's odd…

Until I realized I wasn't feeling my discomfort but that of my sister's.

Kat.

She needed me.

84

JORDAN

Ithaca, New York, Present Day

I focused on the Sentinel and charged forward. We clashed again, this time both of us picking up speed. Our swords hummed as they whizzed through the air, and our feet danced over the wet stone. At the same time, we disarmed each other, but it didn't stop either of us. We just used our fists to continue the fight.

He punched me in the ribs, but I managed to crack him across the face. However, it did little to sway him. The Sentinel was so unnatural, I didn't know what was going to break his stride.

I ducked one of his kicks and spun on the ground, only to see Uncle Aeron approaching. The Sentinel noticed and grabbed his sword to meet my uncle's.

"Jordan, go!" Uncle Aeron demanded through gritted teeth. "This is my fight!"

"But he's unkillable. Let me help!" My words went unheard, the two men consumed by their revenge.

It didn't take long for their weapons to fall to the wayside. Instead, they used their fists, too, to pummel one another.

"Why?" Aeron raged. "Why did you do it?"

The Sentinel flipped him onto his back. "Because you treated me like shit!" He cracked Aeron across the face. "I always had to take your orders!" He landed another punch. "I always had to clean up your messes!" His next strike hit Aeron's ribs. "And not once did I get a favor returned, even when I was sick!" He let go of Aeron's shirt, dropping him to the ground and standing tall above him.

Aeron writhed in pain but managed to wheeze out. "I let you into my family."

The Sentinel sneered. "The whole lot of you are self-righteous pricks. You all deserved what you got."

That's it! I couldn't stand here any longer as the Sentinel insulted my family. He had done enough to us already.

I knelt for my sword and grasped the hilt, prepared to spar with him once more. But what good would that do? There had to be a way to stop him.

A bloodstone arrow sat next to my sword. One of the archers must have shot it and missed their mark. I picked it up and inspected it. If this was what would take down Lilith, then maybe it would work on the Sentinel, too.

I tightened my grip on the arrow and advanced on him from behind. "Silas!"

He paused his fight with Uncle Aeron to turn and face me. And, as soon as he did, I plunged the arrow into his chest.

He sucked in a breath and faltered. The wings at his back receded. His red eyes went wide and returned to their normal hue. Everything unnatural and abnormal about him vanished, the bloodstone undoing any blood magic Lilith had performed on him.

The Sentinel was becoming Silas again. And when the transformation was complete, I thought there might be a chance to reason with him. But it turned out Silas had never been a friend.

He reached for the gun at his hip, intending to shoot me. I ducked for cover, but there was nothing to hide me. Other than my uncle, who stepped in front of me with his own gun raised.

"This is for Arthur!" Aeron shouted.

My eyes widened. "No, don't!"

But it was too late. Two gunshots sounded.

I flattened myself along the rocks, missing the bullets but seeing one hit its mark. My uncle's shot landed right between Silas's eyes.

I shut my own, unable to stomach the sight. His body thumped to the ground, and I reopened them, not expecting to hear a second thump. But I did.

No...

I turned around to find my uncle on the ground.

I leaped to my feet and raced to his side, at which point I collapsed to my knees and reached out to put pressure on his neck.

Silas's shot had nicked an artery. Blood seeped through my fingers.

I opened my mouth to reassure him, to try to keep him holding on, but his eyes were like glass. He was already gone.

In their final acts, two best friends turned brothers turned enemies had killed each other. In a way, they both got their justice.

85

SOPHIA

Ithaca, New York, Present Day

"Arrows! I need more arrows!" I cried.

"Which kind?" Dafne asked from behind.

"Normal ones. I can't keep wasting our bloodstone supply until I have a clear shot."

Dafne handed me one and I nocked it in my bow, taking aim. Meanwhile, she filled the quiver at my back. Uriel had given me a special one with two compartments so I could keep bloodstone arrows on the left and normal ones on the right.

We were above the waterfall, the riverbed at our feet, its waters spilling over the cliffside. Around us was a dense forest that provided protection. Overall, it was the perfect spot.

I let the arrow loose, hitting a demon. I reached for another when Uriel raced from the woods.

"Fall back!" he commanded.

The archers on either side of me grasped their weapons and retreated into the surrounding foliage.

I stood my ground.

"Sophia, we need to go!" Dafne shouted.

"Not yet! I have a shot!" I grasped a bloodstone arrow, ready to nock it in my bow.

Someone snatched my arm and pulled me into the forest.

"What's your problem!"

Uriel flung me against a tree. "That was an order!"

I sprang forward and inched close to his face. "You told me it was up to us to stop Lilith. Wasn't that an order, too?"

Dafne had followed us into the woods, and her head swung back-and-forth as we argued.

Uriel gritted his teeth. "It was, but we have a more pressing issue."

"Which is?"

He pointed to the other side of the riverbed.

I peered across the distance, my Nephilim senses kicking in. There were beings over there. A lot of them. They weren't angelic or demonic.

"What are they?" I asked.

"Lilith's experiments," Uriel said.

Dafne blanched. "You mean the unkillable ones?"

Uriel nodded. "We don't stand a chance. There's too many of them and not enough of us."

He was right. There was only a small group of us up here.

I looked down at the bloodstone arrow still in my hand. "What about this?"

Uriel glanced over. "What about it?"

"Maybe it can kill them," I suggested.

He shook his head. "We can't take that risk. Those arrows need to be saved for Lilith."

"But—" I didn't have time to finish.

Lilith's soldiers surged out of the woods and through the riverbed.

Uriel slung his bow on his back and drew the axe hanging at his waist. "Attack!" He charged and the others followed.

Dafne pulled her sword from its scabbard. "I guess it's time to test our training."

I grabbed her arm. "No one would blame you if you left."

She shrugged me off. "I would." She took a deep breath. "I'm not deserting. I'm a Delucci. I've got this." Then she attacked.

I replaced the bloodstone arrow I still held in my hand and put away my bow. Dafne was right. It was time to test ourselves.

I removed my sword and stormed into the fight, joining my friends in what felt like an impossible task. No wound would kill these enemies. I knew, though, that they would grow weak as they sustained more injuries, so I inflicted as many as I could. Except their numbers kept pouring from the forest opposite the riverbed.

"Retreat to the trees!" Uriel instructed.

Everyone in our group was angelic so they quickly alighted into the air and took refuge among the woods. All but Dafne, who happened to be at my side.

She slashed her opponent, sheathed her sword, and held out her arms, which I clutched, lifting us both into the air before anyone could harm her.

I set us down in a nearby tree. We nestled between the branches and took a moment to regroup.

Lilith's soldiers remained on the ground. None of them had wings like the Sentinel so they couldn't reach us unless they decided to climb. From here, it was easy to see that some weren't nearly as invincible as the Sentinel, either. A handful of casualties covered the forest floor. Until their bodies convulsed and they rose once more.

Dafne gasped. "Are you seeing this?"

I nodded.

Now that their numbers had regenerated, Lilith's soldiers approached the trees we were hiding in, ready to chase us out. Some attempted to scale the trunk. Others used their weapons to chop at the roots.

Uriel and the rest of our group started firing arrows to stop them.

I adjusted my footing and reached for my bow, but the branch I was perched on broke.

"Sophia!" Dafne yelled.

I fell through the branches, unable to get my wings out and save myself since they were trapped beneath my weapon.

Finally, I collided with the ground. Right in the middle of the enemy's ranks.

86 SATAN

Ithaca, New York, Present Day

Lucifer and I flew through the thick of battle, ascending higher until we found an open patch of air. I sped up, ready to collide with him and brawl, but he swooped down low to avoid the attack.

We were above the forest, skimming the tops of trees, when I realized we were heading north, away from the waterfall and toward the lake that lay at the edge of the national park.

I stopped midair. Was I *really* going to let him do this to me again? Bait me so I would follow him without a care?

It was highly unlikely he was leading me into a trap this time. Instead, he was distracting me, taking me away from the war.

My eyes narrowed. Which is exactly what Lilith wanted.

I was the one who could destroy the scepter. And Lucifer was the biggest thorn in my side. No wonder Lilith kept him around. It was all a ploy to divert my attention and incite my anger, something she had done since the day I had met her in Eden.

Well, that wasn't going to happen anymore.

"I know what you're doing, and I'm not falling for it!" I called out to him.

He chuckled. "You're still as spineless as when I left you!"

"I disagree!" I stretched my arms out wide. "What I'm doing takes a lot of strength. I would love nothing more than to incinerate that egotistical head of yours into ash. But I'm refraining."

"Why?" he challenged.

"Because you're not worth it. You never were." I sighed and pointed behind me. "Whereas they are." I raised both hands in the air and flipped him my middle fingers. "Fuck you, Lucifer!"

For once, I turned my back on him and left. Did I want him dead? Yes. But there would be plenty of opportunities to do that beyond this day. Right now, I had more important matters to attend to.

Banking over the forest again, I returned to the waterfall and the battlefield, but before I could land below and resume the fight, a skirmish in the woods caught my attention.

It looked like a group of Lilith's soldiers had overwhelmed the archers. That wasn't good, considering we were relying on them to stop Lilith.

I sighed. I had to find Dane, but this matter seemed more pressing at the moment, given that I wasn't even sure if Dane still had the scepter.

As I drew closer, I noticed these opponents were Lilith's experiments, the ones who weren't easy to kill. Me interceding wouldn't help much when no weapon or amount of force worked on them. But I had to try something because they had the archers cornered in the trees.

On my right, I spied a cistern of anointing oil. I headed for it and landed undetected. I bent over and grabbed a handful of twigs and leaves. Standing, I dunked my hand in the oil and ignited the Hellfire. It set the debris ablaze.

Suddenly, a body came crashing through a tree and collided with the ground.

Shit! It was the girl, Sophia. And she was completely surrounded by foes.

For once, I was trying to be discreet, but all bets were off now.

"Hey, assholes!" I shouted.

They turned their attention to me, briefly ignoring her.

"I hope you like it crisp," I said. I turned the cistern over. Oil spilled out onto the forest floor, and I threw my fireball directly into their horde.

In seconds, our surroundings were aflame. Lilith's soldiers fled, and my allies soared down from the trees.

"What were you thinking?" Uriel asked. "We're going to have a whole forest fire on our hands."

Sophia eased up from the ground. "Can someone please help Dafne?" she cried.

One of the angels flew up and rescued her, returning her safely to the ground.

"Thanks," Dafne said.

"Hello?" Uriel waved his hands in front of my face. "What do you have to say for yourself?"

I glared at him. "I don't answer to you! Besides, I was saving you," I said. "The least you can do is show a little gratitude."

"Oh like you do?" Uriel challenged.

My blood boiled. "Fine. Next time I'll let them slaughter you." I glanced at the flames. "It was only meant to be a distraction. It's not that big anyway," I said, gesturing around us.

"Right now it isn't!" Uriel yelled as a tree caught fire. "See!"

"All right! I'll work on putting it out," I conceded. "If we get Abbadona or Naomi up here, it'll be doused before any damage is done."

Uriel tensed. "I'll work on the fire." He pointed across the riverbed. "You deal with them."

I followed his indication and saw that Lilith's soldiers had merely taken cover to regroup.

"Fine," I ground out.

I whistled and waited.

"What's that going to do?" Uriel asked.

I held up a hand to silence him.

Eventually, the hellhounds came racing through the trees and wasted no time attacking Lilith's soldiers.

"That should hold them off for now," I said, drawing my sword. "But I'll make sure they won't disrupt you."

"Archers!" Uriel commanded. "Resume your places!"

They all shuffled over to the cliff edge to rejoin the battle while Uriel went to deal with the fire.

I guessed our conversation was over. I faced the forest, ready to assist the hounds.

"Thank you."

Surprised, I turned around. It was Sophia.

"I appreciate you saving us… Although I imagine it's probably out of temporary obligation," she said.

I shrugged. "For them it is." I met her eyes. "For you it's not."

Her brow furrowed. "What do you mean?"

"So long as you're involved with Dane," I paused, "then you're protected by the Fallen."

"Oh…"

"I didn't mean that as a threat. I'm just stating a fact," I said.

She nodded. "I know."

The mention of Dane had an effect on her. Her eyes grew distant and her face sank in worry.

"I'm sure he's fine," I assured her. I reached for a bloodstone arrow and handed it to her. "It's time for you to focus and finish this."

She took it from me without touching my hand. "I will."

We went in opposite directions, the war still waiting for us.

87 DANE

Ithaca, New York, Present Day

Flying seemed like the best way to flee with the scepter, except the sky, like the ground, had become a battlefield.

Angels fought angels, and while most of the Blessed and Fallen had teamed up to attack the gray-feathered beings from Purgatory, some had turned against one another, getting the rematch they never thought was possible.

I wove through their skirmishes the best I could, trying to avoid any confrontations. I wanted to ascend to the top of the cliffside to get a better vantage point so I could see where Satan was. Landing in the woods, I took a moment to collect myself.

Holy shit, is this thing powerful!

The energy from the scepter kept pulsing through my hand and up my arm.

If only I could destroy it myself...

I closed my eyes and searched inside for the Hellfire. I knew I had it. The fever I'd suffered through had been too extreme to be anything else.

I tried to focus, but all I could feel was the energy from the scepter, this time radiating all the way up to my shoulder. Something wasn't right. I panicked and dropped the scepter to the lush, green grass.

"Blood mages can't handle bloodstone."

I tensed at the voice and gritted my teeth. "It's not bloodstone."

"Not completely," Lucifer said, "but one of the thirteen spheres is, and it's now swirling around in there." He pointed to the Sovereign's Orb. "Why don't I take that off your hands before it does any more damage?"

He lunged for the scepter, but I stopped him by throwing out my hand and summoning my blood magic. He froze in place, but it was a struggle to keep him back since I still didn't have control over my powers. My hand shook and was unsteady, a visible sign of my weakening hold.

The trees around us rustled as another angel alighted behind me. I heard the unmistakable scrape of a sword unsheathing.

"Dane, let him go," Michael said. "I'll take care of him."

"No!" I shouted. "Get the scepter to Satan!"

He hesitated.

I was losing control.

"Michael!"

He snatched it from the ground and sprang into the sky just as I let Lucifer go. The fallen angel braced himself to leap into the air and go after Michael, but I drew my sword and swung it his way, narrowly missing his neck.

Lucifer fell backward and rolled, my blade connecting with the ground, making a loud thump. I pulled it free and advanced, not giving him a moment to rest.

He drew his weapon, and it met mine, metal clanging against metal.

"I see you're trying to follow in your father's footsteps," Lucifer taunted, eyeing my sword.

I ignored him and swiveled free.

"It's a shame you'll never succeed," he continued, feinting up then striking down and grazing my ribs.

I jumped back with a grimace, grateful that the armor I was wearing had protected me.

"You're a disappointment to both your parents," he sneered. "Not living up to either of their expectations."

Resuming the fight, I performed a sequence of steps around Lucifer, eventually nicking his shoulder in a moment of vulnerability and disarming him. However, the closeness worked to his advantage, and he pulled a dagger from his sleeve and slashed my leg.

This time I wasn't so lucky. Blood welled to the surface.

I faltered but managed to hop back out of reach.

Lucifer laughed. "Do you really think you can beat me?"

No, you can't do anything.

I braced myself against a tree and held a hand to my head. One of the two voices on my shoulders was back. And it happened to be the self-deprecating one.

You've never amounted to anything.

"You're still that same desperate boy in the park, aren't you?" Lucifer asked.

My eyes flashed.

"The little leech that would cling on to anyone who showed a remote interest in him, let alone gave him affection."

I slammed my sword in the dirt, unable to deal with both internal and external mockery. It was too much. Instead, I swung my fist, connecting it to Lucifer's jaw. He lurched backward, stunned. But then he just seemed to become more energized.

He raised his hands, dancing in place on the balls of his feet. "You should have come with me. I would have put you out of your misery long ago."

Something inside me snapped.

No one's ever wanted you.

No one's ever cared about you.

You're always second best.

I seized the knife at my belt and flipped it toward myself.

"Do it!" Lucifer cheered. *"Do it!"*

And just when I'd convinced myself I should, tears streaming down my face, the supportive voice on my shoulder kicked in, remembering every encouraging remark I had ever received.

Don't hold it back. Your feelings matter. Let them out.

I dropped my knife and heeded Jordan's advice, releasing a primal roar and allowing every suppressed emotion to escape.

Don't ever apologize for who you are.

With Satan's words in my mind, I composed myself and leaped at Lucifer. I clutched him by the shirt and began to pummel him. I leveled punch after punch across his face, not giving him a chance to move or breathe.

You matter.

Sister Helen's reminder gave me pause. Still clutching Lucifer's shirt, I looked down at the fallen angel. His face was bloody and swollen, and yet, he still smiled.

"I finally see where you get it from," Lucifer spit out. "That bitch of an old nun was as spineless as you are."

His insult aligned everything inside me, igniting a feverish heat. I clenched his throat with both my hands and let the inferno rage. He writhed and shrieked, but I didn't back down. He had burned Sister Helen to death, and it was only right for him to suffer the same fate.

"You are unworthy to live a second life in Purgatory, even wandering the Wastelands," I said.

I intensified the Hellfire to a temperature no being—human or otherwise—could handle.

Lucifer's skin turned ash gray and started to crack.

"And for that reason, you shall cease to exist."

Before my eyes, Lucifer slowly disintegrated into a pile of embers.

I sat back, winded, but having no regrets. I brushed the ash from my hands. Finally, I could sense the rush of Hellfire running through my veins, never feeling more content or sure of myself.

88 JORDAN

Ithaca, New York, Present Day

I hardly knew my uncle Aeron, so I wasn't wrecked the way I had been with Sister Helen, but at the same time, he *was* my uncle, and I couldn't help but feel solemn.

I closed his eyes and stood, assessing the battlefield. It was easy to detect our forces were growing thin and weak. Bodies covered the ground, blood and gore stained the water red and black, and flashes of light continuously struck around us as angels perished. There was a small stream of smoke coming from the woods above the waterfall, and I imagined it indicated a fire.

Meanwhile, Lilith's army kept spilling forth from Purgatory, her numbers only increasing as it was hard to slay the majority of her troops.

We had to finish this.

Picking up my sword, I inspected my surroundings. Lilith was only a few feet away engaged in a confrontation with Kat. Abbadona and Naomi were helping her by providing constant distraction with streams of water and spikes of ice, which allowed Kat moments of reprieve from Lilith's blood magic.

I quietly approached from behind in the hopes to sneak up on her.

"Enough!" Lilith bellowed, sending Kat, Abbadona, and Naomi to their knees. She stepped over to them. "The three of you have been so bothersome." She stared vehemently at Kat. "You in particular, though." She knelt in front of her and squeezed her cheek. "You're going to die." Lilith straightened and moved on to Abbadona, tipping up the fallen angel's chin. "You'll be tortured." She continued down the line, placing her hand on Naomi's head. "You I might spare so long as you pledge allegiance to me."

"Leave her alone," Abbadona ground out. The water at her knees was swirling. She was resisting Lilith's magic.

Lilith cackled. "I guess you figured out you're her mother and feel the need to protect her now." She sneered. "How admirable." Her eyes focused on the water. "I should have never taught you anything." She reached for a knife at her belt.

"I don't think so," Kat said, rising.

Lilith was stunned. "That's not possible…"

"You might be manipulating me," Kat said. "But you're not manipulating my brother. He's giving me the strength to fight you." Kat grabbed her sword and stepped forward.

Lilith lost it. "Gabriel!" She flung down her hands, and Kat froze in place, struggling against Lilith's magic. "Show yourself so we can end this!"

He didn't appear.

"Ugh!" Lilith screeched. She slammed her hands down, and Kat dropped to her knees in the water again.

Clearly whatever connection Kat and Gabriel had was only a momentary defense against Lilith's blood magic. That or he had gotten distracted with the chaos around us.

Either way, I had enough. First the Sentinel and his big mouth and now Lilith's. I didn't think I could handle anymore insults and threats. Besides she was controlling Kat, Abbadona, and Naomi, and there was no telling when her antics might turn deadly, much like I had witnessed in Hell.

Lilith hadn't sensed me yet, so I continued to approach her from behind until I was close enough to slam her across the head with the pommel of my sword.

She went soaring to the ground.

Kat, Abbadona, and Naomi rose from the shallow waters, grateful for the assistance.

"Is the arrow still in her?" I asked.

"No," Kat said, "she pulled it out once the Sentinel engaged you, which is why I came over to detain her."

"Crap," I said. "We need another shot."

Kat nodded. "They're trying."

I tightened my grip on my weapon, advancing on Lilith while she was still down. She lifted herself from the water before I could strike, though, throwing out her hand.

Her wave of magic hit me. I could feel its warm energy. But it did nothing.

"You're forgetting something," I said, lifting my neck to reveal my mother's silver chain.

Lilith shrieked and straightened up, throwing out her arm again and sending Kat, Abbadona, and Naomi sprawling behind me. "How? I destroyed it!"

Above, on the cliffside behind her, I saw Sophia draw back an arrow and take aim.

"A mother's love never dies," I said, maintaining the distraction. "Except in your case."

She sneered. "I'm not a mother!" Lilith drew a weapon from her belt that looked like a spike attached to a hilt. "I'm a god!"

And as she screamed the words, Sophia's arrow soared through the air, hitting its mark between Lilith's wings.

Bull's-eye.

She gasped and twisted in an attempt to pull it free.

Abbadona and Naomi froze the water at her feet to trap her. Kat and I rushed forward to finish her, but Gabriel must have known Kat's intentions because he arrived before we got to Lilith. Dropping from the air, he grasped the arrow and snapped off the shaft just as Lilith lifted her weapon over her head. She drove it down into Gabriel's chest. Lilith fell forward to her knees while Gabriel stumbled back.

My feet didn't stop advancing, even though everything slowed around me. I reached out and clutched him, holding him steady. He drew his scythe and pushed it into my hand. I took it, and he grabbed his chest as his head rolled back.

"No!"

His full weight came down on me, and my knees buckled.

Kat caught us both, her strength far greater than mine, taking Gabriel's body and easing it to the ground. The sight of him forced a sob from my throat, and my whole body shook. I had never felt more broken.

I raised the scythe and grasped it with both hands, tightening my hold. Without hesitation, I stepped over to Lilith and swung. The scythe's blade was sharp and easily cut through her skin, striking her neck and taking her head clean off.

As the appendage rolled and her body slumped forward to the ground, I dropped the weapon and returned to Gabriel. Crashing to my knees, I seized his shirt and wept over his chest, my tears falling over his wound. I tried to wipe them away but they kept coming, even as I detected the faint rise and fall of his chest.

My eyes opened wider, the tears slowing. "Raphael!" I bellowed the angel of healing's name, knowing he would come if called.

"Jordan," Kat whispered, "it's no use."

"He's still breathing! We have to try!"

Thunder rumbled overhead. I looked to the sky, but there were no clouds.

Thinking Abbadona or Naomi was summoning another downpour, I said, "Help me shield him from the rain."

Kat shook her head, mouth agape. "That's not a storm. It's the Factions of Faith."

89

MICHAEL

Ithaca, New York, Present Day

I flew high over the woods, scanning the ranks below. It took every fiber of my being to leave Dane, but I had to trust him and his ability to defend himself.

You trained them right. It's time to let them flourish.

From my vantage point, I searched the throngs of bodies for a being clad entirely in black.

Satan, where are you?

I finally spotted him among the trees atop the cliffside, surrounded by a horde of Lilith's soldiers. It looked as if they were the unkillable ones since many had sustained injuries, yet they kept on fighting like nothing was wrong.

I remained in the sky and shouted, "Satan!"

He briefly set his focus on me and I waved the scepter in the air.

Immediately, he came to join me. "Give me that!" He demanded. "I need it!"

I pulled back. "Why?"

"The archers were under siege. I came to assist them so they could focus on Lilith, but it's impossible to slay these bastards." He held out his hand. "Unless I use that."

"What?!" I hesitated as Metatron's warning came to mind. He had been right that Satan had started the war in Heaven for the very object I held in my hand. Should I really give it to him so he could wield it?

"Swear to me you'll do nothing more than stop them," I commanded.

"I swear," he said.

"And you promise to destroy it afterward?"

He rolled his eyes. "Of course."

I pulled back. "Satan, please take this seriously. I'll kill you myself if you don't do the right thing."

His eyes narrowed. "Those are some harsh words coming from a brother who betrayed me."

"We betrayed each other," I said. "Don't act like you didn't play a part in it."

"I never denied that," Satan stated. He smirked. "After all we've been through, after all this division, it's ironic to see how much I'm still needed in Heavenly matters."

"Meaning?"

"Meaning you need me. Meaning my existence as the Devil is necessary to solve your problems." He pointed to the scepter. "And *that* is the perfect example. You all created it, you all allowed it to exist, but in order to destroy it, you turn to me." He shrugged. "You're lucky I'm so accommodating because I could just wash my hands of it all and refuse to help you."

"Why don't you? That would certainly give you greater satisfaction."

"It would. But the consequences are too steep. If I let the scepter remain, someone could use its power to overthrow me, to make it that I don't exist anymore. And I much prefer my current situation compared to that."

"Then why not use it for yourself?" I asked.

He chuckled. "At one point, that's all I wanted to do. But now I realize much of what made me so obsessed with the Union of the Spheres was Lilith's influence. Since the day she bit me in Eden, she has had more sway over me than I care to admit. Now that it's gone, I don't seek to use the scepter because if I did, I would have no purpose. There would be nothing left for me to attain. I would have everything I ever wanted or needed, and I much prefer a struggle to gain something rather than have it handed to me. It builds greater character. It makes me who I am, and I like what I've become."

"Fair enough," I conceded, handing it to him. Because more than anything, I trusted his words. He wasn't a liar. Never had been. Our betrayal hadn't lain in the fact that neither of us trusted the other. Quite the opposite, as we trusted each other too much. So much so that we had expected one to follow the other, and when neither of us did as the other anticipated, it was a difference of opinion that had driven us a part.

Satan grasped the scepter and wasted no time in pointing it toward Lilith's soldiers. "Those that are unkillable, may you return to your former selves and perish from your wounds."

Bodies dropped in the forest below.

"It worked," I said.

Satan nodded. "It did." He turned to me. "But that's enough. This power is unnatural, just like Lilith's experiments. It's time to destroy it."

He ignited the Hellfire and his hands glowed against the black-and-white rod, a small stream of smoke billowing into the air.

Moving his hands upward, Satan's blaze consumed the rod, pulverizing it to ashes. The smoke cloud grew and turned darker. Eventually, all that remained was the winged topper holding the Sovereign's Orb. He cupped it in both his hands and increased the heat.

The metallic wings on the topper melted, soon the only remanent of the orb itself. The light swirling inside it became fainter and fainter. Satan's hands drew closer together until he clasped them and annihilated whatever was left.

90 JORDAN

Ithaca, New York, Present Day

I glanced behind me and saw angels from every religion cascade over the waterfall. The Factions of Faith were enormous, and they soon went to work vanquishing any remaining opponents.

Sandalphon appeared through the chaos with a smile on his face. "Finally! Our connection is restored!" He stood before the waterfall and shouted, "Father, I summon thee to close this gateway to Purgatory!"

Clouds rolled in fast, and a beam of light struck the cliffside.

"Jordan!" Raphael yelled, landing in the shallow water. "What did you—" He stopped when he saw Gabriel lying limp and wounded.

Rushing over, he dropped next to his brother and inspected the injury. "Oh no," he whispered.

"What is it?" I asked.

"There's nothing we can do," he said softly.

"No! There has to be!" I yelled. "Where's Dane? He can fix him."

"He can't," Raphael said. "The weapon used was—"

"Dark? Then we'll get some holy water," I stated.

Raphael shook his head. "No, it was ancient and obscure…full of shadows and death. No magic can hold against it."

"There has to be something we can do!" I repeated. "There has to..."

A group of angels formed around us, none of them familiar faces until one by one the family I knew well joined us.

Chamuel and Zadkiel were first, pushing through the others. Then Uriel and Sophia arrived, followed by Dane. Dafne was next, along with Naomi. And finally, Michael and Satan appeared, the former visibly stricken by the sight.

Each of them joined me on the ground and surrounded Gabriel. Satan knelt, too, and the Fallen mimicked his move. The Blessed did the same, all taking a knee beside their rivals. Everyone was silent and solemn.

I was the only one making noise. I couldn't stop sobbing, especially as I thought about all Gabriel and I had been through. He had been my savior the night the Fallen had chased me, giving refuge to a helpless and frightened teen. There had been our travels together around the world to collect the angels. His endless violin interludes. The calm way he handled every scenario, even when I'd done things I probably shouldn't have. For the past two years, he had been a constant in my life.

I refused to give up on him.

Up above, the roiling clouds still lingered. I'd had a religious upbringing as a kid, but I never asked, let alone begged, for God to intercede on my behalf. I had believed in Him, but seeing the almighty and immense power before me forcing shut a portal within the cliffside certainly changed my perspective and increased my faith.

For that reason, I had to try.

Raising my head to the sky, I shouted, "Please! Save him!"

The clouds kept churning, and the beam of light held strong over the waterfall.

I dropped my head to Gabriel's chest, his breath a small rattle. "Please," I pleaded to no one other than myself.

Why?

A strong voice rang through my mind.

My eyes flashed open and I raised my head again.

"Because he doesn't deserve this," I demanded. "He's been loyal to You and committed to the cause from the beginning. He did whatever it took, no matter the cost."

And if I save him? What then?

With assurance, I said, "He will do whatever You ask."

There was a moment of pause.

It shall be done.

A bright light shone down on us.

I edged back.

The beam shot over Gabriel's chest, repairing the damage done by Lilith's blade. As the skin healed, a healthy color returned to his body, wiping out the sickly paleness. Suddenly, Gabriel's eyes opened, and he wheezed in a rush of air.

The entire Heavenly army banged their weapons against their armor, celebrating the miraculous act.

Gabriel eased up on his elbows, and I clutched him in a hug. He returned it and smiled softly. "Thank you."

I pulled back. "Of course."

Michael came over and patted him on the back. "You can't do that ever again, you hear?"

"I have no plans to," Gabriel assured him.

Gazing around the battlefield, I saw all that remained of the war—wounded soldiers, casualties, sadness, relief. But more importantly, I saw a sea of beings who had looked past their inherent differences to come together to defeat a greater evil.

91 SOPHIA

Ithaca, New York, Present Day

A week had passed since the battle, the wreckage finally cleaned up and the many souls laid to rest. A mass ceremony had been held for those who had fought with us gallantly but did not make it. My dad one of them.

Delphine and my mom had been hit the hardest by his death. Jordan and I were sad to have a family member taken so soon after meeting them, but there was also a feeling of detachment since we hardly knew him. A part of me regretted that I had never made amends with him, and another part didn't because even if I had, I don't think we would have ever been close. There was too much unspeakable strain between us, and an apology or forgiveness could never shake it.

As for our allies, they had departed shortly after the burial services. The Factions of Faith had returned just as swiftly as they had come, without saying a word. The Fallen had left in a much louder ruckus, energized from winning the war, while the Blessed traveled back to Heaven content with closure for a conflict that had been mounting for centuries.

Kat, Aziza, and Yadira said their goodbyes, assuring us they would always be around if needed, but matters closer to Aziza's and Yadira's realms were currently calling them away.

All that remained in terms of angelic beings were our six friends who had become family. Even they had to leave us soon, but they stayed on a bit longer to make sure everything had been taken care of.

I sat on the dock by the lake in the afternoon sun, looking out across the water and watching the many birds that flew high overhead.

Footsteps sounded down the wooden planks, and a figure came to sit beside me.

"I'm going to miss having you around," Jordan said.

I met his eyes. "I'm only temporarily going to stay at Delphine's house. Our aunt and I decided it's the best thing for my mom right now. I won't be that far away."

"I know, but then you're back to Harvard," he said.

"And you're off to Cornell," I pointed out.

He shook his head. "No, I'm not."

I was shocked. "What? You never answered that e-mail, did you?"

"Actually, I did," he confessed. "I thanked them for the opportunity but told them my plans had changed and I wouldn't be attending after all."

"Really?" I asked, amazed. "And what do you plan to do?"

"I'm going to the University of Cape Town in South Africa. I applied in the spring and received my acceptance e-mail five weeks ago. I didn't have a chance to share the news with everything going on."

My mouth dropped open. "Jordan, that's wonderful! You must be thrilled."

He smiled. "I am. I love my parents more than anything, but I need to make my own way. Cornell was my mom's path, and while it's a great school, I really loved seeing Africa on our travels and I want to spend more time there."

"This sounds perfect for you, then," I said.

He nodded. "Before you go, there's something I want you to have." He handed me a rectangular object wrapped in a burlap cloth.

I took it and untied the rope woven around it. Peeking underneath, I saw a title, *The Book of Prophecies*.

"Why are you giving me this?" I asked.

"Because it's a Conway heirloom," he answered.

"Right, but *you're* a Conway," I told him. "If anything, you should keep this. It was your dad's."

"It was only my dad's because the family seat had been passed to him," he explained. "And if it was ever passed to us, it would go to you, not me."

"You're the one with the visions," I said.

"Yeah, but you're the eldest," he countered.

"What about the angels?" I asked. "Don't they want to bring it back to Heaven?"

Jordan shrugged. "They told me to keep it. It's been here for centuries anyway, and the missing page was never found."

"What do you think Lilith did with it?" I asked.

"I don't know. It may never turn up, but the book needs to remain in our family," he said.

"Except I'm like my dad. I don't have the gift," I told him.

"Says who?" he asked, grinning. He rose from the dock and sauntered back to the house.

I looked down at the book. When I was in the Sea of Galilee, one of my visions of the future contained two books held by different angels. Was this one of those books? I secured the cloth again and settled the book in my lap. What made Jordan think I had the Conway gift?

More footsteps sounded down the dock, and someone else came to sit beside me.

Dane and I sat in silence, looking out at the water.

So much had happened during battle that when the two of us saw each other again, we nearly ran into one another's arms until we stopped ourselves. We settled for some intense staring instead. In the week since, we spent every day together like usual, except he had grown quiet. I suspected something had happened during the fight he had yet to tell me about.

"I killed Lucifer," he admitted.

My head turned fast. It was hard to hide my shock. I wasn't expecting that to be his confession. So I waited for him to say something else.

There was another long pause. Eventually, he looked at me. "Do you hate me?"

My mouth dropped open. "Of course not. Is that why you've been quiet?"

He nodded. "I didn't want to ruin anything between us."

I smiled and put my hand next to his on the dock, our fingers inches apart. "Don't worry I can handle a lot." I drew serious. "You forget that I killed things, too. Maybe not a fallen angel, but certainly enough of Lilith's beings."

"I know." He stared longingly at me. "I keep telling myself I'm not good enough for you, but all I want is *you*." He shook his head. "I'm afraid I'm going to ruin everything."

"Dane, stop," I whispered, scooching closer.

He slid back a little. "Sorry. I don't want to chance it. I don't think we can get by with clothing barriers. My Hellfire burns more than my dad's."

"So... Are you saying we're over?"

His eyes widened. "What? No!"

I sighed. "Good, because you had me worried."

He ran a hand through his hair. "See... I'm messing this up."

I nodded. "I agree with you there. But not for the reasons you think." I placed my hands on top of the book in my lap. "I'm not some porcelain doll that's going to crack the moment I'm faced with evil or darkness or anything heavy for that matter. To be honest, those circumstances are only going to make us stronger because we'll be by one another's side no matter what."

His eyes flashed. "Promise?"

I thought about it for a second and my heart fluttered.

I would do anything for you.

"Promise," I said, trying to contain my enthusiasm.

He exhaled a deep breath of air and lay back on the dock. "Well, that's a relief."

I laughed and joined him, gazing up at the sky.

"Can you even believe our lives right now?" he asked.

"No," I murmured. "I never thought we'd be here dealing with angels and demons, Heaven and Hell."

"But I wouldn't change it," we said together. Our eyes met and we beamed at one another.

"By the way, thanks for the birthday gift," he said.

"I'm glad you liked it." I had gotten him an easel and set it up in his room so he could paint more.

I waited for him to say something else. He didn't.

"Dane," I whispered.

"Hmm..."

"Are you still thinking about art school?"

He shrugged. "I don't know. Maybe. I'm not sure what the future holds." He rolled onto his side and stared down at me. "Other than you."

Damn, did I want to kiss him.

I settled for pressing one to my hand and blowing it his way. He pretended to catch it and placed it to his lips with two fingers.

"You're not making this easy," I said.

He smiled devilishly. "Neither are you."

A sharp cawing sounded overhead.

Dane rolled his eyes. "I have to go."

My brow furrowed. "What do you mean?"

He pointed to the raven on the roof. "Dad's calling." He got to his feet. "I'll be back."

92 DANE

Ithaca, New York, Present Day

I flew up to the roof of the house and sat on the turret. The expansive view of the horizon was a much nicer sight than the lake. This scenery gave me hope that everything would be all right while the water reminded me of the battle, and I didn't need to keep reliving that day.

I glanced at the raven. It cawed in my face.

"If you want to see me, just come yourself," I told the bird.

It squawked and flew away, only to be replaced by Satan seconds later. "What are you doing up here, Ace?"

I smiled. "I could ask you the same thing."

"I was just checking on you," he said, taking a seat.

"Really?"

"Yeah." He reached into his pocket. "I know I'm a week late, but there was a bit of a conflict we had to take care of on your birthday so I never had a chance to give you this." He handed me a small square box.

Surprised he'd even thought to get me anything, I took it from him and opened it. It was a silver Ace of Spades ring. I removed it from the box and slipped it on my finger. "This is awesome! Thank you," I said.

"Don't mention it," he answered, sliding another small square box my way.

"What's this?" I asked.

"The second part of your gift."

I grabbed the new box and opened it. A skull ring stared up at me.

"I'm not saying you have to take the position," Satan said, "but it is yours since you killed Lucifer."

I met his eyes. "What does that mean exactly?"

He shrugged. "You'd be the leader of Pride, my second-in-command."

"What would I do?"

"Attend to the spirits, keep the fallen angels in line, do some occasional work for me here on Earth," he said. "And the hounds would be with you all the time."

Wow, I was actually being offered a place in Hell. I knew most people would balk at such a thing, but I didn't, mainly because I knew how well I would fit in. Except what about Sophia? She had told me she was by my side no matter what, but our relationship was already hard to manage without touching one another. Now I was going to add long-distance to it. So long that you had to travel to another realm. And one that wasn't even desirable to go to.

While the offer was tempting, I knew I couldn't decide in this moment. Especially without talking to Sophia first.

"Do I have to answer now?" I asked.

"Not at all," he assured me. "I just wanted to lay out the proposition since you so rightfully earned it. I'm really here to see you and give you your gift."

I admired the Ace of Spades ring. "This means a lot to me."

He slung his arm over my shoulder. "You mean a lot to me."

Finally, I was no longer second best.

93 JORDAN

Ithaca, New York, Present Day

"Do you want to do London or Rome before we go to Paris?" Dafne asked me.

"Uh... London I guess."

"I agree. It's closer, and we can always do Rome another time." Dafne took notes in her planner. "And what about Cairo? Maybe spring break?"

I tore my eyes away from the picture I was holding. "Sure."

Dafne set the planner aside. "Sorry. I'm trying to keep your mind off it."

I smiled weakly. "I know."

The moment I had been dreading came much sooner than I would have liked. It was time for the angels to depart.

Dafne was distracting me with our travel plans. We only had four weeks together before we had to arrive at our colleges, and we were planning to make the most of it. Our first week would be spent in New York City. Then we were going to travel to London and from there we would finish the last two weeks of our trip in Paris.

While I was going to miss my house, I knew it would be hard to live in without the angels. Their presence had filled it since the day I had discovered it. Already it felt strange as they had packed up their rooms, either taking their personal belongings with them or discarding things entirely. No trace of their existence was left behind. So much so they had even settled whatever earthly affairs remained, leaving behind the lives they had made and preparing to return to their old ones.

The only reminder of their time here was the picture Sophia had given me. The one I was staring at now.

A part of me wished to go back to that moment when we were all together. It was a time when thoughts of war were far from mind, when the unbindings were still a mystery. Deep down I knew it was better to be past those hardships. But now we were here, having to say goodbye.

Upon their return to Heaven, the angels would resume their seats on the Council of Archangels, with two exceptions. One, Michael would become Head of Council, replacing Metatron, and two, Gabriel would be raised in rank to Head Seraphim taking Seraphiel's spot. Both positions came with tremendous responsibility, but Gabriel's had far more. That had been the agreement between him and God in exchange for Gabriel's life, and he was prepared for the challenge.

Dafne came over to the bed and sat down next to me. "Before we go downstairs, will you promise me something?"

I took my eyes off the picture and glanced at her. "Anything."

She put her hand on top of mine. "Promise me you won't run away from your life."

My brow furrowed. "What do you mean?"

Dafne sighed. "I mean traveling and spending time with one another is important, but don't do it because you can't handle the thought of being here." She paused. "Don't do it as a way to escape your mind."

I frowned. "A part of me might be doing that. But that doesn't mean I don't want to be with you. Actually, I think I need this trip. These past two years have been a whirlwind, and I haven't had a chance to live my life. Don't get me wrong. I would never change what has happened, but I also know I need to move forward." I squeezed her hand. "And you're the focus of my next chapter."

She grew meek. "Really?"

"Yes, really." I caressed her cheek. "I can't wait to spend every minute with you."

She smiled softly. "And what about when we have to leave one another? Long distance isn't easy."

"You're right. It isn't. But my parents survived it, and I think we will, too."

She took my hand away from her cheek and placed it between her palms. "How can you be so sure?"

I tilted her chin up with my finger. "Because I believe in us. Promise me you will, too."

"I promise—I truly do. I'm just nervous. Everything is so uncertain."

"It is." I knew that more than anyone, especially after I had died. I was still coping with that experience along with my visions. If anything, though, it all had taught me that nothing is guaranteed, so it was important to seize the opportunity while you could. "Dafne?"

"Hmm?"

"I love you."

She grinned. "I love you, too."

We leaned toward one another for a quick kiss.

When we eased back, Dafne whispered, "It's time. Are you ready?"

"No. I'll never be ready," I said, but I grabbed her hand anyway and headed downstairs.

Everyone was gathered outside, the six angels already saying goodbye to Martha, Deborah, Peter, Emily, and Delphine. Naomi and Sophia were next to exchange hugs with them, the latter much more teary-eyed as Sophia had grown close to the angels much like I had.

Dane flew down from the roof of the house and landed in front of Dafne and me.

"This sucks," he said.

I nodded. "Tell me about it."

Dafne let go of my hand and joined in on the round of farewell hugs.

I sighed and stepped forward with Dane.

The angels waited until they finished saying their goodbyes to Sophia and Dafne before setting their sights on us.

"Dane," Michael said, "we all would like to give you your birthday gift." He handed him a thick envelope.

Dane opened it and pulled out a stack of papers, shuffling through them. His eyes widened. "What is this?"

"All of Jophiel's earthly assets," Zadkiel explained. "We knew the two of you were close, and we couldn't think of a better person to pass his legacy on to."

Dane shook his head. "I can't take this."

"Jophiel would have wanted you to have it," Chamuel said.

"Besides, we have no use for any of it," Uriel added.

Chamuel elbowed him.

"I'm just being honest!" Uriel defended.

"I don't know what to say other than thank you," Dane said.

Raphael smiled. "You're welcome. You're more than deserving of it."

Then they turned their attention on me.

My face contorted, and I started crying before I even hugged any of them.

Chamuel grabbed me and held me tight. "I'm so glad you were the sign we were waiting for." We both laughed. "We certainly needed you."

I pulled back and moved on to Zadkiel, exchanging a quick hug. "It has been a great privilege to teach you everything I know. You were the best pupil I had."

Uriel was next. I got a mere handshake from him. "It was good knowing you, kid."

Raphael's hug made up for Uriel's lack thereof as he squeezed me tight. "You've made me very proud. I can't wait to see what you become."

I smiled and turned to Michael. "There's a lot I can say to you," he told me, "but I'll settle for 'always keep swinging.'" He pulled me in for a bear hug, giving me one last reminder of his strength.

Letting go, I knew there was one angel left, and it would be the hardest.

I practically fell into Gabriel's arms and clutched him close. "Don't be upset," he said as I sobbed. "This isn't goodbye. It's just a brief departure. And while I might not be with you physically every day, I'll always be with you in spirit, watching over you, guiding you, and protecting you." He patted my back and slipped something into my hand. "By the way, the apartment in New York is yours."

I drew back and smiled. "Thank you. For everything."

The angels lifted their storage chests, and one by one, they disappeared as their portal devices transported them to Heaven.

Six beams of light shone down from the clouds, marking an end to my angelic adventure. Except it wasn't really an ending. It was only the beginning.

Reference Guides

Cast of Characters

Humans

Aeron Conway: Sophia's father; Jordan's uncle; an honorary member of the Sacrarium, Beta classification; connected to the Ten Families

Allen Clark: an informant who alerts Michael to Geneloom's operation; Aeron Conway's alias

Arthur Conway: Jordan's father; Sophia's uncle; an honorary member of the Sacrarium, Beta classification; connected to the Ten Families

Cecil (SEE-SILL) Wallace: a member of the Sacrarium, Beta classification; connected to the Ten Families

Dafne Delucci (DEL-LU-CHEE): Sophia's best friend and roommate at Harvard; Jordan's love interest; connected to the Ten Families

Dane: an orphan; grew up with Jordan and Sophia; Jordan's roommate at Holy Trinity; a blood mage

Darcel: Dane's alter ego

Deborah Barnes: Naomi's mother; a member of the Sacrarium, originally Beta classification, now is the new Alpha

Emily Conway: Sophia's mother; Jordan's aunt; was presumed to be a member of the Sacrarium and is a confirmed member, Gamma classification

Evangeline Conway: Jordan's mother; Sophia's aunt; a descendant of the holy bloodline

Jordan Conway: an orphan; grew up with Dane and Sophia; the heir of the holy bloodline

Martha O'Reilly: Jordan's housekeeper; Sister Helen's biological sister; a member of the Sacrarium, Gamma classification

Mr. and Mrs. Delucci (DEL-LU-CHEE): Dafne's father and mother; connected to the Ten Families

Naomi Barnes: Jordan's neighbor; set up to date Jordan by her mother and Martha; an intern at Geneloom; a Sacrarium Novice; a Supernal

Peter Barnes: Naomi's father; a member of the Sacrarium, Gamma classification

Silas Sharp: Aeron's best friend; was training to be a member of the Sacrarium but never finished; died from cancer

Sister Delphine (DEL-FEEN): a nun who helped run Holy Trinity with Sister Helen; Jordan and Sophia's aunt; an honorary member of the Sacrarium, Beta classification; connected to the Ten Families

Sister Helen: Head Sister at Holy Trinity; Martha O'Reilly's biological sister; member of the Sacrarium, Alpha classification; full name is Helen O'Reilly

Sophia: an orphan; Jordan's best friend; training to be a member of the Sacrarium; grew up with Dane and Jordan; a Nephilim

Tamar: Evangeline's friend; Naomi's surrogate mother

Theo Sinclair: Evangeline's brother; Jordan's uncle; a descendant of the holy bloodline

Tony: a friend of Gabriel's; Gabriel's "assistant"; Dafne's grandfather; connected to the Ten Families

HEAVEN

Father: ruler in Heaven; creator of all angels; otherwise known as God

ANGELS

Araziel (AH-RAZZ-EE-EL): a male Angel; an angel of music

Ariel: a female Archangel; an angel of power; former member of the Council of Archangels; sent to Purgatory

Azrael (AS-RYE-EL): the angel of death

Cassiel: a male Archangel; an angel of power; new member of the Council of Archangels

Chamuel (CHAM-U-EL): a male Archangel; an angel of the home; member of the Council of Archangels; lives on Earth; alias is Cam Angel

Chastity: a female Virtue

Gabriel: a male Archangel; an angel of music; member of the Council of Archangels; lives on Earth; alias is Gabriel Maestro

Grace: a female Virtue

Griel (GREE-EL): a female Angel; an angel of music

Haniel (HAN-EE-EL): a female Archangel; an angel of healing

Hope: a female Virtue

Jophiel (JOE-FEE-EL): a male Archangel; an angel of art; member of the Council of Archangels; lives on Earth; alias is Jo Crane

Justice: a male Virtue

Kushiel: a male Archangel sent to Purgatory

Metatron: a male Archangel; an angel of teaching; former member of the Council of Archangels; elevated to a Seraphim and now a member of the Council of Seraphim

Michael: a male Archangel; an angel of power; member of the Council of Archangels; lives on Earth; alias is Michael Lyons

Peace: a female Virtue

Raphael: a male Archangel; an angel of healing; member of the Council of Archangels; lives on Earth; alias is Dr. Raphael Wolf

Raziel (RAZZ-EE-EL): a male Archangel; an angel of teaching; former member of the Council of Archangels; elevated to a Seraphim and now a member of the Council of Seraphim

Sandalphon (SAN-DAL-FON): a male Archangel; an angel of nature; former member of the Council of Archangels; the Warden of Purgatory

Seraphiel (SER-REF-EE-EL): a female Seraphim; Head Seraphim

Tzaphkiel (ZAHF-KEE-EL): a female Archangel; an angel of the home; member of the Council of Archangels; interim Head of Council

Uriel (YOUR-EE-EL): a male Archangel; an angel of nature; member of the Council of Archangels; lives on Earth; alias is Uri Reed

Zadkiel (ZAHD-KEE-EL): a male Archangel; an angel of teaching; member of the Council of Archangels; lives on Earth; alias is Zak Leid

THE TRIUNE

Aziza (AH-ZEE-ZAH): a female member of the Triune; represents Islam

Katriel (KAT-TREE-EL): a female member of the Triune; represents Christianity; otherwise known as Kat

Yadira (YAH-DEER-AH): a female member of the Triune; represents Judaism

Hell

Abbadona: a female fallen angel; resides in the Eighth Cavern; the only angel not affected by the Rivers of Hell; practices the healing arts

Asmodeus (AS-MO-DEE-US): a male fallen angel; member of the Six; leader of Lust

Astrid: a spirit; a witch; one of the Witchcraft Sisters; practices black magic; blind; Tabitha's sister

Balberith (BALL-BURR-RITH): a male fallen angel; attends to spirits in the throne room by watching them, recording their requests, and escorting them back to where they belong

Beelzebub (BILL-ZE-BUB): a male fallen angel; member of the Six; leader of Gluttony

Belphegor (BELL-FA-GOR): a male fallen angel; member of the Six; leader of Laze

Cerberus (SIR-BER-US): three-headed dog in Hell; Leviathan's "pet"

Duke: a hellhound; Dane's "dog"

Haborym (HA-BORE-RIM): a female fallen angel; helped Satan manipulate divine light to create his portals, barriers, and shields; forges the weapons in Hell

Leviathan: a male fallen angel; member of the Six; leader of Envy

Lilith: the snake in Eden who bit Satan; the mother of blood magic; Dane's mother

Lucifer: a male fallen angel; member of the Six; leader of Pride; Satan's second-in-command; alias is Luc Helton

Mammon: a male fallen angel; member of the Six; leader of Greed

Mulciber (MUL-SIB-BURR): a male fallen angel; escorts spirits from Misery to the city they will reside in

Murmur: a male fallen angel; interrogates spirits in Misery to determine what city they will reside in

Nehema (NAH-HE-MA): a female fallen angel; promoted to leader of Misery

Satan: a male fallen angel; the ruler of Hell; leader of the Six; leader of Elysium; former Archangel; former angel of power; former member of the Council of Archangels; given name was Samael (SAM-MY-EL); alias is Samuel Cross; Dane's father

Tabitha: a spirit; a witch; one of the Witchcraft Sisters; practices black magic; Astrid's sister

Connected to Nephilim Operations

Jazema Grigori (JAZZ-EM-AH GREH-GOR-EE): owner of Geneloom; Penelope Grigori's "sister"; a Watcher; given name was Semjaza; Moriko's mother

Moriko: Sophia's only friend as a child when she was at Geneloom

Parvati Irin (PAR-VAH-TEE EYE-RIN): former owner of Giant Heart Healing Center; died in a lab accident

Penelope Grigori: presumed owner of Giant Heart Healing Center; Jazema Grigori's "sister"; a Watcher; given name was Penemue; Sophia's biological mother

Rajani (RAY-JON-E): a teenage Nephilim girl

Salma Amir: a doctor and geneticist hired by Jazema; died in a lab accident

Sentinel, the: a person employed by Jazema to kill people and tie up loose ends; secretly working for Lilith

Siena: a Nephilim girl at Geneloom

Others

Angelica: Tony and Francesca's granddaughter

Angelo: works in Gabriel's apartment building

Benny: a footman in Gabriel's apartment building

Bianca: Simon Price's assistant at the Met

Carmen: Dafne's friend at TKTS

Carmine: a footman in Gabriel's apartment building

Claudia: Tony and Francesca's daughter

Daisy: Uriel's coworker

Doug: a mailman

Dr. Parr: Raphael's colleague

Dr. Reynolds: Raphael's colleague

Enzo: Tony and Francesca's grandson

Ethan: Jordan's former coworker

Francesca: Tony's wife

Gigi: Preston's mother

Ivan: works at Geneloom

Laila Barnes: Naomi's sister

Marcus: Jordan's former boss

Margaret: a student at Oxford

Matthew: Uriel's coworker

Nonna Bea: Tony's mother; real first name is Beatrice
Preston: Sophia's mother's boyfriend
Sheila: Uriel's coworker
Simon Price: curator of the Department of Ancient Art and Antiquities at the Met
Simone Barnes: Naomi's sister
Umberto: maître d' of the restaurant where Chamuel worked

Glossary

34 Central Park West: The address of Gabriel's apartment.

520 Oak Harbor Road: The address of Jordan's house.

1055 Applegate Road: The address of Sister Delphine's house.

Alpha: The highest classification for a Sacrarium member; distributes information to all other members; has taken oath to protect the holy bloodline; there is only one Alpha.

amulet: The necklace Astrid and Tabitha created for Satan so he can travel to Earth.

ancient wonders of the world: Locations around the globe from the ancient world; many no longer exist; where the classic keys are hidden.

angel of art: Angel that possesses the capability to create artistic works or inventions.

angel of healing: Angel that possesses the capability to heal.

angel of music: Angel that possesses the capability to play any musical instrument.

angel of nature: Angel that possesses the capability to protect and care for nature.

angel of power: Angel that possesses the capability to fight.

angel of teaching: Angel that possesses the capability to teach and learn.

angel of the home: Angel that possesses the capability to nurture and care for the home.

angelic script: Language of angels that is mainly written.

Angels: Ranked nine out of nine classifications in the Celestial Hierarchy; part of the Third Choir; known as Heaven's messengers; reside in Low Heaven; duties are to act as guardian angels.

anointing oil: Holy oil used to rub on the body for ceremonial purposes.

Archangels: Ranked eight out of nine classifications in the Celestial Hierarchy; part of the Third Choir; known as Heaven's messengers; reside in Low Heaven; duties are to watch and protect humankind.

ascensio: A Latin word meaning "rise."

astrological constellations: Twelve (formerly thirteen) star signs; otherwise known as the zodiac; a member of the Council of Archangels represents each sign.

barriers: Divine light that has the ability to barricade things; made by angels of art with God's permission; otherwise known as divine light barriers.

Beta: The second classification for a Sacrarium member; given covert duties and aware of almost all confidential information; has taken oath to protect the holy bloodline.

black magic: A dark type of magic practiced by Astrid and Tabitha.

Blessed, the: A term used to describe the angels in Heaven.

blood mage: A person who wields magic and draws their power from blood

blood magic: A force stronger than black magic; created and mainly used by Lilith.

Brooklyn Heights: A neighborhood in Brooklyn, New York, where Holy Trinity Home for Disadvantaged Youth is located.

Castle Key, the: An item that went missing from Heaven; needed to open the tower of the castle in High Heaven.

castle: The structure in High Heaven where the Seraphim, Cherubim, and Thrones reside.

cathedrals: Two structures in Low Heaven where the Principalities and Angels reside.

celestial energy: Holy energy emitted by anything divine; usually undetectable by most humans.

Celestial Hierarchy: The classification system in Heaven that organizes different types of angels and their duties.

Celtic tree astrology: Similar to astrological constellations but based on trees and nature instead of stars; a member of the Council of Archangels represents each sign.

chakram: A sharp, disklike weapon that separates into two identical pieces.

Cherubim: Ranked two out of nine classifications in the Celestial Hierarchy; part of the First Choir; known as Heaven's counselors; reside in High Heaven; duties are to provide input on decisions made by God and relay messages to the Second Choir.

circle of vocation: A grouping system for angels in the Third Choir that determines their skill set; there are seven circles of vocation in total.

classic key: A metal key that was hidden at the ancient wonders of the world; this key is needed for the Union of the Spheres; each member on the Council of Archangels has one.

confinio: A Latin word meaning "confine."

Core, the: A void in the center of Purgatory, ravished by the elements.

Council of Angels: Consists of a group of Angels appointed by God; implemented for order.

Council of Archangels: Consists of a group of Archangels appointed by God; implemented for order; thirteen members in total until Satan fell.

Council of Cherubim: Consists of a group of Cherubim appointed by God; implemented for order.

Council of Dominions: Consists of a group of Dominions appointed by God; implemented for order.

Council of Powers: Consists of a group of Powers appointed by God; implemented for order.

Council of Principalities: Consists of a group of Principalities appointed by God; implemented for order.

Council of Seraphim: Consists of a group of Seraphim appointed by God; implemented for order.

Council of Thrones: Consists of a group of Thrones appointed by God; implemented for order.

Council of Virtues: Consists of a group of Virtues appointed by God; implemented for order.

dark beings: Humans that are infected with dark matter but are still alive.

dark energy/dark matter: An evil substance that can infect and pollute humans; lethal to angels and the Fallen.

dark energy weapon: A weapon that has been created from the river water in Hell and sanctified in dark matter; otherwise known as a dark weapon; lethal to humans, angels, and the Fallen.

deadly sin rings: A piece of jewelry worn by Satan and the Six.

demon cash: A currency in Hell.

demons: Humans that were turned into dark beings that are now dead.

divine light: A type of energy that comes from God.

divine markings: Another name for angel tattoos.

divine wisdoms: All knowledge contained in Heaven.

Dominions: Ranked four out of nine classifications in the Celestial Hierarchy; part of the Second Choir; known as Heaven's governors; reside in Middle Heaven; duties are to uphold laws and relay messages to the Third Choir.

Eastern Region, the: A region in Purgatory connected to Qliphoth.

Eden: The Garden of Eden; created by God and located on Earth.

Eighth Cavern, the: Eighth level of Hell; where the five rivers reside; Abbadona dwells here since she is immune to the tempting whispers of the waters.

Elysium: First city in Hell ruled by Satan; otherwise known as the Royal City; where fallen angels reside.

Envy: Third city in Hell; run by Leviathan; where spirits that succumbed to envy reside.

exilium: A Latin word meaning "banish."

exitus: A Latin word meaning "exit."

Factions of Faith, the: Angels from every religion in the world.

fallen claps of thunder: The sound heard when the Fallen travel to and from Hell; can impair the hearing of humans.

fallen forces/Fallen, the: A term used to describe Satan and his army of fallen angels and demons.

First Choir, the: A hierarchical designation that contains the highest level of angels—the Seraphim, Cherubim, and Thrones.

fleur-de-lis: A three-pronged symbol associated with the Sacrarium.

Flood, the: The biblical story of how God sent a massive storm to wipe out the Earth so that He could create it again.

Forge, the: The place in High Heaven where all divine objects are made.

fourteenth sphere, the: A gemstone sphere whose true existence is unknown.

Gamma: The third classification for a Sacrarium member; only called upon when needed and informed on a need-to-know basis; has taken oath to protect the holy bloodline.

gemstone key: A gemstone that is hidden at the natural wonders of the world; needed for the Union of the Spheres; each member on the Council of Archangels has one.

Geneloom: A genetic-testing company that conducts secret experiments.

Giant Heart Healing Center: A rehab facility that works with Geneloom for the same aims.

Gluttony: Fourth city in Hell; run by Beelzebub; where spirits that succumbed to gluttony reside.

Great Tree, the: A large tree housed in the Council of Seraphim's chamber used to commune with Father.

Greed: Fifth city in Hell; run by Mammon; where spirits that succumbed to greed reside.

Guardians of the Lost Souls: Angels in Purgatory who assist lost souls in passing on to a new realm.

Hall of Law: A structure in Middle Heaven that contains all heavenly laws; where one of the stolen objects was placed.

halls: Three structures in Middle Heaven where the Dominions, Virtues, and Powers reside.

Head of Council: A designation given to Metatron that signifies he is the leader of the Council of Archangels.

Head Seraphim: a designation given to Seraphiel that signifies she is the highest angelic authority.

Heaven's counselors: A designation for the type of angelic duties given to the First Choir.

Heaven's governors: A designation for the type of angelic duties given to the Second Choir

Heaven's messengers: A designation for the type of angelic duties given to the Third Choir.

Heavenly Gates: An entrance located in High Heaven that leads to another heavenly realm.

heavenly light: A type of energy that comes from angels.

Hellfire: a mixture of heavenly light and divine light; the angels of art accidentally created Hellfire by mixing together mass quantities of heavenly light and divine light, creating dark matter; the type of fire that rages in Hell; Satan's punishment; lethal to almost everyone and everything.

hellhounds: Dogs in Hell that guard caves between cities.

High Heaven: Where the Seraphim, Cherubim, and Thrones reside.

holy bloodline: A living descendant of Jesus and Mary Magdalene; also known as the heir.

Holy Trinity Home for Disadvantaged Youth: The orphanage where Jordan, Sophia, and Dane grew up; more commonly known as Holy Trinity.

holy water grenade: Clear glass balls filled with holy water.

holy water: Sanctified and purified water that is lethal to the Fallen.

Horn of Assembly: A long, gold horn used to send messages to angels or Heaven.

incarnation: A person meant to represent a deity.

inferos: Latin word meaning "Hell;" the Fallen must place a hand to the ground and say this word in order to open a portal to travel back to Hell.

Ishim, the: Angels who were once Watchers; also known as good Watchers; sent to Earth to teach humans and pass along their wisdom; five in total; much of their knowledge is gained through visions and conditioning of the mind.

keeps, the: Structures in Purgatory once guarded by archangels.

Keys, the: Nickname for the classic keys and the gemstone keys.

Laze: Seventh city in Hell; run by Belphegor; where spirits that succumbed to laziness reside.

leader of the army: A designation given to Michael that signifies he is in charge of the heavenly army.

light energy/light matter: A pure substance that is lethal to humans, angels, and the Fallen.

light energy weapon: A weapon that has been created from divine light and sanctified in light matter; otherwise known as a light weapon; lethal to humans, angels, and the Fallen.

lost souls: Spirits sent to Purgatory because they need help moving on or have unfinished business.

Low Heaven: Where the Principalities, Archangels, and Angels reside.

Lust: Sixth city in Hell; run by Asmodeus; where spirits that succumbed to lust reside.

Metatron's Cube: A formation of circles linked together; created by Metatron; the placement required for the Union of the Spheres.

Middle Heaven: Where the Dominions, Virtues, and Powers reside.

Misery: located in the ninth cavern of Hell; where all spirits must complete their sentence of torment before they can move into a city; all spirits who succumb to anger remain here eternally.

modern wonders of the world: Locations around the globe from the modern world; many are not necessarily modern but are popular tourist sites; where the spheres are hidden.

natural wonders of the world: Locations around the globe that are natural phenomena; where the gemstone keys are hidden.

necessary evil: Something unpleasant that must be done to achieve a particular outcome; in the context of this book series it is the notion that evil was intentionally created by God.

Nephilim, the: Half-human, half-angel beings; their forefathers were Watchers and their mothers were mortal women.

neque heredis exponere: Latin phrase meaning "Do not expose the heir;" the motto of the Sacrarium.

Northern Region, the: A region in Purgatory connected to Heaven.

Novice: The lowest classification for a Sacrarium member; taught rudimentary information in preparation for taking the oath to protect the holy bloodline; a member must remain at this level for five years to determine their dedication and trustworthiness before they take their oath.

novissimum: A Latin word meaning "hinder."

Operation Pure Form: The secret experiment Geneloom is conducting to achieve the untainted genetics of the Watchers.

Pit, the: A large, dark void that spans throughout Hell and is sometimes used as punishment by Satan.

Ponds of Purgatory, the: Small bodies of water located in the Southern Region.

portal room: A room in Hell connected to Satan's private quarters where his portal to Earth resides; also where Satan keeps prisoners.

portals: Divine light that has the ability to transport things; made by angels of art with God's permission.

Powers: Ranked six out of nine classifications in the Celestial Hierarchy; part of the Second Choir; known as Heaven's governors; reside in Middle Heaven; duties are to uphold laws and relay messages to the Third Choir.

Pride: Second city in Hell; run by Lucifer; where spirits that succumbed to pride reside.

Principalities: Ranked seven out of nine classifications in the Celestial Hierarchy; part of the Third Choir; known as Heaven's messengers; reside in Low Heaven; duties are to interact with members and institutions of the church.

Prophecy of the Three Heirs, the: A foretelling of how Jordan, Dane, and Sophia can discover who they are.

pure form: A term Geneloom uses to signify the untainted genetics of the Watchers.

Purgatory: A realm between Heaven and Hell.

Qliphoth: A realm of evil where dark forces reside.

red blaze, the: A term Satan uses for Hellfire.

Rivers of Hell, the: Located in the Eighth Cavern of Hell; five rivers in total—the River of Pain, the River of Lamentation, the River of

Forgetfulness, the River of Fire, and the River of Hate; the waters tempt beings into their depths for eternal punishment.

rondel dagger: A long, slim blade that tapers into a needle point.

Royal City, the: A nickname for Elysium.

Sacrarium: A secret society meant to protect the holy bloodline.

Sacred Heart High School: The high school that Jordan, Sophia, and Dane attended.

sai: A pair of handheld weapons that have three-pronged blades.

sanctuaries: Seven structures in Low Heaven, each designated for a circle of vocation.

Sanctuary of Art: A structure in Low Heaven that houses the angels of art; the symbol to represent this circle of vocation is an artist's palette.

Sanctuary of Healing: A structure in Low Heaven that houses the angels of healing; the symbol to represent this circle of vocation is a caduceus.

Sanctuary of Music: A structure in Low Heaven that houses the angels of music; the symbol to represent this circle of vocation is a music note.

Sanctuary of Nature: A structure in Low Heaven that houses the angels of nature; the symbol to represent this circle of vocation is a tree.

Sanctuary of Power: A structure in Low Heaven that houses the angels of power; the symbol to represent this circle of vocation is a helmet.

Sanctuary of Teaching: A structure in Low Heaven that houses the angels of teaching; the symbol to represent this circle of vocation is a scroll.

Sanctuary of the Home: A structure in Low Heaven that houses the angels of the home; the symbol to represent this circle of vocation is a hearth flame.

Second Choir, the: A hierarchical designation that contains mid-level angels—the Dominions, Virtues, and Powers.

Sefirot: A realm of wisdom where light forces reside; where the teachings of the Ishim originated.

Seraphim: Ranked one out of nine classifications in the Celestial Hierarchy; part of the First Choir; known as Heaven's counselors; reside in High Heaven; duties are to provide input on decisions made by God and relay messages to the Second Choir.

Seventh Day Gathering: A celebration in Heaven meant for camaraderie.

shields: Divine light that has the ability to cloak things; made by angels of art with God's permission.

Sight, the: An ancient gift that gives a person the ability to have visions.

Six, the: Satan's fallen angels that execute his bidding—Lucifer, Leviathan, Beelzebub, Mammon, Asmodeus, and Belphegor.

skull ring: A piece of jewelry worn by Satan and the Six.

skull tattoo: An identifier of the Six; Satan and each member of the Six has it on the back of their hands.

Son of God: Signifies God's incarnation on Earth; mainly used in reference to Jesus.

Southern Region, the: A region in Purgatory connected to Hell.

Sovereign's Orb: The orb that is created during the Union of the Spheres; the thirteen spheres combine to make it.

Sovereign's Scepter: A scepter that holds the Sovereign's Orb; needed for the Union of the Spheres.

spheres: Round stones the size of a grapefruit; thirteen in total; needed for the Union of the Spheres; each member on the Council of Archangels has one.

spirit coin: A currency in Hell.

spirits: Deceased people in Heaven or Hell.

St. Michael medallion: A small pendant worn on a necklace that depicts Archangel Michael.

storage chest: A large, rectangular case that an angel travels with.

subsisto: A Latin word meaning "stop."

Supernals: Beings who are full celestial since both of their parents are angels.

Temptress: A being in Purgatory; also known as temptations.

Ten Families, the: Families chosen by the Ishim to pass along their teachings.

terra: Latin word meaning "Earth;" the Fallen must place a hand on a portal and say this word, along with their intended location, in order to travel to Earth.

The Book of Prophecies: A book from Heaven that contains prophecies and other divine wisdoms; it was also an item that went missing from Heaven.

Third Choir, the: A hierarchical designation that contains the lowest level of angels—the Principalities, Archangels, and Angels.

throne room: A room connected to Satan's private quarters where he receives visitors.

Thrones: Ranked three out of nine classifications in the Celestial Hierarchy; part of the First Choir; known as Heaven's counselors; reside in High Heaven; duties are to provide input on decisions made by God and relay messages to the Second Choir.

Tree of Good and Evil/Tree of Knowledge, the: Located in Eden.

Tree of Life, the: A symbol of growth and ancestry for Jordan, Dane, and Sophia.

trial of trust: A task given to a Sacrarium Novice to prove they are dedicated and trustworthy; occurs after their training is finished; a novice can take the oath to protect the holy bloodline upon successful completion of a trial of trust.

trinity: A Christian notion meant to signify the three parts of God—Father, Son, and Holy Spirit.

Triune, the: A group of angels meant to protect the holy bloodline and anything related to it; connected to the Sacrarium.

Union of the Spheres, the: The process of combining thirteen spheres into one in order to make the Sovereign's Orb; the ceremony gives the wielder immense power.

Virtues: Ranked five out of nine classifications in the Celestial Hierarchy; part of the Second Choir; known as Heaven's governors; reside in Middle Heaven; duties are to uphold laws and relay messages to the Third Choir.

vivo: A Latin word meaning "live."

Warden of Purgatory, the: A designation given to Sandalphon that signifies he is meant to keep order in Purgatory.

Wastelands, the: A vast desert in Purgatory filled with lost souls and other creatures.

Watch Towers: Three structures in Low Heaven; one contains the Council of Archangels, and the other two are where Archangels stand watch over the world; where Archangels reside.

Watchers, the: A group of angels sent from Heaven to Earth in order to teach humans; fell in love with mortal women and produced the Nephilim; now considered fallen angels.

Western Region, the: A region in Purgatory connected to Sefirot.

wonders, the: A nickname for the ancient, natural, and modern wonders of the world.

ACKNOWLEDGMENTS

It’s bittersweet to write these acknowledgments because while it makes me happy to share this book with all of you after that massive cliffhanger, it's also sad knowing that this book is an ending.

When I set out on my writing journey, I always imagined this day would come, the day when the Empyrean Trilogy would be officially complete, but I never imagined it would come this soon.

This series is the first I’ve ever attempted to write, and I’m so proud of what it has become. The story itself is everything I imagined and more, and the experience has been extraordinary. I’m so grateful to all the readers who have found this series and loved it. I never expected the reach these books would have, and I know it’s only going to continue to grow as more and more discover it.

Now it’s time to do my thank-yous. As always, thanks to the family unit—mom, dad, and Anthony. I know I say this every time, but I really couldn’t do any of this without you. Whether it’s reading, brainstorming, supporting, or even lending physical help either for events, packing boxes, or putting together merch items, you all are there no matter what. I cannot express how grateful I am to have each of you in my life. Our family is the true definition of ride or die.

A shoutout to my grandfather whose artwork lives on to this day in everything that I do. He drew the angel that has become my logo, but he also created the compass artwork featured on the cover of this book.

To Franklin, who not only produced another amazing book trailer, but also has become a vital part of the team. I cannot thank you enough for your behind-the-scenes work, whether it's tech support and logistics, physical help during an event load-in, or even just the fun times in-between.

Also, thank you to Albert. You've been a big supporter from the beginning and continue to believe in me and spread the word about my books.

Next, a huge thank you to my fantastic editor, Danielle, and the entire Double Vision Editorial team (www.doublevisioneditorial.com). Danielle, you are exceptional. To me, it's easy to see how my writing has evolved ever since I started working with you, and your guidance has truly made me a better writer.

Thanks to all the virtual tour companies I've partnered with (Divine Book Tours, MLC-Mágico Libro Casa Tours, Between the Spines, Raven's Bookish Network, Feather and Dove, Book Tour Gals, MTMC Tours, Prism Book Tours, Storygram Tours, Literary Bound Tours, NBB Book Tours, and Starlight Book Tours). The reach of my books would not be what it is without you all. You all are wonderful to work with, and I look forward to partnering together again in the future.

Zach, thank you for another awesome voiceover (www.zachhoffmanvoice.com). I hope we can continue to collaborate and bring these characters to life.

Joselyn, Stella, and Andrea, thank you for doing live author chats and interviews with me.

Thank you to FanExpo Denver, C2E2, New York Comic Con, and LA Comic Con for having me as a guest and exhibitor.

To the readers, you all are phenomenal! Thank you for reading, reviewing, and loving these books.

And finally, to the angels. Thank you for inspiring me every day in all that I do.

While this might be an ending, it isn't goodbye, as more stories will be coming.

Wings up!

CPSIA information can be obtained
at www.ICGtesting.com
Printed in the USA
JSHW031203201122
33194JS00002B/4/J

9 781732 516267

Storygram
1-18